MEN AND WOMEN IN A TIME OF AMERICA'S SEARING TRIAL AND SHINING TRIUMPH

Jeremy—heir to the great plantation of Oakhurst, violently torn from his birthright, and forced to prove his manhood in a world of brutal action and savage passion.

Sarah—pledged to Jeremy in marriage, unsure whether he was alive or dead, and facing an ultimate testing of her love in the arms of another man.

Tom—hot-blooded and hot-tempered, with no woman out of bounds to his driving desires, and no man safe from his naked steel.

Margot—the sensual beauty who played the tease with one lover too many, and almost lost her last chance for happiness.

These were the Beauforts of Oakhurst Manor—a family as powerful and passionate as the dreams and realities that made America great.

Big Bestsellers from SIGNET

OAKHURST

By

Walter Reed Johnson

A SIGNET BOOK

NEW AMERICAN LIBRARY

TIMES MIRROR

COPYRIGHT © 1977 BY BOOK CREATIONS, INC.

Produced by Lyle Kenyon Engel

SIGNET TRADEMARK REG. U.S. PAT. OFF. AND FOREIGN COUNTRIES
REGISTERED TRADEMARK—MARCA REGISTRADA
HECHO EN CHICAGO, U.S.A.

SIGNET, SIGNET CLASSICS, MENTOR, PLUME AND MERIDIAN BOOKS
are published by The New American Library, Inc.,
1301 Avenue of the Americas, New York, New York 10019

FIRST SIGNET PRINTING, JANUARY, 1978

1 2 3 4 5 6 7 8 9

PRINTED IN THE UNITED STATES OF AMERICA

Prologue

Sarah walked slowly through the Georgian brick house— her house—and marveled at it, as she did every day of her life. Built almost a half-century earlier, when South Carolina had still been a British colony, Oakhurst Manor was more than a private dwelling, more than the core of a vast plantation. It had a life of its own, an identity of its own, and it was alive.

She emerged onto the portico, and for a moment she leaned against one of the sturdy, white Doric columns, seeking the comfort and strength that only Oakhurst Manor could give her. She had learned to love this place, just as she loved the endless acres of Beaufort land.

At the far end of the manicured lawn stood rows of live oaks draped with Spanish moss, and beyond were groves of palmetto and cypress. Sarah's slender hand rose to the gold chain at her throat, and she absently fingered the heavy ring that rested against her milk-white skin between her firm, high breasts. Jeremy was always in her mind, but she couldn't allow herself to think too hard and too long about him or—as experience had taught her—she would get nothing done all day.

Jeremy belonged to the night. Only then could she indulge in her hopes and give free expression to her fears. The days belonged to Oakhurst Manor.

In the fields beyond the lawn she could see the slaves already at work, the men stripped to the waist, the women in long shifts. There were hundreds of them, and they provided the raw power that made Oakhurst Manor a viable entity. They picked the cotton, cut and hauled the lumber, made pitch and turpentine, and grew the foodstuffs that not only made the great plantation self-sustaining but also enabled Sarah, with the help of her brother-in-law, to sell large quantities of produce in the Charleston market.

There were fields of wheat and corn and rye, large tracts of sugarcane, their pliant stalks waving in the gentle early-morning breeze that swept across South Carolina. There were vegetable gardens, and beyond them the groves of peach trees. And behind the handsome brick house, not visible from the portico but clear in Sarah's mind, stood the smokehouses where bacon and ham were cured, the sheds where cattle were slaughtered and poultry prepared.

She smoothed the low-cut collar of her pure silk dress, made from one of the last bolts of cloth imported from England eighteen months ago, before the outbreak of the War of 1812 had cut off all commerce between the young United States and her former mother country. Somehow she managed a wry smile.

It was odd, even now, that she who hated slavery and yearned for its abolition should be the mistress of a vast estate that was supported and sustained by slaves. It was her duty, uncompromising and unavoidable, to work with the tools at hand, to prevent in every way she knew how the collapse of Oakhurst Manor.

After all, she was a Beaufort.

That was the irony. In the eyes of God and man she might be a Beaufort, but under the law she was . . . well, she wasn't really sure of her identity. At moments like this, she wanted to weep. But, as she knew so well, tears accomplished nothing. Giving in to sudden impulse only made matters worse. She had to behave in the Beaufort tradition that went back to Jeremy's grandfather in America and through long generations back to Cornwall, a tradition that had originated eight hundred years earlier, when a Beaufort had accompanied William of Normandy in his successful invasion of England.

I am a Beaufort, Sarah thought. My son is a Beaufort. For his sake and for Jeremy's, I shall stand firm, no matter how great the odds against me. I shall not only survive, but I shall succeed. Because I must. Because I no longer have an alternative.

Her words were courageous, but Sarah nevertheless felt grave doubts. Could she, at the age of only twenty-three, overcome the circumstances that were piling up, the crises that threatened to inundate her and Oakhurst Manor?

"Yes!" she exclaimed aloud. "I'll succeed because I have no real choice!"

Slowly she turned away from the white marble steps that led up to the house, and although she wasn't superstitious, she touched the nearest white column for luck. This was not the moment to remind herself that slaves had cut and shaped the timber for the columns and for the sloping, shingled roof, three stories high, that towered over everything in sight. Slaves had quarried and polished the marble. Dear God, how she despised an institution that deprived fellow humans of the liberty that was the supposed birthright of all Americans. And the slaves were as American as everybody else in the United States. She had known it back in Boston, and she knew it now. Perhaps she was the only person in all the South who realized it.

No matter what she knew, however, she was honorbound to support the system that made it possible for Oakhurst Manor to exist.

Entering the stately house, Sarah paused to glance at her reflection in the long, slightly smoky pier glass that stood in the spacious front hall. If she concentrated on herself for a moment or two she might forget her problems, so she subjected herself to a critical examination.

Blond hair, the color of wheat, that tumbled down her back. Enormous green eyes that Papa—and Jeremy, too—had said were the true indications of her character. Firm. Strong. A thinking woman who took pride in herself, her mind, her accomplishments. But, as she had learned all too well, there was another quality reflected in her eyes. A sultriness hidden deep beneath the surface. An impulsiveness, the quality that seemingly motivated her sister at all times, and that took possession of her, too, when she least expected it.

A figure that Jeremy had called perfect. Not only Jeremy . . . but she couldn't think of that, or she'd go mad. Tall and slender, with full, high breasts, a tiny waist that a man could span with two hands, rounded hips, and incredibly long legs. Oh, she was vain, all right. If she weren't, she'd be wearing the full skirts and petticoats of other plantation women. Instead she insisted on dressing only in the style that the Empress Josephine and the Emperor Napoleon's sister, Pauline Bonaparte, had made so popular in France in recent years. They called it an Empire style, dresses that hugged the bustline and were gathered beneath it. With a low décolletage, they made her breasts so prominent. Perhaps her sister was right, after all, when she insisted that Sarah actually enjoyed showing off her breasts.

Her whole body, for that matter. The dress, narrow and fluid, fell in soft folds to her ankles, subtly revealing every line of her body when she moved. Only a girl with a truly perfect figure could wear such a costume, and Sarah well knew it. Vanity, vanity, all is vanity. That was Ecclesiastes, of course. Papa had seen to it that she knew her Bible. For all the good it was doing her these days.

Yet, she had to depend on the Almighty. And on herself. There was no one else to whom she could turn.

All at once, Sarah straightened and stood erect, her shoulders pulled back, her delicate but square-cut chin jutting forward. She had moped long enough.

She would go to the kitchen outbuilding to see how Amanda was coming along with the preparation of breakfast. Then a chat with the overseer, Mr. Higby. Then the hour she dreaded, a tour of the sickrooms with Dr. McPherson. A long session with the inevitable ledgers that haunted her. Finally, if she was lucky, a few precious moments to play with her baby before she took her place at the head of the dinner table.

4

Oakhurst Manor might be the envy of neighbors as far away as Charleston and Columbia and even Savannah, far to the south. But there were times when Sarah felt inundated by her cares and her responsibilities.

Chapter 1

More than mere miles separated Oakhurst Manor and Boston; the distance was immeasurable. Jeremy Beaufort settled his bicorne more firmly on his head, wrapped himself securely in his cape to protect himself from the winds that were the one constant factor of the weather in Massachusetts throughout the winter, and stamped the snow off his boots.

His immediate problem was simple: should he take the long route to Beacon Street, or should he brave the foothigh snow and tramp across the Common? As he hesitated, he heard the bells on the Old South Church chime the hour, seven o'clock in the evening, and that made up his mind for him. Sarah Benton was waiting for him, so it didn't matter in the least if he risked frostbitten toes.

Jeremy was so lost in thought that he was startled when someone loomed up beside him, brushing against him.

The harlot was young and pretty, with rouge accenting her lips, rouge on her cheeks, and some black substance smeared on her lashes. Her black hair was loose, blowing in the breeze, and her half-open cloak revealed more than

7

it concealed of a figure clad in a sleazy satin. She was very cold, but her false smile was steady.

"I have a room with a fire just off the Common," she said. "I'll bring you a mulled rum, and I have other ways to warm you, too. All for a fee of only fifty pennies, though you can pay me more if you've a mind to it."

There had been a time when Jeremy would have leaped at the opportunity. The harlot reeked of sensuality, in spite of the cheap perfume in which she had bathed herself, and the night was so raw that any man of twenty-two would have gladly sought the warmth provided by a woman's body. But his life had undergone a profound change.

There were trollops in Charleston and Savannah, too, girls far more subtle than the Boston wenches, and in those days he would have accepted such an invitation without delay. Now, however, he was in love with Sarah Benton, and that made the difference. All the difference in the world.

He reached into the money pouch at his belt and found a Rhode Island quarter-dollar. The truth of the matter was that he felt sorry for this young whore, who had to sell her body in below-freezing weather in order to survive. It had never occurred to him that he was a compassionate man, and he would have been embarrassed had anyone accused him of such feelings, but they were an integral part of him, all the same.

He handed the silver coin to the astonished harlot, tipped his bicorne to her, and plunged into the snow of the Common.

Unaccustomed to such generosity, the trollop stared after him for a moment, then began to laugh, and the raucous sound echoed across the deserted pastureland.

Jeremy had already dismissed her from his mind. For reasons he had never bothered to fathom he was a natural target for women of every class: broad-shouldered and lithe at six feet, two inches in height, without a spare ounce of flesh on his hard body, he was spectacularly handsome, with dark brown hair, penetrating hazel eyes, and a quick, easy smile. But it had never crossed his mind to think of his appearance; the intellect was all-important to him, and he left frivolous concerns to his younger brother, Thomas.

A gust of icy wind cut through Jeremy's woolen cloak, and he shivered. It was one of his principles that a man could become accustomed to anything in life, but he was beginning to doubt it. He had spent the better part of two years in Boston, coming to Massachusetts soon after President James Madison's inauguration in the spring of 1809, but he would never learn to like the damnable cold.

One year as a student of law at Harvard, in Cambridge, and the better part of this past year as an apprentice in the law office of Isaish Benton here in Boston. In another six months, with luck, he would be admitted to the bar, and then he could go home to Oakhurst Manor, never to be chilled to the bone again.

Taking Sarah Benton with him as his bride, to be sure. Thanks to Sarah, the abominable weather of New England was palatable. Thanks to Sarah, the sun never stopped shining.

It was odd, Jeremy reflected, how much his romance with this headstrong, stubborn girl had altered his whole approach to life. He had made his plans with such care. He and his father, Paul Wellington Beaufort, had concluded after endless hours of talk and analysis that, in a world that was becoming increasingly complex, one of the Beaufort sons should study law, then open a practice in Charleston.

That had meant Jeremy. Thomas had the brains but lacked the willpower and drive of the brother who was twenty months his senior. Neither Paul Wellington Beaufort nor his elder son could understand Thomas, and they sometimes speculated that the death of Mama in childbirth had influenced her infant in some mysterious way. Paul and Jeremy were sober, hardworking and industrious, prizing the mind of man above all else on earth. Thomas was a hedonist who sought nothing but his own pleasure, hunted and fished, made love to every pretty girl he met, and didn't give a hang about Oakhurst Manor.

It was Jeremy's absence from the plantation, combined with his love for Sarah, that had convinced him how much Oakhurst Manor meant to him. According to the original

9

plan, Thomas would have become the manager of the estate, while Jeremy practiced law in Charleston, but all that was changed. Jeremy would take over his birthright himself, install Sarah as its mistress, and, using his knowledge of the law to help him, enlarge the profits and buy still more property. He would hand on to his own sons a plantation unequaled anywhere in South Carolina, which was the same as saying anywhere in the world.

The crest of Beacon Hill loomed directly ahead, and Jeremy couldn't help chuckling under his breath. Near the top stood the magnificent mansion of Governor John Hancock, the wealthiest man in the state of Massachusetts, wartime president of the Continental Congress and universally admired and respected as one of the greatest of Revolutionary War patriots.

It didn't matter a tinker's dam to any of Hancock's neighbors, friends, or fellow New Englanders that he, like his uncle before him, had earned a vast fortune as a smuggler. Northerners, it seemed, cared nothing about a man's ancestors.

That wasn't true at home, however, and even after spending twenty-one months in Cambridge and Boston, his own lifelong values remained what they had always been. A man never forgot his roots, not for a moment, and tried his utmost to live up to the standards that had guided his ancestors for generation after generation. Oakhurst Manor would be just another large plantation, one among scores in the Carolinas, Georgia, and Virginia, were it not for the significance of the Beaufort name. The original Baron Beaufort, a younger son, had come to the New World, established Oakhurst Manor, and lost his life fighting as a colonel under General Francis Marion in the War of Independence. His son Paul Beaufort, Jeremy's father, had served as a junior officer under his father and later expanded and solidified the estate, and was preparing to hand on the torch.

Jeremy was willing to admit to himself, if to no one else, that Sarah Benton was largely responsible for the fierce pride he had developed in Oakhurst Manor. The very thought of installing her there as his wife, showing her off to the neighbors, and showing off the plantation to her, sometimes made him dizzy.

He forgot the cold when he saw the trim white house looming directly ahead, two doors from the Hancock mansion. He still regarded it as almost miraculous that, among almost four and a half million Americans, he and Sarah had found each other. A man and girl with the same serious approach to life, the same respect for the human mind, the same craving for knowledge. Had he spent the rest of his days searching for a wife, he could have found no one as perfect as Sarah.

Jeremy's fingers tingled as he raised the polished brass door knocker.

Sarah Benton herself answered his summons, and he had no idea she had been watching for him from behind the velvet draperies of the formal parlor.

She stood before him in the open door, and as he stared at her, he knew, not for the first time, that she was perfect in more ways than one. Her blond hair was piled high on her head, caught in the back with a Spanish comb of ebony, and she was wearing a gown of soft silk that, in some magical way, showed off every line of her supple, beautifully proportioned body.

"Well, Mr. Beaufort," Sarah demanded tartly, "do you intend to stand on the stoop until I freeze?"

Jeremy kicked the door shut behind him. "You're lovely," he murmured, taking her in his arms.

Their bodies pressed close as their lips met and parted, and Jeremy's ardor caused him to forget discretion. His tongue probed and explored as he felt an overwhelming desire to devour this girl whom he adored.

Sarah responded with a passion that matched Jeremy's. She, too, was convinced that the development of the human intellect came before all else in life, but some strange magic was at work whenever she saw her beloved. She wanted him with all her heart and soul and mind, and everything else was blotted from her consciousness.

At last they drew apart reluctantly and stood staring at each other.

"Be good enough to remove the snow from your boots

in the entrance hall, sir. I cleaned these tiles myself this very morning."

Jeremy obeyed, then removed his bicorne and cape and hung them on an entrance-hall peg. "I must protest, ma'am, that you're unkind to a country boy from the Carolinas."

Sarah tossed her head and had no idea that her manner was arch. "In what way?"

"Your gown puts ideas in my head. Ideas that shouldn't be there until you become my wife."

Her smile was unconsciously seductive as she fingered his gold signet ring, which she wore on a chain around her neck and which she would transfer to her finger when their betrothal became official. "I take it you like the new Empire dress I just made. It was all the rage in Paris last year when Margot and I went there with Papa. Because the Empress Josephine and the Princess Pauline Bonaparte introduced it."

All Jeremy knew was that the green silk matched her eyes, her breasts looked as though they would burst through the thin, clinging fabric, and he felt an uncontrollable desire to make love to her. He took a single step toward her.

"Mind your manners," she told him, and led him into the parlor, where a wood fire was blazing in the hearth.

Trying to distract himself, Jeremy thought that New England drawing rooms were incredibly small. Judge Benton, who had served as a justice of the Massachusetts Supreme Court before retiring to private practice, was one of Boston's first citizens, but his parlor was no bigger or more impressive than that of an inconsequential Charleston dry-goods dealer or produce merchant.

"Papa told me to offer you a drink. Two, if you're thirsty."

"He isn't here?" Jeremy followed her to a sideboard.

Sarah eluded him by ducking around the carved oak cabinet to the other side. "He was asked to deliver a lecture to the association of shipowners on President Madison's new tariff laws, and he took Margot with him." She laughed. "He's still determined to educate her, you know, even though she refuses to learn."

He joined in the laugh. Margot Benton reminded him of his brother. Like Thomas, she sought pleasure for its own sake, never read a book when she could find something else to do, and instinctively flirted with every man she met, including her future brother-in-law. "I can hardly wait until Margot and Thomas meet. Both of them will explode."

"Then it's our duty to keep them apart. Will you have sack or rum toddy?"

Rum, the standby of New Englanders, was too strong for Jeremy at a time when it was difficult enough for him to keep his feelings in line. "Sack, please. Will you join me?"

Sarah poured him a glass from a crystal decanter. "I don't know how often I have to keep reminding you that ladies in this part of America don't drink."

He accepted the glass and grinned at her. "Well, it won't be long before you'll be calling Oakhurst Manor home."

"I still don't intend to drink liquor," she said. "It just isn't seemly." Afraid she might be overwhelmed by her own desires, Sarah chose a chair, rather than the sofa, where he would otherwise join her. "I hope you aren't too hungry."

"As long as I can look at you, I don't give a damn about food."

She knew he meant it and accepted the compliment gracefully. "Well, we'll eat as soon as Papa and Margot return. Provided Amanda doesn't become disgusted waiting for them. If she does, she might go off to her own room for the night."

Jeremy chuckled and shook his head before raising his glass to her in a silent toast. "Whoever heard of a cook becoming impatient? That's what comes of hiring free servants. I can promise you that at home our kitchen help prepare dinner or supper whenever we want it. At midnight or later, if that's what pleases us."

Sarah's sense of euphoria faded somewhat. "I refuse to become involved with you in another argument about slavery. We've had more than enough of them."

"Amen."

Sarah's chin always became square when she set it. "All the same, my dear," she said, "I just cannot accept the very idea of human beings being owned by other human beings. As though they were horses or pet dogs. Or inanimate objects."

He tried to exercise patience. "You live in Boston, the third-largest city in the country. It's very easy for people to feel as you do here. Or in Philadelphia. Or even in brawling New York Town. The South is strictly an agricultural region, and the economy of our plantations is founded on the base of slaveholding. It's that simple."

"I wonder if you read President Adams' last message to the Congress on the subject of slavery before he retired." She was becoming annoyed.

Jeremy genuinely wanted to avoid a fight, so he concealed his amusement. "I'm not familiar with the message, but I'd like to remind you that President Washington, our greatest citizen, owned several hundred slaves."

"That doesn't make it right," she said. "Just today I was rereading Thomas Jefferson's *Declaration of Independence*. When he wrote that all men are created equal, surely he included black men. When he wrote that all men are entitled to life, liberty, and the pursuit of happiness, surely he included black men."

"Apparently not," Jeremy said, trying to keep the triumph from his voice. "When we travel down to Oakhurst Manor, we'll make a little side journey to President Jefferson's estate, Monticello, in Virginia. And you'll see for yourself that he owns several hundred slaves who work on the property. What's more, President Madison is a slaveowner. So is Secretary of State James Monroe—"

Sarah cut him off by clapping her slender hands over her ears. "I won't listen to you, and I don't care who owns slaves! Something is wrong, terribly wrong, when a country that pays such constant lip service to the cause of freedom not only permits the institution of slavery to exist inside its borders, but actually endorses it."

He sighed and made no reply. It was impossible to answer her arguments, just as he had been unable to debate slavery with his law-school classmates from New England.

Emotions crowded both sides of the issue, making it difficult to discuss the problem on its merits.

She knew she should drop the subject, but a perverse streak in her nature caused her to demand, "Will you admit I'm right?"

"May I help myself to another glass of sack?" He went to the sideboard, refilled his glass, and faced her. "When you come to Oakhurst Manor you'll see this institution you regard as dreadful, and I'll wager you a pair of diamond earrings against a kiss that you'll change your mind. You'll discover that my father and I do treat our slaves as people. They aren't beaten and cowed."

"That's because you're humane."

"Maybe so," Jeremy said, "but there's more to it than you realize. Slaves are valuable. We depend on them for our living. It wouldn't make sense to mistreat them!"

She understood what he was saying, even though she couldn't accept it, but her own innate wisdom asserted itself. It was stupid to engage in a bitter quarrel that neither of them could win.

Jeremy became aware of her invisible flag of truce, and going to the sofa, he drew a letter from his pocket. "This is for you."

Sarah went to him and sat beside him. Taking the letter, she recognized the seal on the wax as being the same as that on his signet ring, the seal of Oakhurst Manor. It bore a Latin inscription, *Aspera ad virtutem est via,* and she needed no one to translate it for her: "It is a difficult road that leads to virtue."

The letter had been written by Jeremy's father, and its bluntness, with no words wasted, was typical of his nature:

Mr dear Daughter:

I look forward with eager anticipation to the visit you will pay to us this spring in the company of your father and sister. I only regret that the passing of your mother three years past deprives us of her company also.

I look forward with even greater joy to the day,

this coming summer, when you will marry Jeremy and settle at Oakhurst Manor.

    I am, ma'am,
    Yr. obdt. svt.,
    Paul Wellington Beaufort

Sarah read the letter a second time. *My dear Daughter*. What a sweet, generous man, and no wonder he had such a wonderful son. Her eyes misted.

"Are you weeping?" Jeremy asked.

She blinked away her tears and shook her head. "I'm happy, that's all."

He wondered if he would ever understand her mind, much less her mercurial changes in mood. One moment she was so serious, full of high purpose, and the next she was as giddy as her sister. No matter. He put his hands on her shoulders and drew her to him.

His touch was a spark that inflamed Sarah, and although she recognized the danger, her lips parted for his passionate kiss. She allowed him to pull her closer, yielding eagerly to him, her desire as great as his.

Jeremy's self-control deserted him. His last conscious thought was that he had no more scruples than Thomas.

Sarah felt his hand close over a breast, and she wanted more, much more. She was behaving like a shameless wanton, showing as little discipline as Margot, and in Papa's parlor, at that. But she no longer cared. Every fiber of her being demanded Jeremy Beaufort.

She pulled down the upper portion of her dress, then ripped off her breastband, and the hand that performed the act was almost disembodied, as though completely separate from her and her own will.

Jeremy blinked, and was dazzled. He bent his head, his lips caressing her bare breasts, and when her nipples hardened, he knew he could no longer curb his own desires.

They behaved like puppets, impelled by forces stronger than their own inhibitions, stronger than the curbs that society placed on the conduct of ladies and gentlemen.

They lay naked together on the sofa in front of the roaring wood fire, and the only law they knew was that of their union. They were a woman and a man whose love surmounted every obstacle.

Their mutual desire mounted until they could tolerate it no longer. They became one, and their erotic yearnings became intolerable. Then, suddenly, they found release together, and their union was sealed.

Chapter 2

Sarah felt no guilt, no remorse, no regrets. Sitting in front of the pier glass in her bedchamber as she repaired her appearance before her father and sister returned home, she had only one thought in her mind. She and Jeremy had consummated their union, and she felt that she had already become his wife. She had been surprisingly impulsive, to be sure, demonstrating the sort of behavior that was typical of Margot, but it didn't matter that she had broken the rules by which she had always lived.

In a few short months she and Jeremy would stand up before a minister and formalize their marriage. But that was only a technicality. Their love was so deep, so certain, that, in spite of her Puritan upbringing, she was convinced that God could not disapprove of what she and Jeremy had done. They belonged together and would spend the rest of their lives together. Nothing else mattered.

Sarah brushed her hair vigorously, removed tiny gold studs from her ears, and substituted the hoops that Jeremy had given her as a Christmas gift. The color of her cheeks was already high, so she used only a small amount of lip rouge, placed tiny dabs of kohl on her eyelids, and lightly dusted her face with rice powder.

When she went into the parlor, she found that Papa and Margot had just returned. Isaiah Benton, a tall, spare man who tied his graying hair at the nape of his neck with an eelskin, in the old-fashioned way, stood in front of the fire with a hot rum toddy in one hand. He was immersed in a discussion with Jeremy of a recent United States Supreme Court decision, and acknowledged his elder daughter's presence with a wave.

"Chief Justice Marshall's brief has set another precedent," he said in his deep, mellow voice. "I urge you to read it carefully, Jeremiah."

"I shall, sir," his future son-in-law replied. "Do you have a copy?"

"The New York *Intelligencer* reprinted it in full, and I have it on my desk."

Sarah was amused to note that Margot, bored by the legal talk, nevertheless couldn't resist flirting with Jeremy. She, too, was wearing an Empire dress, and had tugged it down off her shoulders as far as she dared without calling Papa's attention to the fact. Her hair, the color of burnished copper, fell forward on both sides of her neck, artfully enhancing her pale skin, which was further emphasized by her gown of mauve silk. She was tiny, several inches shorter than her older sister, and small-boned, but her figure was equally attractive, within proportion. And she knew how to utilize it to the full. She was in a provocative pose, as always, conscious of her sexuality and its powers.

Only her eyes were like Sarah's and were the same shade of deep green. But their expression was different: Margot found it necessary to challenge every man she met, and lurking behind her sensuality was an almost hidden amusement at the gullible frailty of the opposite sex. She took nothing seriously, herself included, and her sister sometimes suspected she laughed at herself as heartily as she laughed at the men who fell all over themselves and each other in pursuit of her.

It was the pursuit that meant everything to Margot. She felt compelled to prove that she attracted every male who crossed her path, but the relationship always stopped with a flirtation. Sarah had lectured her for years, trying to convince her that she was playing with a scorching fire, that someday she would encounter a man unwilling to be dismissed with a kiss. Fortunately, she was still a virgin, but she walked a delicate tightrope, and Sarah was convinced she was headed for disaster.

Even her makeup was far heavier than most young ladies wore. She used grease on her lashes and heavy applications of kohl on her eyelids. She wore ample quantities of rouge on her cheeks and on her lips, and she brought out her high cheekbones with a beauty patch, sometimes of black velvet, sometimes of a snippet of material that matched her dress.

Even Papa had been known to observe that she used cosmetics with the lavishness of a waterfront whore. But Margot went her own way, listening to no one, secure in the inner knowledge that she was capable of handling any situation that might arise. It was that sense of security that gave her ultimate protection, Sarah thought; behind her inviting facade was a hard core of purity. Well, of innocence, if not of purity in the true sense. Margot not only had confidence in her own charms but assumed that every man was a gentleman, that he would stop making advances at her request. Heaven help her when she met someone who was less than a gentleman, who would demand that she live up to the promise implicit in her lazy smile.

Even though Sarah came into the room, Margot continued to flirt with Jeremy, watching him sleepily through half-lowered lids as she curled up on the sofa. A faint suggestion of a smile touched the corners of her full, ripe mouth, and she had permitted her skirt to ride above her sandals, displaying more of her ankles than was proper. She had twisted her body artfully, too, simultaneously emphasizing her breasts, tiny waist, and the long, graceful line of a thigh.

She had no way of knowing, of course, that less than a half-hour earlier Sarah and Jeremy had made love on the very piece of furniture on which she was displaying herself. Unconsciously touching the heavy signet ring hanging between her breasts, Sarah had to conceal a laugh.

Isaiah Benton cut his discourse short. "It's high time we dine," he said. "I think we've kept Amanda waiting long enough, and we don't want her to leave and find other employment, which she'll do if we don't keep regular meal hours." He offered his arm to his younger daughter.

Sarah took Jeremy's arm, and they went into the dining room, a Spartan, utilitarian chamber. Even the linen, silverware, and glasses on the table of polished maple were plain. The late Mrs. Benton had shared her husband's unpretentious tastes, and although Sarah would have preferred something slightly more ornate, she deferred to Papa's continuing regard for his wife's memory.

Amanda came into the room as soon as they were seated, carrying a steaming tureen. She was approximately Sarah's age, an agile girl with delicate features and a good figure that was concealed beneath a crisp black, white-trimmed serving maid's uniform. Jeremy had known at a glance, the first time he had seen her, that she was not a full-blooded black. He suspected that a white grandfather lurked in her background. Whatever her heritage, her attitude was unlike that of any of the slaves at Oakhurst Manor, and her approach to life never failed to amaze him. She was sturdily independent, proud of her free birth in Boston, and she not only was treated as the equal of the Bentons, but she herself assumed an air of easy familiarity with them. At Oakhurst Manor only a slave woman like the principal cook, Cleo, who had nursed Thomas when his mother had died, was on such intimate terms with members of the family.

Isaiah Benton ladled out the thick, fragrant fish chowder, which the serving maid carried to each plate. "Amanda," he said, "we invited you to come with us when we go to South Carolina to visit Mr. Beaufort's family. Have you decided as yet whether you want to join us?"

"No, sir." The black girl paused in her work and stood beside Jeremy. "I need to know a little more first. Mr. Beaufort, if I was to make that trip, is there any chance that your folks would keep me there and turn me into a slave?"

Jeremy could sympathize with her concern, but was shocked by the suggestion. "Under no circumstances, Amanda," he said. "South Carolina is as much a part of the United States as Massachusetts, you know, and we obey the same federal laws."

"I wasn't saying your folks would be like to kidnap me," Amanda replied, "but I do get some flutters in my stomach."

"You have nothing to fear from my family," he assured her gravely.

Isaiah Benton intervened. "If you wish, Amanda, I can provide you with a notarized document stating that you're freeborn."

"Then I'll think about the invitation," the girl said, and disappeared into the kitchen.

"I must admit," Isaiah Benton said, speaking in a low tone, "that the prospect of taking Amanda with us has made me a trifle uneasy, too."

Jeremy shook his head. It was astonishing that even one of New England's most distinguished attorneys completely failed to understand the South. "I'll grant you," he said, "that slavery is involuntary servitude. By definition. I won't make any attempt too argue that virtually all of the blacks who came here from Africa were the losers in tribal wars who were sold to traders by the victors and who would have been either enslaved or murdered had they remained in their own world. I will say, though, that most of them are ignorant savages who benefit by their exposure to our civilization."

Sarah couldn't help challenging him. "Do you teach the slaves at Oakhurst Manor to read and write?"

Jeremy grinned at her. She was a spitfire who refused to concede defeat. "Those who show the ability to learn are taught," he said. "Others become carpenters, bricklayers, mechanics—they pick up many trades. I won't predict that all slaves will become literate or become skilled workers in our lifetimes. But it will happen. In the time of our sons or grandsons, and they'll be better off than those who were left behind to die of starvation and disease and war in the African jungles."

"I hope you're right," Sarah said.

22

"Make no judgments until you see Oakhurst Manor for yourself," he told her.

"Jeremy is right," Isaiah Benton said. "One of our most pronounced New England faults is our tendency to pass judgment on others without trying to accumulate all of the evidence and then weighing it. It's no secret to any of you young people that I don't approve of slavery in principle, but I refuse to condemn it outright until I see your system at Oakhurst Manor in operation."

Margot was bored. "Surely you don't spend all your time at Oakhurst Manor studying slaves! What will there be for me to do?"

Jeremy chuckled. "There are local assemblies and balls and routs. We visit friends in Charleston and Savannah. We have parties after we go on hunting and fishing trips. Every weekend, someone in the neighborhood holds an informal barbecue or picnic or jamboree. And if the organized social life isn't enough for you, I'm sure you'll keep busy making eyes at my brother, Tom, or flirting with the oldest of the Emerson boys, who live nearby. Unless I'm mistaken, you'll have plenty to keep you busy."

Sarah and her father joined in the laugh.

Margot was unabashed. "If your brother and this Emerson person are half as handsome and seemly as you, Jeremy, I'll have no complaint."

Isaiah Benton glanced at her. "I'm surprised," he said wryly, "that you haven't asked for the right to bring home one of the young officers from the British squadron of warships that's anchored in the harbor."

The girl had an elfin-like grin. "The only reason I haven't, Papa," she said, "is because I haven't met any of them."

"I should hope not, miss." Sarah was indignant. "Those warships stop honest American merchantmen on the high seas and take any cargo they believe is being sent to the Emperor Napoleon."

"That's not all," her father added. "There have been any number of cases of American seamen being impressed into the Royal Navy, because the British have been at war so long they're short of sailors."

"But that's illegal, Papa!" Sarah exclaimed.

"I'm afraid we live in a world in which might makes right," the attorney said in a weary voice. "President Madison and Secretary Monroe have sent countless complaints to London, but the king's government pay no attention. We had to fight one war to win our independence, and it wouldn't surprise me if we're forced to fight another to maintain it."

"South Carolina," Jeremy said, "would answer a call to arms without hesitation. Which is more than can be said for some New England towns like Hartford and Providence. I'm startled whenever I read that a great many people up here would be just as happy to leave the Union and establish a new affiliation with Great Britain."

"There are some, to be sure." Isaiah paused for a moment to watch Amanda bring in a platter of salt beef that had been boiled with potatoes, carrots, onions, cabbage, and other vegetables, a typical Boston main dish. "I'll even grant you that the same sentiment can be found right here, as well as in Worcester and Springfield. But the people who feel that way are in a minority. I'm certain you'll find that if a real crisis develops, the people of New England are as patriotic and as eager to serve the United States as the citizens who come from other parts of the country."

"From my own observations, sir. I'm sure you're right," Jeremy said. "Our territory has expanded enormously since the Revolution, thanks principally to the purchase of the Louisiana Territory from France eight years ago, but our population hasn't yet grown all that much. All the same, even though there may not be many of us, most Americans are willing to defend our liberty with their lives!"

The young people were hungry, and conversation languished. The men washed down their meal with mugs of locally brewed ale, while the girls sipped small glasses of new wine that came from New York State. They finished the meal with dishes of syllabub, a custard-like dessert mildly flavored with rum. They retired to the parlor to drink strong West Indian coffee, and when the clock on the mantel chimed nine o'clock, it was time for Jeremy to take his leave.

He arranged to pick up Sarah the following evening to

attend a lecture on the establishment of new factories and industries in major American cities and towns, a subject that interested both of them. Isaiah gladly gave his consent to the engagement and shook the hand of his future son-in-law.

Margot raised her face, and it was evident that she intended to kiss Jeremy on the mouth.

He grinned at her and lightly brushed her cheek with his lips. Her only motive was that of making her sister jealous, and he had no intention of playing her game.

Sarah accompanied Jeremy to the front door. "I have no regrets over what we did tonight," she murmured as they embraced.

"Nor have I," he said. "I love you."

A moment later he stood on the stoop, pulling down his bicorne and closing the loops on his cape. But this was one night he didn't feel the penetrating cold. He, too, was filled with the wonder of what he and Sarah had done, and, like her, he felt no sense of guilt. Their betrothal would be announced when she came to Oakhurst Manor, and this summer they would be married. He could ask for little more.

Again he cut across the Common en route to his own lodgings, and he was so indifferent to the weather that he took his time. Ultimately, as he made his way down narrow, twisting streets, his boots echoing on the cobblestones, it occurred to him that he was thoroughly chilled.

Directly ahead was a tavern, and on sudden impulse he decided to stop in for a small glass of brandywine for the purpose of warming himself. Besides, he thought in sudden exultation, I owe me a drink to celebrate. Sarah is mine. All mine!

The tavern wasn't the place he ordinarily would have chosen for a celebration, but it was convenient. Like so many others in Boston, it served a clientele of fishermen, sailors, and mechanics, an all-embracing term that included the men of many trades who earned their living with their hands. An oak log was burning in a large hearth at the far end of the taproom, and workingmen in homespun linsey-woolsey sat in twos and threes at the tables of scrubbed Massachusetts pine, most of them drinking ale or a local version of mead, a brew made from honey.

A trollop who sat alone smiled at Jeremy and raised her glass to him.

He wasn't even aware of the wench's presence. He had eyes only for Sarah Benton, and had no interest in any other woman on earth.

Three men at a corner table, all attired in the blue woolen uniforms and pea jackets of the Royal Navy, looked with interest at the newcomer. The eldest of the trio, whose cuff markings identified him as a boatswain, ran a heavy hand through his thinning hair, then rubbed his thick chin.

"A lively specimen, lads," he muttered. "He's tall, young, and has a right good build."

One of his companions demurred. "Oi don't rightly fink 'e's for us, Talbot," he said. "Looks to me loike that there one is gentry."

Boatswain Talbot hated to be crossed, and his face darkened. "Those that come from the gentry are the best," he said. "They don't have much fight in them, and once they learn their place, they'll do as they're told, as docile as lambs." He watched Jeremy give his order to a haggard, middle-aged barmaid, and then summoned the woman.

"Not again," she said.

Boatswain Talbot's lips parted in a bloodless smile, and gaps showed between his remaining front teeth. "Mollie, m'love, how would you like to earn another shilling of his majesty's silver?"

"The price has gone up," she replied. "Two shillings, paid in advance."

He did not argue, but reached into a pouch at his belt and handed her a coin.

She bit it to test its authenticity, slipped it into a pocket, and went off to the bar.

The trio continued to watch as Jeremy Beaufort was served his brandywine. He raised it in a silent toast, then downed half of the contents.

A few moments later he slumped forward and sprawled across the table.

The trio were on their feet instantly and joined him.

"Our friend has had a bit too much," Talbot said in a loud voice. "We'd best see him to his house." While he paid the barmaid for the drinks, his companions half-carried, half-dragged the unconscious Jeremy out into the street.

By the time Talbot had joined them, they had hoisted him into the saddle of a rented horse, and the three did not delay as they headed toward the waterfront.

"Full alert," one of the sailors muttered. "Constable ahead."

Talbot took the lead and greeted the officer of the peace with exaggerated courtesy. "A cold night to be making your rounds."

"That it be." The constable showed little interest as he glanced at the crumpled figure on horseback. "One of your mates is ill, is he?"

Talbot laughed and winked. "Nothing wrong with him that a night of sleep and a day or two of drying out won't cure. You know sailors when they come ashore."

The constable chuckled and wandered off down the street, his heavy staff tapping the cobblestones.

The seamen quickened their pace, and soon they reached the waterfront, making their way to a stone wharf that stood apart from the docks used by commercial merchantmen. A longboat rode the cold, black waters, six sailors resting at their oars.

While Jeremy was unceremoniously dumped into the boat, Talbot handed a sixpence to a small boy who happened to be passing and instructed him to take the horse back to his stable.

Then he lowered himself into the boat. "Push off," he directed, hauling in the line that held the craft fast. "Lively, now!"

The oarsmen bent to their task, rowing in unison, and the longboat glided across the silent harbor. A cluster of Royal Navy ships was anchored about a half-mile from shore, and Talbot, at the tiller, directed the boat toward the nearest of them, HMS *Dolphin*, a sloop of war.

When they reached the vessel, he hauled himself onto the deck with the easy grace of a man who had spent most of his life at sea and went straight to the quarterdeck.

"Boatswain Talbot at report, sir," he said, saluting the officer of the watch, whose single epaulet indicated that he was a lieutenant.

"What luck?" Lieutenant Gough was impatient.

Talbot grinned self-importantly. "I got another, sir. The fourth of the night, and the best of the lot. They're taking him 'tween decks now."

"Ah, then we have a full complement at last. We'd best put out to sea before the bloody Americans send a search party aboard." He turned to the boatswain's mate who shared the watch with him. "Rouse all hands!"

"Aye, aye, sir."

"You may weigh anchor when ready."

"Aye, aye, sir."

"My compliments to the captain, and ask him to join me here, if he will. Helmsman, sail to the leeward of the flagship, close enough so the captain can notify the commodore that we've fulfilled our mission and are putting out to sea."

Orders were shouted, and sailors swarmed onto the deck.

The unconscious Jeremy Beaufort lay crumpled in a hammock below, unaware that he had been impressed into the British Navy and was being carried out to a harsh new life at sea.

Chapter 3

Isaiah Benton ate his usual light breakfast, which consisted of porridge with sausages, broiled scrod, and honey cakes. With his meal he drank a mug of porter, and, fortified for the day ahead, he walked the short distance down Beacon Street to his law offices. The early-morning air was raw, and a glance at the leaden sky told him that snow would fall again before the day ended. He would miss Sarah when she moved to Oakhurst Manor, but he was pleased for her sake that she would be spared the rigors of New England winters. He was tempted to move to a warmer climate himself, but Margot was still single, so it was premature to think in such terms.

Three of his four clerks were already at work in the outer room, and Isaiah was surprised to see that Jeremy Beaufort's desk was unoccupied. Isaiah's future son-in-law was so eager to learn that, most days, he was the first to appear. "Tell Mr. Beaufort I want a word with him as soon as he comes in," he said, and went on to his large private office, where a coal fire had been burning for more than an hour.

Reading the morning newspapers that awaited him,

Isaish noted that work was almost completed on the new Park Street Church, which was being built by his friend Peter Banner. In Connecticut a new organization called the Moral Society had just been founded by the Reverend Lyman Beecher to fight rum selling and the failure of citizens to observe the Sabbath.

The national news from Washington City was grim. Great Britain was insisting that the young United States terminate her trade relations with France, while the Emperor Napoleon was demanding that America halt trade relations with Britain. The new president was asserting his nation's right to trade with anyone it wished. Meanwhile, the State Department complained that seven more kidnappings of Americans who had been impressed into the Royal Navy had just been unearthed and authenticated. The British government followed its usual policy of making no reply of any kind to these accusations.

Isaiah read his morning's mail, which was light, and then turned to a brief for a pending lawsuit that required his attention. It was after ten A.M. when he glanced at the clock on the mantel over the fireplace, and he reached for an ivory-handled bell on the desk.

The senior clerk answered his summons.

"I'm still waiting for a word with Beaufort."

"He hasn't come in, sir."

Isaiah was concerned. "He's never been this late, so he may be ill. Perhaps you'd do well to send a messenger to his lodgings. On second thought, go yourself."

The better part of an hour passed before the senior clerk returned, and one look at his face told Isaiah that his news was bad.

"Jeremy didn't return to his lodgings last night, sir," he said.

"But he left my house at nine!"

"All of his clothes and other belongings are still in his room, so it's plain he intended to go back there. I took the liberty of stopping at the constabulary headquarters to report that he's missing. They tell me that they've had similar reports about several others."

"Young men?"

"Yes, Mr. Benton."

"So suspicion points in the direction of the British naval squadron at anchor in the harbor."

"I'm afraid it does, sir."

Isaiah sighed heavily, then donned his greatcoat and tricorne. "Attend to anything that may come up here," he said. "I'll need to go down to the waterfront myself to see what I might be able to learn." He refrained from mentioning that he hoped to pick up some crumbs of information before going home to tell Sarah the catastrophic news.

He walked quickly down to the docks, and although it wasn't yet noon, the taverns were doing a roaring trade, with seamen from merchant ships and a scattering of Royal Navy sailors drinking. Waterfront trollops were patrolling their beats in sleazy finery, and in spite of the cold, the beggars were out in force.

Isaiah questioned everyone he saw on the streets, but neither the beggars nor the prostitutes could tell him anything about the missing Jeremy. He scoured the area near the wharves used by the Royal Navy, refraining only from questioning the tavern keepers themselves. His experience on the bench had taught him that the owners of drinking establishments who connived with the Royal Navy always lied in order to protect themselves from possible prosecution.

Finally he found an unshaven dockworker who gave him a lead. "My little boy, he got a tip from some English sailors last night to take their horse back to the stable. Mayhap he can tell you something."

"Where is your son right now?"

"He's to home, sir, a-waitin' for his dinner." The man pointed toward a dilapidated house that stood adjacent to a warehouse.

A few moments later, Isaiah confronted the child in the shabby parlor, the boy brightening when he was given a new ten-cent piece recently minted by the Commonwealth of Massachusetts.

"There was three English sailors," he said, "and a fourth who was sleeping off his ruff-scuff. They bundled him into their boat and took him out to their warships, they did. And they give me money and a tip to return their horse to Mr. Harder's stables."

"Could you describe the man who was sleeping?" Isaiah managed to speak calmly.

"I didn't rightly get a good look at him, mister, but he was a big one. It took two of the sailors to carry him."

"Was he dressed in a Royal Navy uniform like the others?"

The boy scratched his head as he pondered. "Now you mention it, mister, I don't rightly recall that he was. I didn't pay all that much attention to him, so I couldn't swear that he was or wasn't dressed in a uniform."

"So you wouldn't know whether he was a sailor. Or, perhaps, a gentleman."

The child knew why he was being questioned so closely, and sighed. "I wish I could help you, mister. Pa always tells me to keep my eyes open, but this is one time I didn't. I reckon the reason is that it was late, and I was sleepy."

Isaiah's hopes were dying. "Could you recognize the English sailors if you saw them again?"

Again the boy hesitated. "I ain't sure, mister. I don't like them lobsters, even when they be a-wearin' blue sailor suits, so I got me out o' there right quick."

There was nothing more to be gained from the boy, so Isaiah's next stop was Harder's Stables. He was acquainted with the liveryman, whom he had represented in a civil lawsuit some years earlier, but could glean nothing of substance from him.

"Ever since the British squadron put into port," he said, "I've been renting ten to fifteen mounts a day to their officers and men. I'm afraid I can't distinguish one from another."

Isaiah went home with lagging footsteps, dreading the necessity of telling his elder daughter that the man she loved had vanished.

Margot greeted him at the front door, but discreetly took herself elsewhere when he said he wanted to talk to her sister.

Sarah looked radiant when she joined him in the parlor, and his heart ached for her.

"You're home early for dinner, Papa," she said.

Isaiah knew only one way to tell her what had happened, and broke the news to her without preamble.

Sarah clenched her fists, her arms rigid at her sides, and a white line showed around her mouth, but in no other way did she indicate that she was stunned. "If highwaymen or footpads robbed and killed Jeremy," she said, speaking in a low, controlled voice, "I assume the constables would have found his body."

"Probably."

"Then he was kidnapped by a Royal Navy press gang, Papa. He had no reason to disappear. Quite the contrary," she added, remembering every detail of her lovemaking with Jeremy on the sofa.

Her father shrugged.

"There are few men in Massachusetts more prominent than you. Can't you win his release?"

"I'll do what I can, but I make no promises. The British never admit they've impressed a man, just as they never deny it, either, but perhaps I can bring some extra weight to bear. My influence was partly responsible for Elbridge Gerry's election as governor of Massachusetts last month, so he's very much in my debt. I'm sure he'll do everything in his power to help. Unfortunately, the British are in command of the situation, and there's little we can do to force their hand."

Sarah stood straight. "I know Jeremy will come back to me," she said. "I know he'll allow nothing in this world to stand between us. Do what you can, Papa, and may the Almighty keep watch over Jeremy."

A sixty-foot cutter flying the ensign of the Commonwealth of Massachusetts, her sails furled, was rowed across Boston harbor, and a complement of royal marines in scarlet-and-white uniforms stood on the deck of HMS *Unicorn,* awaiting the governor of Massachusetts and his companion. Commodore Sir Francis Browning had learned of the impending visit only minutes earlier, but everyone aboard his forty-two-gun flagship had been alerted.

The marines stood at stiff attention, their muskets at present arms, and the shrill pipes of a boatswain welcomed the visitors.

The commodore and Governor Gerry exchanged flowery greetings, Isaiah Benton was presented to Sir Francis, and the trio repaired to the spacious aft cabin, which had twenty windows of square-cut glass on each of three sides. Although it was late afternoon enough daylight entered so that it was as yet unnecessary to light the oil lamps. High-ranking officers in the Royal Navy enjoyed luxuries that few other men knew ashore.

"Americans haven't been partial to tea for the better part of forty years," Sir Francis said, "but I trust you'll permit me to offer you some of the East India Company's finest."

An orderly brought three steaming mugs into the cabin.

Isaiah Benton and Governor Gerry refused offers of rum in their tea, indicating that their call was not social.

"Sir Francis," Gerry said, "we may be wasting your time on a wild-turkey chase, but I feel certain we can rely on your help."

"I'll gladly do what I can, gentlemen."

The governor was blunt. "Judge Benton's future son-in-law disappeared last night, and we have reason to believe that one of your press gangs may have caught him."

Isaiah told his story in firm, undiplomatic language. "The Boston constabulary," he concluded, "informs me that Jeremy Beaufort is only one of four young men who have vanished here in the past twenty-four hours. We have reason to believe that your men may have kidnapped all of them."

The commodore looked pained. "My country," he said, "is carrying the entire burden of the war at sea against the tyrant Bonaparte. We wish the nations whose interests we're protecting would be more appreciative of our efforts."

"The United States," Governor Gerry observed, "would be far more grateful if you left her citizens in peace to resolve their own destinies."

"We realize, Sir Francis, that you aren't personally responsible for your government's policy of impressment," Isaiah said. "All the same, you could do the cause of Anglo-American friendship a great deal of good. If one of your gangs has taken young Beaufort, I'm sure his impressment wasn't a personal vendetta. He's a splendid young man who is due to be admitted to the bar this spring, and is scheduled to marry my elder daughter soon afterward. So I'm sure you can understand my concern."

"To be sure." Sir Francis' sigh was exaggerated. "Britain has been bled white in her sea war with Bonaparte, so some of our patriotic boatswains may be guilty of . . . ah . . . overzealousness in their recruiting methods. But nothing of the sort has taken place in Boston, so we're not guilty of abusing your hospitality. My captains are required by Royal Navy regulations to notify me—personally—whenever the press gangs pick up new apprentice seamen. As you saw when you sailed across the harbor just now, there are four of my ships at anchor right now, including this one, but I've had no notice from any of my four captains that they've found any local recruits."

Isaiah had expected no coöperation or help, but was nevertheless disappointed.

"I don't even ask you to take my word, gentlemen," the commodore went on. "If you wish, you may send a committee of your own naval experts—if you have any—to inspect all four of my ships."

Isaiah exchanged a quick glance with Elbridge Gerry. The commodore was clever, no two ways about it. Inasmuch as he was anchored in American waters, he was required to submit to a ship-by-ship search if his hosts demanded such a hunt. So he was making the best of the situation by placing them on the defensive.

Governor Gerry was aware of the helplessness of his own position, knowing how easy it would be to hide kidnapped men in the holds or elsewhere on board the warships. He drank the last of his tea, stood, and bowed. "We're thankful for your offer, Sir Francis, but we're obliged to accept your word. If it should come to your attention that young Beaufort or any of our other citizens have been impressed, we rely on you to release them at once."

"Of course." As Sir Francis accompanied his guests to their waiting boat, he did not explain that the names of impressed seamen were irrelevant. Nor did he mention that four had been picked up the previous night and had been carried out to sea on board the fifth ship of his squadron, the *Dolphin*, which he had dispatched on detached service.

A heavy winter rain seeped in through the thick walls of red brick, and even the study was damp. This chamber, lined with leather-bound books from floor to ceiling, was Paul Wellington Beaufort's pride, and he often said that no other plantation in South Carolina boasted a library as extensive as Oakhurst Manor's. An unopened novel by Sir Walter Scott, whose work was now the rage in the United States, lay opened beside him as he sat with a gout-ridden foot propped on a stool in front of a small wood fire. It was the same foot in which he had suffered a wound during the War of Independence while serving with the irregulars under Brigadier General Francis Marion, and experience had taught him that he would be immobilized for four or five days.

Paul ran a strong hand through his still-dark hair, sipped steaming beef tea from a pewter mug, and, after sending a servant to fetch his younger son, sat and stared into the fire. Life at Oakhurst Manor had been so harmonious of late, with the plantation more successful than ever before, that he should have been on his guard. As Cleo, the black housekeeper who ran the domestic staff, so often said, the Lord always took care to afflict those who appeared to have risen beyond trouble.

A chill crept up Paul's spine, and he tried to ignore it, loosening the stock at his throat and vigorously rubbing his hands together. At the moment, he was helpless, unable to attend personally to the sudden crisis that had arisen, but perhaps that was just as well, too. As soon as he could ride a horse again, later in the week, he'd be needed to supervise the cutting of timber on the backland. Mr. Higby might be a competent enough overseer, but selecting the right stands of pine to be cut, fashioned into planks, and sent off to Charleston was a task that only the owner of a plantation could perform. Oh, Scott Emerson, at nearby Trelawney, might assign the job to an overseer, but Paul Beaufort was too conscientious. Maybe that was why he had built up Oakhurst Manor until no other estate in the Carolinas or Georgia was its equal.

He had twenty-one thousand acres, and more than five hundred slaves worked the land for him. He could have been a power in the state legislature and even been sent to the United States House of Representatives, had politics interested him. But Oakhurst Manor had been his whole life, just as it had been his father's before him.

His elder son had felt precisely the same way, loving the plantation as fervently as some men loved their women. But now Jeremy had disappeared, and only the Lord knew what had become of him. If the British had taken him into their navy, it might be years before he came home. Provided he survived. Jeremy was tough, resourceful, and resilient, but he'd need all of those qualities and a number of others as well to live through an experience in the Royal Navy.

Damn the crown, its troops, and its sailors! Ever since the treaty of peace had been signed in 1783 and Great Britain had recognized the independence of her former colonies, Paul had been willing to forget the long war. But the freedom of the United States wasn't being respected, and his own son, in all probability, had been forced into involuntary servitude.

The worst of the situation was that neither he nor Jeremy had any recourse under the law. Secretary of State Monroe could protest to the Foreign Office in London until he was purple in the face, for all the good it would accomplish. The British had learned nothing in the Revolution and would have to be taught a lesson again.

Paul stirred when his younger son came into the study, clad in boots and an open-throated shirt, his long hair tied with a bit of cloth at the back of his neck. He was tall and husky, looking and sounding like Jeremy, but there the resemblance ended. Jeremy was serious and hardworking, proud of the Beaufort name, and devoted to Oakhurst. Tom cared only for his pleasure of the moment, gave no thought to the future, and could not be bridled.

He saluted his father with his riding crop, then faced him in front of the fire. "They found me at the stables just as I was about to ride off to Trelawney. Young Scott and I are going to try our luck in the duck blind."

"In this weather?" His father raised an eyebrow.

"Never fear, sir. We'll fortify ourselves with a few drops of rum before we go out."

"Are you sober now?"

Something in the older man's attitude caused Tom to pause, and his grin faded. "What's amiss, Papa?"

Paul handed him the letter he had just received from Isaiah Benton, telling him of Jeremy's disappearance.

Color rose in Tom's face beneath his heavy tan as he read the letter. "Damn those British bastards. I'll . . ." He choked and stopped short.

His father watched him in wry amusement. "Just what is it you'll do, lad?"

"If I must, I'll go to London and put a charge of gunpowder under the royal palace."

"That won't bring your brother home a day earlier, I'm sorry to say." Paul's voice was heavy. "No, lad, you'll sit tight here. Jeremy will look after himself, provided they give him half a chance and don't murder him. I'll write to our senators, of course, and they'll notify the State Department, but that will accomplish nothing. We're obliged to wait until Jeremy works his own way out of his troubles."

"I hate waiting!" Tom slapped his thigh with his riding crop.

"You can start paying more attention to affairs here at Oakhurst, as I've been urging you to do ever since Jeremy went off to study law." Paul did not raise his voice. "As soon as you come back from your journey."

"What journey, sir?"

"I'm sending you off to Boston tomorrow. Scott Emerson and I have chartered a merchantman loaded with sugarcane that sails from Charleston on the morning tide. You'll be aboard her. You'll meet the Bentons and make your own investigation of Jeremy's disappearance."

Tom had long wanted to make the trip to Massachusetts, and his eyes gleamed. "Yes, sir!"

"I'd go myself, but my confounded foot has crippled me again. Just remember, this is no pleasure trip, lad."

"I'll remember."

"I'll want you to take Willie with you." Willie was a slave, the son of Cleo and an expert cabinetmaker. He was two days older than Tom, and when the late Mrs. Beaufort had died in childbirth the slave woman had nursed both babies. Tom and Willie had grown up together; they had been inseparable as boys, and were still close.

"I reckon you don't trust me, Papa," Tom said, and laughed aloud.

His father's smile was tight. "Well," he said, "if you start tasting too many of Boston's joys and forget why I've sent you there, Willie will haul you back into line fast enough."

"I'll be glad to have Willie's company, Papa, but I won't need anybody to remind me of why I'm going north. If Jeremy can be found, I aim to find him!"

Chapter 4

Margot Benton heard someone pounding on the front door and peered out through the parlor curtains, but it was snowing so hard she could see only the boots, bicornes, and capes of two tall men. More of Papa's clients pestering him at home instead of going to his office, she assumed, and went to answer the summons, annoyed because the pounding didn't stop.

She opened the door and stared when she saw two young men, one white and one black. "There's no need for you to break down the door, you know!" she said angrily.

"We'll freeze out here. We're not accustomed to this weather." Tom Beaufort stepped into the entrance hall, with Willie close behind him, and both bowed as they removed their hats.

The white man's resemblance to Jeremy was uncanny, and Margot gasped. "You're obviously a Beaufort, and you must be Tom."

"You're right, Miss Sarah."

"I'm Margot."

"Aha!" Tom inspected her with greater interest. "Jeremy never told us that Sarah's sister was beautiful."

"That's Jeremy for you," Willie said with a chuckle. "Probably never got his nose out of his law books long enough to recognize a pretty girl when he saw one."

"This is Willie, Miss Margot," Tom said, but offered no further explanation of his companion's identity.

"Leave your capes on the pegs yonder," the girl said, trying to compose herself. "Then scrape the snow off your boots and go into the parlor. That way. I'll get Papa and Sarah."

She hurried off before they could reply, and after notifying her father and sister of the guests' arrival, she raced to her own room. There she dabbed grease on her lashes and kohl on her lids, added rouge to her cheeks and lips, and removed the combs from her hair. She didn't want to take the time to change into an Empire gown, which would have meant changing her shoes and stockings, too, so she did the next-best thing and pulled her dress down to bare her shoulders. Tom Beaufort had been expected, his father's letter having arrived some days earlier, but no one had indicated that he was even more strikingly handsome than his brother.

Tom and Willie, wearing identical suits of black broadcloth, were warming themselves in front of the wood fire in the parlor as Isaiah Benton told them of his own investigation of Jeremy's disappearance.

Sarah sat as though in a trance, and seemed mesmerized whenever Tom spoke. It really was uncanny that he sounded so much like Jeremy.

"So you had no trace of him, Mr. Benton?" he asked.

"Not until it was too late," Isaiah said. "The British squadron left port two days after the governor and I saw the commodore and made our futile plea for his help. Only then did it dawn on the harbormaster that one of the warships, a sloop of war called the *Dolphin*, had sailed much earlier. On the very night that Jeremy vanished. Or early the next morning, at the latest."

"So he was abducted and taken on board the *Dolphin*?" Tom asked.

"That's our surmise, but we have no way of proving it. Even if one of our warships encounters the *Dolphin* at sea, it would be impossible to halt and search her. We're simply not in a position to challenge the Royal Navy."

"The day will come—and soon—when that's exactly what we'll be obliged to do," Tom said angrily. "Willie and I would go after them alone, if we could.".

"Barehanded," Willie added, "and we'd put up one whale of a fight."

Sarah, who had been very quiet, joined in the conversation for the first time. "We won't allow you to go to an inn while you're in Boston, Mr. Beaufort. We insist that you stay here with us, although we aren't sure we can offer adequate accommodations for you and your . . . ah . . . friend."

"Willie? He's my slave," Tom said.

Willie nodded cheerfully.

Sarah was embarrassed. "We have only one guest bedchamber, with an oversized double bed . . ."

"That's plenty big enough for Willie and me," Tom said, unaware of the hesitation being shown by his host and his daughters.

"Sure is," Willie added. "Sometimes, when we go hunting, Tom and I sleep in a tent that's scarce big enough for one."

They were interrupted when Amanda came into the room carrying a tray heavily laden with platters of baked clams, smoked herring, buttered brown bread fresh from the oven, and a raisin pie.

Margot immediately went off to the kitchen for another tray, on which there were pitchers of coffee and hot chocolate. "I hope you're not too partial to tea in the afternoon," she said to Tom. "Boston stopped drinking it long before I was born, and I don't think I've even tasted it more than once or twice in my life."

Willie was staring at Amanda.

The serving maid was conscious of his scrutiny, and her hips swayed as she left the room.

"That slave girl," Willie said, "is as pretty as the ladies of the house."

"Thank you," Sarah replied with a smile, "but she isn't a slave. She's as free as we are."

Tom and Willie gaped at her.

"Amanda works for us," Isaiah explained. "She earns wages, and she comes and goes as she pleases. She's a citizen, with the same rights that every citizen enjoys. There is no slavery here. It's prohibited by law."

The two South Carolinians were stunned.

Margot couldn't help laughing aloud, but clapped a hand over her mouth when Tom turned to look at her.

Willie rose to his feet and adjusted his stock of white linen. He grinned at Tom, then turned to their host. "If you don't object, sir, that free girl in the kitchen may appreciate some help. Not that I know much about cooking, but I can clean dishes and offer her encouragement." He sauntered off to the kitchen.

Tom chuckled. "That Willie is a terror. I've yet to see a girl who can resist him."

Margot bridled. "Amanda can take care of herself." She glared at him.

He looked her up and down, his expression insolent. "It's said back home that Willie and I are as alike as two peas in a pod. It's been rumored that I have an unerring eye for the ladies, too."

"I wouldn't doubt it, sir." Margot was deliberately challenging him.

Sarah intervened as she served the high tea, a term that was still used, even though no tea itself was ever in evidence. "What I don't understand, Mr. Beaufort," she said, "is that you and Willie seem to be on such friendly terms."

"We're the best of friends, Mistress Benton. I'm as close to Willie as I've ever been to my brother. Closer, maybe."

Sarah shook her head, and Margot seemed bewildered, too.

"My daughters," Isaiah said, "obviously don't grasp the subtleties of the relations between masters and slaves."

"I don't rightly think there are many subtleties," Tom said. "I was nursed by Willie's mama when I was a baby, and we grew up together. I'd give my life for him, just as I know he'd give his life for me. He's the best cabinet-maker you'll find anywhere in this country, and in his spare time he earns a fortune crafting furniture for folks in Charleston. Legally that money is mine, but that's only a technicality. It belongs to Willie, and he can spend it or save it or do what he pleases with it."

"You and he," Margot said, "must have an unusual relationship."

Tom shook his head. "Sorry to disappoint you, Miss Margot, but you'll find the same thing happening all over the South."

Sarah knew that Jeremy had told her the same thing on many occasions. She hadn't believed him, but now she was seeing for herself that he had spoken the truth, and she wished she could tell him as much.

Margot was not ready to concede. "Now that you're both in Massachusetts, what would prevent him from running away and establishing a life of his own as a freeman? If he's as clever a cabinetmaker as you say, he could earn a good living in Hartford or Providence—or any one of a dozen towns where the antislavery feeling is so strong that you could never win a court ruling that would return him to your custody."

It was Tom's turn to be bewildered. He took his time replying, eating a thick slice of the hot brown bread and reaching for another. "I can't imagine why Willie would ever do a fool thing like that," he said. "He has his own snug house at Oakhurst, and his living doesn't cost him a copper. This past half-year he's made a chest of drawers that my father gave our neighbors, the Emersons, as a gift, and the rest of his time has been his own. His food and clothes and drink are free, and he goes hunting or fishing with me a couple of times every week. He knows he can sell his cabinets in Charleston and Savannah at his own prices, and he has more girls than he can handle. What more could a man want?"

"What indeed?" Margot murmured, acid in her voice. "As long as he has girls!"

"There is one thing he lacks," Sarah said, and was reminded of her many fruitless talks with Jeremy on the subject. "He doesn't have his freedom."

Tom was becoming restless. "With all due respect, ma'am," he said, "I'm blamed if I can see why he needs it."

All at once Sarah could see the essential difference between him and his brother. Jeremy had an intellect and loved to exercise it, often debating for pure pleasure of arguing for its own sake. Tom was far more shallow, and it was obvious that his one real aim at this moment was to make an impression on Margot. She, of course, had little genuine interest in the slavery issue, and was preening for Tom's benefit, changing her position every few moments to show off the different angles of her face and the lines of her bare shoulders.

They were two of a kind, just as she and Jeremy had suspected, and if not controlled, they would explode together. That explosion could be bad for everyone concerned.

Papa, of course, was unaware of the tensions that were building between Margot and Tom. But Papa belonged to a different generation of ladies and gentlemen, a generation that failed to understand changing times and the freer, franker relations that young men and young women were establishing. During the Revolution and the years immediately following it, social life had been conducted according to the rules established for the aristocracy in England. Or the colonists' conceptions of those rules.

Now, however, the morality of the frontier was becoming dominant. People were more blunt, saying what they felt and believed. Anyone who didn't like an attitude or an opinion could lump it and turn elsewhere for friendship, business associations, companionship, and even love.

Later, when Sarah had an opportunity to speak alone with her sister, she would warn Margot to proceed with caution in the development of a relationship with Tom.

Oh, how she wished Jeremy were here! He could put his brother in his place with a few words, then keep him in that place. Without Jeremy, life was drab, dull, without savor. He was constantly in Sarah's mind and heart. For all the good that did. She realized she should try to live as normally as possible, but her grief was a constant source of pressure, and not until she was reunited with the man she loved would she become whole again.

Tom Beaufort left the Benton house on Beacon Street early each morning and made the rounds of officialdom.

He visited the chief of the constabulary and the harbor-master, he had an interview with Governor Gerry, and he spoke at length with the little boy who had been paid by British sailors to return their rented horse to its stable. Doggedly attempting to find some lead to the whereabouts of his missing brother, he made it his business to question the proprietors of every Boston tavern, but there were more than one hundred and fifty such establishments in the city, and not one could or would provide him with any information.

Bostonians, like most Americans, ate their heaviest meal of the day in the early afternoon, and Tom quickly discovered it was a waste of time to do business after dinner. Professional men like Isaiah Benton returned to their offices, where they could work and study without interruption, and unskilled laborers toiled until long after sunset. But civil servants and other members of the growing middle class did as little as they could after dinner, so Tom needed no persuasion to seek his own pleasure.

Margot Benton acted as his guide, showing him the sights of Boston and Cambridge, but she well knew, as did Tom, that it was she herself who was the magnet that attracted him. In spite of her sister's repeated warnings, she flirted with him outrageously.

"He likes me," she said. "Very much. And I may be growing fond of him. We're doing no harm to anyone, so why should I stop?"

Only Isaiah Benton was blind to complications in the developing relationship. He had accepted the invitation of Paul Beaufort to bring his daughters to Oakhurst Manor for a visit, so he was putting his own legal affairs in order, and in whatever time he could spare he was pressing the search for Jeremy. He tried, too, to keep up Sarah's lagging spirits, but it was a lost cause. She slept poorly, ate very little, and soon became haggard. It proved impossible to persuade her to follow her normal routines, and she was so short-tempered that Margot avoided her, as did Amanda. They sympathized with her plight, but nevertheless saw as little of her as they could.

One afternoon when the sun made a rare appearance in the sky, Margot took Tom to a pond in the Common for ice-skating, a sport in which he had never engaged. While she flew around the pond, he struggled, losing his balance and sprawling on the ice, and she didn't help matters by laughing at him.

Ultimately Tom's natural grace asserted itself, however, and all at once he acquired the knack. For the next hour and a half he and Margot skated together, and only when she began to tire did he reluctantly agree to leave the pond.

They were warmed by their exertions, and, their faces flushed, neither noticed the cold as they strolled back to the Benton house on Beacon Hill. Tom carried their wooden skates and examined them with care. "I reckon Willie could make sharper blades than these," he said. "The sharper the blades, the more you can do on skates."

"Jeremy learned of a company in Philadelphia that makes metal skates," Margot said. "He was telling us about it at supper that last night."

The mention of Jeremy cast a pall over them, and they were silent on the rest of the walk. After they reached the house, Margot made hot chocolate, and as they drank it in front of the parlor hearth, their natural exuberance reasserted itself.

"Would you like a splash of rum in your drink?" she asked. "Many of my friends seem to like it."

"They're entitled to their tastes," he said, and frowned.

She was delighted that the mention of other men made him jealous.

"I don't drink spirits very often," Tom continued, "but when I do I prefer my rum or brandywine unadulterated. Of course, if you'd care to join me . . ."

"I would not, sir," Margot replied, and tossed her head. Now he was trying to tease her, and even the knowledge did not prevent her from becoming annoyed. Certainly he well knew that although a lady might drink limited quantities of wine, under no circumstances did she touch strong liquor.

"Don't tell me that people in Massachusetts abide by the standards of South Carolina," he said.

She saw the light in his eyes and became even angrier. "Why are you mocking me, Tom?"

"Why did you mock me at the pond?" he demanded.

Margot looked innocent, and her green eyes grew larger. "Did I?"

"For a full hour, until I caught on to the principles of skating, you did nothing but laugh at me."

"That's because you were so clumsy. You just can't imagine how awkward you looked!"

He flushed and glared at her. "When we get to Oakhurst Manor," he said, "we'll see how well you can ride cross-country."

"I assure you I won't disgrace myself," Margot replied hotly. "I learned to ride when I was very small, and I've rarely been thrown." Her expression became mischievous. "You'll have to find some other way to prove me inferior to you, sir."

"If you insist, ma'am." Before she quite realized what was happening, he reached for her, drew her into his arms, and kissed her.

For a moment Margot clung to him, returning his kiss. Then, after a brief struggle, she managed to free herself, and was doubly upset when she discovered she was breathless. "Is that how you prove yourself superior to a girl?" she demanded, her voice filled with scorn.

Tom was breathing hard, too, but managed to grin broadly. "No, now you mention it," he admitted.

"Well, then!"

"It proves nothing whatever," he said. "But I can think of nothing I've ever enjoyed more, and from the way you reacted, I know you liked it as much as I did." He reached for her again.

She eluded him and retreated across the parlor. His expression told her he was serious, that he intended to bed her if he could, and too late she recalled Sarah's warnings. He had misinterpreted her flirtatiousness, and now she faced a real problem. "Halt, sir!" she commanded. "Don't you dare come a step closer."

Tom chuckled and continued to advance.

"If I scream," she said, "Amanda and Willie will come into the room."

"In the first place, you won't scream. But even if you did, they won't hear you. I fear you've forgotten that your sister sent Amanda off to the butcher, the greengrocer, and the fishmonger, and Willie decided to go with her so he could carry the food parcels for her."

Only now did it occur to Margot that they were indeed alone in the house, and she fought off a sense of panic. "I beg you to remember that you're a gentleman, Mr. Beaufort," she said, managing to place a coffee table between them.

"It would be far easier to remember, Mistress Benton, if you'd behaved like a lady. But you've been playing the tease ever since we've met, and the time has come to find out what you mean and what you don't."

She reached for a large bowl of sterling that Paul Revere, the silversmith, had made for her grandfather, and brandished it over her head. "I warn you, Tom!" she cried. "You come one step closer at your peril!"

He snatched the bowl from her before she could throw it at him or strike him with it. Then, while she was still off balance, he pulled her to him, and holding her close, kissed her again.

Margot melted in his arms. The worst of her situation, she realized, was that she wanted him as much as he wanted her, and when she felt something hard pressing between her legs, growing larger, she knew she would be lost if she hesitated.

Tom enveloped her still more tightly when she began to struggle.

She had no choice. Either she had to act like a vixen or she was lost. Suddenly she bit his lower lip, and her long, carefully buffed nails raked the side of his face.

He released her, took a single step backward, and stared at her.

"If it weren't for Sarah becoming a Beaufort when she and Jeremy are married," he said, raising a hand to his cheek, "I'd beat you for that!"

Margot had regained the upper hand, so her instinct compelled her to taunt him. "Is that how you'd prove you superiority?"

"No, ma'am." He fought hard to recover his poise and his sense of humor. "I'd do it for the sheer joy of hearing you squeal and beg for mercy."

Margot stood erect, her high breasts outthrust, her eyes stormy. "No man in this world," she said, "will ever hear me beg. For anything."

Tom stared at her for a long moment, and suddenly he laughed. "Now you've spoken the truth," he said. "What a spitfire you are, and how I'd love to tame you!"

"You won't, sir, nor will any man!" She remained defiant.

He looked at her again, hooking his thumbs in the pockets of his embroidered waistcoat, and all at once he became rueful. "That's also true, I fear," he said.

He looked so woebegone that Margot's defenses crumbled. "I—I'm sorry I was mean to you, Tom. I didn't intend to be so violent."

"You treated me as I deserved. I'm the one who must apologize, and I do."

She took a tiny handkerchief from her cuff and wiped a thin streak of blood from his cheek. "I'd best get some linseed ointment for your face."

He shook his head. "There's no need to bother, thank you. I'll heal fast enough."

Margot's touch was tender as she again raised her hand to his face.

Tom caught hold of her wrist and gently kissed the palm of her hand before releasing her.

Their eyes met in unspoken acknowledgment that they were playing with fire, and with one accord they drew farther apart.

"Perhaps you'd like a drop of rum now," Margot said.

"I think not. I'm finding it difficult enough to control myself."

She knew they couldn't take the risk of staying in the house alone any longer. "Papa has invited you to visit his office," she said. "I do believe this is the best of all possible times for me to take you there."

"I agree."

She allowed him to place her cape around her shoulders, then turned to him with a self-denigrating smile. "If Papa and Sarah should ask," she said, "we'll tell them you cut your face on the ice while you were learning to skate."

"You're clever," Tom said, "and I salute you."

"It's the least I can do to make up for the injury I've caused you."

"There's only one way you'll ever make it up to me, and one day my opportunity will come."

The cold locker was a wooden, metal-lined box that stood against the outer wall of the kitchen, and at this season of the year a tray that sat on the bottom was filled each night with hard-packed snow. Amanda placed the meat and fish she had purchased in the box, then strung the onions and carrots she had bought in a windowless pantry that adjoined the kitchen.

Willie leaned against the kitchen table, smoking a Caribbean *cigarro* as he watched her, and marveled at the natural sinuousness of her movements. "What can I do to help?"

"Not a thing," Amanda told him. "You carried all the packages and bundles home for me, and that was enough."

"I can do more."

"I'd rather not be in your debt."

"Why is that?"

Amanda's glance was arch as she looked at him over her shoulder. "Because you're going to demand payment. So I'm keeping the debt as low as I can."

For a few moments Willie's face was obscured by a cloud of tobacco smoke. "You want that payment as much as I do."

She made no reply, and continued to busy herself in the pantry.

"You may be free," he said, speaking slowly and distinctly. "You may vote in elections. You may even copy the manners of the white ladies who pay your wages. But you're still black, so you know how to behave natural-like."

Amanda became defensive. "How would a slave know what's natural and what isn't?"

"The only difference between you and me is in words," Willie said. "If I wanted freedom, Tom would give it to me, and so would old Mr. Beaufort. I'm as free as you. More free. I don't have to slave away to earn a roof over my head and food for my table."

"You talk big," Amanda said. "But you couldn't go off

to set up a homestead in the Indiana Territory if you had a mind to it. I could."

Willie was annoyed. "Why would I want to live in a cabin out in the wilderness of the West when I have my own house? Four big rooms, and I made every stick of furniture myself."

"It isn't the same," Amanda said as she emerged from the pantry.

He watched her as she poured water into a bowl and washed her hands. "Don't judge until you come to Oakhurst and see for yourself. There's a difference between me and the ignorant field hands who are just a few years out of the African jungles. They can't read or write, they have no trade, and they can't even speak English."

"They'd be better off back in the jungles."

"Now," Willie said with heat, "you sound like the abolitionists who come calling on the Bentons, and you're dead wrong. There are almost no middle-aged men, no old men in the African tribes! They're killed off in wars against each other. They die of starvation. They die of disease. They're a blame sight better off here. My grandpa was a field hand, and look at me. Yes, and your grandpa had to be a field hand, too. You'll understand when you come with the Bentons to South Carolina."

Amanda reached for a linen towel to dry her hands. "I'm none too sure I'm going there," she said.

"Afraid?" Willie chuckled.

"Maybe," she conceded. "Let's just say I enjoy my freedom, so I'm being cautious."

"I'll protect you," he said.

"You?" She began to laugh. "What could you do?"

He stared at her back for a moment, then placed his *cigarro* in an ashtray and silently advanced across the kitchen toward her. "Seeing you'll be visiting the Beauforts, no harm could come to you. But if I had to, I'd do anything for you. I'd even kill for you." He reached around her from behind, and his hands closed over her firm breasts.

Amanda had been awaiting this moment, and with a sigh she leaned back against him.

Willie buried his face in her neck.

"Not here," she said. "Sarah and Margot could wander in at any time." She led him off to her own bedroom and closed the door behind them.

"Nobody will interrupt us here?"

"Hardly. That's one of the advantages of being free. This room is mine." Amanda began to remove her clothes without embarrassment.

Willie followed her example. "Free or slave, white or black, you have the prettiest face and body I've ever seen."

"Well," she replied, "you may not be a field hand, but you're built like one."

They met on the bed, and their lovemaking was as simple and uncomplicated as their emotions. They lived in a white civilization and had acquired something of its patina, but at moments such as this their basic honesty asserted itself. They wanted and they took, they gave and they received, joyously and freely, and therefore they were content.

Sarah kept her feelings under control through the long hours of the day and evening only because, late each night, in the privacy of her own room, she cried herself to sleep. Life had no meaning and no purpose without Jeremy, and only the hope that he would return to her continued to drive her forward.

At moments such as this, however, she found it difficult to prevent herself from becoming hysterical. Papa and Tom were discussing the complicated French embargo on American shipping and Mr. Madison's reaction to it, but she paid no attention to the substance of their talk. It was torture to hear Tom's voice, close her eyes for an instant, and imagine that Jeremy was speaking. It was torment to glance obliquely at Tom in the candlelight and imagine that it was Jeremy who sat opposite her. The Almighty had been cruel to give two brothers such striking similarities.

The very worst of her situation, Sarah reflected as she picked absently at her codfish cakes and liver dumplings, were the constant reminders that she was alone.

A subtle change had taken place in the relationship of

Margot and Tom. She could see it as well as sense it. Margot's attitude was less blatantly flirtatious now, and Tom's aggressiveness toward her had become muted. Something had happened between them to make them cautious, but Sarah wasn't sure that was to the good. Both were still spoiled, demanding children, and their caution might cause them to forget the potential dangers they faced jointly.

She wished she could discuss the problem with Papa. But he saw nothing, as usual, and droned on about the Emperor Napoleon and his correspondence with Mr. Madison.

Sarah was willing to wager that Papa didn't even realize that Amanda and Willie had become lovers. She herself could see it in the way they looked at each other, the way they touched, seemingly by accident, as they carried dishes to and from the kitchen.

How she envied them. Yes, and how she envied Margot and Tom, too. Never had she been so isolated, so completely cut off from all feelings. She could smile or even force a laugh without pleasure, just as she would know no pain if a needle were driven under her skin.

Please, dear God, she prayed silently, bring Jeremy back to me. Alive and well. And soon, before I expire.

Chapter 5

The incident blew up out of nowhere, and the worst of it was that it couldn't be justified or even explained on rational grounds. Bostonians approved, to be sure, although they were somewhat bewildered, but responsible men shook their heads and told each other that difficult days lay ahead for the United States.

A reception was held at the Governor's Mansion, facing the Common, the first in a series that Elbridge Gerry planned to give. Isaiah Benton and his daughters were on the guest list as a matter of course, and as a courtesy an invitation was also extended to Thomas Beaufort, their houseguest.

Sarah would have preferred to stay home, saying she had no desire to engage in an active social life until Jeremy returned safely to her, but her father insisted that she accompany him. It wasn't healthy for her to remain in her bedroom behind a closed door, grieving for Jeremy and brooding, and he told her it was imperative that she lead as normal a life as possible.

So, although her heart was heavy, she donned one of

her new Empire dresses, applied a little makeup, and made an effort to be polite, if not cheerful.

Margot, however, was in a party mood. Her gown of green velvet and long jade earrings set off her red hair and pale complexion, further emphasized by a deep shade of lip rouge, and she was radiant as she went through the receiving line. Then she took the arm that Tom extended to her, and they made their way through throngs being served a mild rum punch and honey cakes by servants in black livery. Proudly showing off Tom, Margot presented him to her friends, and knew from their reactions that they shared her opinion of him. He had a flair that expressed itself in the way he walked, in his quick smile and affable manners. Bostonians were reserved, in the main, but the handsomely rugged young South Carolinian suffered no inhibitions and chatted amiably with everyone he met.

Suddenly he stiffened.

Margot followed his gaze and saw that he was staring at a man in his late twenties who was wearing the blue uniform, trimmed in white, of an officer in the Royal Navy. The single silver epaulet on his right shoulder identified him as a lieutenant. "Do you know him?" she asked.

Tom had grown taut, and replied in a deep growl, "I've never seen him in my life; but I wonder what the devil he's doing here."

"A British frigate put into port yesterday, so I'm sure her officers have been invited as a matter of course. There may be as many as twenty of them coming here today."

"They have no right to associate with decent folk." Tom continued to glare at the officer, who was chatting with a pretty girl in an old-fashioned, full-skirted gown.

Margot tried to draw him away, but Tom refused to budge.

"They kidnap our citizens and force them to serve in their damned navy," he said. "Then they enjoy our hospitality, eat our food, and drink our punch. They're hypocrites, and it's high time someone exposes them."

"Don't make a scene, Tom." Margot was alarmed. "This isn't a private party, remember, it's the governor's reception."

He turned to her, his hazel eyes glacial, and his smile was bloodless. "I have too much respect for your father to abuse his courtesy," he said, "and I have no intention of embarrassing the governor of this commonwealth. All the same, we can't allow these scoundrels to get away with their two-faced approach to us. Their bluff must be called, and they've got to be taught that they aren't welcome in this country until they change their ways." He began to move slowly across the room.

Margot continued to hold tightly to his arm. "What are you going to do?"

His chuckle was dry, totally lacking in mirth. "I aim to serve due notice on the scum who abducted my brother."

She realized she couldn't stop him, and she knew, too, as her excitement mounted, that she wasn't all that anxious to halt him. Obviously he had something in mind to avenge Jeremy, and the dramatic situation appealed to her.

Tom approached the officer, bowed, and spoke in a low, almost conversational tone. "My name is Beaufort."

The lieutenant broke off his conversation and returned the bow. "Hillier," he said, a hint of contempt for American manners in his voice.

Tom had no intention of presenting him to Margot. "Mr. Hillier," he said, "I've been admiring your audacity." He spoke so softly that people standing nearby couldn't hear him.

Margot knew he was avoiding making a public scene, and thought him remarkably clever.

"In what way am I audacious, sir?" The British officer held himself stiffly, as though undergoing a quarterdeck inspection, and even his dark hair seemed to bristle.

"You don't seem to fear abduction, Lieutenant."

Hillier regarded the remark as odd, and looked puzzled.

"Our navy is still small and undermanned," Tom said. "So far we've had more applications from men who want to serve than our government can handle, but one of these days we may start impressing you Englishmen to serve as common seamen. You appear to have had some experience, so you might be sufficiently able to become an apprentice seamen in the United States Navy."

Hillier grasped the hilt of his dress sword, and his

knuckles grew white, but he did not raise his voice, either. "May I inquire why you go out of your way to insult me, sir?"

"I have reason to believe that my brother was kidnapped and forced to become a sailor in your naval service. Not only is your conduct unlawful, but your arrogance in believing you can treat Americans in this high-handed manner is outrageous. A halt must be called, and I'm calling it, sir!"

Lieutenant Hillier smiled. "What do you intend to do about it, may I ask?"

"I've chosen you to set the example," Tom said, "and I brand you a coward."

"Be good enough to tell me where you may be reached, and at what hour, and my second will call on you."

Tom pulled the gold watch that had been his grandfather's from a waistcoat pocket and glanced at it, then gave the officer the Benton address on Beacon Hill. "My second will be waiting in an hour and a half."

Both men bowed, then turned away from each other, and no one in the milling throngs other than Margot and the girl to whom Hillier had been speaking realized that a challenge to a duel had been issued and accepted.

Tom's eyes were brighter now, and his spirits were high. "I knew he wouldn't be able to resist."

"You're actually going to fight him?"

"Certainly! That was the whole idea of speaking to him in the first place. He'll have the choice of swords or pistols, but it doesn't much matter which he prefers."

Margot stared at him, her heart pounding. "But he's a Royal Navy officer. He must be expert in handling any kind of a weapon."

"No matter. I'm a Beaufort." Tom grinned, and his shrug indicated his indifference. "I'm aware of only one problem. I've been in Boston such a short time that I'm not even acquainted with anyone who might act as my second."

The girl looked around the room and laughed when she saw an old friend. "I know just the fellow. Come along."

A few moments later Tom was shaking hands with Addison Adams, a young Harvard College graduate who was a member of the illustrious Massachusetts family headed by John Adams, who had been the nation's second president.

"Beaufort," he said, slapping his thigh. "I like your gall, even though you may be killed for your pains."

"I think it unlikely." Tom seemed supremely confident. "But the risk must be taken. Someone has to teach the lobsters a lesson, particularly the lobsters who wear blue. London seems to have forgotten we're no longer colonies. They ignore the protests of our president and State Department, and only the Almighty knows what my brother may be suffering at this very moment as a result of their cold-blooded and inhumane policies. The wounding of just one of their officers in a duel might seem insignificant, but it will embarrass them and prove to our own people that they're human, just as we are. This fight may not bring my brother back to us any sooner, but it might cause them to think twice before they abduct anyone else."

He was so firm in his conviction that he acquired greater stature in Margot's eyes. Never had she known a man willing to risk his life for the sake of upholding a principle in which he believed.

Addison Adams grinned. "I'll be honored to act as your second, Beaufort," he said.

Isaiah Benton and his elder daughter didn't learn of the impending duel until they were walking home from the reception an hour later, and Sarah was aghast. She managed to wait until they reached the Benton house and were settled in the parlor, however, before she expressed her opinions.

"Tom may not realize that our laws are strict," she said, addressing young Adams, "but you know it, Addison, and you know this fight is madness. The British can claim immunity for their officer, so he can sail away in safety. But Tom could be sentenced to several years in jail, and there he'd stay until the end of his term."

Tom smiled and made no reply, and Addison Adams seemed equally resolute.

Sarah turned to her father. "Tell them, Papa. Maybe they'll listen to you."

Isaiah ran a hand through his hair, a gesture that indicatèd he was deep in thought. "It's true enough," he said, "that the Commonwealth of Massachusetts has a firm law. The statute is both specific and all-inclusive. 'No person shall fight in a duel for any purpose, no matter what he might regard as a just violation.' The term of imprisonment for the first violation is three years. The law grants no exceptions."

"If my only aim was the vindication of Jeremy," Tom said, "I might allow myself to be talked out of this duel. I won't be helping my brother, and I'll be placing my own life in jeopardy. But the way I see it, the honor of the United States is at stake!"

"I know every member of the bench in this state," Isaiah said, concealing a smile. "If you fought a duel over a woman or to settle a quarrel over a gaming debt, not one of them would show you mercy, and off you'd go to jail for the maximum sentence of three years. The law would be upheld to the letter. But once your motives are made public—"

"I'll see to that," Addison Adams interjected.

"—then I'm equally positive that every judge in Massachusetts will look the other way. Circumstances make it necessary sometimes to ignore every law we keep on the books, and the laws against dueling aren't all that sacred."

Sarah was angry. "Suppose Tom should be badly wounded or even murdered!"

"That's the one thing that bothers me," her father replied. "If something untoward happened to Tom on the heels of his brother's tragic disappearance, I don't quite know how I'd be able to face Paul Beaufort."

"I plan to stay alive and healthy," Tom said. "You can take my word for it."

A half-hour later a British naval officer stood at the door, announcing that he was Lieutenant Hillier's second, and he retired with Adams to the library, where they conferred. Only after the visitor departed did Addison Adams return to the group waiting in the parlor.

"I agreed to swords," he said, "preferably a pair of the lightest weight attainable. Hillier's second told me in so many words that his principal has fought a half-dozen duels and has won all of them. So I hope you'll know what you're doing, Beaufort."

Tom was still unworried. "If I had to, I'd fight him with my bare hands. This is one duel that can't be left to chance."

"We'll meet in the pine woods behind Harvard College at dawn tomorrow. Also, I've agreed to provide the physician. Each contestant is allowed to bring two persons other than his second as witnesses."

"I'll bring Willie," Tom said. "He's never missed one of my fights."

Margot said nothing, but her green eyes became opaque.

Isaiah produced a bottle of his best Madeira wine, and toasts were offered to Tom's success. Only Sarah refrained from taking an active, vocal part in the festivities. The duel had become important for its own sake, and she alone seemed to realize that, regardless of the outcome, Jeremy's plight would not be affected.

Tom needed no one to awaken him very early, and he washed in a basin of cold water, shaved with care, and donned his best shirt of fine lawn cotton. Members of the Benton household were still asleep, but Willie had prepared a light breakfast of bread, smoked herring, cold roasted beef, and cheese, and they ate together, drinking mugs of mild beer brewed in New York.

An hour before dawn they stood together in the front vestibule, awaiting the arrival of Addison Adams. He was prompt, and when they heard his carriage pull up outside, they opened the door.

Both were astonished when a short, slender figure materialized beside them and left the house with them.

Margot's feminine figure was concealed in a man's boots, breeches, and swallow-tailed coat, and aside from her man's shirt, which was too large for her, her disguise was effective. Her long red hair was pinned up beneath a tricorne, and she was muffled in a cloak that fell to her ankles. Her face, scrubbed clean of cosmetics, was shining, and she looked like a boy of about thirteen.

"I demand the right to go with you," she said before Tom, Adams, or Willie could speak.

Tom was the first to recover, and seemed amused. "On what grounds?"

"Why should men have all the pleasure in this world? It won't suffice to hear later about the duel. I want to enjoy watching you win it. I warn you, if you send me back into the house, I'll alert the Cambridge constables, and they'll stop the duel before it can be fought."

Tom and his second exchanged glances.

"Margot," Adams said, "you surely realize this duel is going to cause a great deal of talk. If anyone should learn that a woman was one of the witnesses, there would be a double scandal."

"I won't create a scandal, I won't cause trouble for anyone, and I promise you I won't say a word, so no one will know that a girl is a member of your party."

"I'm against it," Adams said.

"You would be!" she retorted. "You're as stodgy as everybody else in Massachusetts."

Tom knew she was making a deliberate attempt to arouse his sympathy, but he saw no harm in allowing her to accompany them, and it didn't occur to him that his decision was emotional rather than logical. "Let the boy come," he said, and climbed into the carriage.

Adams and Willie followed, purposely forcing Margot to bring up the rear, and she had to take the tiny jump seat, the only place left. But she had won her victory and didn't care.

The coachman headed for the Charles River ferry, and they made the short trip without incident. Then, as the coachman directed his team onto the dirt road that led to the woods behind the Harvard buildings, Adams broke the silence.

"I made it my business to check into Lieutenant Hillier's background last night," he said. "And I can't help wishing you'd selected a less formidable opponent, Beaufort. He's won every one of his six duels, and killed two of his foes. He's regarded as the best swordsman—or one of the best, anyway—in the entire British fleet now on this side of the Atlantic."

Tom seemed as impervious to the odds against him as he was to the bitter early-morning cold, and he chuckled, rubbing his hands together. "So much the better. There will be all the more talk, and my victory will be more notable."

For the first time, Margot felt a pang of doubt, even though his confidence in his talents was unimpaired. She had forced herself onto the party as a lark, but now it occurred to her that two men would actually fight with dangerous weapons until one drew blood. There was a chance that Tom would be seriously wounded, at the least, and she regretted the impulsiveness that had led her to disguise herself. She had been carefully protected against the world's ugliness and brutality, and never had she witnessed an act of violence.

But it was too late to back out now. No matter what happened, she warned herself, she could not scream or otherwise betray the fact that she was a woman. If the duel became too grisly, she could close her eyes.

Sitting very still, Margot shuddered.

Her companions thought the cold was responsible, and offered her their cloaks.

She refused with as much dignity as she could muster.

The coachman pulled his horses to a halt beside a path that led into the pine woods.

"This is it," Adams said.

They took care to let Margot dismount by herself, but Willie walked close behind her on the dark path, ready to catch her if she stumbled. It was still so dark that she could see only a few inches ahead, but she walked with great care, not allowing herself to become a burden.

After a ten-minute walk they came to a clearing about sixty feet long and perhaps half as wide. They were the first to arrive, and moved to one end, where they stamped their feet in order to keep warm.

Tom was the calmest member of the group, and when he took a *cigarro* from a leather case, his hand remained steady as he lighted it with a small flint and tinderbox.

A short, stubby man appeared in the clearing, a black bag of medicines and instruments in one hand, a long, narrow case under his other arm. He did not speak, but bowed and stood apart.

Margot realized that Dr. Carlton Kramer had been a

perfect choice, and silently congratulated Adams. Kramer was one of Boston's most prominent young physicians; a sports enthusiast who rode in the winter and swam in the summer—he himself was rumored to be an expert swordsman, having learned the art while attending medical school in Edinburgh.

Lieutenant Hillier, his second, and two other officers, all of them in civilian attire, came into the clearing just as the first streaks of muddy daylight were showing in the dark sky. Members of both parties bowed, but the principals refrained, and Hillier stood at the far end of the clearing.

Margot thought the silence was uncanny.

Dr. Kramer advanced to the center of the open space and summoned the seconds. "In the absence of anyone else capable of officiating," he said, "I shall assume that role, provided there are no objections from either side."

Adams nodded, and so did the British second.

"You know the rules, gentlemen, and I presume your principals are well acquainted with them. The duel will begin when I give the signal, and not until then. It will continue until one or the other draws blood, at which instant it will cease. If necessary, should the principals be carried away by their feelings and continue the duel, it will be your duty to intervene, too. Do you wish to ask any questions, gentlemen?"

The seconds shook their heads.

Tom seemed to take no interest in the proceedings and puffed his *cigarro*.

Hillier stared up at the sky, which was growing still lighter.

Margot marveled at their calm, even though she realized it was contrary to the male code to reveal one's emotions in a time of stress.

Dr. Kramer opened his sheathlike case and withdrew two long swords of finely crafted Toledo steel, supple yet strong and equipped with small cross-barred handles.

Even a girl who knew nothing about swords could tell they were superb blades, and Margot felt queasy.

Dr. Kramer offered Adams a choice, since, under the protocol that governed such matters, the opposition had elected to fight with swords.

Testing one, then the other, Addison Adams quickly discovered they were truly identical, with perfect balance. He took one, returning the other to the physician, who handed it to the British second.

"No duel may be waged," Dr. Kramer said in a loud voice, "until an attempt has been made to reconcile the two parties. Lieutenant Hillier, are you willing to be reconciled with Mr. Beaufort?"

"No, sir," the British officer replied.

"Mr. Beaufort, are you willing to be reconciled with Lieutenant Hillier?"

"I am not, sir." Tom removed his cloak, hat, and coat, which he handed to Willie, and in spite of the raw cold, he opened his lawn shirt at the throat.

Then, with a grin, he handed his glowing *cigarro* to Margot and winked at her.

The gesture was so unexpected that, in spite of her growing concern for him, she had to swallow a giggle that might have revealed her identity.

Adams handed his principal the sword.

Tom balanced it, examined it with great care, and gripping it experimentally, slashed and cut several times. The blade sang.

Again Margot shivered.

"The principals will advance to me," Dr. Kramer ordered.

They obeyed, with the British officer moving at a slow march and Tom sauntering casually, a picture of indifferent indolence.

Dr. Kramer stood with his own sword raised as a barrier.

The participants stopped short of his blade, and taking cognizance of each other for the first time, raised their swords in salute.

"*En garde!*" the physician said crisply. "You may begin, gentlemen." He whisked away his sword and retreated to the side of the clearing.

Both blades were raised, half-extended, and the pair in the center of the open space circled each other warily, each wanting to test the other's style.

Suddenly Hillier feinted twice, then lunged, but Tom

parried easily, and the Englishman's blade slid harmlessly along the length of his own. The purpose of the swift attack was not difficult to divine. Tom had taken great care to study the ground while he had been waiting for the duel to begin, and he knew that directly behind him was an icy patch. Had he allowed himself to be forced onto it, he might have slipped, and the fight would have ended before it really started.

There was no reason he couldn't use that ice patch to his advantage, so he pretended to be unaware of it and skirted its edge as he moved backward step by step.

Hillier followed, ready to lunge again.

It was Tom's turn to counterattack first, however, and a wicked slash drove his opponent onto the ice.

The lieutenant lost his footing and skidded.

Tom could have skewered him then and there, but instead he stood back, giving his foe a chance to recover. Raising his blade in a mocking salute, he had the temerity to laugh aloud.

These gestures created precisely the effect he sought. Hillier was angry and drove forward, death in his eyes.

Tom's sharp thrust halted him abruptly, and he parried just in time to avoid serious injury. Now it was the turn of the Englishman to back away, inviting pursuit while he altered his tactics. He used the interlude to regain control of his feelings, and something in his manner changed, too. He realized that this American bumpkin was an exceptionally capable duelist, so he had his hands full, and he treated his foe with a new, cautious respect.

Steel clashed against steel, the sound echoing through the pine woods.

Margot watched in terror, her own discomfort from the cold forgotten. Men were brutes, and the sheer excitement of the duel was unbearable, but her fear for Tom numbed her. Had she discouraged and deterred him from the outset, she might have been able to persuade him not to quarrel with the British officer. Now it was too late, and at any moment the Englishman's sword might enter his body. She would never forgive herself if Tom died, and for the first time she could sense her sister's suffering over the disappearance of Jeremy.

Just thinking of Jeremy reminded her of Tom's reason for seeking this fight. Suddenly Margot wanted to shout encouragement to him. She had never thought of herself as bloodthirsty, but at this instant she hoped with all her being that he would destroy this man who was the symbol of injustice and cruelty. For the moment she forgot that if she spoke her soprano voice would reveal her sex, but it didn't matter. She couldn't catch her breath and therefore was rendered incapable of speech.

Tom was learning a great deal about his opponent. The Englishman was strong, technically proficient, and seemed to specialize in face-high thrusts. He seemed somewhat less sure of himself when placed on the defensive, but that might be a ruse. A man who overextended himself could be placed in a position from which there was no retreat.

Parrying repeatedly, until his arm grew tired, Tom realized he had to experiment and create an offensive opening before his opponent's bull-like strength wore him down and made him an easy prey.

Twice more they circled the clearing, with Tom moving backward step by step and Lieutenant Hillier seeming to have a distinct advantage.

So it appeared to Margot, but she wasn't certain. The tensions in the faces of Addison Adams and Willie told her nothing, Dr. Kramer's face was blank, and the English officers on the far side of the long clearing were not yet ready to cheer for the victory of their champion.

Slowly Tom halted, continuing to parry thrust after thrust, until, all at once, he launched a whirlwind attack that rapidly used his reserves of strength and energy. He slashed and cut viciously, his blows aimed at the Englishman's face and neck.

The astonished Hillier looked alarmed, and for a moment his guard was raised too high.

Tom recognized his opportunity too late to utilize it, but at last he understood how to unlock the door to victory. The Englishman was vain, and was afraid that a cut across the face would mar his appearance. Jeremy, who had taught his younger brother how to fight with swords, had consistently preached one theme: "Every man has his weakness. Find it, play on it, and you'll win."

So be it. For Jeremy's sake as well as his own.

Pretending to act with reckless abandon, Tom unleashed a whole series of wild slashes to the face, knowing but not caring that he wouldn't land even one of these blows.

Again the British officer raised his guard a fraction of an inch too high.

Tom's manner and style changed instantly, and a delicate, neatly delivered thrust caught Hillier in the fleshy upper portion of his left arm.

Blood had been drawn, so Tom had won the duel. He leaped backward and lowered his blade.

Dr. Kramer started forward into the arena.

Hillier stood still for a moment, looking at the growing smear of blood that soaked the upper part of his left sleeve. Humiliation and pain momentarily deprived him of his reason, and he started forward again, intending to kill the American who had demeaned him.

Margot's hand flew to her mouth, and she discovered later that she had bitten her knuckle.

Dr. Kramer managed to intervene, and the two seconds raced into the clearing, too.

They needed only a short time to disarm Hillier, who apologized to the physician as soon as he recovered his senses.

"There's no permanent harm done," Dr. Kramer announced as he inspected the wound and started to bind it.

"Just stop the bleeding, sir, that's all I ask," Hillier said. "I'll go straight back to my ship, where our surgeon will do the rest."

"As you wish," Dr. Kramer replied.

The English second handed the physician Hillier's sword and bowed to Tom, who continued to stand, sword in hand. In a few seconds the officers were gone.

Tom surrendered his blade, and the physician lost no time in leaving the clearing, too. The sounds of swordplay had been audible for a considerable distance, and it was now broad daylight, so he would have too much to explain if the Cambridge constabulary found him here.

Willie hugged Tom and pounded him on the back; then Adams solemnly shook his hand.

At last Tom turned to Margot, who had not moved. There were tears in her eyes, and as she tried to blink them away, she couldn't decide whether she was weeping for joy because Tom had won or whether she was relieved that he had escaped injury.

He saw that she was still holding the burning stub of his *cigarro,* and taking it from her, he threw it into a pile of soft snow. "This was no ordinary duel," he told her. "The lieutenant and I should have been reconciled after the fight, but I was damned if I wanted to shake that bastard's hand, any more than he wanted to shake mine. No matter, though. I beat him, and the story will soon be known in every state and territory."

Margot tried to speak, but hadn't yet recovered her voice, and could only nod.

Tom looked at her more closely, then suddenly took her in his arms and kissed her.

She pressed close to him for an instant, unmindful of the presence of Adams and Willie.

Not until later did she wonder why she had allowed the intimacy. He had deserved the kiss as a reward for his victory, and perhaps it had no significance. On the other hand, she wasn't certain whether it had a deeper meaning, or what it had meant to Tom, either.

Chapter 6

They went from Boston to New York by commercial stagecoach, and Tom Beaufort was stunned by the brawling city of fifty thousand persons, now second in size only to Philadelphia and growing at such a rapid rate that it was certain to become the nation's largest within a few years. Isaiah Benton had to confer with some local attorneys, so they stayed for several days at an old inn near the Battery. Willie went exploring on his own initiative and announced that, second only to the plantations of South Carolina, he thought the vegetable-raising farms of Staten Island offered the best commercial possibilities in America.

"It's the cost of transporting produce that raises prices," he said, "and that's what makes Staten Island just about perfect. The farmers there have a natural market in New York for their beans and corn and onions, and the green-grocers send their barges across the harbor and pick up what a man grows right from his own wharves. Some of those little places have only forty acres, but the farmers who own them earn a mighty good living."

Sarah, long familiar with New York, spent her time quietly. She went her first morning to the shop of her favorite dressmaker, returning daily for fittings, and she browsed in the bookshops located in the narrow lanes off Broad Street. Jeremy was still ever-present in her mind, but she found that talking about him made her even more depressed, so she preferred to be alone with her private thoughts.

Margot showed Tom the town, and they loved every minute of the experience. They attended an afternoon performance of Shakespeare's *Romeo and Juliet,* and neither could understand why all four of New York's theaters were featuring English plays. Americans, it appeared, were too busy building cities, establishing factories, and conquering the wilderness to write plays.

They explored the tiny waterfront shops of the harbor, where Margot counted the flags of eleven nations on merchant vessels, and when they stopped at a tavern for a bowl of soup, they were fascinated by the many languages they heard. One day, in spite of the cold, they had a picnic in the woods about Nineteenth Street.

Between the Battery and Governor's Island they could see a mammoth British ship of the line, her seventy-four gun ports discreetly closed, riding at anchor. New York still had bitter memories of the redcoat occupation of the city through the better part of the War of Independence, however, so no crew members were granted shore leave. Anyone who wore the uniform of the Royal Navy ran the risk of a beating on the streets of New York.

At Tom's insistence they rented a carriage of their own before setting out on the next stage of their journey, and he and Willie took turns acting as coachman. They could travel more rapidly because they could set their own pace, he said, and he proved to be right. Changing horses twice each day, they reached Philadelphia without incident. Still the country's largest city, it was staid and sedate, and except for the appearance on the streets of Indians from various Pennsylvania tribes, it reminded Sarah and Margot of London, which they had visited with their father.

Continuing to travel by rented coach, the party went on to Washington City, the nation's new capital, and they were able to obtain accommodations at O'Neale's Inn and Tavern only because the Congress was not in session. When the Senate and House were at work, there were so few rooms in the community that most ordinary travelers were required to stay in nearby Georgetown.

Even the proudest of Americans had to admit that Washington City was a mess. No cobblestones had yet been laid, and the two principal thoroughfares, Constitution Avenue and Pennsylvania Avenue, were rutted dirt roads. The President's House, made of dark wood, was one of the few graceful buildings, in the community, and the Capitol, which might someday be impressive, was an unfinished structure. Only the Treasury and the State Department had separate buildings of their own. The Navy and the War Department shared a two-story structure, as did the Post Office and the Justice Department.

Isaiah Benton paid a courtesy call on President Madison, and because it was raining, Sarah remained in the bedroom she shared with her sister and read in front of an open fire. Images of Jeremy intruded constantly, however, so she gazed into the fire and daydreamed, even though she knew such dreams would not return him to her side.

Tom and Margot went off to a local stable, where they turned in the rented coach and hired horses for the rest of their journey. In all, Tom estimated, from the time they had left Boston until the day they arrived at Oakhurst Manor, they would have spent a full month on the road.

Ever since Tom had fought his duel with the British officer, he and Margot had become virtually inseparable. They always sat beside each other in the taverns where the party ate their meals, and they went sightseeing together at stops along the way. Often oblivious of the presence of others, they spoke in low tones, and they laughed at private jokes incomprehensible to anyone else.

By the time they reached Washington City, Sarah felt the time had come for her to talk with her sister, and that night, as they undressed before a coal fire that warded off the damp chill of the town on the banks of the little Potomac River, she opened the subject with startling abruptness.

"Margot," she asked, "what are Tom's intentions toward you?"

The younger girl smiled as she seated herself in front of a small dressing table and began the nightly ritual of brushing her hair one hundred strokes. "We haven't discussed such things."

"Well, if he's serious, it's his obligation to speak to Papa and get his permission to pay court to you."

"Tom would be too embarrassed, and I think I'd just curl up and die."

Sarah's hand crept to Jeremy's ring at her throat. "There are obligations that ladies and gentlemen are required to fulfill. Jeremy wouldn't have dreamed of courting me until Papa gave his approval, and I wouldn't have permitted it myself. It's a dangerous business to ignore the standards that were established for the protection of everyone concerned."

"I suppose those standards are necessary," Margot said with a sigh, "but they're such a bore."

"If Tom isn't serious," Sarah said firmly, "you'd be wise to watch your step."

The younger girl bristled and for the moment stopped brushing her hair. "I'm not certain I know what you mean, but I'm quite certain I don't like it!"

"I'm sure you do know." Sarah's voice remained even. "You're with him from breakfast until bedtime, and your relationship can grow complicated."

"I resent that," Margot said. "Just because you and Jeremy are such somber, good people doesn't mean everyone else must behave as you do. I'm willing to wager that after you're married, you'll go to church every single Sunday for the rest of your lives. I may or may not go to church. I'll do what I feel like doing. And I'm sure Tom is the same kind of person I am. We believe in doing our duty, but that doesn't mean we've got to wear hair shirts. There's no crime in seeking and enjoying life's pleasures." She began to brush her hair again with more vigor than was necessary.

Sarah remained silent. Vividly recalling her last day with Jeremy, when they had made love on the parlor sofa, she knew they were far less staid and somber than her sister imagined. How shocked Margot would be if she knew of that occasion! Sarah was preaching because of her own greater experience, but she couldn't discuss it with Margot or anyone else. What had happened that day was strictly between her and Jeremy, and even to mention it would be a violation of a trust.

She had to try again to make Margot behave with greater propriety. "I'm not asking you to seek fewer pleasures. But you're tempting Tom when you flirt with him so incessantly, and one of these days you'll tease him beyond his endurance. Then, watch out. You'll face a situation you can't handle."

"I can handle Tom," Margot said, and giggled. "Besides, I love to tease him. He takes the bait every time."

Sarah climbed into bed and slid her feet down to the warming brick. "Are you in love with him?"

Margot's smile faded slowly, and she pondered the question. "I've asked myelf that same thing. Many times. And I honestly don't know. Except for passing fancies when I was younger—and I don't count them—I doubt that I've ever been in love."

"When it happens," the older girl assured her, "you'll know it. You won't wonder about it any longer."

"Perhaps, perhaps not," Margot said. "You're very definite in your approaches. You're just like Papa that way, and you and Jeremy are remarkably similar. You have positive views of everything, and you always know what's right and what's wrong. You never guess. I may spend my whole life never really knowing whether I love someone."

Sarah had no intention of becoming involved in a theoretical problem. "Is Tom in love with you?"

"He hasn't said, although he acts that way. I'm sure you've noticed that he doesn't exactly avoid my company. It appears that Benton women have an irresistible fascination for Beaufort men."

"What we're discussing, dear sister, is the fascination that Beaufort men have for Benton women. If you aren't serious about Tom, if you have any doubts, don't let the relationship become too involved. There are hundreds of little ways you can signal to a man that, much as you enjoy being with him, you're not interested in a romance with him."

"Who says I'm not interested in a romance with Tom?"

Margot demanded as she completed her hair-brushing chore and climbed into her side of the featherbed.

Sarah sighed. "You're incorrigible."

Margot blew out the candle, and discovered it was easier to be candid and truthful in the dark. "Sarah," she said, "I'm frightened."

"By what?" The older girl spoke softly.

"I'm not as giddy and foolish as I seem to be. Sometimes I playact, which is like wearing a sweater under a party dress for protection from the cold. I . . . I think I am falling in love with Tom. And what frightens me is that I'm not certain how he feels. Oh, he wants to tumble me, of course, as every man does. I've learned to expect that. If that's all Tom wants from me, he's going to be disappointed, because I won't let him bed me until we're married. I'm not Papa's daughter and your sister for nothing, and I believe, deep down, in your standards."

I'm a hypocrite, Sarah thought, clenching her fists. I've created a false front for my sister, and she has faith in it. And in me. Yet, I gave in to the temptations of the body. But why should I feel ashamed? I love Jeremy, he loves me, and in God's sight we're man and wife. Only the terrible thing that has happened to him, whatever it may be, prevents us from becoming one in the eyes of man.

"I flirt with Tom because I can't help myself," Margot said. "There's a she-demon inside me that forces me to do it. I realize I should wait until someone with Jeremy's qualities comes my way, but I couldn't find happiness with such a man. I thrive on excitement, even danger. It's more important to me than food or sleep. There's something of Beelzebub in Tom. I recognize the quality, but it doesn't matter. It's one of the magnets that draw me to him. I've tried to overcome it, to put him out of my mind, but I can't. I'm drifting on a tide so strong that I can't swim the other way, and I don't know what will become of me or how all this will end. I can swear to you, though, that I'll be chaste. Neither Tom nor any other man will have me until he puts a wedding band on my finger."

Sarah wept silently, and fell asleep clutching Jeremy's precious ring.

Never, as long as Sarah lived, would she forget her first sight of Oakhurst Manor. She was tired after spending long days on the endless roads through Virginia and the Carolinas. Jeremy should have brought her here himself to be his bride, and without him she felt like an impostor. The salt had lost its savor.

They rode inland from Charleston, a lovely, gracious town, and her depression intensified because she wasn't seeing it for the first time with Jeremy. They rode past fenced fields, and in the distance she could see slaves at work under the supervision of overseers, a sight that made her ill. It had been a mistake to come to South Carolina, she thought; she should have remained in Boston and waited there for Jeremy to return.

Suddenly they turned off the main road onto a narrow lane, and Tom spoke with quiet pride. "We're home," he said.

Willie began to sing an ancient song of his ancestors, his voice strong and strangely sweet:

> *Tola m-bena, toa m'bwana,*
> *Mengano, rangano m'bwana.*

As he continued to chant the African incantation with its emphatic rhythms, Tom softly translated the words into English for the benefit of the Bostonians:

> *This land is rich and sweet,*
> *Holding me close like a mother.*
> *She nourishes me, she gives me strength,*
> *This rich, sweet land.*

The fields looked like scores of others Sarah had seen in recent days. She had already learned to identify tobacco, the principal crop, as well as cotton and rye. Rice grew in the wet soil adjacent to small streams and ponds, and she found it easy to identify the thick rows of sugarcane. Why anyone should feel emotional about this land was beyond her ability to understand.

The furious barking of a dog interrupted her thoughts, and she was startled when a huge creature sped down the lane toward them, its ears flattened and its tail extended. Tom and Willie leaped to the ground, and Sarah thought they intended to kill the beast before it could attack.

Instead they began to shout. "King N'Gao, King N'Gao!"

The dog's tail began to wag, and the animal, as large as a pony, jumped on them with such force that someone smaller and weaker would have been knocked to the ground. Tom hugged the creature, as did Willie, and the delighted dog raced in circles around them.

"Mr. Benton, Miss Sarah," Tom said, "this is King N'Gao, the real master of Oakhurst. N'Gao, I have the honor to present you to Mistress Margot Benton. See to it that no harm comes to her."

The dog approached Margot, its manner wary.

She leaned low from her saddle and patted the beast.

King N'Gao's tail began to wag again, and a new compact was formed. Then, still elated by the return of his closest friends, the dog proudly moved to the head of the procession, which he led down the lane.

Directly ahead, the path became somewhat wider, and at either side stood double rows of fifty-foot Carolina hemlocks, their shining, deep green leaves extending a welcome of their own. At the end of the lane stood a three-story house of red brick, fronted by a gracious white portico with Doric columns, and all at once Sarah felt a rush of emotion. Oakhurst Manor looked exactly as Jeremy had described it to her.

Paul Wellington Beaufort stood alone at the top of the steps, his back ramrod stiff, resembling an older version of Jeremy. He greeted his son and Willie, shook Isaiah Benton's hand, and bowed to Margot.

He had saved Sarah for the last, and needed no introduction to her. He placed his hands on her shoulders, looked deep into her eyes, and then embraced her. "Welcome home to Oakhurst Manor, daughter," he said.

Tears stung her eyes.

Gradually she realized that someone else stood on the portico, a black giantess of two hundred and fifty pounds, clad in a gown of soft, French silk. She hugged Willie and Tom in turn, curtsied to Isaiah, and inspected Margot without comment. Then she turned her attention to Sarah, her dark eyes probing, and the girl felt she could keep no secrets from this woman.

"You be Jeremy's lady," Cleo said. "So this place b'long you. Cleo b'long you."

Again Sarah was embraced.

The dog became excited and leaped on her.

"Down, N'Gao," Cleo said, and the beast subsided.

House slaves in black livery with silver buttons were carrying saddlebags and other luggage into the house, black stable boys were leading the horses to an outbuilding, and everyone was talking at once.

Cleo, it appeared, was annoyed, and jabbed a finger at her son. "Willie," she said, "you write me a black girl come, too. Where she be?"

The usually glib Willie was tongue-tied.

"Where she be, Tom?"

Tom shifted his weight from one foot to the other. "It's a long story, Cleo," he said.

It occurred to Sarah that Tom was as afraid of this formidable housekeeper as was her own son. "Amanda," she explained, "is a free woman, and she was nervous about coming to a land of slaves. But she promised to join us if I write to her that it's safe."

"Missy write," Cleo said. "Cleo here, so girl be safe."

"I'll write her before the day ends," Sarah promised, and Willie grinned in appreciation.

Before they could go into the house, a heavyset man of about forty appeared from a side yard. His face was heavily tanned from long exposure to the sun, the sleeves of his shirt were rolled above the elbows, and there was a coating of dust on his boots.

Paul Beaufort paused to present his overseer, Mr. Higby.

Jeremy had never mentioned him to Sarah, but she took an instant dislike to him, perhaps because he was in direct charge of Oakhurst's slaves and forced them to work. She was being unfair to the man, but her instinct told her she was right. Something in his pale, red-rimmed eyes sent a chill up her spine as he looked hard at her, then bowed to her.

At the far end of the entrance hall stood a magnificent staircase with marble steps. Tom insisted on showing Margot to her room before going off to his own quarters, Cleo conducted Isaiah Benton to his suite, and Paul Beaufort lingered behind, an arm around Sarah's shoulders.

King N'Gao was torn. He looked at Margot climbing the stairs, gazed at Sarah for a moment, and then made a decision, racing up to overtake Margot and Tom.

"You'll have to pardon our spoiled dog," Paul said with a chuckle. "He doesn't yet realize that you're the new mistress of Oakhurst Manor."

"My feelings aren't hurt," she said with a smile, already marvelously at ease with her future father-in-law. "Tom told King N'Gao to look after my sister."

"He did, eh?" Paul whistled under his breath, looked bemused, and then laughed aloud.

Sarah waited for his explanation.

"Tom, Willie, and N'Gao have formed a very private triumvirate," Paul said. "The dog minds Cleo because he knows she'll throw him out of the house bodily if he misbehaves. N'Gao has barely tolerated Jeremy and me, and I sometimes like to think he senses that we own this place. No matter. If Margot has been admitted to the magic circle, it means Tom has been smitten at last."

"I wonder."

"We'll find out, won't we?" Paul offered his arm. "I waited until the others were taken to their rooms because I want to give you a choice," he said as they mounted the stairs. Falling silent, he started down a wide corridor and opened a door.

Sarah saw a handsome bedchamber with a pale rug on the floor, a large featherbed, and windows with curtains that she recognized as New England's most expensive product.

"This is our best guest room, and it's yours if you want it," Paul said, then took her in the opposite direction.

Sarah stood in the entrance to a small suite that consisted of a sitting room lined with bookshelves from floor to ceiling, and beyond it a bedchamber dominated by a four-poster bed. The furniture was heavy, masculine, and she knew without being told that these were Jeremy's quarters.

"I prefer to stay here," she said, her voice thickening, "and thank you for thinking of it."

Paul's eyes misted, and he turned away quickly.

For a long time Sarah stood and looked at the volumes that lined the shelves. There were writings of Ben Jonson and John Locke, the controversial books by Dean Jonathan Swift and Thomas Paine, all the works that Jeremy had discussed with her so eagerly. These books were her friends as well as his, and by reading them during her sojourn at Oakhurst Manor, she would assuage her loneliness a little.

Eventually she walked into the bedchamber, and to her surprise, saw one of her nightgowns already laid out on the bed.

Someone appeared in the frame behind her, and Sarah turned to see the housekeeper, who stood with folded arms, watching her.

"My things have already been unpacked, before I even decided I wanted to stay here," Sarah said, and felt bewildered.

The giantess smiled. "Cleo know," she said.

Sarah thought it unlikely that anyone had ever been able to fool this woman with the wise, penetrating eyes.

"Missy rest now," Cleo said, pointing to the bed. "Cleo send maid with herb tea, then missy sleep."

Sarah shook her head. "I promised I'd write to Amanda today. If she hurries here by ship, she can be here in time for Christmas."

"Missy write tonight," Cleo said. "Willie take letter to Charleston tomorrow." She opened a window, then closed the jealousie-shutters that darkened the room. "Now missy rest."

Sarah thought it likely that, if she disobeyed, Cleo would undress her and force her to get into bed.

Not until she began to remove her clothes did the housekeeper depart.

Some of the things Jeremy had said about slavery started to make sense to Sarah for the first time. Cleo was a slave, and regarded herself as one, but in actuality she was the real mistress of Oakhurst Manor. It was unlikely that even Paul Beaufort would dare to cross her will.

As soon as Sarah settled herself in the four-poster bed, a serving maid brought her a large cup of fragrant herb tea. It was delicious, unlike any she had ever tasted, and the thought flicked through her mind that perhaps it had medicinal qualities. She would not put it past Cleo to decide that she needed medication of some sort to enable her to sleep more soundly.

The truth of the matter was that the long journey from Boston had exhausted her. Perhaps the constant strain of her separation from Jeremy, her fear for his welfare and safety, had weakened her.

Whatever the reasons, she relished the feeling of stretching out beneath the canopy of this huge featherbed. Jeremy's bed. With pillows on which he had rested his head.

In the distance, Sarah heard voices chanting, and as the sound grew louder, she guessed that the field hands were coming home after their day's work. Tomorrow, she hoped, her future father-in-law would take her on a tour of those cabins so she could see for herself that the slaves of Oakhurst were adequately housed.

All at once she recognized the words, the same that Willie had chanted when they had first arrived at the plantation:

> *Tola m-bena, toa m'bwana,*
> *Mengano, rangano m'bwana.*

With almost no effort Sarah recalled Tom's translation:

> *This land is rich and sweet,*
> *Holding me close like a mother.*
> *She nourishes me, she gives me strength.*
> *The rich, sweet land.*

It was true, apparently, that the slaves thought of Oakhurst as their home. There was pride in the voices of the field hands, as there had been in Willie's. There was something else in their tone, too, and all at once Sarah recognized it: joy.

Oakhurst truly was their home, and although Sarah had

been here only an hour, she knew how they felt. Oakhurst was Jeremy's heritage, so it was her home, too, and she already felt fiercely possessive of the stately manor house, the fields that extended as far as one could see.

Her sense of depression lifted somewhat, and for the first time since Jeremy had vanished, a sense of joy pervaded Sarah. She was smiling as she dropped off to sleep in Jeremy's bed.

Chapter 7

Cleo ruled Oakhurst Manor from her own domain, a small house of red brick that was a miniature version of the great house and was located only a stone's throw from the kitchen outbuildings. The entire household staff and the gardeners reported to her, and she was everywhere, making certain the furniture was polished and the rugs beaten, weeds removed from flowerbeds. She supervised the preparation of all food, ordered such needed provisions from Charleston as sugar, salt, and flour, and took care of the feeding of the slaves as well as those who ate in the manor.

Paul Beaufort automatically deferred to Cleo's authority in all things, and it would not have occurred to Tom to defy her, much less argue with her. She attended to Isaiah Benton's comforts, saw to it that a filled carafe of rum was placed in his suite at all times, and even directed that he be given a firm, hard mattress when she observed that sleeping on a featherbed gave him a stiff back.

Apparently Cleo had not yet made up her mind about Margot Benton. She treated the girl with respect, to be sure, without ever becoming servile, but she kept watch on

Margot when no one else was aware of her activity. Only Sarah noted what she was doing, and was privately amused.

It soon became clear to Sarah, however, that Cleo had taken Margot under her protective wing. Late one afternoon, when Tom and Willie returned from a hunting trip laden with bags filled with wild ducks, Cleo inspected their kill near the kitchens, then abruptly dismissed her son.

Neither Cleo nor Tom realized that Sarah stood only a few feet from them at the entrance to the smokehouse where hams and bacon were prepared. She had just inspected it for the first time, and stepped back into the shadows of the interior when Cleo had appeared with the two young men.

"What have I done now, Cleo?" Tom's manner was joking, but there was an undercurrent of uneasiness in his voice.

"Not do yet. Cleo say no do."

"What?" He sounded like a small boy being disciplined.

"No sleep with girl!"

"Wait up, now, Cleo." Tom seemed to recover his poise. "Since when do I need to ask your permission before I make love to a girl?"

"Tom no sleep with red-hair girl," Cleo said, her voice severe and uncompromising. "If Tom do, Cleo know. Cleo tell Mr. Paul. Tell father of girl. Make great trouble for Tom."

"By God," Tom said, "I really believe you'd do just that."

"Cleo do," the housekeeper said.

Hickory smoke was causing Sarah's eyes to water, and she was afraid she might cough, revealing the fact that she was eavesdropping, but she quietly blessed Cleo.

"If you're so all-fired smart," Tom said, displaying bravado, "what makes you think Margot would allow me to make love to her?"

"Cleo no know. But Tom no try."

That was the end of the matter, and Sarah waited until Cleo disappeared into the kitchens and Tom went to the front of the house before she emerged.

Jeremy, it seemed, had been Cleo's favorite, and she

smothered his betrothed with attention. It was customary for the Beauforts and their guests to be served breakfast in their individual quarters, and for several mornings Sarah contented herself with a thin slice of toasted rice bread and a cup of the strong West Indian coffee that had a flavor all its own in South Carolina.

One morning, about a week after her arrival, she sat in Jeremy's leather chair near the windows reading one of his books in the bright morning sunlight, when Cleo entered, not bothering to knock.

"Good morning," Sarah said, and smiled.

Cleo had no interest in preambles. "Missy eat," she said, and pointed a thick forefinger at breast of smoked turkey, a goat cheese made on the premises, and a platter of fried ham and hard-boiled eggs.

"Thank you for your concern," Sarah said, "but I never have much of an appetite this early in the day. I'm never hungry until it's time for dinner."

"Missy eat!" Cleo commanded, and folded her arms. It was evident that she intended to stay in order to ensure that her order was obeyed.

There was no escape, so Sarah took a token bite of turkey and another of ham.

"More," Cleo said.

Sarah ate until she thought she would burst, and hoped that was the end of the matter.

She was doomed to disappointment. Thereafter Cleo came to Jeremy's suite herself with the breakfast tray each morning and made sure that Sarah ate.

The housekeeper's concern extended far beyond Sarah's eating habits. One day she returned from a canter with Margot, Tom, and young Scott Emerson, the high-spirited son of a neighboring plantation owner, and she found a disapproving Cleo awaiting her on the portico.

"When missy ride on horse," the housekeeper said, "horse walk. Not run."

That evening Sarah spoke to her future father-in-law. "I don't know what I've done to deserve Cleo's smothering attention," she said, "but she treats me as though I were made of fragile porcelain. Yesterday she lectured me for running down the stairs, and today I was told not to canter."

"You'll be marrying Jeremy when he comes home," Paul said, almost slipping by saying "if he comes home."

"I know, but—"

"As the mistress-to-be of Oakhurst, you have no choice," Paul told her, and chuckled. "Cleo has taken you under her wing, so you'll just have to do as she tells you. I'm afraid you have no choice."

About a week before Christmas, Sarah had her first confrontation with Cleo. The brig that brought Amanda to South Carolina landed at Charleston one morning, and Willie was on hand to escort the girl to Oakhurst. They arrived that afternoon, and Cleo assigned Amanda a small but substantially built house near her own dwelling.

"No," Sarah said, "Amanda will live in the manor."

"Black woman no live in big house," Cleo declared.

"Others may not," Sarah said, setting her jaw. "I know nothing of the rules that govern the conduct of slaves, and where they sleep is none of my business. But Amanda is a free woman, as free as I am, and she'll sleep where she pleases. Where I please."

Amanda settled the matter by moving into Willie's house with him.

The next day she came to Sarah to help her arrange her hair, and confessed, "Willie's mother is a strange one. I was afraid she'd tear my head off when I told him to take my luggage to his house, but she's been nice to me all day. Willie says you're the only one ever to make her toe the mark. Not even Mr. Jeremy could do it."

"Just so she doesn't try to give you orders, we'll have no trouble," Sarah said. "As I wrote to you, we'll be paying you full wages while you're here, and you're free to leave anytime you decide you've had enough."

"So far, I like it fine," Amanda said, and giggled. "That Willie is a special man."

That evening Sarah dressed with care in an Empire dress with a bodice made of Belgian lace. Paul Beaufort was giving his annual pre-Christmas party, neighbors and friends had been invited, and Sarah knew she would be a focus of attention. Jeremy's absence overwhelmed her, and she felt empty inside, devoid of feeling. But for his sake she was determined to put up a cheerful, pleasant front.

She had already met Scott and Julia Emerson, who lived at neighboring Trelawney, and she felt at home with the bluff, hearty couple, even though she couldn't share the gray-haired Julia's mania for fishing. Never before had Sarah known a woman who preferred fishing to more feminine activities.

The Emersons were a strange lot. In spite of Julia's predilections, all three of her daughters were delicate, dark-haired girls who enjoyed such activities as embroidery and playing the piano. Yet, they expressed their individuality in striking ways. Alicia, the eldest, who was approximately Sarah's age, wore shockingly low-cut bodices and had invested an inheritance from her grandfather in Mississippi River barges that carried the farm products of the frontier to New Orleans. Ann, the second daughter, had invented a new type of saw that was being used at both Trelawney and Oakhurst for cutting wood, and she was currently at work on a new project, a machine that would dig postholes for fenceposts. Ardeth, the youngest, who was in her early teens, spoke Latin, Greek, French, and Spanish, and insisted she planned to study law, even though the profession was closed to women.

The Emerson sons appeared to be less talented than their sisters. Young Scott, a contemporary and close friend of Tom Beaufort's, was a hellion who had no interest in the management of Trelawney and spent most of his time in the pursuit of pleasure. His younger brother, Julius, had just come home from the college at Princeton for the holidays, and Sarah was not impressed by him. He talked constantly about his drinking escapades, and showed little or no interest in his studies.

"The Emerson boys will settle down, as Tom will," Paul Beaufort had told Sarah. "Our young men are less inhibited than you New Englanders, and we have our own traditions here. Our boys raise Cain for a time before they turn to more serious matters."

"But Jeremy never followed that pattern."

"Hardly." Paul's smile was proud. "Jeremy has always been in a class by himself. I believe he was born with a sense of responsibility, as your father tells me you were. He never needed prodding, just as he never had to be curbed. You and Jeremy are exceptional, daughter, and it's miraculous that you found each other."

The real miracle, Sarah thought, would occur when Jeremy returned to her.

Knowing he would want her to appear at her best when she first met various friends and neighbors, she had dressed with care tonight in a new ankle-length Empire gown of pale gold silk that set off her hair and skin. It had tiny cap sleeves, and she wore it off the shoulders, with Jeremy's gold earrings and his signet ring on the chain around her slender throat as her only ornaments. Ordinarily her shoes were made for her, but this evening she wore sandals of pale gold kidskin that she had purchased in Philadelphia on the journey to South Carolina, because they were a lucky match. Her hair was piled high on her head in a style that enhanced her youth while making her look more mature.

Sarah knew she was ravishing, and she walked slowly down the marble stairs with the poise of one who realized that no other woman would outshine her. Jeremy's absence would make the evening difficult for her, but she was determined to conceal her inner feelings from the company.

The ladies of South Carolina hadn't yet been introduced to the new Paris styles, and without exception they wore full-skirted gowns with low-cut, tight bodices. Sarah's dress created a sensation, as did her natural beauty, and gentlemen as well as ladies stared at her openly as she made the rounds of the company on Paul Beaufort's arm. He proudly called her "my daughter," and she held her head high.

Three fiddlers from Savannah, brought to Oakhurst for the occasion, were playing lively airs in a far corner of the solarium, adjacent to the main drawing room; house servants circulated with trays of punch under the direction of Cleo, who had established her command post in the dining room. The scent of flowers was sweet on the soft air that drifted in through the open windows and French doors, and Sarah, who was partial to jasmine, vastly preferred the natural odors to the harsher smells of perfume worn by some of the ladies.

There were guests in every room, and Sarah dutifully accompanied the master of Oakhurst to each. They came at last to his magnificent library, its shelves lined with leather-bound books, and she was relieved to see that she was already acquainted with everyone in the room, so there were no more names to memorize. No, there was one exception.

In a corner, engaging in a spirited conversation with her father, Sarah saw a handsome woman of about forty, with dark hair, intelligent eyes, and a vivacious smile. It was obvious at a glance that she was more sophisticated than the wives and daughters of the planters: she was wearing a gown of soft yellow velvet unstiffened by horsehair padding or whalebone stays, and her still-youthful figure was shown to good advantage.

Paul Beaufort went to her at once, holding her hand somewhat longer than convention required as he bent over it. "Mistress Small," he said, "I'm happy to present my daughter—and Mr. Benton's. And I can't begin to tell you how delighted I am that you've come down from New York."

As Sarah acknowledged the introduction, she knew the lady was the "Aunt Lorene" about whom all of the younger generation of Emersons spoke so frequently. She was Lorene Small, Julia Emerson's sister, who had been left a substantial sum of money by her late husband, a New York merchant. She had grace and charm as well as the veneer that came from the years she had spent in the nation's most active city, and Sarah could understand why the Emersons admired her so much.

As they chatted about inconsequentials, it slowly dawned on Sarah that Lorene Small held a special place in Paul Beaufort's affections, and that her own father was strongly attracted to the lady, too. They vied for her attention, trying in genteel ways to outmaneuver each other, and Sarah was all but forgotten. She couldn't help giggling when Paul and Isaiah simultaneously snatched silver cups of the mild, wine-flavored punch intended for the ladies, and simultaneously offered them to Mistress Small.

"For shame, gentlemen," she said, laughter in her eyes. "Is Mistress Sarah a mere child, too young to drink punch? How cavalier of you to ignore her when she has no escort of her own." She snatched both cups, showing no partiality, and handed one to the amused girl.

Sarah couldn't remember when she had seen her father so flustered.

Paul was equally embarrassed.

"Now, gentlemen, I want to become acquainted with the girl Jeremy had the good sense to find, so I trust you'll leave us." A large diamond ring flashed on her hand as Lorene Small dismissed the two men with an airy gesture.

They had no choice, and withdrew.

Lorene linked her arm through the younger woman's and led her to a high-backed leather sofa that faced the rear of the library. "We won't be disturbed here," she said as they sat. "Julia and Scott have raved about you, as have the youngsters, so I was prepared to find you an exceptionally attractive person. But I wasn't prepared for your sense of humor."

"I couldn't help it," Sarah said, and giggled again. "Papa looked like a little boy trying to show off, and so did Papa Beaufort."

"My dear, all men are boys, you know, regardless of their age. I thought my life was ended when my husband died three years ago, but I discover it's just beginning."

Sarah looked at her, and sobered. "You aren't just making conversation."

"Indeed I'm not, and I knew you'd be intelligent enough to understand."

"You're doing what no one else has dared to even try. You're preparing me for the possibility that Jeremy won't come back. Ever."

"I believe in facing reality. Oh, I may sound glib, my dear, but I assure you I suffered. I've loved only one man in my life, and when I lost him, I thought the world would end. It didn't, and here I am."

"If I allow myself to think that Jeremy won't return, I doubt if I can survive." Sarah spoke slowly, with deep conviction.

"I happen to know something about the shipping

business, because my husband traded with merchants in London, and most of my funds are invested in foreign trade right now. The Royal Navy is cruel. Her sailors are subjected to more dangers than I can count. A man can die of abuse if he fails to accept his lot and conform. He might be swept overboard in a storm and drown. Or he might be killed in a battle with the French. Frankly, the odds that Jeremy will live aren't too good. Provided, of course, that he was actually impressed into the Royal Navy. You can only guess what may have happened to him."

"You're torturing me," Sarah said.

Lorene shook her head. "I'm doing you the greatest possible kindness. I've known Jeremy since he was born, and I'm fonder of him than I am of my own nieces and nephews. So I can guess how much he means to you, and I'm not speaking lightly. I wanted to have this talk with you, and the moment I saw you, I knew you had the strength of character to view your situation factually."

"What should I do, then?"

"My dear, I'm not suggesting that you abandon hope or try to forget Jeremy. That would be stupid, and a waste of your efforts. All I'm trying to do is to urge you to keep—in the back of your mind—the possibility that he won't be seen again. Don't dwell on it, but admit to yourself that the chance exists. That will make the tragedy easier to bear if you should ever have your hopes extinguished."

"I can't promise that I can do it, but I can try," Sarah said.

The older woman placed a hand on her arm. "Forgive my interference, but I've just wanted to help. For Jeremy's sake, and now that I've come to know you a little, for your sake, too. I'm living proof of the resilience of the human spirit. I've spent the past hour talking with your father, and I enjoyed every minute of it."

A mischievous smile touched the corners of Sarah's mouth. "You don't need me to tell you that Papa liked it, too."

Lorene laughed. "I find him fascinating. Not many Americans care what happens beyond our own boundaries, but your father understands the world."

"I know. My sister and I are fortunate, even though Papa seldom is aware of what happens at home."

"Will it surprise you to learn he's invited me to ride to Charleston with him? He's just discovered one of our local delicacies, she-crab soup, and he wants to take me to an inn that serves it."

"I . . . I hope you've accepted, Mistress Small—"

"Lorene, if you please."

"Thank you. Lorene." Sarah felt shy. "Papa has been lonely, far lonelier than he's realized, since Mama died."

"I guessed it. In spite of his knowledge and his worldliness, he was ill at ease with me. Why, he was even worse than Paul Beaufort, whom I've known since I was a child. I grew up not twenty-five miles from Oakhurst."

"I needn't tell you that Papa Beaufort likes you, too."

"Between you and me, Sarah, since we're confiding in each other, I suspect that Paul is in love with me, although he hasn't had the courage to bring it into the open." Lorene made no attempt to conceal her glee. "Is it any wonder that I feel alert and alive? I'm forty-one years old. There are more than a hundred men here tonight, and the only two who are worth a hill of rice husks are dancing attendance on me. When I was your age, I took the attention of men for granted, just as you undoubtedly do. Today I'm grateful for it, and I don't know when I've enjoyed myself more."

"Any man who didn't fall in love with you would be stupid," Sarah said.

"Thank you, my dear. That's the nicest compliment I've had in years, and I can only return it by saying the same is true of you."

"I want only one man on earth," Sarah said. "Jeremy."

"We've talked long enough." Lorene drained her punch cup and stood. "If we go on any longer, you'll become morbid. No, don't come with me. You're not interested in the talk of the old about excise taxes and the price of sugar, much less the lack of respect that the young are showing their elders. You need people of your own generation this evening." She gestured toward the open French doors that led to the beautiful lawn. "They're all outdoors, I'm sure. As I'd be if I were twenty years younger."

Sarah hesitated. "It's my duty—"

"You've met everyone here, so you've done your duty. Remember what I've told you. And go!" Lorene turned away, and as she left the room, every mature man watched her departure.

Sarah envied the balance she had achieved. She could understand Papa's interest in Lorene. Paul Beaufort's, too. It would be dreadful if they became competitors for her hand, because one—or both—would be hurt.

Right now, however, she had to think of herself. The advice Lorene had given her was sound, and she would follow it, to the best of her ability. She stepped into the open, where the strains of the music mingled with the laughter of the fifty or more girls and young men who stood in small groups.

At moments such as this, Sarah missed Jeremy so much that she felt physically ill, but she tried to overcome it by moving forward, and soon she was surrounded.

A young captain of cavalry who had just returned from an expedition against warring Indian tribes that had taken him into southern Georgia and across the border into the Spanish Floridas brought her an unwanted cup of punch. The son of a neighboring plantation owner offered to show her the oleander and rose gardens, and a young physician who had recently established himself in a Charleston practice was equally attentive.

She realized she should be flattered by the interest of the unattached males, but she didn't really care. Those who knew she was betrothed to Jeremy were respectful, while the others were somewhat bolder, but she treated them in the same way, smiling automatically and absently replying to their comments.

Gradually, in the light of the oil-soaked torches that illuminated the lawn, Sarah became uncomfortably conscious of a drama being played out only a few yards from the spot on which she stood. Unfortunately, one of the principals was her sister, and another was young Scott Emerson.

Margot was in one of her more outrageous moods, and was flirting recklessly with Scott. Her lashes fluttered, and she moved toward him and then edged away again; as she talked with him, she sometimes brushed a hand against his velvet lapel for emphasis, and once she caught hold of a pewter button on the front of his swallow-tailed coat and twisted it.

Young Scott was a perfect foil. He knew only that a pretty girl with red hair and green eyes was making a fuss over him, and he was enjoying himself. What he failed to realize was that Margot was just using him for her own purposes.

Tom Beaufort stood alone in the shadows, watching every move she made, and his clenched fists, the set of his jaw, and his blazing eyes told Sarah that her sister was succeeding in making him wildly jealous. She excused herself from the group that surrounded her and joined Tom.

"Does the family give many parties this large?" she asked.

He muttered something unintelligible, and glancing at her for barely an instant, continued to watch Margot.

Sarah made another attempt to distract him. "Cleo showed me some of the food that will be served later, and I've never seen such opulence. Gallons of she-crab soup and gallons of smoked oysters. Platters of a white, flaky fish I've never seen before—"

"Kingfish, we call it here." Tom glared at the back of the laughing, gesticulating Margot.

"Right. There must be a dozen smoked hams. Roasted turkeys. A side of beef basted with Cleo's special sauce as the spit turned, and a side of barbecued venison, too. Not to mention all the Italian salad greens and fruit and cheeses and cakes. Will people actually eat all that food, Tom?"

"They usually do." He was still absorbed, and his rudeness was unintentional.

Sarah realized she had to resort to a more direct method, and took his arm. "I've had more offers than I can count to see the oleander and rose gardens in the moonlight, but I didn't quite trust any of my guides. I wonder if my future brother-in-law would show them to me."

"Later, Sarah." His teeth were clenched.

Her temper flared. "Tom Beaufort, stop behaving so idiotically! Margot is making a scene for the sole purpose of arousing your jealousy, and you're making it obvious that her little game is effective. Just because she chooses to act like an adolescent is no reason you've got to do the same. Pay no attention to her! Show her you don't care a fig, and she'll stop."

For the first time that evening Tom looked hard at his missing brother's betrothed. "By God, Sarah, you're right! I'm obliged to you for the advice!"

To her consternation, he stalked off, and she realized that instead of behaving sensibly, he intended to retaliate in some way.

Sarah's guess was right. Tom marched up to Alicia Emerson, whose décolletage revealed the deep cleavage between her breasts, and who, as a consequence, was winning more than her share of male attention. Tom said something to her, and Alicia nodded, then took his arm, and they wandered together toward the fringes of light cast by the leaping flares.

Margot was aware of Tom's movements, and flirted even more energetically with Scott.

Tom and Alicia halted, and as they conversed, they too flirted.

Sarah was reminded of the mating dance of birds that landed on the Boston Common in the spring. She thought it obscene that people should behave in this manner, particularly when they didn't mean it, and she marched back into the mansion.

Her father and Paul Beaufort were engaged in a lively conversation with Lorene Small, and she made no attempt to interrupt. The energetic Julia Emerson halted her for an exchange of a few words, and then several other members of the older generation talked with her.

But Sarah was worried about the scene in the garden, and felt compelled to find out what was happening. Something in her manner was so grim, so determined as she made her way out through the open French doors of the library, that Paul Beaufort followed her at a distance.

Most of the young guests had taken themselves elsewhere, and with good cause. Margot and Tom stood facing each other directly beneath a torch, arguing violently.

They were speaking at the same time, so neither heard a word said by the other.

Sarah did not hesitate, and pushed them away from each other. "That's quite enough!" she said. "You're making spectacles of yourselves. If Jeremy were here, Tom, he'd tan your hide for your rudeness and lack of courtesy to your father's guests. Being a Beaufort is more than bearing a name. It entails a sense of responsibility. As for you, Margot, your conduct has been inexcusable, and you're not too old for me to take a hairbrush to your backside."

Her fury stunned the squabbling couple, and they gaped at her.

"If you care for each other," Sarah said, "I'm sure you can find better ways to express your feelings. Flirtations with other people for the sake of making each other jealous are childish and contemptible. But if you don't really care for each other, be adult enough to admit the truth. No one is forcing you to come together."

Tom found his voice. "Margot started it," he said. "She leaned all over Scott."

"You more than made up for my innocent little chat," Margot said. "The way you fawned over Alicia was—"

"As disgusting as you're both being right now." Sarah's rage was icy. "All I ask of either of you is good manners, and I more than ask it. I demand it. I'm going to be a Beaufort as long as I live, and I hope to live at Oakhurst until I die. I refuse to permit my sister and my brother-in-law to make laughingstocks of the Beaufort name. Or the Benton name."

They began to wilt, and Tom became embarrassed. "I meant no harm, Sarah. I have a hot temper—"

"Then learn to control it!"

"The fault was mine," Margot said. "Tom was so busy ogling the pretty girls that I thought I'd teach him a lesson."

Sarah did not relent. "If there's any more nonsense, I shall ask Papa to take you straight back to Boston immediately after the new year." Not waiting for a reply, she turned on her heel and headed back toward the house.

A chuckling Paul Beaufort emerged from the shadows

and enveloped her in a hug. "Spoken like the mistress of Oakhurst Manor," he said.

Sarah was abashed. "Oh, dear. If I'd known you were listening, Papa Beaufort, I wouldn't have—"

"I'm delighted you did. It's precisely what Jeremy would have done, and they deserved it."

She took his arm, and they started back toward the house. "I really think they're falling in love," she said, "but I don't believe they realize it, so they express themselves in immature ways."

Paul patted her hand. "You startled me, too, when you spoke of going back to Boston, daughter. I wish you'd think of staying here until Jeremy comes back."

"But he'll expect me to be waiting for him up there."

"Not necessarily. He knows me, so he undoubtedly realizes that I want you to make your home here—and become the mistress of Oakhurst in fact. Don't make a decision now. Ponder well, daughter, and you'll know what's right for you."

Chapter 8

Paul Beaufort changed his habits of a lifetime. Each morning, arising at his customary early hour, he went to nearby Trelawney, and after escorting Lorene Small on a canter, brought her back to Oakhurst Manor for breakfast.

Isaiah Benton concluded that he didn't enjoy eating alone in his suite, so each morning, when he heard the sound of approaching horses, he came down to the dining room for breakfast. The trio stayed at the table for a long time.

Later, when Paul went off with Mr. Higby for his regular morning inspection of the plantation, Isaiah strolled with Lorene, discussing law cases in which he had participated, literature, and the rapid deterioration in America's relations with Great Britain.

More often than not, after Paul's return, he persuaded Lorene to stay for dinner.

Conversation, particularly in the presence of the Benton sisters, Tom, and some of the young Emersons, who were frequent visitors, was general. Isaiah and Paul agreed that the possibility of war between the United States and Great Britain was becoming greater. Conversely, the threat of hostilities with France was fading. The Emperor Napoleon, who was preparing for a major campaign against imperial Russia, had become less belligerent toward the Madison administration, principally because he could not fight simultaneously on two continents.

But, as Isaiah Benton said, Napoleon's preoccupation with Russia was the factor that made war between America and Britain more likely. The Royal Navy constituted Britain's most powerful weapon, and she was determined to tighten her embargo on Europe, making it as difficult as possible for Napoleon to obtain raw materials in trade. If that meant Britain had to fight a secondary war against her former colonies, it appeared she would take the plunge.

Lorene reluctantly agreed with the men. "I had to take over portions of my husband's business after he died, so I've had many dealings with the English. They're splendid merchants, and their own trade is very important to them, but their determination to crush Bonaparte has become a mania. They intend to be rid of him for all time, even if the effort ruins them."

Sarah, who knew little about world affairs, not only was impressed by Lorene's knowledge but also noted that her father and Paul listened to her with respect. Someday, the girl hoped, she would be capable of winning such attention for her intellect, too.

Two days before Christmas, Alicia and Ann Emerson joined their aunt at Oakhurst Manor for dinner. When the meal ended, Paul and Isaiah remained at the table for glasses of port, while Tom and Margot went into the solarium with the Emerson girls for a game of whist. Lorene and Sarah upheld tradition by adjourning to the drawing room for coffee, and Cleo put the stamp of approval on their friendship by serving their coffee herself.

The development of that friendship had been rapid, in spite of the difference in their ages, and undoubtedly had been sparked by their frank talk on the night they had met. Neither put up any false fronts, and by unspoken agreement they were candid, totally honest; if a subject was broached that one or the other wanted to avoid, it was dropped.

Lorene took a *cigarro* from a cedar-lined box and lighted it neatly with a tinderbox and flint.

Sarah stared at her in astonishment.

The older woman laughed. "Do you find it so surprising? My husband imported *cigarros* from the Dutch West islands, and I picked up the habit of smoking them from him."

"Actually," Sarah said, "I admire your courage. There are too many restrictions on women, and sometimes I grow so sick of being a lady that I want to scream!"

"Then why don't you?" It was apparent that Lorene enjoyed her *cigarro*.

"I fully intend to. Tomorrow night, after we come home from Christmas Eve services at church, I intend to scream myself hoarse. In the privacy of my room, of course. It's the only way I'll be able to bear Jeremy's absence."

"Do it, by all means. But it won't help, Sarah. I know. About a month after my husband died, I spent an entire night screaming, but it didn't bring him back to me. What may I do to help you tomorrow night?"

"I hope you'll be spending the evening here. Just having you near will be a help."

Lorene laughed as she sipped her steaming coffee. "My dear, I'm going to spend the night here. Paul and Isaiah were so insistent that I had to agree so they'd stop hammering at me. Julia and Scott are delighted, of course. They keep urging me to remarry—without expressing any preference, which is wise of them."

"I'll confess something dreadful to you. Tom and young Scott are accepting wagers from Margot and the Emerson clan."

Lorene threw back her dark hair and laughed. "Which of my suitors has the better odds?"

"I don't know. I've refused to have any part of such idiocy."

"To tell you the truth, my dear, I wouldn't want to place a wager myself. I'm not certain where I stand, and it's too soon to find out."

"That's what I've thought. I've watched you reacting to both of them."

"You're very shrewd," Lorene said. "I'm enjoying being

courted, naturally, but I'm not ready to decide whether I want to marry again, much less which I'd choose. Time will make up my mind for me. Time is what you need, too."

Sarah remained silent. She stayed sane only by telling herself that each passing day brought the return of Jeremy closer.

Lorene realized she didn't want to talk about Jeremy, so she brought the conversation back to herself. "One of the factors that holds me back," she said, "is the knowledge that when and if I choose one, I'll hurt the other. I guess it boils down to a question of which will suffer the lesser hurt."

"I honestly don't know." Sarah realized they were being too solemn, and spoke in a lighter vein. "I'm dying to see how they'll react when they join us and see you're smoking that *cigarro*."

"Oh, they'll hide their surprise and pretend everything is normal and natural, of course. When a man—any man— is trying to win a woman's favor, he pretends to approve of anything and everything she does. He waits until they're married before he tries to mold her to his concepts of right and wrong."

"I wonder if I'll ever be as wise as you."

"Wiser. Just follow your natural instincts."

"You know," Sarah said, "I'm the only person who has everything to gain and nothing to lose in this romantic triangle you've become involved in, Lorene. Regardless of whether you become Mistress Benton or Mistress Beaufort, you'll be related to me."

St. John's Anglican Church, a red brick structure with a towering white steeple, had been burned to the ground by redcoats in the last year of the War of Independence, and had been the first structure in the parish rebuilt late in 1783. General Francis Marion had worshipped there after his postwar marriage, as had various members of the Pinckney family and other South Carolina notables. The interior was plain and unadorned, painted white, and Sarah, reminded of Boston churches, felt at home.

The congregation sang Christmas hymns and carols,

then knelt for the Eucharist, and Sarah prayed hard and unceasingly for Jeremy's safe return.

When she left the church, she felt exhausted but refreshed. She intended to go to bed as soon as she reached Oakhurst Manor, but she no longer felt the need to scream herself senseless, and she knew she would sleep. She felt strangely comforted, and she knew Jeremy was alive, just as she knew he was in no danger tonight. She had no idea how the conviction had formed within her, but it was there.

Members of the Emerson family and several other neighbors were invited to a late supper by Paul Beaufort, and all gladly accepted. The ladies rode in carriages, as did the elderly rector of St. John's, the Reverend Dr. Edward Alan Gibney, with the men on horseback forming an escort. The younger people sang Christmas carols, their voices echoing across the fields of tobacco and cotton, rice and sugarcane.

Sarah sat in a corner of the lead carriage, with Lorene beside her, and sighed, then rested her head on the older woman's shoulder. For the first time in the months since Jeremy had disappeared, she was at peace within herself, her torment at least temporarily allayed.

Lorene knew how she felt, and patted her hand.

When they reached Oakhurst Manor, Sarah wished her father, future father-in-law, and Lorene a happy Christmas, then slipped off to her own suite. Cleo claimed the honor of tucking her into bed, and within minutes she was asleep.

Members of the older generation gathered in the drawing room, while their juniors occupied the solarium, and Isaiah Benton provided a Christmas surprise. He had arranged for a client now residing in Martinique to send him several cases of French champagne, which had been unavailable in the United States for years, and it had arrived the previous day in Charleston on board a privateer that had managed to slip through the ever-tightening British blockade. Willie had picked up the wine, and for more than twenty-four hours it had been cooling in a stream that meandered through the fields behind the manor house.

Willie took several bottles to his house for a private

celebration with Amanda, and insisted that Cleo join them, even though she didn't care for the taste of wine.

In the drawing room, everyone stood as the Reverend Dr. Gibney offered a brief invocation. He ended his prayer with a plea that the young nation be allowed to remain at peace in 1812. Gifts were exchanged, but in the tradition long followed by the Beaufort and Emerson families, they were inexpensive tokens. Lorene Small came in for her fair share. Isaiah gave her a leather-bound collection of the works of Dean Jonathan Swift, which he had purchased for her in a Charleston bookshop, and Paul presented her with a new set of spurs for their morning canters.

The festivities in the solarium were less restrained. Someone conceived the idea of mixing three parts of champagne to one part of brandywine; later the young people were agreed that either Tom Beaufort or young Scott Emerson was responsible, but no one could remember which it had been.

In any event, the drink was potent, and the young men soon were feeling its effects. Only two of the girls, Margot Benton and Alicia Emerson, dared to sample the concoction, and even though they drank considerably less than the men, they became slightly tipsy, too.

After a time, Margot found herself sitting next to young Scott on a divan, and, her lesson unlearned or forgotten, she couldn't help flirting with him again. He was such an easy mark, responding so eagerly whenever she smiled at him, that she couldn't resist playing up to him.

The brandywine and champagne made her careless, and it didn't occur to her that Tom was becoming increasingly sullen.

Only Alicia was aware of the growing storm, but she was under the influence of the drink, too, and made no attempt to interrupt the couple conversing in low tones on the divan.

Margot said something that Scott found particularly amusing. He roared with laughter, and when they leaned closer together, he grasped her bare upper arm.

Margot neither moved away from him nor removed his

hand. Later she confessed that she had scarcely been aware of his touch.

Suddenly an enraged Tom stood before them. "Emerson," he said in a hard, clipped voice, "be good enough to join me outdoors."

The laughter died in young Scott's face, and he jumped to his feet.

The other young men followed the pair onto the lawn, and Margot stood with Alicia at the open French doors, one hand at her throat. "Now I've done it," she murmured.

Alicia was sobering, too. "They've had too much to drink, and they're going to fight."

"We've got to stop them." Margot was near tears.

"How can we? They've become like two stallions, with bad blood between them."

Tom drew himself to his full height. "Emerson, I've tolerated your insolence for the last time. I'll permit no familiarity with Mistress Benton."

Young Scott looked him up and down. "Do you have a proprietary interest in her, sir? If not, tend to your own affairs."

Margot felt ill.

"You'll give me satisfaction, sir!" Tom said.

"Gladly, sir!"

"Dear Lord," Alicia murmured. "They're going to fight a duel."

Margot wanted to race onto the lawn and stop the grim farce, but it was too late.

Other young men acted as seconds and quickly began to arrange the details.

A hysterical Margot fled the scene.

Sarah was awakened from a deep sleep by her weeping, sobbing sister. Finally understanding what she was being told, she donned a quilted dressing gown. "Go straight to your room and stay there!" she commanded. "You've done enough damage for one night."

Margot went off, still weeping.

Sarah hurried down the stairs.

Most of the guests had departed, the champagne and supper forgotten, and the atmosphere in the drawing room was funereal. The elder Scott Emerson paced the room, and Paul Beaufort stood at a window, his fingers drumming a tattoo on its sill. Julia Emerson looked stunned, and Lorene Small seemed unable to console her.

Only Isaiah Benton remained relatively calm. "There must be some way under the law to prevent this duel from taking place. I don't care how obscure the statute is. We can wake up Judge Campbell down the road, and he'll issue a restraining order that will place those young hotheads in contempt of court if they proceed with the duel."

"There is no such statute in South Carolina," Paul said. "No legislator would vote for a law that prevents a man from defending his honor."

"Honor, indeed," Lorene murmured.

"And even if there were such a law," Scott said as he continued to pace, "those young fools would ignore it. They'd rather risk being in contempt of court."

Julia seemed on the verge of collapse. "How can they fight a duel on Christmas Day?"

Paul stared out at the lawn with unseeing eyes. "The worst of it is that the Beauforts and the Emersons have been the closest of friends for generations. Those boys grew up together, and I can't understand how they can do this to each other. And to us."

"There will be no duel," Sarah said.

Until that moment they had been unaware of her presence, and with one accord they turned to look at her as she stood in the arched entrance to the drawing room.

"Papa," she told Isaiah, "this is Margot's doing, but I'll attend to her later. When and where is this fight supposed to take place?"

Scott Emerson was the first to recover. "At the old mill-pond," he said, "at the dividing line between Oakhurst and Trelawney. They're meeting at dawn."

"I'll want two horses," Sarah said, "and the services of Willie to guide me there. Will you arrange it, Papa Beaufort?"

The unexpected complication increased Paul's uneasiness. "What do you have in mind?" he countered.

Her reply was indirect. "I shall also require the loan of

two pistols," she said, "and as I know nothing about firearms, I'll be obliged to you if they're loaded."

Isaiah, who knew his elder daughter's moods, was alarmed. "There's been enough insanity, Sarah."

"You're right, Papa." She was unyielding. "I refuse to stand by idly while a Beaufort and an Emerson maim or kill each other. If Jeremy were here, he'd knock the heads of those two boys together until they heard church chimes pealing. He isn't here, more's the pity, so I intend to act in his stead."

Isaiah and Paul started to speak simultaneously.

"Enough!" Lorene ordered, cutting them short. "I've listened to all of you wailing, and I've watched you wringing your hands. Isaiah wants to rely on laws that don't exist. Paul and Scott speak of the satisfactions of sacred honor, as though that were important when the lives of two boys are at stake. Not to mention the friendship of two families. Do as Sarah asks!"

The fog was so thick that Sarah had to ride close behind Willie as they made their way to the far reaches of Oakhurst, and occasionally he turned in the saddle to make certain he hadn't lost her.

Never had she known such a Christmas. The weather was as balmy as Boston in late May or early June, and the fog reminded her of the thick blankets that rolled in from the Atlantic in September. She was taking unprecedented risks, she knew, but she had no choice, so she was resolute. Paul, Isaiah, and Scott had wanted to accompany her, but she had refused to accept them as escorts on the grounds that their presence would merely postpone the fighting of the duel.

She had no clear-cut idea of what she planned to do, but she had made up her mind to stop the fight, and she intended to rely on her instinct. Her disgust with everyone involved in the incident was overwhelming, and she gave no thought to herself or the role she had elected to play. For the moment, even Jeremy had receded from her mind.

A dilapidated building of unpainted pine loomed up directly ahead, and beside it Sarah caught the dull silver-black gleam of a body of water.

"This is the old mill house," Willie told her. "Nobody has used it, as far back as I can remember."

"Take me to a side where we won't be seen."

Willie led her to the rear, where they dismounted.

"It will be your responsibility to keep our horses quiet," she said.

"You can depend on me."

"I do. Willie, do you know anything about duels?"

He was thankful for the dark as he answered, "No, Miss Sarah. I've never played those games."

"Neither have I. Oh, well. I'll have to decide for myself when to act."

"You won't have long to wait," he replied, lowering his voice. "The Trelawney party is coming."

A few moments later, she heard the approach of several horses and heard several men speaking in low voices.

"Here comes Tom," Willie whispered.

The second group approached.

It would be at least an hour or two before the fog lifted, but the sky was beginning to brighten, and Sarah could see a little more clearly. She was wearing a shirt, breeches, and boots, with a short cloak thrown over her shoulders, and in her belt she carried the two French dueling pistols that Paul had given her. Slowly she edged around to the side of the barn so she could see what was happening.

All of those taking part in the proceedings were young men she had met at the Beaufort and Emerson mansions, and they were so pompous that she thought them absurd. The official in charge produced a pair of swords, which the seconds weighed and examined while Tom and young Scott stood apart, facing in opposite directions.

They were given the weapons and told to face each other.

Sarah's moment had come, and she threw back her cloak, then moved forward. "Put down your swords," she said quietly.

Tom stared at her. "Sarah! What in hell's own name are you doing here?"

"Don't interfere, Sarah," young Scott said. "Go home."

"Do as I say," she told them, "and drop those swords to the ground." She drew the pistols from her belt.

Tom recognized them. "They're my father's," he said, "and they have hair triggers. Be careful, Sarah."

"They're loaded," she declared, "and I urge all of you to be careful." She waved the pistols.

The seconds and the other observers began to back away.

"Watch what you're doing!" the alarmed Tom exclaimed.

Sarah's smile was cold. "You haven't yet obeyed me. Both of you. Now."

The two blades fell to the ground.

She turned to the others. "Have you nothing better to do on Christmas Day than watch blood being shed? I'm sure you have parents and other relatives who'll expect you to have breakfast with them."

No one moved.

Sarah cocked the pistols, as Paul had taught her, and the clicking noise seemed to reverberate across the fields. "You strain my patience," she said, and again raised the pistols.

Two young men went quickly to their horses, and the rest followed their example more slowly.

The girl stood still until they had ridden off.

Tom's dignity had been shattered. "Sarah, please. The whole state will be talking about this farce."

"It's no farce," she said. "It's a tragedy when two lifelong friends allow a silly, addlepated girl to come between them. Make up your differences!"

They faced each other, two proud young men who were being made to appear ridiculous.

"I was told how to aim these pistols," Sarah said. "It looks quite simple."

Tom began to laugh. "Scottie," he said, "don't be surprised if she wings both of us."

"Or shoots herself in the foot," Scott said with a grin.

They shook hands, then embraced.

The relieved Sarah lowered the pistols.

Tom snatched them from her and examined them. "I'll be damned. Scottie, they're not loaded."

"That was the one thing your fathers wouldn't permit,"

Sarah said. "I've never touched a pistol before, and they were afraid someone might be hurt."

The pair stared hard at her, their sheepish expressions, almost identical.

"You owe it to your families to patch up your friendship," Sarah said.

"I . . . I reckon I was overhasty and lost my temper," Tom said.

"No," Scott told him, "I gave you cause."

"Neither of you is to blame for anything except being stiff-necked," Sarah said. "Tom, you're coming back to Oakhurst Manor with me. Willie," she called, "will you take charge of this arsenal?"

Willie found it difficult to restrain his own laughter as he appeared from the side of the mill house and collected the various weapons.

"So you're a party to this conspiracy, too?" Tom demanded.

Willie winked jauntily.

Sarah took charge again. "Scott, your family is waiting for you at Trelawney after a sleepless night. Go to them. And hurry, so they'll be spared more pain."

Scott squared his shoulders. "A happy Christmas to all," he said, and after wringing Tom's hand again, he mounted his horse.

Tom and Willie flanked Sarah as the trio headed back toward Oakhurst Manor, and for a time no one spoke. The mist was thinning, and the early-morning air was sweet and clean.

Tom broke the silence. "What would you have done, Sarah, if we hadn't heeded you?"

Willie shook his head. "Miss Sarah is like my mother," he said. "Some women, when they tell you do this or that, you do it!"

Sarah couldn't remember when anyone had paid her a greater compliment.

"Anytime you want a job as an overseer," Tom said, "I'm sure Papa will send Mr. Higby away and hire you."

Her goal accomplished, Sarah refused to rise to the bait.

Cleo awaited them on the portico, and promptly vanished into the house when Sarah waved.

They dismounted, and Willie gathered the reins.

"Tom," Sarah said, "you'll go first to the solarium, and then we'll expect you at breakfast." She went off to join the haggard Paul, Isaiah, and Lorene.

Tom was still too shaken to question her command, and went to the solarium.

A red-eyed Margot awaited him there in a full-skirted dress of yellow linen cut in the style that was popular in South Carolina.

He stopped short when he saw her.

"I don't ask your forgiveness," Margot said in a low tone. "If you had been killed or hurt, I wouldn't have forgiven myself."

His face became masklike.

"I accept the full fault for what happened," Margot said, "even though I scarcely knew what I was doing. You shouldn't have given me that mixture of brandywine and champagne. My head still aches."

Tom returned her glare. "A lady," he said, "doesn't drink more than she knows she can handle."

"A gentleman doesn't deliberately give a lady too much to drink!"

"You came between Scottie and me, and it's only because of Sarah that we didn't hack each other to pieces."

"I've already expressed my regrets." Margot placed her hands on her hips and looked at him defiantly. "Don't expect me to grovel, because I won't!"

"I thought about last night all the way back here from the millpond just now. And I can't say I blame Scottie for behaving the way he did when you threw yourself at him."

"Who are you to criticize my conduct, Mr. Beaufort?" Margot knew she was behaving absurdly, but she was so relieved he was safe that she needed an outlet for her feelings. "I'm not one of your field slaves. In fact, you and I mean nothing to each other. When my sister and your brother are married—assuming he comes back some day— you and I will be related, in a manner of speaking. But that's all. I'm free to be friendly with anyone I please."

Tom hadn't intended to become embroiled in yet another quarrel with her, but the vixen was goading him beyond endurance. "I'll be damned if you will, Mistress

Benton. I forbid you to smile in that special way you have at any other man, ever again!"

"You forbid? Really!"

He could tolerate no more, and grasping her by the shoulders, he began to shake her.

"You bully!" Margot struggled in an attempt to free herself.

His excitement mounting, he drew her close and kissed her with passionate fury.

She continued to fight for a moment or two. Then, inexplicably, she yielded and pressed closer to him.

Tom wanted her so badly that he was deterred only by the knowledge that they were locked together in a public room.

Margot sensed his yearning and responded to it without shame. Suddenly, miraculously, her greatest problem had been solved, and she knew she loved this impulsive, spoiled young man.

He felt her beginning to tremble, and his grip slackened, but he continued to hold her. "When we're married," he said, "you'll smile at no one but me in that way."

Margot's instinct for flirtation reasserted itself, and she pretended surprise. "Are we being married?"

"We are!"

"Am I to have no chance to refuse, or even to think about it, sir?"

"None."

She sighed gently.

Tom realized he had neglected to say something important. "I do love you."

Margot returned his fervent gaze. "I truly believe you do, and that's most convenient, because I discover that I love you, too."

He tried to kiss her again.

This time she wriggled free. "Not now. They're waiting for us at table."

Their smiles revealed more than they knew as they walked arm-in-arm into the dining room.

As they took their places, Paul and Isaiah congratulated Tom on the peaceful, civilized resolution of his quarrel with Scott.

"You have Sarah to thank," Lorene added quietly.

"Indeed I do, ma'am." Tom turned to the older girl. "For a minute or two down at the millpond, Sarah, I reckon I could have broken your neck, and I'm sure Scottie felt the same way. But I'm in your debt for the rest of my days, and so is he. I don't aim to make the same fool mistake again."

"I'm glad," Sarah said.

Her sister looked at her in wonder. "Weren't you terrified?"

"Not until it was all over. I was too angry."

Tom turned to Isaiah. "Mr. Benton, after breakfast I'd like a word with you in private."

"I think it can be arranged." Isaiah's broad smile revealed his answer to the unasked question.

"We're going to remember this as one of the jolliest of happy Christmases," Paul said.

Sarah felt as though she had been turned to stone. She was being selfish now, but Margot's radiance, and the joy of Tom, who so closely resembled his brother, were wounds that cut deep. Only by exerting the utmost self-control was she able to refrain from racing from the table and bursting into tears.

Never had she missed Jeremy as she did at this poignant moment.

Chapter 9

Aspera ad virtutem est via. It is a difficult road that leads to virtue.

The family motto should be changed, Jeremy Beaufort thought as he ran aft on the main deck of HMS *Dolphin*, and, barefoot, as usual, began to climb the rigging to unsnarl the lines of the mainsail high overhead. It was a difficult road that led to survival itself. Two and a half weeks had passed since he had been kidnapped and taken aboard the sleek British sloop of war, and it was almost as though he had never known any other existence.

The new apprentice seaman slept in a hammock between decks, with other seamen crowding into the narrow space on either side of him; he had no clothes other than the sailor's pants and shirt the Royal Navy had provided him; and his meals consisted of salt beef, salt fish, and, when he was fortunate, the juice of lemons or limes to ward off scurvy. He had learned quickly to tap a hard biscuit on the table to rid it of weevils, and to the amusement of other seamen, he insisted on putting himself through the daily torture of sloshing himself with buckets of seawater, the only type of bathing that was available.

A feeling of slow-burning anger over his kidnapping and impressment into the Royal Navy was ever-present, and only his determination to live prevented him from creating a furor. In the short period of time he had been on board the *Dolphin*, he had already learned that protest was useless, that there was no appeal. On three occasions he had demanded the right to speak to the captain, Viscount Saunders, but had been told that the ship's master did not converse with ordinary seamen. Even the first mate, Lieutenant Gough, was unavailable.

Several of the younger officers, junior lieutenants and ensigns who were approximately his own age, seemed to sympathize with him because he was a man of education and breeding, but they kept their distance from him, too. He had been told by other seamen that it was a waste of time to complain to anyone but the captain or his mate, and common sense told Jeremy they were right. Lord Saunders was the final, absolute authority, and could be approached only with the permission of the boatswain.

Jeremy knew better than to ask any favors of the burly, swaggering Talbot, a man he loathed with all his heart and all his might. Talbot, who had the unenviable task of training the new members of the crew, was his tormentor and nemesis, always nearby with a length of line soaked in seawater that he did not hesitate to lay across the back of any man who failed to obey an order instantly and without question.

Several times each day, on some occasions without reason, Jeremy was forced to feel that lash, and the excruciating pain was bad enough, but the injury to his pride was even worse. It was almost inconceivable that he, an American citizen, should be subjected to such outrageous treatment. He had been abducted, but had no legal recourse; he was being forced to serve against his will in the naval forces of a foreign nation, and sheer physical force was being used to compel him to do what he was told. Anytime he disobeyed or failed to please his masters, he could be beaten insensible, perhaps emerging from the ordeal crippled for life. The ship's company lived on widespread rumors, and according to the scuttlebutt passed from sailor to sailor at meals or late at night in the forecastle, at least six or seven seamen had been maimed by Talbot in recent years.

So Jeremy kept his mouth shut, did as he was told, and tried to suppress his fury. When he had an opportunity, perhaps he could desert and find some way to work his passage back to the United States. At the very least, he might have the chance to meet Talbot on equal terms, and when that happened, he fully intended to beat the boatswain to a pulp.

Meantime, he missed Sarah Benton so much that the very thought of her was a torture he could scarcely endure. She was beyond his reach now, perhaps for all time, but in spite of his great efforts to discipline himself, he could not help thinking about her. Or about Oakhurst Manor. Only the Almighty knew how Sarah was faring without him, only the Almighty knew what was happening at the plantation that, by rights, someday should belong to him.

If he was being cautious, it was only because of Sarah and his yearning for her and his home. He willed himself to live. He willed himself to learn as much as he could about warships and the sea. Ultimately he would return to Sarah and take her to Oakhurst Manor as his wife. He made the promise to himself when the boatswain's blasphemous shouts awakened him every morning, and he renewed them when, exhausted after long hours of work on deck, he fell into his hammock each night.

What Jeremy failed to realize was that his ordeal was responsible for his physical transformation, and that he was already in the best condition he had ever enjoyed. His years of studying law at Harvard and in Isaiah Benton's office had softened him. Now, active for twelve to sixteen hours per day, he had developed the muscles in his arms, legs, and torso. Never overweight, he had grown even leaner and stronger.

Boatswain Talbot had already learned that Beaufort was the man on whom to call when sheer physical strength was needed. Only a few days earlier, one of the ship's eighteen cannon had broken loose from its moorings and had slid across the deck. It had needed to be returned to its place, and Jeremy had been given the assignment, with two others assisting him. To the astonishment of many members of the crew who had been watching, he had accomplished the feat almost single-handed.

He was aware, of course, of certain changes. There were heavy calluses on the soles of his feet, and his hands had become as toughened as those of a Boston dock worker. It was odd that he, who had always taken pride in his intellect, should be nothing now but a strong body.

In a sense, he knew, he had become a slave in the service of the British crown. The irony of his situation was not lost on him, and he couldn't help wondering if his attitudes toward the slaves at Oakhurst Manor might be changed as a result of what he was currently experiencing. He found it impossible to dwell on such matters, however. He was too busy.

He was in the crow's nest, acting as the lookout, when he saw a smudge on the horizon. As it grew a trifle larger, he could make out land directly ahead. Doing precisely what he had been told, he shouted, "Land, ho!"

As nearly as he could judge, the *Dolphin* was approaching what appeared to be an island. He had no idea what it might be, however, and knew only that the weather was much warmer than it had been in New England when he had been kidnapped. Therefore, the sloop of war had sailed south.

Not until the anchor was dropped was the word spread through the crew of more than one hundred and eighty men. The *Dolphin* had reached the British colony of Bermuda, where food, water, and various supplies would be taken on board. Boats would bring the necessary items to the ship, which would remain at the outer end of the harbor. Only authorized members of the crew would be permitted to go ashore, this group consisting of the officers, the noncommissioned officers, and sailors who had spent a minimum of eight years in the Royal Navy.

The reasons for this unusual order were not difficult to understand. In recent years, numerous seamen had deserted in Bermuda, commandeering smaller craft in an attempt to make their way to safety elsewhere, so Lord Saunders was taking no unnecessary chances.

The ruling was applied with greater emphasis to the

four Americans who had been abducted in Boston than to any other members of the crew. Jeremy had enjoyed little contact with his illiterate compatriots, but he stood with them now at the main-deck railing as Lord Saunders, Lieutenant Gough, and several junior officers were rowed ashore in the captain's gig.

"By God," muttered one of the Americans, a former blacksmith named Davis, "they aren't the only ones who can go ashore. I've been a-waitin' for the chance to get off'n this damn ship, and I'm a-goin' tonight."

"You're deserting?" Jeremy kept his own voice low.

The man nodded. "Come along with me, lawyer man."

"I think you've chosen the wrong place," Jeremy said. "This is a small island, so there are few places to hide. It's a British colony, so you'll find few people here, if any, who will be willing to help an American. There aren't many, I'm sure, who would agree to hide an American, and even fewer who would connive in your escape."

"I'll take the chance," the former blacksmith said, his voice curt.

He wasn't being sensible, and Jeremy felt compelled to dissuade him. "Look here, my friend. All of us feel just as you do. In fact, if I could plant a load of gunpowder in the hold of this ship and blow her out of the water, I'd do it without hesitation. But the odds are against you."

"To hell with odds."

"I urge you to wait until we find ourselves in a better situation. We may put into some North American port. Even Halifax or Quebec would be preferable to Bermuda. We could make our way overland back to the United States. With luck."

"I'll make my own luck," Davis replied.

Jeremy frowned. "We were less than twenty-four hours out of Boston, you may remember, when Lieutenant Gough read us the articles of war. The penalty for desertion in time of war is death, and you're courting it by leaving the *Dolphin* here."

His words made sense to the other two impressed seamen, both of whom nodded gravely.

"I'd rather be dead than spend another day in the Royal Navy. My pa was wounded in the War of Independence, and my grandpa lost a leg. The way I see it, the worst the damn lobsters can do to me is murder me, which would be better than doing their dirty work."

Jeremy was torn. He couldn't help admiring the courage of a man who was willing to take such a reckless gamble for the sake of his own freedom. On the other hand, Davis didn't have as much to lose. He didn't have Sarah Benton waiting for him, he didn't have Oakhurst Manor beckoning. "I wish you good luck and Godspeed," he said.

Long after midnight, in the small hours of the morning, a junior lieutenant made his way through the forecastle, and Boatswain Talbot, who accompanied him, held an oil lamp close to the face of each sailor sleeping in the long row of hammocks. No one spoke, but the tension became almost unbearable. Not until the pair left did anyone dare to break the silence, and then a single word rippled through the narrow space: "Deserter!"

Jeremy felt ill. Davis had made good his threat, but in some way his absence had been discovered before the *Dolphin* weighed anchor, and now that a head count had been made, a major manhunt would begin in earnest.

The seamen began to speculate on the identity of the deserter, and by a process of elimination it became evident that the missing sailor was an American.

A wizened little man with a thick cockney accent, who tended the galley fires and otherwise assisted the cook, spoke for all of his colleagues when he blinked at Jeremy. "You bloody Yanks," he said, "ain't got the sense the good Lor' gived ye when ye was borned. There ain't nobody wot likes the life we lead, but them as loves us would weep all the more if we wasn't drawin' breath."

Unable to sleep, Jeremy dressed and went up to the deck. The island of Bermuda looked dark and forbidding at the far side of the harbor, lanterns and candles in private homes and inns having been extinguished hours earlier. His heart heavy, and a sense of foreboding enveloping him, he went to the galley and helped himself to a mug of tea from the wood stove that burned day and night. Then he returned to the deck and resumed his vigil.

Somewhere ashore, perhaps a mile or more from the anchored warship, a string of lights appeared and moved slowly off to the left. There was no need to wonder what was happening. Jeremy knew that a search party was engaged in an intensive hunt for Davis.

All at once a voice only a few feet away down the deck broke the silence. "Be you praying for your friend, Yankee?"

Even before Jeremy turned, he recognized the deep voice of Boatswain Talbot. "If I'm praying for him," he said, "that's my business and the Lord's. But I'm afraid that prayers won't be of much help to him."

Talbot's lips parted in a thin smile. "I thought you'd be the first to run."

"Not I," Jeremy said, then added recklessly, "At least, not here." He saw that Talbot, too, was drinking a mug of steaming tea, so he realized the man was keeping a vigil of his own. He was responsible for members of the crew, and if Davis was not found, the captain well might demote him to the ranks.

"You knew his plans," Talbot said.

Jeremy's heart pounded. "No, he didn't confide in me."

"Either he's a madman, or he may have confederates on the island. There's no other choices."

Jeremy shrugged.

"Yankee, life will go easier for you if you tell me whatever you know of this insane scheme."

Jeremy turned away from the rail and faced his tormentor. "As it happens, Boatswain," he said, "I know nothing of Davis' plans. I have no notion of how he made his way ashore, or how he intends to hide out now he's there. I hope with all my heart that he succeeds in evading you. He's a free man, a citizen of a nation at peace with Great Britain, so it happens to be his right to protect himself in any way he can. I freely admit I want him to outsmart you, the captain, the whole navy, and the crown. What's more, even if I knew his plans, I wouldn't reveal them to you. You may have kidnapped me and forced me into crown service, but my rights are as great as those of any Englishman on board this ship. So no one—not the captain and not you, either—could compel me to speak up against my will."

"It's come to my ears that you be a lawyer," Talbot said. "You sound like one."

Jeremy merely shrugged.

There was a hint of grudging admiration in the voice of the boatswain. "You know your rights, Yankee. So be it. But I'm keeping my eye on you. I know your kind, and the first time you err, the first time you step out of line, may God have mercy on you!"

Jeremy moved off down the deck, relieved that the night was too dark for the boatswain to see the hatred in his face that he knew he could not conceal. He envied the escaped Davis, and wondered if he himself was a coward. His father, who had fought under the Swamp Fox, General Francis Marion, in the War of Independence, frequently had told him, "There's a difference between wanting liberty and fighting for it." Perhaps, Jeremy thought, he was being denied his freedom because he wasn't willing to risk his life trying to win it for himself.

In spite of his lack of sleep, he didn't feel tired, and just as the first streaks of a gray, dirty dawn appeared in the sky, his patience was rewarded. A flare lighted the sky at least a mile or two behind the harbor, and he felt a surge of excitement, followed by an overwhelming sense of dismay. The flare could mean only that Davis had been captured.

The low, satisfied chuckle of Talbot at the far end of the deck confirmed his guess.

Jeremy could not tolerate being anywhere near the gloating boatswain, so he went below, shaved, and was the first in line for a breakfast of salt fish and hard biscuits, the juice of two lemons, and another mug of tea. He could not allow himself to think about the fate of the captured American.

Soon after breakfast, the entire crew was given work to do, and Jeremy was on his knees cleaning the teak planks of the main deck with a holystone when a boat pulled alongside the *Dolphin*. A white-faced ensign was in command of the party, and it was difficult to recognize Davis as he was hauled on board. His eyes were half-closed, his lips were puffed, and there were streaks of dried blood on his face and torn shirt. It was obvious that he had suffered a severe beating after he had been taken. Stumbling as he was dragged and pushed, he passed within a few feet of Jeremy as he went below, but he was so dazed he failed to recognize his fellow American.

Immediately thereafter, the order was given by the captain himself to weigh anchor, and Jeremy was sent aloft. The sloop of war set sail, but a short time later, with Bermuda still visible on the horizon, the anchor was dropped again.

The entire ship's company was mustered on the main deck, aft.

Lord Saunders and his oficers appeared on the quarterdeck above them, all wearing their dress bicornes, swords, and white gloves.

Jeremy guessed what was coming, and felt ill.

A boatswain's mate blew on his pipes, and the shrill sound echoed across the deck. Then another played a roll on his drum, and a half-conscious Davis was hauled up onto the deck through a hatch. Supported by two burly, veteran British seamen, he was led to a spot directly below the quarterdeck.

The captain donned a pair of spectacles and read several passages from the articles of war to the assembled company. Only a few words made sense to Jeremy. The first was "desertion," soon followed by the phrase "death by hanging." As a student of law, he wanted to intervene on Davis' behalf and plead his case. But he had spent enough time in the Royal Navy to know that he not only would be advancing a lost cause but also would be assuring himself of severe punishment, too. He wouldn't be murdered, as the Royal Navy intended to murder poor Davis, but his back would be opened with a rawhide whip.

Ashamed of himself and furious, he remained silent.

Davis was asked by the captain if he had any comment to make, but the blacksmith was too groggy to speak.

A gibbet was erected on the main deck, a hood was thrown over Davis' head, and he was lifted onto a small platform. Then a noose was dropped over his head and made secure at the side of his neck.

The ship's company stood in rigid silence.

Lieutenant Gough recited the Lord's Prayer in a voice devoid of expression.

Captain Lord Saunders drew his sword, raised it high, and then lowered it, with the point aimed at the deck.

A boatswain's mate kicked the small platform from beneath the feet of the unfortunate Davis.

The former blacksmith dropped, breaking his neck, and less than two minutes later the ship's surgeon pronounced him dead.

Jeremy's stomach heaved.

The other three Americans who had been kidnapped in Boston the same night were ordered to leave the ranks and wrap the dead man's body in a sheet. They did as they were ordered, and Jeremy shuddered when he realized that Davis' body was still warm.

"No prayers are said over the remains of a deserter," Lord Saunders said in the drawl of a British aristocrat. "You may throw the deceased overboard."

Jeremy and the other two Americans carried the body to the rail and unceremoniously heaved it into the Atlantic Ocean. There were tears on Jeremy's cheeks, and he knew he was weeping for himself more than he was on behalf of a man he had scarcely known.

There was a flash of silver below, then another, followed by a great churning of the water. Sharks were making certain that Davis' body neither floated nor dropped to the bottom of the sea.

All at once Jeremy's fury could no longer be contained, regardless of the consequences. He walked boldly to the base of the quarterdeck, then pointed a forefinger at the captain.

"Milord," he said in a ringing voice that shook with fury, "I accuse King George of murder. I accuse you and your officers of murder. An innocent man, a citizen of the United States of America, was abducted and carried on board this vessel against his will. He was compelled to serve an alien power. Seeking the freedom that was his birthright, he attempted to escape. You have rewarded him by killing him in cold blood. May the Lord have mercy on your souls!"

There was a moment of stunned, disbelieving silence.

Captain Lord Saunders was the first to recover. "Young man," he said, "I admire your fortitude. I must respect you for it. But the disciplines of his majesty's navy must be maintained, and on my ship they shall be maintained. Who are you?"

"American citizen Jeremy Beaufort, sir!"

"Apprentice Seaman Beaufort, I condemn you to a punishment of ten lashes, said punishment to be administered at once, in the presence of the ship's company. Boatswain, do your duty."

"Aye, aye, sir," Talbot said, and motioned several of his mates forward.

Strong hands took hold of the unresisting Jeremy and dragged him to the mainmast. His arms were extended around it, then tied, and someone stepped up behind him and ripped off his shirt.

He could feel the warm sun on his back, and tried to shut out his feeling of apprehension. At least, he had spoken his mind, proving to himself and the entire ship's company that he was no coward, so he was satisfied. He had raised his voice in the cause of justice, and it was not his fault, certainly, that justice was not being done this day on HMS *Dolphin*.

Boatswain Talbot approached the mainmast, and out of the corner of his eye Jeremy saw that the man was carrying an ugly cat-o'-nine-tails, a whip with several strands of rawhide extending from the handle, each of them a quarter of an inch thick and at least three feet long.

Lieutenant Gough moved to the quarterdeck rail. "May the assembled ship's company observe and benefit," he said in his high, thin voice. "No seaman may speak to the captain without permission. Due respect will be shown at all times by members of this company to his majesty's personal representative, your commander. Prisoner, take heed, and be glad the captain did not decree that you suffer an even more severe punishment."

Jeremy held his head high. To hell with the captain, his mate, and the whole Royal Navy.

Talbot stood behind him and to one side, feet spread apart.

"Are you ready, Boatswain?" Lieutenant Gough asked.

"Aye, aye, sir!"

"Then do your duty. One!"

The rawhide thongs sang through the air, and many of the sailors winced when the leather made a cracking sound as the whip landed on the prisoner's back.

The shock of the multiple blow seared Jeremy, and flames of pain shot through him, enveloping his entire body. Never had he known such intense agony, but his anger was even greater than his hurt, and he hated his captors with all his soul.

"Two!"

Again the cat-o'-nine-tails descended.

Jeremy made a supreme effort to show he was beyond pain, but he could not help writhing, and sweat bathed his face, blinding him.

"Three!"

Again the multiple whip hissed.

Jeremy had to bite his lower lip to prevent himself from screaming aloud.

"Four!"

No member of the *Dolphin*'s company moved as the rawhide strips found their target.

Now Jeremy knew how slaves at Oakhurst Manor felt on the rare occasions when Mr. Higby, the overseer, had found it necessary to whip a runaway or a rebel. It was impossible to imagine such terrible torture. Even when undergoing the experience, it was almost as though someone else was being punished.

"Five!"

The whistling of the whip seemed magnified.

Jeremy knew his back had been laid open, that the leather was biting deep into his raw flesh. But he was only vaguely aware of the blood that smeared his entire back and ran in rivulets down into his trousers.

"Six!"

A member of the ship's company moaned aloud in sympathy with the suffering prisoner.

Only the memory of slaves who screamed and begged for mercy enabled Jeremy to clamp his jaws together and remain silent. If the day should ever come when he returned to Oakhurst Manor, he promised himself, no slave would ever again be forced to endure such inhuman torture.

"Seven!"

The sounds of the cat-o'-nine-tails seemed to grow still louder.

Jeremy's back arched, then his knees buckled, and he fell forward against the mainmast. He was uncertain how much more of the torment he could tolerate, and he was thankful that Sarah was not present to witness his total degradation.

"Eight!"

Members of the ship's company were becoming restless, and a number began to shuffle their feet.

In spite of Jeremy's vow to make no sound, he could not help gasping. His whole body felt as though it was being submerged in a fire of intense heat.

"Steady in the ranks," Lieutenant Gough ordered. "Stand to attention!"

The quiet on the deck was deafening.

"Nine!"

The whip screamed.

Jeremy wanted to scream, too, but managed to exercise greater willpower than he had ever known he possessed.

He did not realize it, but Captain Lord Saunders was watching the prisoner with admiration. He had spent more than twenty-three years in the Royal Navy, rising from midshipman to his present exalted rank, and not once during that time had he known any sailor to absorb such great punishment without flinching or crying out.

"Ten!"

The whip shrieked for the last time, Boatswain Talbot putting all of his brute strength into the final blow.

Jeremy's entire body was lifted off the deck for an instant, and then, mercifully, he lost consciousness.

For three days and nights Jeremy remained in the ship's so-called hospital, where the surgeon kept his back covered with a greasy, foul-smelling ointment. For the first twenty-four hours the pain and discomfort were so great that the young South Carolinian could neither eat nor sleep. Then, almost miraculously, the agony vanished and he felt like himself again.

"You're either a fool or the bravest man in the navy, Beaufort," the surgeon told him. "Perhaps there's an element of both in you. I'm told you were a student of law before you were impressed into service, so you must be more intelligent than most. If so, I beg you to listen to me, and heed me well. You've made a certain name for yourself on this ship. If the cat-o'-nine has cured your rebel streak, all will go well with you. If not, you're a marked man, just as your back will be marked for life by the blows you've received."

"I'm not sure I know what you mean, sir," Jeremy replied, shifting his weight slightly on the narrow mattress.

The surgeon loomed over him, a white-haired man who had reached the rank of commander after spending his entire life at sea, healing the sick and tending the wounded. "If you speak out of turn again, Beaufort, you'll be given twenty or twenty-five lashes, more than any man can tolerate. You'll never stand straight again, and you'll be sent to Dartmouth prison for the rest of your days. Try to lead a mutiny or try to desert, and you'll be hanged even faster than your fellow American was hanged in your presence."

"Do you expect me to turn the other cheek when I've been kidnapped and then abused?" Jeremy was bitter.

"You've made your protest, and you've been penalized for it." The surgeon lowered his voice. "Learn a lesson from what you've been made to suffer. Our war with Bonaparte won't last for all time. Both Britain and France are on their last legs, and the war can't last much longer. Submit to authority, because you have no alternative. Learn from your experience, and benefit accordingly."

"You're telling me, sir, to make the best of my situation, I presume."

"Precisely," the surgeon said. "You have everything to gain if you're amenable. But you have your life itself to lose if you remain recalcitrant."

Jeremy weighed the advice before he drifted off to sleep, and reflected that it was sound.

At the end of his third day in the hospital, he was released.

The expression on the faces of his fellow seamen told him they regarded him as something of a hero. At the same time, however, they were apprehensive; if he elected to challenge the captain again, they had no desire to associate with him.

He merely grinned at them as he reported for duty, and his grin faded when he saw Talbot.

The boatswain looked at him impersonally and immediately sent him aloft.

A few moments later, even though his back wasn't yet healed, Jeremy was climbing the rigging high above the *Dolphin*'s deck. There had been an element of the boy in him when he had been abducted, but he was all man now, a coldly calculating man who had to look out for himself in a harsh and evil world.

Chapter 10

Day by day, the weather grew warmer. Jeremy was reminded of the climate of Oakhurst Manor in the spring and summer, and waves of homesickness, combined with his love for Sarah, upset him so badly that he found it difficult to sleep. One night he felt he could remain in his hammock in the crowded, confined between decks no longer, so he made his way up to the main deck.

The air was balmy, the sky seemed filled to overflowing with glittering stars, and he spent a long time staring up at them.

Suddenly his reverie was interrupted by someone on the quarterdeck. "You, there! Sailor!"

Jeremy recognized the voice of Lord Saunders and stiffened to attention, as he had been taught, even before looking up at the captain. "Yes, sir?"

"Aha! It's the American, Beaufort. Come up here."

Jeremy climbed the steps to the quarterdeck, and, as he saluted, found the captain studying him with a half-smile.

"What the devil were you doing just now?" Lord Saunders demanded.

"Star-gazing, sir."

"Your fingers looked as though you were playing a harpsichord."

Jeremy saw no reason he shouldn't tell the whole truth. "The fact is, captain, that I was trying to plot our position by the stars."

Lord Saunders was dumbfounded. "You know celestial navigation, Beaufort?"

"No, sir. But I studied astronomy at Princeton College before I went on to law school, and when I recognized the Southern Cross, I . . . I guess I became curious."

The captain studied him in silence for what seemed like a long time, then abruptly turned the ship over to the second lieutenant, who stood behind him on the quarterdeck. "Come with me, Beaufort," he said as he stalked off.

Jeremy followed him, and became apprehensive. Royal Navy captains were not in the habit of conversing with common seamen, much less fraternizing with them, and he hoped he hadn't offended Lord Saunders in some way. If he had, he would be subjected to another beating at the mast, and the mere prospect made his blood run cold.

The captain led the way into his own quarters.

This was the first time Jeremy had seen the cabin, which was located aft, and he was astonished. The entire aft bulkhead was made up of small panes of leaded glass that looked out over the stern. The captain slept in a real bed; his furniture consisted of elegant chairs, a settee, several tables, handsome oil lamps, and a desk. There were thick Turkish rugs underfoot, obviously made in the Ottoman Empire, and one bulkhead was covered with shelves, which were overflowing with books. Paintings that reflected taste and discrimination were hanging on others, and the entire atmosphere was that of a handsome, compact drawing room rather than a ship's cabin.

"Sit down, Beaufort."

"Very good, sir." Jeremy perched stiffly on the edge of a chair.

"No, there." The captain waved him to the settee. "For the moment, we'll forget you're an apprentice seaman. I believe we can converse more freely in an informal way. Will you drink a drop of sack?"

"Thank you, milord," Jeremy thought he was dreaming

as he watched the master of the *Dolphin* fill two glasses from a crystal decanter.

"You know the stars, I gather, and you must be familiar with mathematics, too."

"I am. The tutor my father hired for me when I was a boy was a stickler for mathematical accuracy, and I continued my studies of the subject at college."

"Amazing." It appeared that something was churning in Lord Saunders' mind. "What do you know about gunnery?"

"Nothing, milord. I'm an expert shot with small arms, and I've hunted countless times with a long rifle, but I've never handled anything heavier."

"Suppose, for the sake of argument, that you were asked to fire one of our nine-pounder cannon at an enemy ship. If you knew the distance from that ship and took the state of the sea and the wind into consideration, as well as gauging the speed at which both we and they were moving, could you work out the proper trajectory for the cannon and the size of the gunpowder charge you'd need?"

Jeremy pondered at length. "In principle, milord, I'm certain I could do it. But it's obvious I'd need practice before I could perfect my marksmanship." Jeremy's reply was honest, but he was bewildered by the turn the unexpected talk had taken.

The captain sighed and leaned back in his leather chair. "Beaufort," he said, "I like to think of myself as a civilized man. I've despised the principle of impressing seamen, regardless of whether we take them at home in England, or, more recently, because a ship may spend years in New World waters without returning to London or Plymouth, in the United States. The policy can be defended on the grounds of necessity, to be sure. Our wars with Bonaparte are a fight to the death, and Britain won't survive if he conquers us. The Anglo-Saxon liberties in which I believe, and to which you're so plainly devoted, will be snuffed out like a candle in the wind."

Jeremy nodded, not knowing what to say.

"Your talents," Lord Saunders said, "which have been honed and developed by your education, have given me a strange idea. The policy of impressment is severely criticized in the House of Commons, you know. You Yankees aren't alone in protesting against it."

"So I've heard, milord. And I understand there's also opposition to it in the House of Lords."

"Correct. I'm going to propose a daring scheme to you, Beaufort, something that will go a long way toward easing the criticism when it becomes known in England. It may even help our cause somewhat in America. I intend to make you a midshipman, effective at once. You're much older than the four midshipman in my crew. They're boys in their mid-teens, so you'll be trained separately. If you progress as I have every right to believe you will, I'll give you a brevet commission as an ensign, or even as a junior lieutenant, depending on how rapidly you advance. You'll be taught seamanship, navigation, gunnery—everything an officer in the Royal Navy needs to learn."

"I'm flattered, sir." Jeremy swallowed hard. "But as an officer, I'd be required to swear fealty to the crown, wouldn't I?"

"You'd be granted a brevet commission, as I indicated. A temporary commission, which would have to be verified and authenticated by the Admiralty in London. So I'm afraid the answer is positive. It would be necessary for you to take the customary Royal Navy officer's oath. Rest assured I'm not asking you to give up your American citizenship and become a British subject. When the war ends, as it surely will in the next few years, you could resign from the navy and return to the United States."

Jeremy was silent for a time, then shook his head. "Anyone who has suffered the hardships that an apprentice seaman must endure in this navy would be a fool not to accept a commission, milord. But I must be a fool."

Lord Saunders laughed as he stood and refilled their glasses. "Permit me to read your mind, Beaufort. You're hoping to find some way to escape and return to your own home. Once you take the oath—which you'd be required to do in order to become a midshipman or officer in training—you'd feel honor-bound to remain in his majesty's service."

"You're right, milord." Jeremy faced the issue boldly. "I

don't take oaths lightly. As things are right now, nothing stands in the way of trying to escape."

"Nothing but common sense. You saw what happened to the American, Davis, after he went ashore in Bermuda."

"I think I might do better than Davis."

The captain's smile vanished. "I am convinced you're mistaken. And I can prove it to you, if your mind is as sound as it appears. We are currently sailing into the Caribbean Sea, where our principal mission will be that of seeking and sinking French warships and merchantmen. When necessary, we'll join a flotilla for major actions, in the event the French send a full fleet into these waters. If all goes as I anticipate, we'll be spending at least eighteen months in these parts. I don't expect to see my wife and children for another two years, at the earliest. At no time will we land on United States territory."

Jeremy stared hard at him and sipped his sack. It was the first he had tasted in many weeks, but he was in such turmoil that it seemed flat, even a trifle sour.

"We shall put into British ports exclusively. Principally Jamaica. Occasionally Barbados. From time to time, if need be, we'll visit the small naval bases on his majesty's islands of Nevis and St. Kitts. Just remember what happened to Davis in Bermuda. I can guarantee you'll find no one to help you, no one to hide you, no one to speed you on your way back to the United States on any of these British islands. You'll be hanged from the yardarm for your pains, more's the pity."

Jeremy realized he was trapped. Certainly he had no desire to serve the British crown as an officer. But the change in his personal situation would be dramatic, and his chance of surviving would be vastly increased.

It was his desire to return to Sarah Benton and go with her to Oakhurst Manor that tipped the scales. He might even be able to argue, to himself, that no oath taken under duress was binding on him or reflected on his honor. He could almost feel Sarah's sweet warmth when he held her in his arms.

He drained his drink, rose, and stood at attention. "Sir," he said, speaking with grave formality, "I am overwhelmed by your generous offer. Only a madman would refuse, and I accept with great pleasure."

The entire ship's company was mustered on deck immediately after breakfast the following morning to witness the ceremony in which the captain administered the oath to Midshipman Jeremy Beaufort. Officers and enlisted men alike were stunned by the development.

Lieutenant Gough, who obviously disliked Jeremy, disapproved. He could not protest a decision made by his superior, however, so he kept his opinions to himself, and like everyone else, he now called the new midshipman "Mr. Beaufort."

The startled boatswain made his own views plain. Whenever he saw Jeremy he smiled sourly and overemphasized the word "Mister."

The changes in Jeremy's day-to-day living were startling. No longer sleeping between decks, he was moved into a tiny cabin that he shared with the other midshipmen, boys so young that they felt constrained to curb their high spirits in his presence.

Theoretically, he could be caned by Lieutenant Gough if he misbehaved. But even the first mate did not give serious consideration to the idea; Beaufort was a man, after all, not a schoolboy.

Jeremy continued to wear a sailor's uniform, but the quartermaster gave him an officer's bicorne, calf-high boots, and stockings. Captain Lord Saunders took pleasure in making the new midshipman a gift of one of his own swords.

At meals Jeremy now sat at the foot of the long table in the officers' wardroom, and although midshipmen were expected to keep silent, several of the junior lieutenants conversed regularly with him, since he was about their own age. The improvement in food was dramatic. Officers ate figs, raisins, rice, and bully beef, known in America as corned beef, all of them delicacies denied to ordinary sailors. There were just as many weevils in the hardtack served at the officers' mess, however.

The captain was true to his word, and the new midshipman was educated privately. Jeremy concentrated on his tasks with his customary serious intent, partly because he discovered he thought less about Sarah and Oakhurst Manor when he was busy. He was a remarkably adept student, picking up navigation and seamanship so quickly that, after only ninety days, the captain sometimes gave him the command and allowed him to sail the *Dolphin*. Regarding him as a personal protégé, Lord Saunders took an active part in his education, sometimes devoting several hours each day to his instruction.

Gunnery took Jeremy somewhat longer to learn. He took part regularly in target practice, but soon discovered, as had so many others before him, that he required more and more opportunities to fire a cannon before he became adept.

He felt completely at home on the quarterdeck now, able to instruct the helmsman and give orders to change sail and direct the vessel toward new places. Even Lieutenant Gough grudgingly admitted, one afternoon, that Midshipman Beaufort was "a natural sailor, with an instinct for the right thing to do." Thereafter, the captain gave him a regular watch, so he shared the responsibility with commissioned officers.

Early in the fourth month of the *Dolphin*'s cruise, the entire company was electrified when the lookout called, "Fighting ship off the starboard bow, sir! She's unidentified!"

The captain ordered all hands to battle stations, and feet thudded on the decks as men raced to their appointed spots.

Jeremy buckled on his sword, slid a brace of loaded pistols into his belt, and took his place at the rear of the quarterdeck. The younger midshipmen would be used as messengers, but he had no specific assignment, and consequently was subject to whatever special duty the captain might have available for him.

The other vessel, at first scarcely more than a speck on the Caribbean horizon, gradually grew larger.

The sea was calm, that unique shade of clear blue-green peculiar to the West Indian waters, and a steady, gentle breeze was blowing from the west. The morning sun blazed in a cloudless sky, and Jeremy told himself that, if there was such a thing, the weather was perfect for a battle.

The captain and Lieutenant Gough studied the strange ship through their glasses, occasionally exchanging a few words.

"She's a sloop of war, little doubt of that," Lord Saunders said.

"She outweighs us, and she has twenty-four guns to our eighteen, sir, so we're slightly outclassed," his first mate replied.

The captain continued to peer through his glass. "Her jib is too long to be one of ours, Gough, and her mainmast is taller than that of any sloop of war in the Royal Navy. She's a foreigner, no two ways about it."

"Stand alert to battle stations!" the mate ordered as a precaution, and his cry was echoed by deck lieutenants.

Jeremy had little interest in the ever-present, continuing quarrel between Great Britain and Franch. Americans thought of themselves as a people who stood apart from the feuds of the Old World, and as the late President Washington had written a decade and a half earlier, the United States intended to make no entangling alliances. All the same, his sense of excitement mounted steadily. The prospect of a fight was in view, looming larger by the moment, and a young man who had been a law student in Boston only a few months earlier, intending to visit his ancestral home with his beloved, whom he had planned to marry within a short time, now stood in danger of having his head blown off. Before that happened, he told himself, he intended to give a good account of himself.

His presence on board the British warship was not of his own doing, and his present status was a direct result of the captain's intervention. Nevertheless, he had accepted instruction, he had accepted a responsibility, and he vowed to live up to it. He was slightly frightened, to be sure, never having heard or seen cannon fired in anger, but one of the senior lieutenants, who had been present with Lord Nelson at the Battle of Trafalgar, had told him that everyone became apprehensive in the hour before a fight. He smiled, promising himself he would tell the story of his feelings to his sons and their sons when he and Sarah reared a family.

The other ship was drawing steadily closer, apparently as eager for a confrontation as the master of the *Dolphin*. Men were lining her deck, staring at the British vessel, but it was impossible to identify either their uniforms or the name of the ship written in gold on her prow.

All at once she raised her colors, and the gold-and-white banner of France fluttered in the breeze.

Lord Saunders smiled. "Mr. Gough, be good enough to raise his majesty's flag."

The first mate repeated the order, and within moments the British Union Jack was hoisted to the topgallants, where it unfurled in the quiet breeze.

There was a spurt of activity on board the French ship, which the first mate was now able to identify as the *Margot*.

Jeremy couldn't help grinning. The French warship bore the name of the tiny red-haired vixen who would become his sister-in-law. He could imagine her delight when she learned of the coincidence.

Lord Saunders remained calm. "Mr. Gough, be kind enough to have your gun ports lowered."

"Aye, aye, sir. Lower gun ports!"

The shields protecting the cannon on the lower deck, actually a part of the hull in foul weather, were removed promptly.

"Mr. Gough, I shall be grateful if you'll order gun crews to prepare for combat."

"Gun crews, make ready!"

Iron shot was heated in large tubs, while other containers of sand were hauled into place to extinguish any fires that might break out as a result of accident or an enemy strike. Boatswain's mates cut and adjusted fuses, and gunners carefully measured gunpowder into beakers.

The two sloops of war were less than a mile apart now, and Jeremy began to fidget. Apparently he had been forgotten, but this was not the moment to call himself to the captain's attention.

All at once the *Margot* maneuvered until she was riding parallel to the *Dolphin*. Then flashes of fire and clouds of smoke obscured her gun deck for a moment, and iron shot soared into the air. The cannonballs fell more than a hundred yards short of their target, an indication that the French gunners were less than accurate.

The crew of the *Dolphin* cheered, jeered, and shouted obscenities that their foes could not hear.

The *Margot*'s gunners sent a second round in the direction of the British sloop of war, but again their aim was short.

Jeremy estimated the distance between the two vessels had been narrowed to little more than a half-mile.

The captain looked as collected and relaxed as he did when enjoying a glass of sack in his spacious cabin. "Mr. Gough, I'll be obliged if your port gunners will fire at their earliest opportunity."

"Aye, aye, sir!" The mate sucked in his breath. "Portside gunners, you may fire when ready!"

A few seconds later the roar of cannon shook the *Dolphin*, her nine port guns sending a salvo screaming in the direction of the French warship.

Jeremy's mind had been racing as he worked out the trajectory and size of the gunpowder charge in his head.

The broadside was short by no more than seventy-five feet.

The captain lost his languid manner. "Fire at will, as fast as you can reload!"

The mate repeated the command.

The gunners responded with gusto, firing and reloading and firing again as rapidly as they could.

The French cannoneers remained busy, too, and an iron ball landed aft on the main deck of the *Dolphin* with a crash, then plowed a furrow in the teakwood before tearing up a section of railing and falling overboard into the Caribbean.

As nearly as Jeremy could judge, the shot had injured no one.

The *Dolphin*'s gunners were the superior marksmen, thanks at least in part to the training rules laid down by the late Admiral Lord Nelson in the years immediately prior to his death. A broadside slashed through the *Margot*'s rigging, which slowed her somewhat, and then a lucky shot sliced through the base of her mainmast, severing it. The mast buckled slowly, then fell, dragging down the mainsail.

The French sloop of war was badly damaged, unable to maneuver with ease, and even more important, unable to escape.

The *Dolphin*'s gunners needed no encouragement as they poured salvo after salvo into the enemy ship, battering her severely and starting a fire in her forward hold.

The *Margot*'s crew continued to fight gallantly in spite of the odds against them, and numerous shots were landing on the decks of the British vessel.

Jeremy heard an English sailor scream in agony, the sound trailing away as the man died.

The roar of cannon became deafening.

"You may continue to close with the enemy, Mr. Gough," the captain shouted above the din.

The *Dolphin* edged closer and closer to the *Margot*.

"Make ready your grappling hooks!"

"Aye, aye, sir!"

Jeremy realized a boarding party would invade the French ship. So far, he had been only an observer, and felt a keen sense of disappointment.

"Mr. Gough, you may take command of the boarders." Lord Saunders turned to Jeremy with a smile. "No, Mr. Beaufort, I haven't forgotten you. If you wish, you may assist Mr. Gough."

Jeremy followed the first mate to the main deck.

There Lieutenant Gough divided the boarding party of forty-two men into two groups. He would lead one himself, while Jeremy would command the other.

The sailors lined the rail, bayonets in place on muskets and pistols cocked.

Jeremy drew his sword and climbed onto the rail, unmindful of the pistol and musket fire that whistled past his head and narrowly missed his body.

Boatswain Talbot shouted an order, and six huge grappling hooks sang through the air, landed, and bound the two ships together, holding them fast.

Never before had Jeremy engaged in such a maneuver, but his instinct guided him, and in the instant before the two ships collided, he leaped across the intervening space onto the main deck of the *Margot*.

"Come on, lads, follow me!" he shouted.

The twenty-one members of his squad needed no urging, and dropped onto the deck of the French sloop of war. Meanwhile, the squad under Lieutenant Gough's personal command was doing the same thing farther forward.

Jeremy had no opportunity to rally his men. Suddenly he came face to face with a French senior lieutenant, a grizzled veteran with graying temples, a man whose scarred face indicated he was no novice in the art of hand-to-hand combat.

Their swords were raised simultaneously and clashed. Jeremy had always regarded himself as a first-class swordsman, far superior to his skilled brother, but he knew as the enemy lunged that he was no match for this experienced French officer. He barely managed to deflect the blow, then backed away down the deck.

The Frenchman followed, the gleam of the kill in his eyes, and after feinting, he lunged again.

The blow grazed Jeremy's left arm, drawing blood, but he felt no pain until later.

Suddenly a hole appeared in the Frenchman's forehead, and he crumpled to the deck, already dead.

Jeremy half-turned and saw Boatswain Talbot racing down the deck with a smoking pistol in his hand.

"Thanks, Talbot," Jeremy called.

The Boatswain's sour grin indicated his contempt for the American whose life he had saved.

There was no chance to dwell on the gratuitous insult. Jeremy summoned his men, who formed a wedge behind him. Then, following the orders that the first mate had given him, he led his squad in a drive down the deck. Lieutenant Gough, in turn, was heading toward him, and between them they had trapped at least one hundred Frenchmen.

The boatswain paused to reload his pistol.

As he did, Jeremy saw a French noncommissioned officer raise a musket.

Before the enemy could shoot, however, Jeremy drew

his own pistol, cocking and firing it in an almost unbroken motion.

The Frenchman sagged and sprawled on the deck.

"Now we're even, Talbot," Jeremy said, as, hacking and slashing, he led his party forward.

Those were the last words he had an opportunity to speak for more than a quarter of an hour. Later, that period remained a blur in his mind, and he could remember only that he wielded his sword until his arm grew weary, sometimes pausing just long enough to reload and fire one of his pistols.

The French were unable to withstand the furor of the twin assault, and when still more boarders appeared, the outcome was no longer in doubt.

All at once the gold-and-white banner of France was lowered. Orders were shouted, and all fighting stopped instantly.

The captain of the *Margot,* a portly officer with a white goatee, stood silently for a few moments on his quarterdeck, tears streaming down his face. Then, with his senior officers forming in a single line behind him, he crossed to the *Dolphin* and climbed to the quarterdeck.

"Sir, you have conquered me in a good fight," he told the master of the British sloop of war, and presented him with his sword.

"You fought well and honorably, sir," Lord Saunders replied.

Jeremy was handed the sword of a French lieutenant, and for the rest of his life he kept and used it. He had won it fairly in his first engagement, so it was a prize he always treasured.

The *Margot* was so badly battered that she could not sail by herself, even when jury-rigged, so she was placed in tow, with a tired Lieutenant Gough supervising the operation. Then, moving slowly under the *Dolphin*'s sail, she headed toward the British island of Jamaica.

The fire in the forward hold of the *Margot* was extinguished. The dead were buried at sea, eight of them members of the English crew and thirty-two of them French, the *Margot* having suffered far greater casualties. The surgeons of both ships tended the wounded, and a prize crew from the *Dolphin* boarded the ship she had taken, disarming the members of the French crew.

Lord Saunders took the captain of the *Margot* to his own quarters for a stiff drink of brandywine and supper.

Some of the Englishmen found pipes of wine on board the *Margot*, but Lieutenant Gough ordered it to remain untouched. Under no circumstances, he reminded the men, would the Royal Navy tolerate looting. The French prisoners, who had fought with honor, would be allowed to keep their personal possessions, and all other property would pass to the crown.

Jeremy realized he needed a drink. After washing himself with seawater, he changed his clothes, then headed toward the officers' wardroom, where a quiet victory celebration was already in progress. He had never been partial to rum, but this was one occasion when he looked forward to a double tot.

Someone was heading down the narrow passageway toward him, and Jeremy recognized the boatswain.

Talbot saw him at the same moment.

Neither was willing to slow his pace, and they squeezed past each other, each taking care to look away.

It was obvious that although each had been instrumental in saving the other's life, there was still deep enmity between them. That grudge would be settled, Jeremy knew, only when blood was spilled.

Chapter 11

The site of Santo Domingo on the Spanish island of Hispaniola had been discovered by Christopher Columbus in 1492, and a number of other Caribbean cities were almost as old. But Kingston Town, the military and commercial capital of Jamaica, was a relative newcomer. Founded in 1693 after Port Royal, reputedly the most wicked city in the world, had been destroyed by an earthquake, Kingston sat at the inner end of one of the finest natural harbors anywhere. The *Dolphin*, her ensign flying proudly and the *Margot* still in tow, sailed up the narrow, landlocked channel, bounded on the inner side by the mainland and on the outer by a thin peninsula known as the Palisadoes.

Jeremy stood near the prow as the sloop of war entered the harbor, and at once smelled the warm, sweet scent of jungle and rotting vegetation that characterized most West Indian islands. Jamaica was one of the largest and most productive, boasting large plantations of sugarcane, tobacco, and coffee. Kingston, with a population of more than fifty thousand, was one of the largest and most bustling cities in the entire western hemisphere.

The spire of the Church of St. Thomas soared high above the many buildings located on King Street, the principal road, and the cannon at Rockfort, a fortress surrounded by a moat and located at the far end of the city, boomed their welcome to the victorious warship. The sun shone overhead in a cloudless sky, the water sparkled, and a small flotilla of Royal Navy boats and private craft, from cutters to gigs to fishing vessels, moved out of the inner harbor to form an escort.

On a dock toward which the *Dolphin* was slowly sailing, a military fife-and-drum corps filled the air with music. Jeremy felt a slight sense of shock when he saw the red-coated soldiers. He and the damned lobsterbacks were united under the same flag now and were fighting for the same cause.

All at once he felt the urge to desert once he went ashore, but he quickly abandoned the idea. People here were loyal to the crown, so he was sure to be captured, certain to lose his life. He heard the shrill whistle of the boatswain's mate, so he walked slowly to his place amidships and fell in with the rest of the company.

A vice admiral, a rear admiral, a major general, and their staffs all came aboard to welcome and congratulate Lord Saunders. Then, after the formalities ended, the captain and officers of the *Margot* went ashore under parole to await exchange for British officers captured in battle. The sailors of the French crew were marched to a plantation in the Liguanea Hills above Kingston, where they would be held in loose captivity until the end of the war. The wounded were carried on litters to King George Hospital and to Headquarters House, both located on Duke Street.

Then the lines that connected the *Dolphin* and the *Margot* were cut, and the French sloop of war was moved by a cluster of small boats to a berth of her own. There she would undergo repairs, and when she was seaworthy, she would go to sea again, this time as a British warship.

Lord Saunders changed into his dress uniform prior to going ashore, where he and Lieutenant Gough would attend a banquet being given in their honor. Before he departed, the captain sent for Jeremy.

It was hot in the spacious cabin, even though many of the windows had been opened.

"I daresay you thought I'd forgotten you again, Mr. Beaufort," Lord Saunders said.

"No, sir."

"Are you going ashore?"

Jeremy was embarrassed. "I may take a stroll for an hour or two, sir, just to feel land under my feet after all these months at sea."

The captain grinned at him. "What's this? You don't intend to dine at one of the fine inns? Or indulge in a sailor's prerogative of wine and women?"

"No, sir." Jeremy could feel himself reddening under his heavy suntan.

Lord Saunders suppressed a laugh. "I assume that a lack of funds is responsible."

"Yes, sir." It hadn't been difficult to guess his reasons, Jeremy thought. As a midshipman, he was paid one guinea per month, but his uniforms and food ate up the entire sum.

"Well, Admiral Lord Martin has assured me the prize money for the capture of the *Margot* and her armaments will be very large. We won't know the exact sum until an admiralty court here passes a ruling in the next few days, but it is certain to amount to many thousands of pounds. Every member of the crew will be given his share, and you'll receive a double share."

"Double, sir?" Jeremy was startled.

"A midshipman's share, of course. And a special share, which I'm awarding to each officer and rating who conducted himself with particular valor. I've been aware of your plight, Mr. Beaufort, so I'm prepared to advance you a small portion of your shares right now." Lord Saunders reached into his purse. "Will five guineas be sufficient for whatever celebrations you may wish to indulge in ashore?"

"More than ample, milord. I'm overwhelmed." Jeremy's own purse had vanished the night he had been abducted, and since that time he hadn't owned a penny in cash.

The captain cut short his thanks, handed him five guineas in coins, then departed.

Jeremy repaired to his own quarters, where he wrote a

letter to Sarah Benton and another to his father, telling them what had happened to him. Then, changing quickly into a clean uniform, he went ashore.

For a few moments the solid ground seemed to rock beneath his feet.

A small boy offered him a coconut for a ha'penny, and he bought it. The boy cut off the outer husk with a machete, a long, hatchetlike knife that he wielded with marvelous dexterity, then cut off the top.

Jeremy drank the sweet milk and ate the soft coconut meat as he asked directions to the post office, then made his way toward King Street, the principal thoroughfare, where it was located.

The street was filled with handsomely dressed ladies in carriages and well-groomed men on horseback. Others were strolling on the street, and if it weren't for the heat, the palm trees, and other tropical foliage, it wouldn't be difficult to imagine himself in Boston.

Duke and King streets were lined with shops, many of them small, and Jeremy was somewhat surprised to see that blacks were in charge of most of them. He hadn't realized there were free blacks as well as slaves in Jamaica. Many of the shops were crowded with officers and men from the *Dolphin*, who were enjoying haggling over their purchases. The entire ship's company had come ashore, and royal marines were standing sentry duty while the crew enjoyed a holiday.

At one corner and beyond it, a covered shed stood in the middle of the street, its sides open. Jeremy saw what appeared to be an auction in progress, and when he realized a black man in a loincloth was standing on a block, with scores of others either standing or huddled on the ground behind him, he remembered that Kingston was one of the western world's major slave-trade centers. The sight was anything but novel, so he hurried on toward his destination, but for the first time in his life he felt deep sympathy for the slaves.

Not that he objected to the institution itself. Slavery was necessary for the operation of plantations throughout the South in the United States, just as it was in the West Indian islands. But the raw welts he saw on the backs of many of the slaves newly imported from Africa were unnecessary and an outrage, an affront to the dignity of human beings. The healed scars on his own back were a constant reminder to him that the beating of slaves was a vicious practice that should be abolished for all time.

A clerk wearing a green eyeshade was lounging behind a wooden counter in the dusty post office, a small one-story building.

"I want to mail these letters to the United States," Jeremy said, "and I'd like them sent on the first packet ship sailing there."

The man raised an eyebrow, and when he spoke, his accent was a blend of cockney and Caribbean singsong. "There's no ships that go to the United States," he said.

Jeremy stared at him. "I don't understand what you—"

"Where you been, sailor? Don't you know what's happening in the world?"

"As it happens, I've been at sea for months."

The clerk sighed. "A royal edict, enforced by the Admiralty, reached us about a month ago from London. The British Empire has stopped all trade with the United States. There's no traffic with her, neither. No merchantmen put in at American ports, and no American vessels are allowed to enter empire ports. No passenger ships from either country call at the other. Even the United States border with Canada has been closed."

"You mean the United States and Great Britain are at war," Jeremy said slowly.

"Not yet they ain't," the postal clerk said, "but they're so close to it that it wouldn't surprise me none if the shooting starts anytime. You'll find out."

"Yes," Jeremy said, knowing he would be trapped in an untenable situation, no matter what he did.

"Anyway, there's no mail being sent to the United States, and no mail coming in from the United States. Because there ain't no way to get it back and forth. There's some little islands offshore where the booby birds nest and hatch, so I advise you to go there, catch one, and train it, sailor. Then he can fly your mail up to America for you. It's the only way you'll get it delivered there."

Jeremy put the letters to Sarah and his father back into

his pocket and wandered out into King Street again. He was dazed, sickened by what he had just learned. He was walking down a hard-packed road in a civilized community, but for all practical purposes he might as well be on board ship in the middle of the Atlantic Ocean. It was almost inconceivable to him that he was totally cut off from the United States, that it was physically impossible for him to communicate with the girl he loved and the father who was surely grieving for him.

Paying no attention to passersby, he bumped into a man wearing a high, hard-crowned hat and the newfangled trousers that the fashion-conscious in London and the major American cities were wearing. The man glared, and Jeremy mumbled an apology as he continued to wander.

A harlot approached him and said something, but he brushed past her, surprised to see that she was white. In this tropical town, where blacks were in the overwhelming majority, he would have assumed otherwise.

The Church of St. Thomas stood directly ahead now, and Jeremy unhesitatingly went inside. He hadn't attended regular services since he had left South Carolina, although he had occasionally gone to church with Sarah and her father in Boston. But he felt completely at home in this quiet place, and realized it was a Church of England cathedral; at home he worshiped as an Episcopalian, which was identical except for a refusal to acknowledge the authority of the Archbishop of Canterbury.

Scarcely aware of the stained-glass windows, and not even conscious of the fact that he was alone in the church, Jeremy entered a pew, placed a small cushion on the stone floor, and fell to his knees. He prayed earnestly and at length for guidance in his time of travail, then asked that those he loved be protected from evil. An inner voice assured him that all would be well if he put his undeviating faith in the Almighty. He continued to pray until his knees and calves ached, and when he finally left the church, he felt comforted. He was still sad, frustrated and angry, to be sure, but the worst of his sense of depression had disappeared.

Royal Navy sailors were everywhere, among them members of the *Dolphin*'s crew whom he recognized. Most were going from one to another of the many taverns on King and Duke streets, and it amused him to see that some were already intoxicated. They had been paid their back wages by the quartermaster before coming ashore, but he knew that by the time they returned to the ship again their pockets would be empty. He couldn't blame the poor devils. They led difficult, restricted lives under conditions of harsh discipline; they were at the mercy of the sea and in constant danger of being killed or wounded in battle. Perhaps they were weak to seek forgetfulness for a day or two, but it wasn't his place to sit in judgment on them.

"Ho, there! Beaufort!"

Someone sitting in the back of a small open carriage was hailing Jeremy, and he shaded his eyes from the glare of the sun. A junior lieutenant on the staff of the *Dolphin* was beckoning to him.

"You look as though you're lost, Beaufort. Where are you headed?"

"No place in particular, Stevens." Jeremy's smile was a trifle sheepish. "I guess I've just been wandering around."

"Then come with me," Lieutenant Stevens said. "I've hired this driver to take me up to the hills, where I'm told the weather is cooler."

Jeremy hesitated.

The young officer laughed. "It's what you need. Join me at once, Mr. Beaufort. That's an order."

Jeremy chuckled as he climbed into the carriage. Soon the driver, gently flapping his reins, was threading through the traffic of the busy city as he headed inland from the southeastern corner of the island. For the first time Jeremy noticed colorfully attired native women in ankle-length dresses carrying baskets, parcels, and various other objects on their heads, walking straight-backed and not holding their burdens with their hands. He was reminded of the slave women at Oakhurst Manor, who did the same thing, and a wave of sentiment swept over him. Somehow, someday, if he did nothing else in this world, he would take Sarah Benton to Oakhurst Manor as his wife.

In a little more than a quarter of an hour they left the city behind, and moving past houses surrounded by vegetable gardens, started up a steep dirt road toward the Liguanea Hills. Now the mountains behind the city were visible, and the driver pointed out Blue Mountain Peak, the highest in Jamaica.

"I'm taking you to a place called the Star Apple," Lieutenant Stevens said. "I went there several years ago, and their meals are the best in the Caribbean. Their liquor and wines are splendid, too."

Jeremy suddenly realized he was hungry.

"Have you ever eaten a star apple?"

The American shook his head.

Lieutenant Stevens chuckled. "Lop off the top, and the meat inside is shaped like a star. It has a sweet, juicy taste, unlike any other that you've ever known. I'm not much of a botanist, but I know it qualifies as a passion fruit, and any man in his senses soon becomes addicted to it." He winked, then chuckled again.

Jeremy was too busy looking at the fields to question him. He saw squash, pumpkins, and a variety of melons growing in profusion, as were black-eyed peas and green and yellow beans; and there were rice paddies, too. His homesickness for Oakhurst Manor grew more intense. There were groves of palms, too, including bananas and coconuts, dates and cacao. Cattle grazed on green fields, goats roamed the rockier slopes, and behind most of the small houses were pens for chickens and pigs. There were few places on earth where the land was more fertile or living as fruitful.

Estates became larger as the carriage moved inland, and at last they turned onto a private road. At its end, high on a promontory with a breathtaking view of the harbor and city below on one side and the high mountains on the other, was a handsome three-story brick house with a portico that featured elaborate Corinthian columns painted white. Again Jeremy was reminded of his family home, and he drew a painful breath.

He and Lieutenant Stevens were admitted to the mansion by a servant in livery, and were conducted to a parlor, a small room with a magnificent crystal chandelier and tapestried French furniture in the style of Louis XIV. Never had Jeremy seen such a lavishly furnished inn.

A ruddy-faced middle-aged woman wearing an attractive dress in the style that had been popular at the time of the American War of Independence came into the room, jeweled rings flashing on both hands, and the two young men rose to their feet.

"How are you, Mistress Ferguson?" Stevens asked as she extended her hand.

"Ach, it's Edward Stevens," she replied, her voice thick with a Scottish brogue. "So you're stationed now on the sloop that arrived this very day."

She kept herself well-informed, Jeremy thought as he was presented to her.

"I know why you've come," Mrs. Ferguson said to Stevens, "and you're in luck. Your friend returned to us only six months ago." She smiled at him, then at Jeremy, and left the room.

A moment later the liveried servant entered, bearing a tray with two tall silver cups.

Jeremy took his cup, tasted the contents, and discovered he was drinking a potent rum mixed with fruit juice. The concoction was very strong, so he sipped it cautiously.

Stevens was more reckless, however, and gulped his drink as he paced the room. For some unaccountable reason, he had become restless.

Jeremy was about to question him when a young woman appeared in the entrance. She was attractive, in spite of very heavy makeup, and was wearing a long, figure-revealing gown. To Jeremy's practiced eye, her chocolate-colored skin indicated that she was a mulatto.

"Anna!" Lieutenant Stevens shouted in a quarterdeck voice as he embraced her.

"I wondered if I'd ever see you again, Edward," the girl murmured.

They wandered out together, arms around each other, the young man they had left behind totally forgotten.

Jeremy cursed himself for being naive. The scene he had just witnessed, Mrs. Ferguson's appearance, and Stevens' sly remarks about star apples being a passion fruit told him this place was a house of assignation.

He had visited bordellos, to be sure, before he had met

Sarah Benton and fallen in love with her, so he was not shocked. But, he wondered, what was he doing here now?

He could not deny to himself that he had felt increasingly strong sex urges, particularly since his status had changed from apprentice seaman to midshipman. He had to admit, too, that he wanted a woman, but he insisted that that woman had to be Sarah, no one else.

Temptation tugged at him, so he wanted to flee, but he had no wish to make himself appear ridiculous. The carriage that had brought him and Stevens to this place from Kingston, far below, had driven off, and he knew he faced a walk of several hours before he could reach the city. Even worse, he could imagine what Stevens would say about him at the officers' mess.

A girl stood quietly in the entrance. "Good day," she said in a cultured, aristocratic voice, her English accent strong. "I am Lisa."

Jeremy turned, and was astonished. She was breathtakingly lovely, with chiseled features, copper-colored hair that fell to her waist, and enormous green eyes. She was tall and slender, her willowy, perfectly proportioned figure and her eyes reminding him of Sarah. He felt as though he were made of stone.

She saw he was ill at ease, and helped him. "You're Mr. Beaufort."

"Yes, Jeremy." He was tongue-tied, too. In spite of himself, he gaped at her in her low-cut Empire dress that revealed every line of her lithe body. A Bostonian or a New Yorker might believe she was white, but a South Carolinian couldn't be fooled. There was a black somewhere in her ancestry, and he jumped to the conclusion that she was a slave.

"Shall we adjourn to other quarters, where we'll enjoy greater privacy?" Her ripe lips parted in a welcoming smile.

Jeremy wanted to fall through the floor. "Mistress Lisa," he said, "when I came here with my friend, I had no idea that . . . What I mean to say is . . ."

"I understand completely," she told him, cutting short his misery, and it was obvious from the look in her eyes that she was telling the truth.

His panic subsided somewhat.

"If you wish," Lisa said, her voice gentle, "I'll have Toby arrange for a carriage to take you back to town. Since you're here, however, it can do you no harm to chat until the heat of the day has passed."

He felt like one of Dean Jonathan Swift's tiny midgets in *Gulliver's Travels*. Under no circumstances did he want this ravishing creature to regard him as a boor. "It will be my greatest pleasure to converse with you, Mistress Lisa," he said, and bowed.

The girl took his hand and led him up a flight of marble stairs to a small but comfortable and handsomely appointed sitting room, where she seated him in an armchair, then took a place opposite him on a divan covered in a white velvet that matched her gown. "Would you care for another cup of punch, Jeremy?" she asked, reaching for a bell rope.

He shook his head. "Thank you, but I find it too strong for my preference."

"So do I," she confessed, and stood again. "We'll both have some sack." Giving him no chance to reply, she crossed the room, her rounded hips undulating, and poured two glasses of the mild wine.

Jeremy accepted one from her with gratitude, and realized he had to make small talk or be considered a hopeless country bumpkin. "I was astonished to find the rum drink was so cold. How is that achieved in this climate?"

"Ah, we have our mysterious secrets," Lisa replied, teasing him, "but I'll tell you this one. It's quite simple. A stream that comes down from the mountains passes through the Star Apple property, so jugs of the rum punch are immersed in the river for hours."

He began to feel a bit less strained, but had to try again. "How long have you been forced to be here, Mistress Lisa?"

A puzzled expression appeared in her green eyes. "Forced, Jeremy?"

"Yes, when your master has ordered you—"

Her light laugh cut him off. "I'm a free woman, sir. No man is my master."

Jeremy was too flabbergasted to reply.

"But you're very shrewd," she told him. "Most of my gentlemen friends assume I'm as white as they are. You know better."

"Only because my father owns a plantation in South Carolina that—if it be God's will—I'll inherit someday."

"You don't shun me because I'm part black?"

"Certainly not!"

Lisa could see his indignation was genuine. "Thank you. I look like a lady, I try to conduct myself like a lady, and I'm grateful when a gentleman treats me like a lady!"

"They should," Jeremy said. "Because you *are* a lady!"

She studied him closely and saw he was sincere. "Perhaps, if you'll pour us more sack, you'd like to hear a story I rarely tell."

"I'd like it very much." Jeremy jumped to his feet, refilled their glasses, and knew he was beginning to feel truly at ease with this charming young woman.

"My great-grandmother was black, as you've realized," she said. "She was a slave who was brought here from Africa. My great-grandfather was the plantation owner who bought her. I know little of their relationship, other than that she died in childbirth when my grandmother was born. My great-grandfather was so grief-stricken he gave her her freedom on the day of her birth and brought her up openly as his daughter."

"I've heard of a very few such cases at home," Jeremy murmured.

"My grandmother inherited her father's small estate, and her son, my father, was an officer in the Royal Navy. He was killed at Alexandria, where Lord Nelson sank the French fleet, and a few months later, after my mother heard the news, she died, too. She had no will to live."

"I see." After hearing the girl's tragic background, Jeremy realized she was an octoroon, seven-eighths white and one-eighth black.

"I doubt if you do. You're wondering why I lead a life like this. You're wondering why I allow men to buy my favors."

Her very candor made him uncomfortable.

"I could live here in Jamaica in genteel poverty on the

inheritance my mother left me," Lisa said. "But I'd never be accepted in local society. And every man—from planter to admiral—would regard me as fair game."

Life in South Carolina was similar, and he knew she was right. "That's an accurate assessment, I'm sure."

"I decided that if I have the name, I might as well reap the benefits, too. Would you like one of our local cigarros?"

"I prefer not to smoke them in the company of a lady," Jeremy told her.

His deference flattered and pleased her. "I select my own clients," Lisa said. "Mistress Ferguson has no voice in the matter, and I turn away from a man if he doesn't appeal to me. Those I permit to stay with me pay very large sums for the privilege. I make my own clothes, so I have very few expenses, and I save my money. It won't be long before I'll be able to retire."

"Surely you don't intend to move to the United States?"

"Indeed I don't. If I lived in the North, I could pretend I was totally white, and no one would know better, but I'm proud of my heritage. And I'm told I wouldn't be allowed to stay permanently in the South as a free woman."

"Quite true. You'd need to be only one-sixteenth black for that. A stupid rule."

His obvious sympathy warmed her.

"It would be difficult for you to remain in Jamaica," he said. "I suspect that too many men here know your background, and they'd be sure to pester you. What's more, I doubt if their wives would accept you."

"You're wise as well as shrewd," Lisa said. "I'll tell you what almost no one else knows. When I retire, I plan to move to another of the British islands in the West Indies. Perhaps Barbados, where there are many visitors from England. I'll find myself a home and live as I please. Ultimately, I'll find someone like myself. When I do, I'll marry him, and we'll bring up a family."

Her strength impressed him. "You have courage, Mistress Lisa."

"Just plain Lisa, if you please. Another drop of sack?"

He glanced through the open French doors that led to a terrace, and saw it was growing dark. The time had passed more quickly than he had realized. "I should go back to Kingston before it grows too late."

"Dine with me here, why don't you? I'm enjoying your company, and you don't appear to find mine unpleasant."

Jeremy hesitated, for the first time aware of the flower-like fragrance she wore. It was difficult for him to think of this lovely girl as a courtesan. "I'd like it very much," he said candidly. "But since I'm not one of your clients—and very much doubt if I could afford to be—I can't allow myself to be beholden to you."

Lisa smiled broadly. "Oh, Mistress Ferguson will charge you for supper, never fear, and her prices are outrageous."

"If I'm allowed to pay for your supper, too, I'll be delighted to stay."

"Agreed," she told him, and held out her hand.

Something stirred within him when he touched her, and he warned himself to be careful. Fortunately, her high fee, whatever it might be, was beyond his reach.

Their meal was served in the sitting room by Toby and a serving maid. Lieutenant Stevens had been right to praise the food: the meal was delicious. The first course, appropriately, was star apple, a purple-colored fruit that had been cooled in the river. After it came a pumpkin soup, the first Jeremy had ever eaten, which had a beeflike flavor. Next came a white fish, native to the Caribbean and known locally as the prince-regent fish. With it, rice flavored with herbs was served.

A fruit sherbet cleared the palate, and then came one of the main courses, fillets of beef covered with a liver pâté and baked in a crust. "This is called beef Wellington," Lisa explained, "because it happens to be the favorite dish of General Lord Wellington, who defeated the French in Spain." With the dish, a variety of vegetables was served.

Next came baked stuffed chicken, accompanied by a fruit compote. Italian salad greens came next, with thin slices of hot buttered toast on the side. The dessert was a pudding with dates, and the last course was a platter of cheeses.

With each course came a different wine.

Lisa ate sparingly, taking only a few bites of each course, but Jeremy was ravenous, hungrier than he had been at any time since his impressment in the Royal Navy. Even though he consumed quantities of the various wines, he was so relaxed after the meal that he gladly accepted a snifter of brandywine.

They chatted about inconsequentials throughout the meal, and after the dishes were cleared away, Lisa displayed delicate skill in drawing Jeremy's story from him. Scarcely aware of what she was doing, he told her about his childhood and youth at Oakhurst Manor, his law studies, and his abduction by the Royal Navy.

Lisa questioned him in detail about his new rank and the battle in which he had fought. Then, shaking her head, she said, "I've never before heard of an impressed seaman becoming an officer."

"I reckon I'll be the first," he admitted.

She changed the subject very gently.

Without realizing it, Jeremy began to talk about Sarah Benton. He had mentioned her to no one in all the months since he had been kidnapped, and he poured out his longing for her.

Occasionally Lisa interjected with a quiet word or two that led him into new channels. He described Sarah in pinpoint detail, even remarking that her eyes were like Lisa's and that their taste in clothes seemed similar. He told the girl his worries about his betrothed. He expressed his fervent hopes for their future together. And he ended his recital by revealing that he had prayed for her that morning.

When he was done at last, Lisa lighted an oil lamp with a tinderbox and flint, then poured more brandywine into his bell-shaped snifter.

Jeremy looked out through the still-open French windows, and was startled by the realization that the night was well advanced. "I'm so sorry," he said. "I've spent at least an hour or two just talking about Sarah."

"You have no idea how glad I am that you did," Lisa told him. "It's wonderful to know that any man could be so much in love with any woman." She excused herself and left the room.

Jeremy wandered out onto the terrace, looking first at the stars with which he had become so familiar in his studies of navigation. The lamps and candles in the windows of Kingston Town homes flickered far below, and in the harbor beyond he could make out the dark shapes of several ships. One had to be the *Dolphin*, and, he reflected as he sipped his brandywine, at this moment his life on the sloop of war seemed as remote as his previous existence.

Soft footsteps sounded behind him.

Lisa joined him on the terrace. She had changed into a semi-transparent negligee of soft, clinging material, the deep V of its low-cut neckline half-revealing her high, firm breasts.

Jeremy gaped at her for a long moment, swallowing hard. "Lisa," he said hoarsely, "I truly can't afford—"

"Ssh, dear one," she said, silencing him by placing a finger over his lips. "Even if you had a king's ransom in gold, I wouldn't accept a farthing from you." Suddenly her peignoir fell to the terrace floor.

She stood before him completely nude, exhibiting her superb body without shame.

Jeremy knew only that he wanted her. Desperately. Urgently.

"I'm not your Sarah," she said, her voice scarcely above a whisper. "But if you'll let me substitute for her, perhaps—at least for a little while—you'll be less lonely for her."

He looked deep into her eyes and was overwhelmed.

Without a word he picked her up and carried her inside, Lisa curling her bare arms around his neck.

A door at the far end of the sitting room was open, and beyond it stood a bedchamber. Jeremy carried the girl there, depositing her gently on the four-poster bed. Thinking he was dreaming, he removed his own clothes and joined her.

Still not speaking, they moved into each other's arms, and Lisa's lips parted for Jeremy's kiss.

He drew her still closer, and the touch of her exquisite body pressing close to his body inflamed him.

She responded to him with a vigor that proved her ardor was no sham.

They became aroused gradually, simultaneously, and when Jeremy could wait no longer, he took her. They seemed to explode together, both of them realizing only that they were finding a wild, golden release.

After they rested for a time, they talked, sitting naked on the bed and sipping brandywine, both revealing their innermost thoughts and hopes. Jeremy had never told anyone other than Sarah his secret dreams, but it was strange that, at this moment, he felt no disloyalty to Sarah, no guilt. In some way he couldn't explain, even to himself, he was closer to her right now than he had been at any time since he had been drugged, kidnapped, and forced to serve in the British Navy.

Ultimately they made love again. Then, their desire at last sated, they fell asleep in each other's arms. Occasionally Jeremy murmured Sarah's name, awakening Lisa, who smiled tenderly and held him close.

Chapter 12

When Jeremy awaked, he saw sunlight streaming in through the open windows of the mansion high in the Liguanea Hills above Kingston Town.

Lisa stirred, opened her eyes, and looked at him.

With one accord they came together and made love again. Then they dozed.

A clock chimed on a bedside table, and Jeremy was astonished to discover it was noon.

Lisa provided him with a robe, and they went down to a natural pool, fed by an ever-bubbling spring, that was completely concealed behind masses of high, flowering poinsettia bushes. They swam in the nude, cavorting like children, and when they returned to the suite in the mansion, Jeremy found that the servants had washed and pressed his uniform.

He and Lisa ate a late breakfast of star apples, grilled meats, and fried bananas, drinking mugs of strong Jamaican coffee with their meal. Then he knew the time had come for him to leave.

"I owe you more than I can ever repay," he told the girl.

"You owe me nothing."

"But our meal last night, and this breakfast—"

"Nothing," she replied with a laugh. "I lied to you about paying for last night's supper because I knew you wouldn't stay as my guest."

She took his arm, and they walked together to the front of the mansion, where a carriage was waiting to take Jeremy back down to Kingston Town. He kissed Lisa, and he clung to him for an instant that felt like an eternity.

"I'll pray, too, that you and your Sarah will be reunited," she whispered. "And I hope that—now and then—you'll think of me."

Jeremy was scarcely aware of the passing scene on the drive to the city. He emerged from his reverie when he descended onto King Street, and without hesitation, he found the shop of a jeweler. There he spent five pounds on a gold cameo brooch, and paid his last few coins to a messenger who would take the gift to Lisa at the house in the hills.

On a card accompanying the brooch he wrote, "With my eternal gratitude and my love." Below it he signed his name in bold letters.

His spirits were high as he emerged onto the street again, but his euphoria was short-lived as he collided with someone. Their mutual force sent both sprawling, and not until Jeremy regained his feet did he realize he had bumped into Boatswain Talbot.

Talbot had been drinking and was in a nasty mood. "Watch where you walk, you clumsy Yankee bastard," he snarled as he brushed the dust of the road from his shirt and breeches.

Jeremy wiped dirt from his bicorne and settled it firmly on his head. "Keep a civil tongue in your head. I've heard enough of your foul-mouthed talk to last the rest of my days."

"Offended your little ears, have I? I'll be glad to beat them off your head."

"You're welcome to try," Jeremy said. This was the man responsible for his abduction, the man who had marked his back for life, and in him was represented all the unfairness, all the cruelty of a vicious system.

A boatswain's mate and a young midshipman, both members of the *Dolphin*'s crew, saw the pair glowering at each other and hurriedly tried to separate them.

"If you fight on the streets," the boatswain's mate told them, "the constables will haul you off to jail, and there you'll stay until we sail."

"I want to teach this bloody American a lesson he won't forget!" Talbot retorted.

"I welcome the opportunity to be your pupil," Jeremy replied.

The young midshipman tugged at his arm. "Please, Mr. Beaufort, don't fight here. There's a vacant lot behind that draper's shop. At least you won't be blocking street traffic there."

"Delighted," Jeremy said, "if Talbot dares to fight me fair and square."

"Dares, say you?" the boatswain bellowed. "Dares? I'll take your head off your neck and separate your neck from your shoulders! By the time I'm finished with you, Yankee—"

Jeremy's icy laugh cut him short. "As we say back home, your mouth is too big. I'll have to fill it with my fist." He stalked off in the direction of the lot.

The teenage midshipman trotted beside him. "Don't do it, Mr. Beaufort. He's a mean brute, and he's as strong as an ox. He's not allowed to touch you on board ship anymore, so he has all the more reason to welcome this chance. He'll beat you to a pulp."

"We'll see about that." A feeling of recklessness filled Jeremy, and he didn't care what happened to him. Here was an opportunity for which he had longed, and he intended to make Talbot pay for every blow with the cat-o'-nine-tails, every whip scar.

The boatswain's mate was worried. "Albert," he said, "the Yankee is the captain's pet now, and he won't take to it kindly if you knock out his teeth and smash his nose. I've found a tavern that serves the best grog in Jamaica. Let's go there for a mug."

"Soon," Talbot said. "We'll go there for a celebration as soon as I tear this . . . this American gentleman into shreds."

When Jeremy reached the lot, he unbuckled his sword belt, handing it to the midshipman with his bicorne, and then began to roll up his sleeves. "I'll be obliged if you'll keep these for me for a few minutes," he said.

Talbot was unable to restrain himself, and as he reached the vacant lot, he emitted an animallike roar, then raced toward his enemy with his fists clenched.

The circumstances were similar to those of a duel, Jeremy told himself. He sidestepped, moving only a few inches, and as the boatswain rushed past him, he unleashed a short jab that caught the English sailor on the side of the head and caused him to stagger.

The boatswain quickly regained his balance, wheeled, and charged again. His eyes blazed, he muttered a string of oaths, and it was plain that he was infuriated. Lowering his head, he resembled a mad bull as he advanced with both arms flailing.

It was a simple matter for Jeremy to dance inside, warding off blows with his elbows and arms. He landed the first solid punch, a smash to the cheekbone that brought blood.

Talbot halted in amazement, wiped his face with the back of his hand, then looked at it for an instant, and the sight of his own blood made him even angrier. Again he charged.

Jeremy moved out of his reach, waited until the other man lowered his guard for an instant, and then landed a long, hard right hook that almost instantly closed the boatswain's left eye.

Talbot threw caution to the winds as he came forward again and landed a hard blow to Jeremy's midriff.

Jeremy realized he had to stand and slug it out now, so he, too, discarded finesse. His physical strength was not as great as that of his foe, perhaps, but he felt confident he had greater stamina, and he was willing to absorb punishment for the sake of giving better than he received.

They stood toe to toe now, exchanging blow after blow, and the sound of fists striking flesh echoed across the lot.

The young midshipman shuddered.

The boatswain's mate was concerned, too. "We've got to stop them before they kill each other."

The midshipman looked around, saw a large wooden bucket filled with rainwater that stood on the ground behind the draper's shop. He ran to fetch it, then threw the contents over both combatants.

They were forced to halt, at least temporarily. Spluttering and trying to wipe away the water that had descended on them, they continued to face each other, both with swollen faces and raw knuckles.

It was plain that both were slightly dazed as they gasped and sucked in air.

The boatswain's mate stepped between them. "There's been enough," he said, authority in his voice.

Talbot peered at the American, unable to see him clearly. "You stood up to me!" he said in wonder. "No man before ye ever did that! You traded me punch for punch, and ye still stand!"

"So do you," Jeremy said. It was painful to smile, because his lip had been split. "But you fought me fair." He refrained from adding that he had expected the boatswain to land some foul blows.

"It seems to me you've had thirsty work," the boatswain's mate declared.

Talbot brightened. "Jenkins, you're using your brains! Where's that tavern you found?"

"I'll show you." His assistant was infinitely relieved. "Come along, Mr. Beaufort, and you, too, Mr. Smithers," he told the young midshipman.

The youth demurred, but was too embarrassed to explain that at his age hard liquor made him ill.

Jeremy was embarrassed. "I have no funds," he said. "I just spent my last ha'penny."

Talbot's roar of hoarse laughter echoed in their ears. "This will be my treat," he said. "When a man has met me honest and fair, and is still on his feet, the least I can do is fill his belly with grog!"

Jeremy retrieved his hat and sword. It would have been a boorish insult to reject the boatswain's hospitality. Strangely, he had no desire to avoid him now. Their fight had rid him of his hostility, and he realized it was wrong to hold Talbot personally responsible for his earlier persecution. The boatswain had his duty to perform in the harsh world of the Royal Navy, and that was that.

The young midshipman took himself elsewhere, and the boatswain's mate led the way to the tavern, a small smoke-filled establishment with dark walls, a bare, scrubbed floor, and tables and chairs of unpainted wood. a fire blazing in a hearth was missing, and the barmaid was black rather than white; otherwise the place bore a strong resemblance to a London tavern. Only two or three other tables were occupied.

"Now," Talbot said, clapping Jeremy on the shoulder, "we'll see if you can drink as well as you can fight."

They were served with large mugs of grob. In New England, where it had been served steaming hot, it was a rum drink with cloves and cinnamon in it. Here it was cool, flavored with spices and a bit of lime juice. As nearly as Jeremy could judge, the concoction was a blend of light and dark rum, and was the most potent drink he had ever tasted.

When he had consumed about half the contents of his mug, his battered face no longer ached, and by the time he started on his second mug, he and Talbot were laughing at each other's jokes like two old friends.

After the third mug, the boatswain's mate decided that discretion was the better part of valor and took his departure.

Jeremy and Talbot lost count of the number of mugs they drank, and no longer cared. They were enjoying themselves, as befitted two men who had saved each other's lives, and if their conversation made little or no sense, neither realized it.

Eventually, the proprietor, a Scot, refused to serve them any more grog. The Royal Navy was lenient with sailors who were on shore leave, but his establishment might be posted as out of bounds if they drank themselves insensible.

They decided they wanted one more mug. "We can pound a bit of sense into the barman," Talbot said.

A fast-fading streak of sobriety convinced Jeremy that such an approach might be dangerous, even though he believed he and the boatswain could win any fight, no matter how many opponents they faced. "To the devil with him," he said. "We'll take our business elsewhere. And, Talbot, when I'm paid the rest of my prize money, I insist on paying my fair share of our little celebration."

"Never." Talbot struggled to his feet. "I don't often have the chance to buy drinks for a future admiral. I don't like it when I'm sent out on impressment duty, Mr. Beaufort, but I'm proud I abducted you."

Swaying and stumbling as they left the tavern, they were surprised, when they reached the street outside, to see that night had fallen. It was astonishing that time had passed so quickly.

"We're due back on board ship at midnight," Jeremy said. "I wonder what the time might be."

Talbot had no idea, and together they pondered. "Mayhap we'd best go back," the boatswain said at last.

Jeremy agreed. "The captain might not like it if we were late. We don't want to vex him."

They had to support each other as they made their way down to the waterfront.

Most members of *Dolphin*'s crew had already returned to the sloop of war, and enjoyed the spectacle of watching the boatswain and the senior midshipman staggering down the pier.

Lord Saunders, who had just returned to the vessel himself, concealed a broad grin and hastily retired to his own cabin so he wouldn't see the pair. It would be difficult to explain to his subordinates that he was relieved that his principal noncommissioned officer and the American whom he intended to promote at the opportune time had ended their feud.

Crew members took the captain's hint, and hauled the pair off to their beds.

When Jeremy awakened with a throbbing head, he was amazed to discover that the *Dolphin* had put out to sea. The sun was shining, and judging from its position, it was now midmorning. He made his way up to the aft deck, attached a bucket to a line, and after filling it with seawater, began to douse himself with it.

Ultimately, he became aware of someone else who had

the same idea, and blinked with bloodshot eyes at Talbot. They exchanged weak grins.

"Jamaica will never be the same," the boatswain declared in a hoarse voice.

"Neither will we," Jeremy was surprised to hear a rasp in his own voice, too.

They toweled themselves vigorously, then dressed. "We put that tavern out of business," Talbot said.

Jeremy nodded, the movement causing new pains in his head. "I doubt if anyone ever drank them out of their entire supply of rum until you and I came along."

He hurried to his quarters to dress for duty, then made his way to the mess, where a mug of hot chocolate and several hardtack biscuits were all he could get down.

It was strange, he mused, making his way to the main deck so that he could report to Lieutenant Gough for duty, that the brief shore leave had made profound changes within him. Boatswain Talbot, whom he had despised, was now his friend, and he no longer felt any hostility toward the man. Even more important, his experience with Lisa had comforted him. He still missed Sarah Benton more than he had dreamed possible, but now he was willing to face reality. He was trapped in a web not of his own choosing, but he was willing to accept his fate. At the first chance, he would return to Sarah, resume his study of the law, and then settle with her in Charleston or some other major city not too far removed from Oakhurst Manor. Until that opportunity arose, however, he would make the best of his situation and would strive to improve his knowledge of ships and the sea. His destiny had taken a totally unexpected turn, and he would no longer fight against it.

He hoped that, someday, Lisa would get all she wanted in the world. She deserved everything good, from a home of her own to a husband who would cherish her. Only a few months earlier he would have scoffed at the notion that a man could find a courtesan so attractive. Now he knew that if Sarah hadn't claimed his heart, it would be easy to fall in love with Lisa.

Jeremy didn't yet realize it, but he was growing mature far beyond his twenty-three years. The square of burnished steel in which he could make out his reflection when he shaved failed to reveal to him the lines that were etched in his face or the sprinkle of gray already beginning to show at his temples.

He was a man, one who was more than holding his own in an alien world. His ambition had been rekindled, and his natural balance had been restored. Thanks in large part to Lisa, he could laugh again and accept each day as it came.

Most of the *Dolphin*'s officers and midshipmen were at breakfast in the wardroom, silently downing fish that had been soaked in water to remove the salt in which it had been packed, then broiled. Some drank coffee, a few preferred hot chocolate, and the majority took tea. Jeremy still could not bring himself to accept a cup of tea. Most Americans still avoided it; this was a legacy they had inherited from their fathers and grandfathers, who continued to regard it as a symbol, thanks to the tax the crown had tried to impose on tea in Massachusetts Bay before the outbreak of hostilities during the War of Independence.

In spite of his devotion to his work, and his determination to rise as high as he could in the Royal Navy, he never forgot he was an American. That, he thought, was the story of his feelings in a nutshell, although he revealed his inner thoughts to no one.

"Strange ship off the port bow," the lookout called, and the cry was repeated.

The shouts were heard in the wardroom, and the officers and midshipmen ate more quickly, anticipating what would happen next.

"All hands to battle stations!" the boatswain's mate roared as he ran through the ship.

Breakfast was forgotten. Officers and midshipmen clamped their bicornes on their heads, buckled on their swords, and quickly emptied the wardroom.

Jeremy ran to the quarterdeck, which remained his assignment. There he would wait until ordered by the captain to perform any service that might be required of him.

The other ship, twin-masted and featuring a square-shaped stern, was executing a turn as the *Dolphin* approached her, and obviously was trying to flee.

"Raise your colors!" Lord Saunders ordered.

The Union Jack was hoisted to the topgallants.

The other ship did not identify herself, and executing her turn, began to beat her way to windward as she ran.

Captain Lord Saunders chuckled. "I think we have a morning's sport ahead, Mr. Gough," he told his first mate.

Jeremy knew the master of the other vessel realized that his ship was no match for the *Dolphin*, and consequently was trying to escape. He shared Lord Saunders' sense of excitement and could feel his pulse pounding, but at the same time he felt sorry for the victim.

As nearly as he could guess, the other ship was a merchantman, not a warship, and consequently was in no position to put up a successful fight.

Suddenly a question filled his mind: what would he do if the fleeing vessel proved to be American? Could he play an active role in capturing or sinking her?

No matter what the dictates of his conscious, he had no choice. He had accepted the rank of midshipman in the Royal Navy, and not only had spent months at his studies but also had taken an active part in one battle. So Great Britain's enemies became his enemies, regardless of his personal feelings, and he had to act accordingly. If he had remained an apprentice seaman, impressed against his will and still protesting, he could have done anything in his power to take action on behalf of the United States. Having freely consented to become an officer candidate, and having enjoyed the prerogatives and comforts of his new position, he was required to obey the orders of the crown's viceroy, Captain Lord Saunders.

Not until now had it occurred to Jeremy that he had placed himself in an impossible position. If he took up arms against his native land, a country he loved, his conscience would give him no peace. If he refused, the captain would be forced to have him executed. His only consolation was that he would face a firing squad rather than die by hanging.

Sloops of war were the fastest, most agile ships afloat, and the *Dolphin* began to close the gap. Lord Saunders and his first mate, watching the running vessel through their glasses, smiled at each other repeatedly.

Jeremy, who had to rely on his own eyesight, at last was able to find out something for himself. The other ship, squat and square-rigged, undoubtedly was a merchantman. This meant she was armed, at best, with a few six-pounder cannon to ward off pirates. Under no circumstances could she dare to engage in a battle with the heavily armed *Dolphin*, whose trained gunners could blow her out of the water.

At Lord Saunders' direction, a curt order was passed to the fleeing brig. Flags were raised to the *Dolphin*'s topgallants that said "Identify yourself!"

It was a fundamental rule of the sea that if the brig refused to comply, Lord Saunders would be within his rights to send her and her entire crew to the bottom. The master of the merchantman was not foolish, and a pennant began to move up a thin line.

The ensign was the gold-and-white banner of France.

Jeremy felt weak. He had no reason to refrain from taking part in a battle against a French ship, military or civilian, and his dilemma was solved. If his luck continued to hold, perhaps he would never be faced with the problem of what to do in a confrontation with an American vessel.

Again the *Dolphin* sent a message. "Heave to," her flags read, "or I shall be obliged to sink you."

The French merchantman continued to run.

Jeremy could understand the reasoning. The brig had changed direction again, and was heading toward the southwest, where increasingly dark clouds were gathering. Newly gained experience enabled the young American to understand the French master's thinking. The squall line was clearly defined, and if he could escape into the storm, fog and rain might lower visibility sufficiently for him to engage in evasive action and get away.

But Lord Saunders knew instantly what was happening, and took steps to counteract the move. First, he ordered the sloop of war to crowd on more sail, and she lived up to her name by leaping forward through the water. No other class of ship could have responded as rapidly.

Then he ordered the gunports lowered and directed gun crews to prepare for action.

The *Dolphin* quickly closed the gap, and the merchant-man was less that three-quarters of a mile away.

A few sprinkles of rain began to fall.

"Mr. Beaufort!" the captain said.

"Sir?" Jeremy stiffened to attention.

"Mr. Beaufort, you've had ample gunnery practice with dummies. The time has come to see how you'll fare against a live target. My compliments to Lieutenant Spinner, and inform him I'm giving you temporary command of his gun crews."

"Aye, aye, sir." Jeremy saluted, then raced down to the gun deck, where he repeated his orders to the officer in charge.

The senior lieutenant frowned, but was in no position to protest. "I'll be watching you, Beaufort," he said, "and if you fail, I'll intervene."

Jeremy made a quick inspection of the nine starboard guns. All were loaded with cold shot, and the crew chiefs were ready, each of them prepared to light a fuse with a small burning flare.

The *Dolphin* continued to narrow the space that separated her from the helpless French brig.

The rainfall was becoming heavier, forcing the chiefs of the gun crews to shield their flares.

Jeremy stood with feet apart and studied the merchant-man. The sea was calm, thanks to the rain, and the swell was slight, which made his calculations simpler. He was being given an opportunity to show how well he could perform, and he welcomed the chance. On the other hand, he warned himself not to feel too confident. He would be firing on living persons on board a real ship, not at a target being towed behind the *Dolphin,* and he couldn't allow himself to forget it.

Depending on the nature of the brig's cargo, the prize money could be considerable, so he could not permit the gunners to sink her or cripple her too badly. Furthermore, his share, as acting gunnery officer, would be far greater than it would have been had his activities been confined to those of an ordinary midshipman. It was small wonder that Lieutenant Spinner was irritated.

A young midshipman arrived at the run with a message from the captain. "Mr. Beaufort, whenever you're ready, you may put a shot across the enemy's bow."

Jeremy walked amidships and told three gun crews to strip for immediate action. Carefully measuring the distance between the two vessels, he ordered the trajectory changed.

"Cannon number one, prepare to fire!" he ordered.

Two gunners made a final change in the trajectory, then threw themselves to the deck and covered their ears.

"Fire!"

The short fuse was lighted, and the crew chief stepped to one side, a precaution always taken to ward off injury in the event the gun exploded.

There was a flash of fire, followed by a deafening roar, and a cloud of smoke billowed across the deck.

Jeremy blinked away the smoke, and was mortified when he saw the shot fall into the sea at least one hundred yards ahead of the brig and a great distance beyond it.

Lieutenant Spinner smiled sourly, and a number of the sailors looked uncomfortable.

"Cannon number two, prepare to fire!" Setting his jaw, Jeremy did not leave the changing of the trajectory to the gun crew, but leaped forward and lowered the elevation himself.

Barely remembering to move aside at the final instant, he shouted, "Fire!"

There was another flash, another roar, and this time the nine-pound cannonball dropped into the sea a scant one hundred feet from the brig, directly ahead of her prow.

That was more like it!

Not waiting for further orders from the quarterdeck, which he could have done, Jeremy quickly ordered small changes in the third gun's aim and trajectory.

He was unaware of the rain that soaked him to the skin.

"Fire!"

This time the shot fell so close to the merchantman that seamen standing on her main deck literally ducked as they were splashed when the iron projectile fell into the sea only a few feet from her bow.

The *Dolphin*'s gun crews cheered. No officer had ever come that close without actually damaging the enemy.

The master of the merchantman had had enough, and raised a white flag.

A boarding party was ordered to take up positions at the sloop of war's rail.

Lieutenant Spinner extended a hand to Jeremy. "Accept my congratulations, Beaufort," he said. "I've been a gunnery officer for eleven years, and I couldn't have done as well."

The boarders were offered no resistance, and a prize crew under the command of Lieutenant Gough was sent on board. Then both ships set sail again, and it was obvious that the *Dolphin* was acting as the merchantman's escort.

A pleased Lord Saunders sent for Jeremy.

"Mr. Beaufort," he said, "the brig was carrying a cargo of arms and gunpowder to the French garrison at Martinique. I know of no richer prize in wartime, and your reward will be greater than you think."

Chapter 13

The *Dolphin* headed back toward Kingston, Jamaica, which she had left four weeks earlier, the captured French brig sailing with her in tandem. Unexpectedly, on the day before they were due to reach port, the entire company of the sloop of war was mustered on the main deck.

The captain stood alone at the quarterdeck rail, looking down at his assembled officers and men, and ordered Midshipman Beaufort to join him.

Several of the senior lieutenants appeared to know what was afoot and were smiling, so Jeremy was relieved, reasoning he had broken no regulation.

"Mr. Beaufort," Lord Saunders said, "your gunnery was responsible for our capture, intact, of a French merchant vessel carrying an exceptionally valuable wartime cargo. In view of your accomplishments on this occasion, as well as your remarkable progress in the sciences of seamanship, navigation, and gunnery in general, I am pleased to grant you a promotion to the rank of junior lieutenant, second class, effective immediately."

Jeremy was stunned. Not only was he receiving a commission immediately, but he was being skipped over the rank of ensign, or third-class lieutenant. Most Royal Navy officers who started their careers as midshipmen were required to serve eight to ten years before being granted the rank he was now receiving.

He managed to stammer his thanks.

The captain pinned a small silver epaulet to his left shoulder, and the entire ship's company cheered.

When the formation was dismissed, the officers crowded around Jeremy to offer their congratulations.

After they, too, went off about their normal duties, Boatswain Talbot came up to him, saluted, and extended his hand. "No two ways about it, sir, you've got the touch," he said. "And if I have my way, I'll ne'er serve with anyone else."

Jeremy knew it was the highest honor he could receive.

That night, regulations were temporarily put aside in the officers' mess, and several bottles of wine were opened and consumed in the new lieutenant's honor.

The following morning, the *Dolphin* and her prize put into the now familiar port of Kingston. There Jeremy was presented to two admirals, who not only offered him their felicitations but also gave him the welcome news that he would be wealthier by one thousand guineas. The *Dolphin*'s paymaster was ordered to give him one hundred and fifty guineas at once, and he was granted a special twenty-four-hour shore leave. Its primary purpose was to give him the opportunity to buy new uniforms befitting his rank. The captain privately made it clear to him that the leave was a part of his reward, and he could spend it in any way he pleased. But, Lord Saunders added with a chuckle, it would be advisable if Lieutenant Beaufort conducted himself with the dignity of his rank and did not return in an intoxicated condition.

Jeremy went first to a tailor on Duke Street who specialized in making uniforms for Royal Navy officers, and there ordered himself a new wardrobe. One complete uniform would be ready for him in an hour, and the rest would be sent to the *Dolphin* that same night. Obviously the tailor knew his business, and gave rapid service to officers whose time ashore was limited.

There was an hour to kill, so Jeremy went to the jeweler

he had visited on his previous stay and purchased a gold bracelet fashioned like a cuff. He watched as Lisa's name was engraved on it, and then, clutching his purchase, he returned to the tailor shop for his uniform.

Attired at last as a full-fledged officer, he engaged a driver and carriage, then headed for the Star Apple in the Liguanea Hills. It was dangerous for him to see Lisa again, and he knew it. Not that he loved Sarah Benton any less than he had on the day he had left her; he was still devoted to her with his whole heart and soul. But he had to admit that Lisa fascinated him, and he was being drawn back to her by a force too strong for him to control or deny.

Mistress Ferguson greeted him like an old friend, and there was no need to tell her why he had come.

After a short wait Lisa came into the parlor, wearing a clinging, copper-colored Empire gown that matched her hair. Her eyes were glistening, but she stopped short when she saw Jeremy.

"Well, it's Lieutenant Beaufort now!" she exclaimed, and saluted him prettily.

He took her in his arms, and they kissed hungrily.

Lisa disengaged herself abruptly, and frowned as she led him up to her suite. She poured two glasses of sack, then took care to sit opposite him rather than beside him.

Jeremy presented her with the bracelet.

"Oh, no!" Lisa said. "I can't accept it!"

"Since it already has your name engraved on the inside, I couldn't give it to anyone else."

The girl looked at the engraving, then shifted the bracelet from one hand to the other. "It's wrong of you to keep giving me lovely jewelry," she said.

"Wrong? I want to do it. I've known no other real pleasure in more months than I can remember," Jeremy told her.

"I realize that," she said, her frown deepening. "I'll accept this on two conditions. The first is that you promise you'll never again buy me any more gifts."

"That's unfair," he protested.

"Nevertheless, I insist."

"Very well," he said reluctantly, "you force me to accept. What's your other condition?"

"That you stop seeing me."

Jeremy was stunned.

"It would create too many problems if we continued to see each other, my dear." Her voice was gentle, her eyes wise. "I know men, unfortunately, and I realize you lack the willpower to stay away from me. I know myself, too, and I'm too weak to resist you. We'd be creating complications that would give rise to an impossible situation."

He hated to admit she was right.

"We're hungry for affection, both of us," Lisa said, "so we may be magnifying the magnetic forces that pull us toward each other."

"I admit that possibility, but—"

"Hear me out, Jeremy. You're an officer in the king's navy now. Obviously you've served with distinction, and you're the sort who is certain to win even more glory. So you would be welcome anywhere in the British Empire when the war ends. Suppose I buy my house in Barbados. Would you come to me there, settle down, and spend the rest of your days with me? As my husband and the father of my children?"

"I . . . I just might," he replied, too startled by her candor to know what else he could say.

"If I exerted pressure, I'm sure you would. You'd give up your claim to your family estates, even though it would be painful. You'd sell your share, perhaps, and use that money, along with your navy pension, to buy a new plantation in Barbados. Yes, and you'd spend the rest of your days with me there."

"I . . . I reckon I would."

"What's more," Lisa said, "you'd be miserable, even when we were making love, and so would I. Because the ghost of a girl named Sarah Benton would come between us. You love her."

"I do," Jeremy said, "but I'm badly confused right now."

"Of course, but after we settled down into mundane, everyday living, the dust would clear away and you'd realize that although you were infatuated with me, you still love her. I saw your eyes and face, and I listened to your voice when you spoke of her. I couldn't compete with her for your love, my dear. I've had too much experience in this world ever to try."

"What you say makes sense," Jeremy admitted, "but I still want you. When I've dreamed at night, I haven't been certain whether I've dreamed of Sarah or of you. One moment I want to make love to her, and the next I want to make love to you."

Lisa clapped her tapering hands over her ears. "Stop, I beg you. I'm not strong enough to resist."

He compressed his mouth until his lips turned white. "I beg your pardon," he said. "No matter what I feel, I have no right to subject you to this ordeal."

"It's no ordeal, really," Lisa said. "What shakes me is the knowledge that you—a slave owner—would marry me if I said the word, even though there's black in my ancestry."

"You're lovely and sweet. You're warm, and a woman of integrity. Color doesn't mean a damn thing to me."

She forced a laugh. "What a pity all of us aren't Muslims who live somewhere in the Ottoman Empire. Then you could marry both your Sarah and me. Except that we'd be so jealous of each other that either she'd scratch my eyes out or I'd do the same to her."

"If you wish, I'll go right now," Jeremy said.

"Not quite yet, but I warn you, I do intend to send you away."

"Before we can make love?"

Lisa hesitated. "I . . . I'm not sure. I'll agree to spend the next hours with you, and you may stay here and dine with me. After that . . . well, we'll see."

He realized she was telling him she would permit him to remain for a time, provided he refrained from forcing his physical attentions on her. "I accept all of your conditions," he told her.

"Good!" Lisa's mood changed swiftly, and she laughed. "Come into the garden with me, and we'll pick our own fruits and vegetables for dinner."

They went downstairs, Lisa found a wicker basket, and Jeremy carried it for her. They went outdoors, and as they wandered through the palm grove, they held hands, their touch innocent. Then they exchanged a glance, and suddenly a current passed back and forth, jolting them. With one accord they drew apart.

"I worry about your future," Jeremy said.

"Don't. I'm a tough harlot, and I can take care of myself," she said.

"You're neither tough nor a harlot."

"If you insist," she replied with a sigh. "But take my word for it, I'll manage. I've known only one man who has the power to hurt me and disrupt my careful plans. You."

He knew she was making it as difficult as possible, deliberately, for them to resume their affair. In one sense, he was relieved and grateful, but that didn't mean he wanted her any the less.

"The worst of my situation," he said, "is that even if I saw you and Sarah standing side by side, I'd still be confused."

"If I thought that was true," Lisa said, "I'd have no compunction about taking you away from her. But I know it isn't. You'd go to her, and you'd never look at me again."

"Suppose I did?"

"I've had married men as lovers," Lisa said, "but I couldn't share you with anyone, regardless of whether I were your mistress or your wife. Here, this pineapple is ripe. Use your sword and cut it for us. It makes a marvelous first course when it's been soaked in a dry wine."

They spent more than an hour in the fruit and vegetable gardens, and the basket was heavy as Jeremy started to carry it back to the mansion.

It was apparent that they had been paying little attention to what they had been doing, and Jeremy's smile was rueful. "We've gathered enough for the entire officers' mess on the *Dolphin*," he said.

Lisa joined in the laugh. "Well, it won't go to waste. There's that much to be said."

After leaving the produce with the cook, they adjourned to Lisa's sitting room, and while they awaited dinner, they carefully avoided the subject of their relationship. The girl took the lead, guiding the talk to Jeremy's experiences at sea since they had last seen each other, and he told her in detail about the gunnery exploits that had led to his promotion.

They drank sparingly, and when their meal was served, both found they had little appetite, even though the dishes prepared for them were delicious. The question of whether they would make love was hanging over their heads, and the depth of their dilemma was making them miserable. Their talk became strained, and the tensions soared.

Then, suddenly, the liveried servant tapped at the door. "Excuse me, Mistress Lisa," he said when they admitted him, "but a sailor is here to see your guest. He says he brings an urgent message."

A midshipman from the *Dolphin* had followed the man, and burst into the room, his anxiety so great that it overcame his embarrassment at finding the officer enjoying a private meal with a provocatively dressed woman.

"Sir," he said, standing at attention and saluting, "we've been searching the whole island for you. Luckily we found the carriage driver who brought you up here. The captain's compliments, sir, and he requests that you return to the ship at once. We're sailing on the evening tide."

Jeremy was on his feet. "What's happened, Calkins?" Obviously an emergency of some kind had developed.

"Lord Saunders hasn't taken me into his confidence, Lieutenant." The midshipman hesitated, then added pointedly, "The carriage is waiting below, sir."

"I'll join you in a moment." When the midshipman and the servant had departed, Jeremy closed the door. "Our problem is being solved for us, it seems."

"I'm glad I don't have to make the decision," Lisa told him. "I'm not sure what I would have done."

"Nor am I," he said, taking her in his arms.

"May God protect you," Lisa murmured. "And if we shouldn't meet again, it might be best. For both of us."

Jeremy kissed her, then tore himself away from her and left the room without a backward glance.

It was already late afternoon, he noted as he climbed into the carriage for the drive back to Kingston from the

Liguanea Hills. He and the midshipman would be reaching the ship without much time to spare.

He was silent on the ride, trying without success to sort out his feelings. What he couldn't understand was how it was possible, when he still loved Sarah and was as devoted to her as he had ever been, to be drawn so strongly to Lisa.

Perhaps the puzzle would solve itself. Certainly the passage of time would help, and he was relieved that he was being recalled to duty. It would be far easier for him to bear the weight of his problem if his mind was occupied.

When they reached the waterfront, Jeremy saw that there was an unusual bustle at the Royal Navy wharves. Supplies were being carried by barge and boat to a huge ship of the line that was anchored in the deeper waters of the harbor, and other small craft were carrying the crew members of a frigate to their sleek, powerful warship.

The *Dolphin* had already taken on water, food, and munitions, and the captain was making a last-minute inspection preparatory to casting off.

Jeremy went directly to him. "Lieutenant Beaufort at report for duty, sir," he said.

Lord Saunders smiled. "I'm pleased we weren't forced to sail without you, Mr. Beaufort."

Less than a quarter of an hour later the *Dolphin* set sail, and as she made her way slowly through the Kingston roads en route to the open Caribbean, all of the ship's officers were summoned to the quarterdeck.

"Gentlemen," the captain told them, "France is no longer our only enemy. Just this afternoon the governor general of Jamaica received word that we are now at war with the United States of America. Henceforth we will engage any of her warships we may encounter, and when possible, we will seize or sink her merchantmen. I anticipate that this is going to be an active cruise."

When the formation was dismissed, Jeremy, who had no duty assignment at the moment, went down to the gun deck, which was deserted, and made his way to the fantail. The situation he had dreaded had come to pass, and he felt ill.

He had accepted a brevet commission in the Royal

Navy, and the circumstances that had led to it were irrelevant. All that mattered was that he was under oath to serve beneath the Union Jack and to fight for the king. Now, however, Great Britain had gone to war with his own country. He would be required to fire on the Stars and Stripes, to kill his fellow countrymen, to sink American ships.

He could not accept the role of a traitor to the United States, no matter what the consequences, and he entertained no doubts regarding his future. The time was not far distant when his loyalty to his native land would compel him to disobey an order. Then he would be subjected to a court-martial, and its outcome was predictable: he would face certain execution by a firing squad. It no longer mattered that he wanted Lisa, even while loving Sarah. He hoped that neither girl would waste her substance by mourning for him.

"All hands to battle stations!"

The shouts of the boatswain's mates awakened Jeremy from a troubled sleep in the tiny cabin he shared with two other junior lieutenants. Looking out of the porthole as he dressed hastily, he saw that dawn was just breaking over the Caribbean. From this vantage point he could see no other ship.

He hoped the enemy that had been sighted was French, but he was afraid his luck had run out. If a battle loomed with one or more American vessels, this would be the last day he would spend on earth. No navy could tolerate insubordination in time of war.

Well, at least he would go down in style. He buttoned one of his new uniform coats, settled his bicorne firmly on his head, and buckled on his sword. Then, expecting the worst, he went to the quarterdeck, where the captain had already assumed the command.

Lord Saunders returned Jeremy's salute but made no comment.

As an officer, Jeremy had his own spyglass now, and making out a speck on the horizon, he studied it with care through the tube. Cannon mounted fore and aft identified her as a warship, and so did her gun ports, which had not yet been lowered for action. As yet, it was impossible to identify her as she moved toward the *Dolphin*, apparently as eager as the British vessel for a confrontation.

What puzzled Jeremy was that the stranger did not resemble any of the warships he had studied during his months as a midshipman. She had three masts, so he supposed that, technically, at least, she qualified as a frigate. But he counted her armaments carefully, and saw that she carried only twenty-four guns. She was tiny, too, a frigate in miniature, perhaps no larger than the *Dolphin*. Frigates in both the British and French navies were a size below ships of the line and carried forty to sixty cannon.

This unorthodox ship had to be American. Jeremy knew it in his bones.

An apprentice seaman appeared with mugs of steaming tea, and as Jeremy sipped the brew, he continued to study the stranger, which was drawing closer. Through his glass he could make out the members of her crew, who were stripped to the waist. They were scurrying back and forth across her decks, battening down in expectation of a battle.

Three officers and the helmsman were standing on her quarterdeck, but it was impossible to identify their vessel from their appearance. Like the officers of all navies, they wore bicornes, blue coats trimmed with gold, white breeches, and calf-high boots. They could be British or French, American or Dutch or Swedish.

The captain broke the silence. "What do you make of her, Mr. Gough?" he asked his first mate.

"Damned if I know, sir. I've never seen a ship like her."

"Nor have I. What's your opinion, Mr. Beaufort?"

"She seems to be a dwarf frigate, sir. I wouldn't know what else to call her."

"Did you ever see such ships in America, Beaufort?" Obviously the captain shared Jeremy's suspicions regarding her nationality.

The young American's smile was pained. "Frankly, sir, I never paid that much attention to ships, and I wouldn't have known one kind from another. I was strictly a land-lubber."

Lord Saunders merely nodded, and all three officers resumed their study of the stranger.

"Her armaments are rather peculiar," Lieutenant Gough remarked. "Her fore and aft guns are nine-pounders, but she carries only two of them. Her principal artillery, judging from the size of her gun ports, can't be much more than six-pounders."

Jeremy had just reached the same conclusion. "I agree, sir. Nine-pounders couldn't be emplaced behind ports that small."

The captain looked pleased. "That means she lacks our range, and will have to close with us if she's to meet us on anything like equal terms. We have a natural advantage."

The stranger was about a mile and a half away.

Lord Saunders abruptly ordered the *Dolphin* stripped for action, and her gun ports were lowered.

Jeremy discovered that his heart was pounding.

The captain motioned him closer. "If this ship proves to be American, Mr. Beaufort, you're placed in a difficult position."

"Indeed I am, sir."

"I sympathize with your plight. So I won't avail myself of your services unless it proves absolutely necessary." Lord Saunders paused, then added in a firm voice, "But if need be, I won't hesitate to call on you. Please remember, Beaufort, that you wear his majesty's uniform, and his cause comes first, before personal considerations."

Jeremy saluted and retired to the far side of the quarterdeck. He had been granted a reprieve, at least for the moment, and could ask for nothing more.

The captain ordered the Union Jack raised.

The small frigate ignored the signal and continued to draw closer.

The *Dolphin*'s gun crews were told to stand ready for immediate action.

Suddenly, when the stranger was still about three-quarters of a mile off the port bow, there were two flashes of fire from her main deck, followed by the boom of her twin nine-pounder cannon, the only guns she carried that were effective at such a distance.

The marksmanship of her gunners was superb. One shot

struck the aft deck, plowing a furrow in it before dropping overboard into the sea. The other glanced off a section of the quarterdeck, and a heavy chunk of splintered wood hit Lieutenant Gough in the forehead, knocking him unconscious.

Two seamen carried him to the surgery, and the second lieutenant was summoned to replace him.

Meanwhile, the other ship finally raised her pennant in a challenge to the British warship, and the Stars and Stripes fluttered in the Caribbean breeze.

Jeremy felt a deep surge of pride. Royal Navy gunnery was first-rate, but that of his fellow countrymen was superior. And the daring of the Yankee captain was breathtaking. Unable to use his smaller cannon at a distance, he had utilized the only guns available, and both of his initial shots had hit their target. No naval commander could ask more of his crew.

The *Dolphin*'s nine-pounders went into action, laying down a furious barrage. But it took two rounds before they began to find the range, and by that time the small frigate had drawn close enough to use her six-pounders. The action was joined in earnest.

The American was close enough now for Jeremy to read her name: *Bald Eagle*.

For one insane moment he thought of jumping overboard and swimming the half-mile to the sanctuary of his own flag. But he abandoned the thought almost as quickly as it occurred to him. Musket fire from the *Dolphin*, or American sharpshooters armed with their magnificent long rifles, would pick him off in the water, and his chances of survival were virtually nonexistent.

For the present he had been reduced to the role of an observer, and had to be content with his lot.

The two ships sailed parallel to each other at a distance of a half-mile and poured shot at each other. The American gunners were far more accurate, but their six-pounders did relatively little damage. The *Dolphin*'s gun crews continued to have difficulty in finding their range, but when a nine-pounder shot crashed onto the decks or into the hull of the *Bald Eagle*, their more powerful blows were effective.

So far, Jeremy reflected, the battle was a draw. The United States Navy was a new force, made up completely of volunteers, and they were giving an amazingly good account of themselves. He had to exercise self-control to prevent himself from cheering them, but he privately hoped they would triumph. His own fate had become unimportant to him.

A six-pounder shot landed on the quarterdeck of the *Dolphin*, only a few feet from the spot on which Jeremy was standing. The impact threw him to the deck, and at the same instant a searing pain shot through his left thigh. He tried to stand, but crumpled again, and he looked in astonishment as he saw a crimson patch spreading across his white breeches. Only then did it occur to him that he had been wounded. But the irony of the situation was not lost on him: the injury had been inflicted by an American cannonball fired by an American gunner.

He had no idea how long he lay on the quarterdeck with the battle raging around him. The roar of cannon was incessant, punctuated by the screams of the wounded and dying, and thick clouds of black smoke filled the air, making it difficult to breathe.

All at once Jeremy felt himself being hoisted into the air.

"You're not hurt bad, Mr. Beaufort," Boatswain Talbot said, as, ignoring the American fire, he carried the injured officer below decks to the dispensary.

There the surgeon and his two assistants, both pharmacist's mates, had their hands full. All six bunks were occupied, and other injured men were stretched out on pallets that occupied the entire space.

By now Jeremy's whole leg felt on fire, and he lost consciousness.

When he awakened, the guns were still roaring.

The surgeon was bending over him. "We've stopped the bleeding for the present, Mr. Beaufort," he said. "A splinter has lodged in your thigh and will have to be removed. But I can't operate until the battle ends, and meantime, there are men who need attention more than you." He began to move off.

"How goes the fight, Doctor?" Jeremy called.

Either the surgeon did not hear him or chose not to answer.

The pain was almost unbearable, but Jeremy clamped his teeth together so he wouldn't cry out. He had no idea that he was bathed in sweat.

All at once he realized that someone was bending over him, holding a small glass that contained a milky, foul-smelling liquid.

"Drink this, sir," the pharmacist's mate ordered.

"What is it?"

"Laudanum, sir."

As Jeremy downed the drink, which tasted as bad as it smelled, he knew that laudanum was an opiate administered in case of serious injury or illness. Perhaps his wound was worse than he had imagined.

"How goes the battle?" he asked, not realizing that the firing on both sides had stopped.

"We're withdrawing, sir, and so is the enemy. Both sides have taken a battering, but neither has the strength to finish off the fight. I've got to hand it to those Yanks," the pharmacist's mate added, grudging admiration in his voice. "We gave them the best we had, but they bloody well don't know when they're beat!"

The laudanum began to take hold, and as Jeremy's pain began to subside, he felt drowsy.

Before he drifted off to sleep, he felt a sudden surge of elation, his wound forgotten. He had been injured by fellow Americans, but he was grateful to them. Thanks to the accuracy of their gunnery, he had not been placed in the position of having to refuse to take up arms against them. An American cannonball had wounded him but had saved him from certain death before a Royal Navy firing squad.

Chapter 14

When Jeremy awakened, he thought he was dreaming. He was lying in a comfortable bed fitted with clean white sheets. Sunlight was streaming into a small, compact room through an open window, beyond which stood a plant of brilliantly flowering hibiscus, and in the distance stood a grove of palm trees. Obviously he had been transferred from the *Dolphin* to a land base.

He remembered his wound, which no longer ached, but his left thigh was heavily bandaged and was sore to the touch. A glance at his hands told him he had lost weight, but he could remember nothing since he had consumed the glass of laudanum on board the sloop of war.

A male orderly in a Royal Navy uniform came into the room with a glass of fruit juice. "Ah, so ye be awake, sir," he said.

"Apparently. Where am I?"

"Royal Naval Hospital, Isle of Nevis, Lieutenant."

"How long have I been here?"

"I ain't allowed t' answer questions, sir. Dr. Carey now, he'll be along soon."

"What's become of my ship, the *Dolphin?*"

"It'll be Dr. Carey who'll give ye the answers he thinks fit, sir." The orderly edged out of the room and closed the door behind him.

Jeremy drank the fruit juice, holding the glass with a hand that—to his surprise—was shaking. Question after question crowded his mind, but he tried to exercise patience until the physician arrived. For the immediate moment, it was enough that he was still alive and, obviously, had been transferred to the largest military hospital in the British West Indian islands.

A quarter of an hour later, the door opened and a portly, middle-aged officer wearing the gold epaulet of a captain came into the room. "Well, Mr. Beaufort," he said, "I'm told you've recovered your wits."

"I was out of my mind, Doctor?"

"For ten days and nights," Captain Carey said. "A large section of the *Dolphin*'s quarterdeck was removed from your thigh in the ship's surgery, and you lost a great deal of blood. But we should soon have you in shape again."

"What's become of the *Dolphin*, sir?"

"She put into the base at St. Kitts, our sister island across the channel, for repairs, which were completed yesterday. Lord Saunders filled out his crew with convalescents I was releasing. The usual system. He stopped in to see you before he sailed yesterday, but I'm afraid you didn't know him."

"I'm sorry."

"Be glad you're alive," the physician said dryly. "Lord Saunders wanted to sail to Jamaica after the battle, but his ship was too battered and he carried too many wounded, so he put in here."

So fate had intervened again. Had the *Dolphin* reached Kingston, Jeremy realized, his reunion with Lisa would have been inevitable during his convalescence. Now, hundreds of miles of Caribbean waters separated them.

"What became of the American ship we fought, Doctor?"

The physician shrugged. "All we know is that she went off under her own sail. If the damned Americans always fight that hard and well, this will be a long and vicious war, I can tell you."

Jeremy was startled by a sudden thought: neither Captain Carey nor the members of his staff quite realized that their patient was an American who had been impressed, then had won his officer's rank under circumstances that were unique. Henceforth he would be treated like any other English officer, and would be deprived of Lord Saunders' sympathy and understanding.

The physician examined Jeremy's thigh, then changed the dressing. "If all goes well now, you'll have no further complications."

"How long will I be here, sir?"

"The very same question all of them ask," Captain Carey replied with a laugh. "I make no predictions, Lieutenant. We'll see how heartily you eat, how soon you start taking exercises to strengthen your leg, and how consistently you work at regaining your health."

"Will I be returning to the *Dolphin?*"

"Anything is possible in time of war, but offhand I doubt it. Lord Saunders has a full complement again. In due time, you'll pay a visit to the base at St. Kitts, and when you're ready for duty, you'll be posted to the first ship that drops anchor at St. Kitts. I needn't tell you that the ways of the Royal Navy, like those of God, are impossible to predict."

Jeremy forced a smile. "Yes, sir." He hadn't known that much about the British Navy, but he was learning rapidly.

After spending another week in bed, Jeremy was allowed to hobble around his room with the aid of a crutch. For the first time he examined his wound, and was surprised to see a livid eighteen-inch scar that he would carry for the rest of his days.

He was regaining his strength, and, still walking with the aid of his crutch, he was finally allowed to go to the mess maintained for officer patients to eat their meals. All patients, officers and rating alike, were issued bathrobes of white cotton, so Jeremy was told to wear his hat to the mess hall for purposes of identification.

He had not shaved in the three weeks that had passed since he had sustained his wound, and he imagined he looked somewhat ludicrous in his full, growing beard, bicorne hat, and white robe. A score of other officers were gathering in the mess hall when he limped in, and as all of them were similarly attired, he forgot his self-consciousness.

"Beaufort!" someone shouted.

Jeremy turned, to see Lieutenant Gough, whose head was bandaged. At no time had they been on friendly terms, the former first mate of the *Dolphin* having resented the American's rapid rise. But both had suffered wounds in the same engagement, and they shook hands with genuine enthusiasm.

"You're looking well, Ben," Jeremy lied.

Gough laughed. "About as well as you do," he replied with a broad grin.

They sat next to each other at the long table, and Lieutenant Gough brought Jeremy up to date. Yet another junior lieutenant, an officer named Sylvester, was a patient at the hospital and was expected to recover. Two others, a senior lieutenant and a midshipman, had died of their injuries.

In the days that followed, Jeremy and Gough became constant companions, and as they walked together on the hospital grounds overlooking the small harbor and town of Charlestown, they fought the battle again.

"Our mistake was closing with the *Bald Eagle*," Gough said. "We underestimated the accuracy of Yankee gunners. We should have stayed out of range of the American six-pounders and inundated them with shot from our six-pounders. There's no other way to beat a crew with their talent for hitting a target."

Jeremy was cautious, and knew better than to express his pride in the *Bald Eagle*'s gunnery.

"At least we weren't battered in vain," Gough said. "You can be quite sure the story of our experience is being spread to every Royal Navy ship in New World waters, and from now on our captains will show a healthy respect for the filthy Yanks. I do beg your pardon, Jeremy. I forget that you were one of them."

In a sense, Jeremy thought, he was being complimented. When he returned to active duty, he again would face the dilemma of avoiding a battle with his fellow countrymen.

Until then, he was being accepted without question as a Royal Navy officer in good standing.

Soon he and Gough were joined by Lieutenant Sylvester, an officer of Jeremy's age, and as they grew stronger, their regimen was changed. Each morning the trio took long walks on the isle of Nevis, eventually climbing to the top of the 3,500-foot mountain that was the highest there. In the afternoons, when the weather was hotter, they adjourned to a beach outside Charlestown and spent two or three hours swimming.

Jeremy's leg healed sufficiently for him to discard his crutch, but he continued to walk with a slight limp that, although it did not impede him in any way, nevertheless would not be cured for the rest of his days. He enjoyed a good appetite again, his walks and afternoon swims restored his health, and he knew he was being kept on the hospital roster only because no new assignment had yet opened for him.

Occasionally Gough and Sylvester went into Charlestown for an evening, but Jeremy refrained from accompanying them. Both drank to excess, which he did not enjoy, and invariably ended their excursions by paying a visit to a local bordello. Sarah Benton was still ever-present in his mind; he thought frequently about Lisa, too; and he wanted no additional complications in his personal life.

One morning the hospital idyll came to an abrupt end. Lieutenants Gough, Beaufort, and Sylvester were ordered to gather their belongings and proceed without delay to a pier in Charlestown, where a Royal Navy gig awaited them. All three went to the wharf, with orderlies carrying their belongings, and were rowed the short distance to the base at St. Kitts.

Only one ship rode at anchor in the harbor, a small but sturdy vessel that was fore- and aft-rigged, with the larger mast emplaced nearer the bow and the smaller set astern. Her name was the *Lark*.

The trio scrutinized the ship at length and in silence, then exchanged glances. None would have volunteered for duty on a vessel that small.

Benjamin Gough broke the silence. "The *Lark*," he said,

"is either a mail ship or a bomb ketch. At this distance, it isn't possible to distinguish."

Jeremy prayed silently. Mail ships, which carried official messages to the various fleets in New World waters, were noncombatants and carried only enough armaments to protect themselves when attacked. An assignment to such a ship well might make it possible for him to avoid battle with an American warship.

The passengers disembarked from the gig at a stone jetty that stood beneath the most imposing building on the little island of St. Kitts. Known as the Fort, it had been built more than a century earlier, when the island had belonged to France.

They climbed the steep hill, and the salutes of royal marine sentries at the entrance to the Fort reminded the trio that they were returning to active duty, although none needed such reminders.

They were admitted without delay to the private office of the base commander, white-haired Vice Admiral Sir Howard Hazeltine. Well past the normal retirement age, the admiral stayed on active duty at a land post in order to free a younger senior officer for sea duty. He welcomed the trio cordially, offered them glasses of sack, and then settled back in his chair.

"I'm sure you're pleased by the prospect of going back to work, gentlemen," he said.

All three smiled and nodded.

"Lieutenant Gough, you're about to become the captain of your own ship. Lieutenant Beaufort, you'll serve as mate. Lieutenant Sylvester, you're posted as armaments officer."

Jeremy's heart sank. A ship carrying a full-time armaments officer was destined for combat duty.

"You've already seen your ship in the harbor, the bomb ketch *Lark*," the admiral said. "Your complement includes an ensign and a midshipman, who await you on board, and twenty-nine ratings. I suggest you inspect your ship and then return here to dine with me. At that time you can let me know what additional supplies and munitions you may need. You'll sleep on board tonight, and tomorrow morning you can come ashore to make any last-minute personal purchases you wish. I urge you to sail on the afternoon tide tomorrow."

An admiral's "suggestion" was a firm order, of course. "May I know my assignment, sir?" a crisp but pleased Lieutenant Gough asked.

"You're being attached to the squadron commanded by Rear Admiral Cockburn, but finding him will be no simple matter. In the past week he's been reported off the southern coast of Hispaniola, near Virgin Gorda, and menacing Guadeloupe. Obviously an impossibility for anyone, even an elusive devil like Cockburn. Don't be surprised if it takes you some weeks at sea before you locate him, Gough."

"I'll find him, sir!"

"I'm sure you will." The admiral dismissed them with a wave. "I'll expect you at my house at four this afternoon, gentlemen."

Gough automatically took the place on the right as they walked down the hill, with Jeremy beside him and Sylvester on the left. It was difficult for Jeremy to realize he had been made second in command of a Royal Navy ship. He tried to console himself with the thought that the primary mission of a bomb ketch was that of blowing up enemy ships at anchor in harbors and destroying land installations. Such vessels rarely took an active part in sea battles, so his situation could have been much worse.

A snub-nosed gig manned by a boatswain and four sailors was waiting at the quay, and all stood at rigid attention as their new commander and the senior members of his staff approached. It was astonishing, Jeremy thought, that in a little less than a year he had risen to the position of first mate on a British warship. The law and the life of a planter were far behind him now, and for as far ahead as he could see, he would pursue the profession of a sailor. He had no choice, so he was forced to accept his destiny.

The new master of the *Lark* was piped aboard the bomb ketch with due ceremony, the pipes of a boatswain's mate twittering and the entire company assembled on the squat main deck. The ensign and the midshipman presented themselves, and Captain Gough spoke a few words.

"I expect every man to carry out his assigned duties," he said. "Do what's expected of you, and you'll have no difficulties with Lieutenant Beaufort and me. Fail to carry out an order, and you'll regret it. We expect no problems, however, and you'll be treated fairly. We're going to make an inspection now, and assuming that everything is in order and shipshape, I'll grant shore leave to the company until midnight tonight. But I'll want a junior officer and six men to volunteer for guard duty. Mr. Beaufort, you may dismiss the company."

"Aye, aye, sir." Jeremy's new position was official now, and he gave his first order: "Company, dismissed!"

While Lieutenant Sylvester went off to make a careful study of the armaments for which he would be responsible, Captain Gough and his mate made a thorough inspection of the entire vessel. Quarters for living and sailing were cramped but surprisingly comfortable. The *Lark* was one of the older ships in the Royal Navy, built prior to the American War of Independence, so the cook's galley, the officers' wardroom, and the captain's quarters were larger than those on newer ketches.

What pleased Jeremy was his own cabin. At last he would have his own private world, to which he could retire when not on duty. Compact but tidy, the cabin was located directly forward of the master's quarters, and contained a full-length bed, two chairs, and a table that folded into the bulkhead. There was ample room in a cupboard for uniforms and other gear, and on the inner bulkhead were several bare shelves. Jeremy intended to fill them before the day ended.

He made notes of equipment that was missing, including spare masts and extra sails, and when Lieutenant Sylvester indicated that some of his bomb fuses were imperfect, he added new ones to his list.

When the inspection was ended, Gough and Jeremy went ashore again, first visiting the commissary to order food staples, which would be placed on board early the following morning. Officers were expected to pay for their own food and liquor, but their basic rations came from the commissary, as did those of the enlisted men.

The next stop was the open market in St. Kitts, and

there Jeremy and his superior purchased a variety of fresh and dried fruits, rice, peas, Caribbean sweet potatoes, and coconuts. They also put in a supply of rum and dinner wines for their own use.

After assuring themselves that their purchases would be delivered to the *Lark* at dawn the following day, they wandered through the town, then went their separate ways, and Jeremy was elated when he found a bookstore.

His pockets still bulging with the wages he had been paid during his convalescence, he splurged on the legal volumes he was fortunate enough to find, including books on common law, torts, commercial law, and international law, all of them the former property of a Royal Navy judge advocate who had sold them when he had retired. The mere fact that Jeremy bought them told him he was eager to return to his own profession at the first opportunity. Now, at least, he would be supplied with reading matter for his spare time and could brush up on the law that he had been compelled to neglect for so many months.

Going on from shop to shop, he purchased a fine oil lamp that would enable him to read in his cabin at night, a sextant and compass for his own private use, and a new pocket watch, his first since the one he had owned had disappeared when he had been abducted.

A sailor from the *Lark* took his purchases back to the ship. Jeremy had an hour to kill, so he sat at a small table on the patio of an inn that faced the main shopping street and ordered himself a nonalcoholic punch.

Most of the passersby were sailors, navy-yard construction workers, and native blacks who appeared to be freemen rather than slaves. There were few plantations on the little island, and the only business of consequence conducted was that of the Royal Navy base. Occasionally an officer walked down the street, but ladies were conspicuous by their absence. St. Kitts was regarded as an advance post, and in wartime, wives and daughters were not allowed to accompany their husbands and fathers here, even when an officer was a member of the permanent base cadre.

There was no absence of women, however. Numerous

harlots were highly visible, some white and some black. A few were surprisingly well dressed, and two or three rode in the back seats of their own open carriages, which they left when they visited shops.

Many of the women smiled at Jeremy, but he was careful to give them no encouragement. It pained him to think of Lisa accepting money from men in return for her favors, and he tried to put her out of his mind, but in vain. It hurt him even more to think of his beloved Sarah and to wonder what she was doing.

Trying to be realistic, he knew he had to face the possibility that she had abandoned hope for him and assumed he was dead. In that event, he realized, she well might have formed a romantic attachment with someone else. Sarah was too lovely, too charming, and too intelligent to spend the rest of her days alone. Suitors would flock to her, and rather than waste her life by grieving for him, it was inevitable that she would marry another man.

The very idea was desperately upsetting, but he told himself he had to face it squarely. All the same, he could not allow himself to dwell on the mental picture of another man making love with Sarah. Displaying great firmness, he shut the image out of his mind.

Promptly at four o'clock Jeremy presented himself at the house of Vice Admiral Sir Howard Hazeltine, the largest dwelling on the island. Gough and Sylvester arrived at the same time, and the admiral was waiting for them. He was a widower, and it appeared at first that he lived alone, but the three young officers soon became aware of the presence, in the background, of a middle-aged Englishwoman in a flower-print silk dress who was supervising the activities of the servants. The officers were not presented to her, and they guessed that she was Sir Howard's mistress.

The meal was the best that Jeremy had eaten since he had last dined with Lisa at the Star Apple in the Liguanea Hills of Jamaica. The first course was a spicy West Indian tripe soup, so thick that it more closely resembled a stew. Next came a grilled fish, remarkably fresh, that had been caught only an hour earlier. It was followed by a succession of principal courses, including roasts of beef and pork, baked chicken, and West Indian meat pies, each accompanied by platters of vegetables. The main dessert was an open-topped fruit pie. A different wine was served with each course, and a rare port followed the cheese.

The admiral ate sparingly, but well remembered his own youth and correctly gauged the appetites of his guests. They did full justice to the feast.

Inevitably the conversation turned to America's entry into the war. "I think the crown's ministers have made a grave error," the admiral said. "We can't fight Bonaparte in Europe and the United States in the New World at the same time. In my opinion, it is a disaster to split our forces. We can muster only a few divisions—at most—in Canada for an invasion of the United States from the north, and even though our navy is the best on earth, we can't do the impossible."

"Impossible, sir?" Jeremy asked, realizing the admiral didn't know he was an American.

"Look at the facts," Hazeltine said. "The United States effectively controls all territory along the eastern seaboard from Maine through Georgia, an enormous distance. Since Spain is so weak, she also controls the waters off the Floridas. She has a long coastline on the Gulf of Mexico, too, and the addition of the Louisiana Territory a few years ago gives her a vast landmass, not to mention effective control of the Mississippi River. Not even our navy can mount an effective blockade of that large a country."

"It's my understanding, sir," Gough said, "that London is following the strategy of first defeating Bonaparte and then turning our full might against the Americans. Surely that makes sense!"

The admiral shook his head. "I wish it did," he said. "But London forgets that America is now a nation of seven and a half million people. We couldn't defeat her in her Revolution when she had only two million and a territory that extended only as far as the Appalachian Mountains. I say the Royal Navy and Army have been given a mission they can't possibly fulfill."

"Then what will be the outcome, sir?" Jeremy wanted to know.

The old sailor's smile was wistful. "No one will benefit, as I've learned after fighting in five wars, but this will be the most frustrating. We'll do a great deal of damage to the young American nation. They'll harm us, too, as they're already doing. In four or five engagements, their gunnery has been magnificent and their seamanship has been more than adequate. If they had the ships, guns, and manpower, they well might fight us to a draw."

"You don't think Great Britain will win the war, Admiral?"

"Neither side will win. Neither will lose. After the fighting stops, which it will, there will be a new legacy of hatred on both sides that will take many decades to overcome. More's the pity, because we're basically the same people, with the same ideals, the same heritage of personal liberty, and the same dedication to the cause of the dignity of man."

"Mr. Beaufort, you may weigh anchor and set sail."

"Aye, aye, sir." Jeremy gave the necessary orders, and HMS *Lark* began to inch her way cautiously out of the St. Kitts harbor.

As second in command he stood on the quarterdeck beside the master of the bomb ketch, marveling at the fate that had led him into his present position. He would take the next watch, and so, after they cleared land, he retired to his own cabin. There, in snug privacy, he lighted a pipe and settled down to a leisurely study of the law books he had purchased. Only now could he begin to appreciate the advantages of his new post.

In the next week he never lost sight of the prerogatives that the mate of a warship enjoyed. His responsibilities were many, to be sure, but he lived the life of a gentleman, he was subject only to the orders of his one superior, and the rest of the ship's company obeyed every command he gave.

During the next week the *Lark* sailed westward to Hispaniola, making a loop around the island and taking care to avoid units of the French West Indies fleet that might be lurking in the vicinity. There was no sign of Admiral Cockburn's squadron anywhere. A number of merchantmen were sighted, and in all probability at least some of them were either French or American, but the *Lark* carried only one nine-pounder and two six-pounder cannon in addition to her bombs. Consequently, she lacked the strength to engage in battle and take prizes.

Benjamin Gough took a philosophical approach when he and Jeremy discussed the matter one evening as they relaxed together in the master's relatively spacious cabin. "Cockburn really is a devil, you know. He never stays in one place, so it may take us a long time to find him. But I'm in no hurry."

Neither was Jeremy. The longer the bomb ketch could avoid an engagement with American warships, the more relief he felt. Nevertheless, he felt compelled to put up a front. "Why is that, Ben?"

"In the first place, you and I are enjoying ourselves." Gough was candid. "If we were stationed on a ship of the line, or even a frigate, I'd be sharing a cabin with two or three other senior lieutenants, and you'd be crowded into quarters with a half-dozen juniors. You'd stand far down the line of command, and I wouldn't be all that much higher. I tell you true, Jeremy, we're little gods, and this assignment will do us no harm on our service records. If this war lasts long enough, I'll be an admiral."

Jeremy did not share his ambition, and prayed that the war would end soon so he could return home, marry Sarah, and resume his own career.

The following day, at noon, the captain was scheduled to relieve him on watch but did not appear. Punctuality was the hallmark of an officer, so Jeremy sent a seaman to the master's cabin to learn the reason for his tardiness.

The sailor soon returned. "Captain Gough lies abed, sir," he said, "and he's loony."

"I beg your pardon?"

"He don't make no sense, sir."

Jeremy summoned Lieutenant Sylvester, and turning the ship over to him, went to the master's cabin himself.

There he found Ben Gough in bed, his cheeks flushed and his eyes bright. The young American had been afraid he had consumed too much liquor, but it was apparent he was suffering from a high fever, which was worse.

A pharmacist's mate, the only man with any medical training on board the ketch, was called to the cabin. He examined the patient, who was babbling incoherently, then turned to the mate. "The captain is stricken with island fever, sir. I've seen it often, and I'm sure my diagnosis is right."

"Island fever?"

"Yes, Mr. Beaufort. I have medication in my stores that I'll give him twice a day, and he should recover. The ailment is sometimes fatal, but rarely when it's caught this early."

"How long will it take him to recover?"

The pharmacist's mate shrugged. "There's no telling, sir. Anywhere from a few days to a fortnight."

Jeremy immediately assumed command of the ship, with Lieutenant Sylvester automatically moving up to the position of mate. For the next week, somewhat to his own surprise, the American performed creditably.

He sailed to the Virgin Islands in search of Rear Admiral Cockburn, and when the hunt proved fruitless, he turned southward, giving the French islands of Martinique and Guadeloupe a wide berth. Twice he saw French warships whose size and armaments would have sent him to the bottom, but he exercised masterful seamanship and slipped away from them.

On the fifth day of his command, an even greater problem confronted him. A scant hour before dusk, he sighted three vessels, one of them a frigate, another an armed schooner, and the third a merchant brig that had been converted into a warship.

The frigate challenged him, raising her colors, and he caught his breath when he saw the Stars and Stripes. Here was his opportunity: he could hoist a white flag of surrender and rejoin his own countrymen at last.

But there were complications. Four British officers and twenty-nine enlisted men would be taken prisoner, and his own impressment in the Royal Navy did not give him the right to send the Englishmen to prison camps for the rest of the war. They were depending on him for their safety, and if he was unfaithful to his trust, he would betray them.

Something else caused him to hesitate, too. How would the squadron leader react when he found a fellow American wearing a Royal Navy uniform and commanding a Royal Navy warship? It would be difficult to explain the extraordinary events that had led to his rise. And if his fellow Americans refused to believe his strange but true tale, they would be within their rights, under the international rules of war, to hang him as a traitor.

The odds were weighted in favor of flight, so he ran.

The American squadron, which could sail faster than the lumbering bomb ketch, gave chase. But the approach of nightfall gave Jeremy the break he needed, and he managed to escape under cover of darkness.

"You're a natural-born sailor," Lieutenant Sylvester told him. "No captain could have managed that feat better than you did."

Jeremy had cause for elation, but instead he felt sad. Day by day, it seemed, his problems were being compounded.

Forty-eight hours later, Captain Gough was sufficiently recovered from his illness to return to duty, and a relieved Jeremy, accepting his superior's praise for a task well done, reverted to his position of mate.

The days that followed were uneventful. Admiral Cockburn's squadron remained elusive, and Gough decided to stop off at Barbados to see if he could learn anything about the admiral's whereabouts.

Jeremy was on watch when the *Lark* changed course, and had a few words with the master, who relieved him at midnight. "I don't like this weather, sir," he said. "The sea is glassy, the wind has dropped away to nothing, and those clouds have a nasty look."

It was true that the sky was heavily overcast, obscuring the stars and moon, but Gough shrugged. "This isn't the hurricane season, so we won't worry. We may be in for a little squall, but it shouldn't be serious. I suggest you turn in and get a good night's sleep. You well deserve it."

Jeremy went off to his own cabin, and, too tired to read, went straight to bed. Within moments he was asleep.

He was awakened by the repeated crash of thunder and the sound of the wind howling through the rigging. The

Lark was rocking and pitching simultaneously in a motion that sailors sometimes called a "corkscrew," and the whole vessel shuddered when a heavy wave slapped her hull broadside.

Jeremy knew instantly that his own premonitions had been right and that the storm was far worse than Ben Gough had anticipated. In the whole year he had served in the Royal Navy, he had never encountered a storm this severe.

He dressed quickly, donned his foul-weather cloak, and then made his way to the quarterdeck. The wind was so strong that he had to cling to the rail to keep from being blown overboard, and he fought his way hand over hand down the main deck. The rain was so heavy that he could see only a few feet in front of him, and it seemed to be blowing almost horizontally, which further impeded his vision. The sea was raging, with mountainous, frothing waves crashing over the prow, washing over the main deck, and even lapping over the stern. Flashes of lightning appeared in the sky, and the intermittent roar of thunder mingled with the shrieks of the wind and the crashing of the waves.

At last Jeremy reached the quarterdeck. There he followed the example of the captain and the helmsman by lashing himself to the rail.

"Damnation, but you were right!" Gough shouted. "This storm is as bad as any hurricane I've ever seen!"

As nearly as Jeremy could judge, the wind was blowing with a force-nine velocity, force ten being the maximum.

The mainsail had been lowered, he noted, and the *Lark* was using only her jib. He realized it was literally impossible for the small ship to remain on course in the freak storm. The problem now was even more fundamental, that of remaining afloat.

The captain tried to head into the wind so he wouldn't capsize, and gave a steady stream of instructions to the helmsman. But the gale was capricious, the wind seemed to shift constantly, and the sea responded accordingly. At times the main deck was awash under as much as a half-foot of water.

"We're battened down as snug as we can make her," Gough said. "All we can do now is ride it out."

The jib looked as though it might break loose at any moment, and Jeremy wondered if it might not be wise to lower this last sail, too. It wasn't his place to make the suggestion, however, and he understood the captain's reluctance to leave the ship completely at the mercy of the storm. The presence of the little jib at least gave him the feeling that he had some voice in the *Lark's* destiny.

Gradually the wind slackened and the rain lessened, although the sea remained exceptionally heavy.

"I reckon we're in the eye of the storm now, sir," Jeremy said, and saw something of a break in the thick clouds that raced across the night sky.

"It may be that the worst is still to come," Gough said. "Take the watch, Mr. Beaufort."

"Aye, aye, sir." Jeremy was surprised.

The captain's smile was weary. "I'll soon be back. I want to see what damage has been done below. I'm particularly interested in seeing whether our gunpowder cargo has shifted. Or has been dampened and ruined by a leak."

He untied the lines that held him fast, then negotiated the steps to the main deck and lurched off.

The *Lark* continued to corkscrew.

Jeremy concentrated on his immediate task, that of giving minute-by-minute and even second-by-second instructions to the helmsman.

He was surprised when a seaman materialized beside him and handed him a mug of steaming tea.

He sipped it gratefully. "How bad is the damage below?"

"We're watertight, sir," the sailor replied. "But this be the last hot drink you'll be taking. The cap'n has ordered the cooking fire put out."

The precaution was wise, Jeremy thought.

The sky grew blacker, the wind velocity increased, and the rain became heavier, with a bolt of lightning appearing in the distance, followed by a long, deep rumble of thunder. Obviously the eye of the storm had passed overhead, and the gale was freshening.

The master of the bomb ketch appeared through a forward hatch, which he took care to close behind him, then began to fight his way aft, clinging to the rail as he moved step by step.

The prow of the *Lark* dipped into a deep trough, and a moment later a solid wall of onrushing water loomed high overhead.

Never had Jeremy seen such a huge wave. It dwarfed the ship, and he shouted a warning, but a peal of thunder drowned his voice.

The wave swept over the entire vessel, drenching Jeremy and the helmsman, and Jeremy knew that only the line that was fastened to the rail prevented him from being washed into the sea.

After the wave had passed, there was no sign of Ben Gough anywhere on the deck.

"Man overboard!" Jeremy cried, but he knew the shout was futile. It was impossible to stand to and pick someone up out of the raging sea.

He looked back and saw the mammoth wave rolling onward across the open Caribbean.

Gough was gone, and Jeremy had to take command of the ship.

The storm became still wilder, and he had no chance to mourn the loss of the officer who had become his friend. He needed all of his strength, all the knowledge of seamanship that he had learned and experienced if he hoped to ride out the storm.

The lightning and thunder were drawing still closer, and the sky seemed to empty itself as the rain fell in torrents.

Suddenly a crack of lightning appeared directly overhead, followed instantly by a deafening peal of thunder. A horrified Jeremy saw that the lightning had struck near the base of the mainmast, tearing it from its moorings. It fell slowly, still partly supported by its lines, and finally crashed onto the main deck. It had barely missed the quarterdeck, and surely would have killed both Jeremy and the shocked helmsman.

Before Jeremy could summon help from below to cut

the mast loose, another bolt of lightning found the ship, confounding the theory that it never struck twice in the same place. This time the lightning hit amidships, and Jeremy's last conscious, rational thought was that it might be eating into the gunpowder magazine.

A tremendous explosion sounded above the roar of thunder and the howling of the wind, and HMS *Lark* was literally blown apart, totally disintegrating in a matter of seconds.

Jeremy had no knowledge of being catapulted into the sea until he struggled to the surface and fought with all his might to remain afloat. The bomb ketch was gone, and in the dark he could make out bits of wreckage that the storm was quickly scattering.

Dazed and scarcely aware of what he was doing, he nevertheless had enough presence of mind to realize he would lose what remained of his strength if he continued to fight the elements. To the best of his knowledge, he was the ship's only survivor, but he, too, would drown unless he gathered his wits.

Suddenly a long, dark shape loomed nearby, and with a pounding heart Jeremy realized it was the mast, which was floating. He managed to remove his boots, then used his last reserves of waning energy as he swam to it.

The base was four feet in diameter, and he hauled himself onto it, gasping for breath, scarcely able to force his body to obey his mind.

Several lengths of water-soaked line were still attached to the mast, and Jeremy worked until there was no feeling left in his fingers, lashing himself to the base. That task accomplished, he lost consciousness.

The storm abated by dawn, the sea became calm, and the Carribbean sun rose in a bright, cloudless sky.

A large ship sailing eastward passed within a quarter of a mile of the still-floating mast, and the lookout in the crow's nest caught sight of the man in the bedraggled Royal Navy officer's uniform who had tied himself to it.

A boat was lowered, oarsmen propelled it across the sea, and the boatswain in charge of the operation was astonished to discover that the man who had lashed himself to the mast was still breathing. Jeremy was cut loose, and, more dead than alive, was placed in the boat as it turned and started back toward its mother ship.

Chapter 15

Three days before the wedding of Margot Benton and Tom Beaufort, guests began to arrive for the festivities, many from Charleston and from South Carolina plantations, some from Savannah, and others from as far as Richmond. Oakhurst Manor was so crowded, with every available room occupied, that the bride-to-be had to move in with her sister. The Emersons lent their full assistance, as always, and the overflow found accommodations at Trelawney, their estate.

The war with Great Britain did not interfere with the celebrations. The South was responding with its usual patriotic fervor to calls to arms, and there were few expressions of the sentiment so common in New England, where the hostilities were called "President Madison's war." The sons of seacoast dwellers, young men familiar with the sea, were volunteering in large numbers for the new, expanding United States Navy. But the army had issued no similar calls. The small standing army was bearing the brunt of fighting on land, and militia units of the individual states had not yet been ordered to serve beyond their own borders. So most young men were not yet in uniform, although most of them were anticipating that, sooner or later, they would serve.

The British blockade of American ports was taking a toll, it was true, so there was a shortage of various goods. No silks were being imported from France or elsewhere, and the importation of cotton cloth from England had been halted. But the young industries of America were resourceful, and there were not only ample quantities of bolts of wool, muslin, and linen, but new factories were coming into being in New England, New York, and Pennsylvania to manufacture cotton.

French wines were in short supply, although limited amounts slipped through the blockade, and many plantations, including Oakhurst Manor, began making their own wine from their own grapes. In general, however, the people of the still-expanding and growing United States were making a remarkable discovery. Paul Wellington Beaufort summed up the situation at dinner the night before the wedding when he said, "Nature has given this country so many good things that we need to depend on the outside world for almost nothing. Our shipyards are building merchantmen and war vessels faster than anyone would have thought possible. We do need more iron and steel products than we're getting, but I'm sure enough new foundries are being constructed to take care of that shortage, too. As General Andy Jackson of Tennessee said the other day in a speech, the United States isn't an infant nation anymore. We're big enough and tough enough to stand on our own feet."

Sarah Benton had no opportunity to think about the war, other than to wonder and worry, as she did every day and every night, how Jeremy was faring. Four and a half months had passed since he had vanished, and a great many things had happened during that time, including the stormy romance, betrothal, and impending marriage of Margot and Tom, but in all that time Jeremy had never for a moment been out of her heart and mind.

Now, however, she had her hands so full that she could not allow herself to dwell actively on the tragedy. Papa Paul expected her to act as the hostess at Oakhurst Manor, and with more than twenty guests in the house, not to mention another twenty at Trelawney and several more housed at other nearby plantations, every moment of each day was occupied.

She was fortunate, as she well knew, that she had the help of Cleo, who was working with an augmented kitchen staff to prepare the wedding feast. Hams and turkeys smoked on the Beaufort property were garnished, and a double pit was dug under Mr. Higby's supervision for the barbecuing of a side of beef and another of ox. Two wagons brought fresh crab and fish from Charleston's waters, and chickens, ducks, and geese by the dozen were baked in the huge charcoal ovens. Sweet potatoes were candied, white potatoes were creamed, and a half-dozen vegetables were cleaned and made ready for last-minute cooking.

At Sarah's insistence, there would be only one wedding cake, which would be mammoth, and no other dessert would be served. Cleo insisted on baking the cake herself, with help from no one else, but she finally relented sufficiently to permit Amanda to assist her. Apparently she had become half-reconciled to the hard fact that Willie and Amanda were living together, and she was forced to respect their reasons for not getting married. Under South Carolina law, a slave could only be half-married, as the phrase was known. Either a plantation owner or someone designated by him said a few words over a couple, and thereafter they were regarded as married.

But Amanda, a free woman from the North, refused to accept such a sham, stating bluntly that she preferred to live with Willie, accepting no ceremony of any kind, until such a time as they could be appropriately joined together by a clergyman. Willie, amenable to her in all things, had accepted her view without question.

Less than forty-eight hours before the wedding, Sarah made a careful tour of inspection of the manor house, and everything she saw was to her liking. A special serving maid had been assigned to take care of the needs of each guest, a gesture she would have regarded as shockingly flamboyant in her Spartan, native Massachusetts. Other servants were polishing the crystal chandeliers in the main drawing room and dining room, and yet others were cleaning the superb silver service and the bone chinaware, the tissue-thin glasses and handsome pewter goblets, the huge serving platters and ornamental crocks.

Ultimately she went out to the kitchen outbuildings, where she found a state of organized chaos. Three women were baking breads and buns, others were basting fowl in the ovens, and a team of four was marinating the sides of beef and ox that would be barbecued, pouring special sauces over them as they rested in mammoth vats.

Cleo, who held herself aloof, had just finished directing three young men in the delicate task of removing the bottom section of the wedding cake, one of four in a rising pyramid, from the special brick oven that had been constructed just for this purpose. The wheel, which stood more than a foot high, was almost five feet in diameter, and its pungent, spicy-sweet scent made Sarah's mouth water.

"You're a genius, Cleo," she said.

"Not do too bad," the housekeeper replied, unable to conceal her satisfaction. "Icing for this layer going to be all white, with yellow roses that Amanda say she going to make." She paused, looking puzzled. "Where that Amanda now? She want to see layer come out of oven."

It occurred to Sarah that she hadn't seen Amanda anywhere while making her rounds. "She must be around the property somewhere," she said.

The housekeeper glowered. "If Amanda and Willie go bed when all the people working, Cleo whup 'em!"

Sarah had to hide a smile. "I'm sure Willie is busy in his workshop making the special chest of drawers he's giving the bride and groom. It's the most handsome chest I've ever in my life seen, and I'm sure nothing would tear him away from it."

"Maybe so," Cleo said dubiously as she returned to an inspection of the savory wheel before placing the next-smaller layer in the oven.

Sarah decided to take the responsibility herself for locating Amanda. Dressed today in one of the low-necked, full-skirted gowns that Southern women frequently preferred to the more fashionable Empire style, she started across the yard to the house that Willie and Amanda now shared. She had to admit to herself that it was possible they were making love, in which case she would beat a discreet retreat, which was not how the indomitable Cleo would handle the situation.

She passed Cleo's solid dwelling, which was empty, but she stiffened as she approached the adjoining house. Someone was weeping, and she recognized Amanda's voice. Not wanting to intrude, Sarah hesitated.

Then she heard the deep rough voice of a man other than Willie, and although she couldn't make out what he was saying, it was impossible to miss the ugly, threatening tone of his voice. Gathering her voluminous skirt and petticoats in one hand, she pushed open the door with the other. The neat living room was deserted.

Sarah heard voices emanating from the adjoining chamber and moved to the entrance. The bedroom was a shambles, with chairs and bedside tables knocked over and one of Willie's prized cabinets on its side.

Crouching in a far corner was Amanda, holding a straight-backed chair in front of her for what little protection it could afford her. Her blouse was torn, half-exposing one of her breasts, and her hair was in disarray. She was weeping, her condition near hysteria, but stubborn defiance still blazed in her eyes.

Facing her, partway across the room, with a long bull-whip clutched in one hand, was Mr. Higby. He swayed slightly, then staggered as he stood menacing the girl with the whip, and it was apparent at a glance that he was under the influence of alcohol.

"I'm nobody's slave," Amanda said, her voice choked. "Get out of here and leave me alone."

"I don't care what you call yourself," the overseer replied in a thick voice. "Any order I give on this plantation is obeyed, and when I want a nigger woman, I take her. Fight me again, and I'll beat you so hard you'll never walk again."

Sarah completely lost her temper. "Mr. Higby!" Her voice was sharper than the crack of his whip.

The overseer wheeled in astonishment, was stunned for a moment, and then grinned. "This is no place for a lady.

Go back to the big house and let me tend to my own business in my own way."

"This is my business." Sarah was so furious she found it difficult to speak coherently. "Amanda is not only my maid and my friend, but she's a free citizen of the United States. As free as you, with the same rights. I refuse to tolerate such conduct for one minute, and I'll take you to court for this."

The overseer laughed aloud. "You ain't spent much time in the South, ma'am. There's nary a court in South Carolina will listen to any rubbish about the so-called rights of niggers."

"No one abuses any human being, black or white, slave or free, at Oakhurst Manor! Leave at once!"

Higby was finding it hard to focus, but the words made no sense to him. "I've seen you acting like you own this place, but you're just a guest here. You ain't married to Jeremy Beaufort, and it looks like you ain't never going to marry him. Because I reckon he's dead. I'm hired to keep blacks in their place, so don't interfere." He raised his whip over his head, menacing Sarah.

Whether he actually intended to strike her with the rawhide was a question the unflinching Sarah was never able to answer. Before she had a chance to reply or move, however, Amanda jumped from the corner and took hold of the overseer's wrist with both of her small but strong hands.

At that moment a gray streak shot across the room.

An instant later Higby was flat on his back, sprawled on the floor, with King N'Gao standing over him. The huge dog's front paws were on the man's chest, and, fangs bared, the animal stood ready to bury his teeth in the overseer's throat.

Higby was badly frightened. "For God's sake, call off this beast!"

Sarah realized she hadn't closed the front door of the cottage behind her. The dog knew she had become the mistress of Oakhurst Manor, even if the drunken supervisor had forgotten that fact, and was offering her his protection.

Sarah's relief was so great that she felt weak, but her voice remained firm. "Steady, N'Gao!"

The dog stayed poised, ready to strike, but did not move.

"Let him kill the bastard," Amanda muttered.

"No," Sarah said. "I won't permit murder at Oakhurst Manor, any more than I'll condone rape. It's obvious that you aren't yourself today, Mr. Higby. So any conversation we have should wait until you're sober. But I have only a few things to say to you, and I'm sure you'll remember them, no matter what your state."

"Call off this damn dog!" the overseer begged.

Sarah was in complete command of both herself and the situation now, and managed a smile. "Steady, N'Gao!" she repeated.

A deep snarl rumbled up inside the animal's chest.

"Mr. Higby," Sarah said, "I haven't interfered in the operation of the plantation, and I prefer to keep my hands off, if that can be managed. Jeremy told me a number of times that you're an efficient overseer, and that's one reason I may be willing to give you another chance. A second reason is that I'd rather not disturb Paul Beaufort this soon before the wedding. Or ask Tom to intervene, because he'd kill you with his bare hands."

Higby lay frozen, afraid the dog would attack if he dared to move.

"Sober up, and stay sober," Sarah said, "and I'll let this incident pass. Annoy Amanda again, just once, ever, and I swear to you that I'll have your hide for it. Just as I promise you'll regret it if King N'Gao is ever poisoned or harmed in any way. I trust I make myself clear."

"Yes, ma'am," the terrified overseer said in a barely audible voice.

"Heel, N'Gao!"

The powerful dog moved slowly to Sarah's side, but was still tense and alert, ready to attack in earnest if necessary.

"I trust you agree to my conditions, Mr. Higby?"

"Yes, ma'am." The overseer cautiously hauled himself to his feet, never taking his eyes off the animal. "No nigger woman is worth that beast's fangs."

"From now on," Sarah told him, "you're on probation. Make one false move, and you'll never hold another position in this state or anywhere else. It may be, as you say, that no black can expect justice in a South Carolina court. But you made an even bigger mistake when you threatened me."

"It won't happen again, I swear it!" The overseer inched out of the room.

The great dog growled again.

"Steady, now." Sarah placed a hand on his head to soothe him.

But he did not relax until the outer door closed, and then slowly wagged his tail.

The two girls embraced and hugged each other, then lavished praise and affection on King N'Gao, who leaped on them, happily licking their faces.

"Are you all right, Amanda?" Sarah wanted to know.

"Yes, thanks to you. My blouse is ruined beyond repair, but a heap worse could have happened."

"I'll repair your blouse. That's the least of it."

Amanda was grateful, but still troubled. "I'm not so sure you did the right thing, letting that overseer off."

"He's learned a lesson."

"Maybe so, maybe not. He treats the slaves decent enough when he's sober, but he's as mean as they come when he has a load of whiskey in his belly. I agree this is no time to tell Mr. Beaufort or Tom what he's done, but I'm not all that sure you persuaded him to behave himself."

"I did very little," Sarah said. "It was King N'Gao who did the persuading."

Amanda stroked the dog's massive head. "Willie said this animal was smarter than most folks, and he's right. One thing he knows for sure. You're the head lady around these parts, and he's not going to let anybody forget it!"

When Willie returned to his house from his woodworking shop shortly before sundown, he was puzzled by

Amanda's mood. Her gaiety was forced, she had little real interest in her discussion of the magnificent wedding cake that Cleo and she were making, and when Willie tried to question her, she became evasive.

Finally she could hold out no longer, and told him in full detail about the incident that had taken place earlier in the day.

He listened in silence, his lips compressed, and slowly flexed his fingers.

Amanda saw his expression, and wished she had kept silent. "Willie," she said, "Sarah and King N'Gao took care of that overseer, never fear. He's a coward, like all bullies, and he won't dare pester me again."

Willie moistened his dry lips. "You can be mighty sure of that, sweetie. Never again."

She stared at him for a moment. "I told you already. Sarah warned him off. You stay out of this."

He made no reply as he crossed their living room to an inlaid box he had made. It was filled with a variety of knives he used in his woodcarving work, and he picked out a curved blade, about eight inches long and double-edged, with a short bone handle.

Amanda became panicky. "Up North you'd get a fair hearing in court, but not here. Maybe you're treated like a free man, like one of the family. But technically you're still a slave. And I've been in this state long enough to know what will happen if you as much as raise your hand to that overseer. They'll hang you! That's the law here, and you know it!"

Willie smiled absently and patted her on the shoulder. "You and my mama have been working on that wedding cake for a long time. Maybe I've had a few ideas of my own about it. Like using a strawberry filling and an inside icing of that good chocolate we make from our own cocoa beans. But . . . have you heard me say one word? Have you or my mama heard me utter even one little bit of advice? No, ma'am. Willie is one fellow who knows how to keep his big nose out of a place it doesn't belong. Now, let's see how you stand. You have a pretty nose. Prettiest little nose I've ever seen. We want it to stay pretty, just

215

like it is, so I can admire it for the next fifty years. Maybe longer. As long as I live."

"You won't live more than a few days if you threaten that overseer or lay a hand on him!" Amanda threw her arms around him and clung to him. "Please, Willie, be sensible. I appreciate your loyalty. I appreciate your love. I appreciate what you want to do for me. But I've told you already, Sarah Benton has taken care of the problem, and you'll just get yourself murdered,—legally—if you interfere."

Willie kissed her, then gently disengaged himself. "I've been thinking hard," he said. "There's so much cooking up in my mama's kitchen that nobody would miss one of those fine chickens that are roasting or baking. Especially if you took it, seeing you're the only one my mama gives the run of the whole kitchen. A roast chicken. Some potatoes we'll bake in the ashes of our own fire. A pan of greens cooked in bacon fat. We'll have us a supper tonight better than any wedding feast."

Amanda was near tears.

"Do like I tell you," Willie said. "You tend to the supper while I look after some man's business, and I'll even be back here ahead of you."

Her voice caught in her throat, and she raised a hand to her mouth as he left the house.

Willie hummed the tune of "The World Turned Upside Down," a popular English song that had become the favorite of Americans after the conclusive Battle of Yorktown in the War of Independence. Fingering the blade of his curved knife, he strolled across the yard toward the far side of the mansion, looking as though he didn't have a care in the world.

Margot and Tom were standing on the lawn, arms linked, sipping glasses of sack as they engaged in small talk with some of the assembled guests. Both saw him and waved, and he raised an arm in return.

But his smile faded as he meandered past the mansion, and the sprightly song died on his lips. His face became expressionless and his eyes grew blank, as only a black man's could when he has lived his entire life in a society ruled by whites. He walked softly, his footsteps making no sound, and he nodded when he saw the light cast by a flickering oil lamp in the dining room of the overseer's house, a dwelling no larger than his own. He knew exactly what had to be done, and his touch was firm when he rapped on the door.

"Who is it, and what the hell do you want?" Mr. Higby's voice was rough after his drinking bout, but he sounded far more sober now.

Willie did not reply, instead entering and closing the door behind him.

The overseer was eating a meal of sowbelly, greens, and boiled chopped sweet potatoes cooked for him by an elderly slave who had departed as soon as she had served him.

Willie glanced at his plate, and thought it astonishing that the overseer, who could have had beef, poultry, or other foods that were commonplace at the mansion, chose dishes that even the most downtrodden field hands refused to touch more often than once a week. Jeremy had often remarked that the ignorant and small-minded descended to the lowest level of those with whom they associated, and as usual Jeremy had been right. Willie missed him, and reflected that if Jeremy were here, his own mission would have been unnecessary.

Mr. Higby saw the husky young black, glanced at the curved knife he held in his hand, and blanched, pushing back his chair and preparing to leap to his feet.

"Don't let me disturb your supper," Willie said in a deceptively calm voice. "You'll get the stomach cramps if you don't eat while your food is hot, and we wouldn't like that to happen."

"My day's work is done." There was a hint of fear in the overseer's voice. "If you want to talk to me, see me at my office after breakfast tomorrow."

"What with everybody getting ready for the wedding, we just don't want to waste your valuable time in the morning. That wouldn't be right, no, sir." Willie drew up a chair.

In spite of his apprehension, the overseer's temper rose. "Who gave you the right to sit?"

Willie remained amiable. "Well, now, I look at it this way. I can sit down in Mr. Paul's library without his giving me an invitation. I've sat all my life around Jeremy, and I do the same with Tom. Seeing as how they're all Beauforts and own this place, I don't reckon I have to stand on ceremony with one of their hired hands."

Mr. Higby had lost his appetite, and pushed his plate away. "I have plans for the evening, so let's hear what you have on your mind. Say it and be done with it."

Willie held his curved knife up to the light, then slowly and carefully tested the inner blade with his thumb. Satisfied with its sharpness, he did the same with the outer blade.

The overseer couldn't help looking in the direction of his bedroom, where he kept a brace of pistols.

The cabinetmaker read his mind, and an expression of mock concern appeared on his face. "There's no need for firearms when Willie comes calling. Willie never for a minute forgets he's a slave, especially when he's talking to the high-and-mighty overseer. No, sir. Not ever. Willie knows the law hereabouts, and he wouldn't raise this knife to a high-and-mighty overseer. Wouldn't even raise his fist without anything in it!"

"I'm glad to hear that." Mr. Higby continued to watch him with care.

"What I like most about Oakhurst Manor," Willie said, "is that everbody here feels just I do. Take the Beauforts. They know their place. So does my mama. So do the field hands."

The overseer sensed what was coming, and grew even more tense.

"My woman is the same way. You wouldn't know her, of course, having nothing to do with the house servants. But she's different. She's not only a ladies' maid to Sarah and Margot, but she's their friend, too. And that's not all. She's a free woman who can come and go as she wants."

"Under South Carolina law," Mr. Higby said, "a free black loses his freedom if he stays in the state more than three months."

Willie smiled bloodlessly and shook his head. "Only if

the owner of the plantation where he's living makes formal application to the courts. Which Mr. Paul wouldn't do. Neither would Jeremy, if he was here. And Tom would never think of doing it."

The overseer began to lose his fear, and grew more belligerent. "How do you know so much?"

Willie remained polite. "Oh, I can read and write well enough to go off to college. I was taught by Tom's tutor all the years I was growing up. That's why I think, sometimes, that my woman is right when she says we ought to go up North so we can be married the proper way by a preacher. But not right off. My mama would be lonely if I left. I like Tom's company, especially with the fishing season here and the hunting season coming up in a few months. And I sure wouldn't want to leave until I know for certain that Jeremy will be coming home and that he hasn't been hurt."

The message was clear, and Mr. Higby understood it: Willie and the black girl from the North had no intention of going elsewhere.

Again Willie held the knife up to the light and lightly ran a finger up the entire length of the wickedly curved inner blade. "Yes, sir," he said, "Amanda and I are happier than I can tell you that we live on a plantation where everybody knows his right place and stays in it. From the Beauforts themselves down to the newest field hand just off the slave ships from Africa. Amanda may be a free woman, but she knows her place hereabouts, and she's glad everybody at Oakhurst Manor treats her with respect. I'm glad, too. I can't tell you how glad I am." Willie slowly pulled himself to his feet and again went through the pantomime of testing the outer edge of his blade.

The overseer's forehead was bathed in cold sweat, and a steady trickle soaked his shirt.

For the first time Willie smiled. "Well, Mr. Higby, I don't want to interrupt your fine supper, so I'll be on my way. I do thank you for this little chat and for your hospitality."

He meandered out, the woodworking knife still in his hand, and soon he began to hum "The World Turned Upside Down." He had not only worked up an appetite for roast chicken, potatoes baked in ashes, and a mess of greens, but he felt he had earned the meal. No two ways about that.

Chapter 16

A smiling Isaiah Benton led his younger daughter up the aisle of the little country church, crowded to overflowing for the wedding. Sarah was her radiant sister's only attendant, and young Scott Emerson took the role of best man. Had Jeremy been present, he would have assumed that function, but this was one day that Sarah refused to allow herself to think about her beloved. Except that he remained ever-present in her mind.

The Reverend Dr. Edwin Humphries, Episcopal bishop of South Carolina, officiated, and after the young bride and groom exchanged vows, kissed, and made their way back up the aisle, the entire party, occupying more than forty carriages, escorted them back to Oakhurst Manor, with the best man and ushers, all mounted, providing a guard of honor.

When the whole party was assembled, the bride and groom were toasted, the wine coming from a shipment landed in Baltimore several weeks earlier by a brig that had managed to avoid the British blockade. Thereafter, for the rest of the celebration, domestic alcoholic beverages, including homemade wines, were served.

Then came the wedding feast, with guests sitting at long tables laid on the trim lawn. Isaiah Benton and Paul Wellington Beaufort made short speeches, as did young Scott Emerson. Tom Beaufort was asked to respond, but became completely tongue-tied for the first time in his life, and everyone laughed and applauded when Margot rose to her feet, kissed him, and then pulled him back into his chair.

A trio of fiddlers from North Carolina provided music in the ballroom, and after the bride and groom had danced alone, Margot radiant in a white gown trimmed with lace that had belonged to her grandmother, others joined in the dancing.

The first on the floor were Sarah and young Scott Emerson. Ordinarily he was a blunt, somewhat crass person, but today he displayed both discretion and a gentle touch. Bowing to her as she curtsied at the start of the quadrille, he said in a low voice, "I'm sorry I'm the one who is your partner today. I just want you to know that everyone here feels as I do."

Sarah thanked him with a fleeting smile and inclined her head. She was grateful that he hadn't mentioned Jeremy's name, and in a vain effort to put him out of her mind, she concentrated on her dancing. She had elected to wear an old-fashioned, full-skirted gown of pale green velvet, her hair was piled high on her head, with one long blond curl dropping across her bosom and pointing toward her cleavage, and she knew from the admiring glances of every man present that she looked ravishing.

She told herself she didn't really care how she looked, but she realized almost simultaneously that she was lying, fooling herself. The attention she received was flattering, and she knew that if Jeremy were here, he would be proud of her.

Returning to the bridal table after the quadrille, she drained her glass of wine, then asked Scott for a cup of the far more potent rum punch. He was a gentleman, to be sure, so he immediately asked a servant to bring her a cup, but he was unable to dissemble, and frowned.

As Sarah downed the punch, drinking it far too quickly, she became aware of her father and Lorene Small surreptitiously observing her. They had danced the first quadrille together, too, and a current was flowing back and forth between them, making it increasingly likely that he was the leading suitor for her hand.

Sarah was too immersed in her own thoughts and feelings to be aware of these subtleties, however. She declined an offer to join in the next dance, instead concentrating on another cup of rum punch, and she was somewhat surprised when Lorene moved down the table from her own seat and joined her.

"My dear," the older woman said, "I know how you're feeling today. But don't give in to it. Wherever Jeremy might be, he wouldn't want you to do it. Hold your head high."

"If I hold it any higher," Sarah replied, again draining her cup, "I'll have a stiff neck for a month." Her feeling of recklessness increasing, she requested a servant to refill her cup.

"Your father and I," Lorene said, choosing her words with care, "are hoping you've had your fill of rum."

Sarah laughed. "Today," she replied, "I could drink from a bottomless cup."

"I daresay you could," Lorene said, "but please remember that rum is a potent drink, especially for those who aren't accustomed to it."

Sarah lowered her voice, and for a moment she became serious. "I know you're right, Lorene. But just this once, I want to empty my mind completely. I must do it."

"Must?" The older woman was puzzled by her attitude, unlike any that she had ever before displayed. "Liquor solves no problems, you know."

"My problems are greater than anyone realizes." Offering no explanation, Sarah took a swallow from her fresh cup of punch.

Before Lorene could question her, they were interrupted by the cheers of the younger people. Tom and Margot had changed into traveling clothes, the bride wearing a dress of yellow linen, with a matching bonnet and stole, and they had just tried to sneak away in a carriage that Willie had brought to the side entrance for them. They had been discovered, however, and as Tom lifted Margot onto the buckboard, then took his place beside her and grasped the

reins, the younger members of the party gathered and
pelted them with handfuls of rice.

A laughing Margot still held her wedding bouquet, and
before they drove off in a shower of rice, she threw it into
the crowd, not aiming it in the direction of anyone.

By accident, or so it seemed, the bouquet landed in
Sarah's hand. She stared at it for a moment, biting back
the tears that threatened to run down her face, and then
returned to the festivities, where she began to drink in earnest.

Her father, Paul Beaufort, and a number of the younger
men tried to distract her, one by one insisting that she
dance with them. She accepted each time, but continued to
drink steadily whenever she returned to the table. By
nightfall, when the candles were lighted in the great chandeliers of Oakhurst Manor and flares blazed on the lawn,
her speech was slurred, she could no longer dance, and it
was apparent that all she had consumed had taken a toll.

Lorene quietly shepherded her into the house and up
the stairs. There Cleo materialized, and it was obvious that
she, too, had been concerned. The older woman and the
housekeeper managed to undress Sarah and attire her in
her nightgown. She smiled incessantly, but without
pleasure, and vaguely aware that her speech lacked coordi-
nation, she remained silent. Even before they drew the
draperies and extinguished the oil lamp, she dropped off to
sleep.

The two women exchanged a long, meaningful glance in
the dark, and there was no need for either to speak. They
communicated without words. Then Cleo turned away
abruptly and went down to the kitchen to supervise the
continuing flow of food and liquor for the guests.

Lorene waited, taking some minutes to compose herself
before she returned to the party.

Isaiah Benton was waiting for her, his expression anxious, and Lorene took his arm, guiding him across the
lawn to the darkness beyond the glare of the burning
flares. "Sarah had too much to drink, which was precisely
what she intended," she said. "She's sleeping now, and I
think it unlikely that she'll awaken again during the night.
If the experience has given her temporary relief, as I hope

it has, no harm is done. Her health is good, so by tomorrow she should be fit again, although she may suffer a headache for a time when she first gets up."

"You're very reassuring," Isaiah said as they halted near a mass of blooming honeysuckle. "She's old enough to look after herself, so I know I shouldn't worry. But Sarah is always so . . . so controlled, that I was surprised."

"Perhaps she's less controlled than you think."

"What do you mean, Lorene?"

She shrugged, her shoulders rising and falling beneath the thin fabric of her gown. "Isaiah Benton, you behave like a mother hen. One of your daughters was married today, and the other is as good as married, so share her faith that Jeremy will return to her someday. Now, sir, isn't it time you think of yourself?"

Isaiah's smile was a trifle rueful. "I can't rid myself of the habit of worrying about my girls. I've done it for so long that the whole process has become second nature to me."

"What will you do now?" she demanded. "Go back to Boston and spend the rest of your days fuming and stewing over matters beyond your ability to influence? Sarah and Margot aren't children anymore. They're women, and they'll lead their own lived in their own ways. I urge you to do the same."

"How I spend the rest of my life doesn't necessarily depend on me alone," Isaiah said.

The light of the flares of the far side of the lawn flickered across Lorene's face as she waited for him to continue.

"When a man reaches my age," he said, "he hates to act like a damn fool. Just about the last thing in the world he can stand is to have somebody laugh at him."

"Is someone laughing at you?"

"No, not yet. But you might," he said.

"I?"

"Yes, Lorene." Isaiah braced himself. "If I were to tell you that I've fallen in love with you. That I want to marry you and spend the rest of our lives together."

"I'm not laughing, dear," she said.

With one accord they embraced, then kissed.

225

Paul Wellington Beaufort stood alone near the portico of Oakhurst Manor, ashamed of himself for spying, yet unable to resist the urge to keep watch on Lorene and Isaiah. He had seen them engage in earnest conversation as they crossed the lawn. Then he had watched them as they had continued to talk. Now, when he saw them kiss, it was too much for him, and he turned away.

He had lost Lorene in fair competition, but a wave of loneliness swept over him, and he felt empty, desolate. For whatever good it did, her hand had been won by a man he could respect, a man who would treat her with all of the gentle love and consideration she deserved.

Without realizing what he was doing, Paul reached out a hand and touched one of the white columns that graced the front of the great house and supported the portico roof. Absently running his hand up and down, he reflected that he still had Oakhurst Manor. His heritage. The heritage he would pass on to his still-missing son and the son who had been married only today. He loved his plantation with all his heart, as much as many men were capable of loving a woman, and no one, ever, could take it away from him.

Returning abruptly to the celebrating guests, he accepted a cup of rum punch and drank sparingly. Congenial and gracious, as he always was, he played the role of host to perfection. But he would wait, he reflected, until Lorene and Isaiah told him their news, and by then, he hoped, he would have recovered his equilibrium sufficiently to offer them his warm and sincere felicitations. His own destiny was clearly defined, and he would accept it without question. A man of courage and integrity could do no less.

At the far end of Trelawney, more than a mile from the great house, stood a small two-story dwelling of red brick, almost hidden from sight by groves of live oaks, cypresses and willow trees. The original home of the plantation's founder, it consisted of a living room and dining room on the first floor and two bedchambers above them, with a compact kitchen outbuilding and servants' quarters in the rear.

Sentiment had impelled Scott Emerson to restore the place in his grandfather's memory, and occasionally it was occupied by distinguished guests. General Francis Marion and his wife had stayed there, and more recently, so had former President Thomas Jefferson. Most of the time it was unoccupied. In spite of the shortage of space caused by the influx of wedding guests, it had been offered to none of them, however, and had been reserved for a special purpose.

Lamps were lighted in every room, a small coal fire burned in the living-room grate, and a supper of cold meats and cheeses was laid out on the dining-room table. Later a cook from the main house would bring in hot breads and pies, too.

Tom Beaufort grinned at his bride as he drove up the narrow road to the house. "We're staying here tonight," he told her, throwing the reins to a waiting groom and lifting Margot to the ground, "and we won't go on to Savannah until tomorrow."

"A surprise? I thought we'd drive straight through to Savannah, and I was sure we wouldn't arrive there before noon tomorrow, at the earliest."

Tom chuckled. "A man is entitled to keep secrets from his wife, particularly when they're intended for her benefit and enjoyment."

Margot placed her hands on her hips as she looked up at him. "Not this husband, sir, and certainly not this wife!"

He waited until a stable boy took their horse, carriage, and luggage to the rear. Then he lifted her into his arms again.

"Put me down, Tom! This instant!"

He paid no attention to her feeble simulated protest, and kicking the door open, carried her into the house. "This is traditional, I believe."

"Only in our own house," she said.

"Ten days is too long to wait."

"Then you shall pay the consequences." Margot curled her arms around his neck, kissed him, and then freed herself from his grasp and stood in front of the fire. "You

227

have no idea how concerned I was, worrying that we'd be spending the whole night on the road to Savannah."

Tom chuckled. "You must learn to trust your husband, Mistress Beaufort."

She thought for a moment, then nodded.

"Ah, you do trust me."

"If you must know," she said, "I was deciding how I like being called Mistress Beaufort. I do like it. As for trusting you, sir, I wouldn't have married you if I didn't."

He reached for her again.

She evaded him. "A stable boy took our carriage. The scent of food being prepared tells me there's a cook on the premises. This room is so spotlessly clean that there must be a serving maid somewhere, too. A married man learns to curb his impulses when outsiders are nearby."

"If they haven't already gone back to the Trelawney manor house, I'll soon be rid of them," he said.

"Are you in so great a rush, sir?" She stood in front of the fire, teasing him.

At the bachelor dinner given for him the previous night, Tom had sworn he wouldn't be prey to the common nervous ailment known as "bridegroom's disease." Now, however, he felt less sure of himself. Margot seemed as poised as she was pretty, but his own stomach was leaping, his hands were clammy, and he was thoroughly ill at ease. "The Trelawney staff is well trained, but I wouldn't want you embarrassed. I suppose it would be wise if I looked around."

He wandered into the dining room, then returned, but by now his apprehension had become so great that he refrained from telling her the servants had vanished. "There's a splendid cold collation on the table," he said.

"Don't tell me you're hungry after the wedding feast we ate!" she exclaimed.

"No, I . . . I don't have all that much appetite," he confessed, then added, "There's also a bowl of a punch that looks very appetizing."

Margot became demure. "I drank two glasses of wine at Oakhurst Manor, and that's more than enough for me. But help yourself, if you wish."

Never had he felt so clumsy, so uncertain of how to proceed. "I'm . . . no longer thirsty," he said.

She was in command now, and knew it. "Alicia Emerson showed me this house last month," she said, "but I don't remember it any too well. So I'm sure you'll forgive me if I explore the upstairs quarters on my own."

Before he could reply, she was gone, lifting her skirts calf-high as she quickly mounted the stairs.

Tom watched her until she disappeared from sight, then wandered aimlessly into the dining room and back. There was enough food spread on the table to provide a half-dozen people with a full meal, but his leaping stomach wouldn't permit him to think of eating. He poured himself a cup of punch, a sniff telling him it had a brandywine base, but the mere thought of liquor made him queasy.

Leaving the cup on the sideboard, he wandered outside and walked around the house. His horses had been stabled, fed, and watered, his carriage had been dusted. But the stable boy was nowhere to be seen. A fire was still glowing in the kitchen-outbuilding hearth, but the cook had vanished, too. He couldn't guess what might have become of the serving maid Margot had mentioned, and he didn't really care. It was obvious the staff was under orders to stay as far as possible from the newlyweds.

Tom returned to the house and stood for a moment in front of the fire, but backed away when he started to perspire. He opened a window, could hear no sound, and not bothering to look up at the sky, he returned abruptly to the dining room. The mere sight of the brandywine punch drove him away again.

He was thoroughly familiar with the little house, and knew there had been more than enough time for Margot to inspect every room with care. Annoyance tugged at him, and he began to mount the stairs.

As he climbed, he reconsidered. Perhaps she had fallen and broken an ankle. Women being delicate creatures, perhaps she had been overcome by the emotions of the day and had fainted. He quickened his pace.

The smaller of the upstairs rooms was empty, its door open. The door of the larger was slightly ajar, and a small light was burning inside the chamber.

Tom thought of tapping on the door, then changed his mind. It was his privilege, as Margot's husband, to enter on his own initiative without first asking her permission. He pushed the door open, then halted abruptly.

A single small lamp was burning on a bedside table, and Margot, seated demurely on a nearby dressing-table stool, was reflected in its glow. She had changed into a nightgown and peignoir of shimmering white silk, and her red hair looked like a soft halo around her head. Never had she been lovelier, more desirable, more feminine.

She looked up, but her attempt at bravado failed, and when she spoke, there was a tremor in her voice. "You're forming bad habits, Master Beaufort," she said. "It isn't seemly to keep your wife waiting for you indefinitely."

Tom's voice was husky. "I shall make up for lost time, Mistress Beaufort," he said, but he remained rooted to the spot, his feet unwilling to obey his will.

Margot looked at him hard and long.

The promise in her eyes unleashed him. In three strides he crossed the room and extinguished the lamp.

In the years that followed, neither could remember the details of what happened that evening. Somehow Tom undressed, somehow Margot shed her nightgown and peignoir, somehow they found themselves locked in a tight embrace on the bed.

At the first touch, both lost their shyness, their inhibitions. Margot's eagerness for lovemaking was as great as Tom's, and her desire mounted as swiftly. Their stormy romance caused them to cast aside their fears, their uneasiness, and their mutual desire soared. Their erotic appetites seemed insatiable, and when they exploded, their universe burst around them.

They made love a second time, then a third. Margot was unpredictable, her demeanor that of a genteel lady one moment, an abandoned bawd the next. All Tom knew was that he wanted her with all his being, that no matter how much he devoured her, he still wanted more.

At last they felt drowsy, and still locked in each other's arms, began to drift off to sleep.

Margot, as always, had the last word. "I knew from the

start that we were right for each other," she murmured, "but I never guessed how *very* right we were."

The wedding guests began to leave Oakhurst Manor immediately after breakfast, and a small army of servants was already at work cleaning the house and grounds. Sarah remained asleep, however, and no one disturbed her.

By midmorning Paul Wellington Beaufort was able to adjourn to his library in order to make notations in the ledgers he had been forced to neglect in recent days. He had no sooner started to work, however, than Cleo came in, availing herself of her special privilege of entering without knocking.

She took a stance opposite his desk, a giantess who stood with folded arms, her face stern.

Paul looked up from his ledgers, still weary from the festivities and heartsick because he had lost Lorene Small to Isaiah Benton. "Don't tell me we have new problems so soon after the wedding," he said.

"Not new," Cleo replied. "Missy have baby."

Paul felt as though a sledgehammer had struck him in the stomach. "How do you know?"

The housekeeper looked at him with undisguised contempt. "Cleo know."

"Who else knows?"

"Missy Small guess, too. Last night, when we put missy to bed after drink too much."

"Where is Mistress Small right now, do you know?"

"On side verandah. With papa of missy."

"Ask them to join me at once, if you please. And thank you, Cleo. I'm not sure yet how we'll handle this situation, but I'm grateful to you for telling me."

The housekeeper departed, and while he waited, he absently shredded a quill pen. His mind refused to function as it should.

After a short wait, Lorene and Isaiah came into the room. They had told him of their betrothal the previous night, but it was still a wrench to see them together. They didn't look like a future married couple, however; their expressions were grim.

Paul waved them to the sofa at the far side of the room.

"I don't know how to say this discreetly," he said, "but Cleo has just told me that Sarah is going to have a baby."

"So Cleo and I suspected last night," Lorene said. "I've just told Isaiah."

"I'm so stunned I don't know what to think," Isaiah said. "If it had been Margot, I wouldn't have been in the least surprised. But Sarah? Never!"

"I feel the same way," Paul replied.

There was a long, heavy silence, which Lorene broke. "I've taken the liberty of sending Cleo to fetch Sarah. The sooner this is brought into the open, the better it will be. Isaiah, my dear, would you prefer to face her alone?"

He shook his head. "No, it's your right to hear what she has to say. And Paul's, too. All of us are in this together, may the Almighty help us."

After another brief wait, Sarah came into the room, looking as vibrant and fresh as though she hadn't touched a drop of liquor the previous night. She was wearing an apron over her full-skirted cotton gown, and the stiff-bristled broom she carried indicated she intended to do her part in cleaning the manor house now that the guests had departed.

She smiled broadly when she saw Lorene and her father, then quickly embraced them. "The whole staff is talking about your wonderful news," she said. "No one can keep any secrets around here." She turned to Paul, sympathy for his plight in her eyes, but it was plain she wanted to wait until they were alone to express her condolences to him.

Lorene and Isaiah thanked her for her good wishes, and then her father said, "Sit down, Sarah."

Their faces were somber, and as she moved to a chair, she felt certain they were going to upbraid her for drinking too much after the wedding.

"It's true," Isaiah said, "that no secrets can be kept at Oakhurst Manor." He choked and could not go on.

It was Paul's turn, and he cleared his throat. "An occasional spree does little harm, provided one doesn't overdo too much and behaves circumspectly. But some people, under some circumstances, shouldn't drink at all." He became confused and didn't know what else to say.

"I remember everything I did last night," Sarah said, "and I'm reasonably sure I conducted myself like a lady."

"We're not speaking of last night," her father muttered.

Men were hopeless, and Lorene took charge. She rose, went to Sarah, and cradled the girl's head in her arms. "What they're trying to tell you is that we know you're going to have a child."

Sarah squeezed her hand in gratitude, then slowly stood, smoothing her skirt and apron. "It's quite true," she said, her head high and her voice firm. "I'm carrying Jeremy's child. I couldn't have kept the news from you much longer, and I'm glad you've heard."

"Does Jeremy know?" Paul asked.

She shook her head. "It happened . . . the very night he disappeared. At first I felt ashamed that we . . . lost our self-control and slipped. It was the only time, and as we were planning to be married, it wouldn't have mattered. If Jeremy hadn't vanished. But now, living with his baby inside me, I'm not ashamed any longer. Even though we're separated, he and I . . . are together."

With a great effort Isaiah went to her and kissed her. "This isn't easy," he said, "but I'm trying hard not to blame you."

Paul kissed her, too. "You're not at fault, really, and neither is my son. If the young weren't impetuous at times, they'd have no right to be young."

"These things sometimes happen, I've learned, when a man and a woman love each other with their whole hearts," Sarah said. "I'll go to Boston at once, if you wish, or I'll take myself somewhere alone and find work to support the baby and me until Jeremy comes back to us."

"I won't permit it," Isaiah said. "I refuse to allow any grandchild of mine to starve."

"Do you think I'd permit a grandchild of mine to want for anything?" Paul demanded. "An absurd notion!"

Sarah smiled in relief.

Lorene found it difficult not to laugh, even though the situation was serious. "You're of one mind, gentlemen," she said. "Now I suggest you make specific plans."

Isaiah blinked. "I'm not sure I know quite how to proceed. The baby will be a Benton, of course—"

"That baby will be a Beaufort!" Paul roared. "Be good enough to remember that my son is the father!"

Lorene could no longer control her laugh.

Sarah's tension broke, and she joined in.

The two men glared at them. "Perhaps you'll share the joke with us," Isaiah said.

"Yes," Paul added, "I'm sure we'd enjoy a laugh, too."

"This situation, gentlemen," Lorene told them, "is no more tragic than you two future grandfathers choose to make it. Allow me to offer some practical suggestions. With Sarah's permission."

"By all means." Sarah was beginning to realize how hard she was leaning on the woman who would become her stepmother.

"There's no need for anyone in this world other than the four of us to know that Sarah's baby is being born out of wedlock. I suggest we tell a white lie, that Sarah and Jeremy were secretly married in Massachusetts shortly before he disappeared. If necessary, I'm sure that documents to that effect could be produced."

"I daresay it could be arranged." Isaiah's agreement was reluctant, although he had to admit to himself that the advice was sensible.

"As for you, Sarah," the older woman said, "start wearing Jeremy's ring on your finger instead of on a chain around your neck. And—beginning today—you'll be known as Mistress Beaufort."

Sarah thought for a moment, then nodded. "It won't be a lie," she said. "In God's eyes, Jeremy and I truly are husband and wife. We're as much married as we'd have been if we'd taken our vows at a church altar. We took them in God's sight."

"That brings up the question of where you'll live until Jeremy comes home," Lorene continued.

Isaiah and Paul tried to interrupt, both of them speaking simultaneously.

Lorene silenced them with a gesture. "I'm not finished speaking, if you please. Sarah, your father and I haven't had an opportunity to tell this to you or anyone else. But just this morning we decided we're going to make our home in Charleston."

"Right," Isaiah said. "So many people hereabouts have asked for my legal help that I intend to move my practice from Boston to Charleston. We'll buy a small house—Lorene already knows the place she wants—and you're welcome to share it with us for as long as you please."

Paul Wellington Beaufort could keep silent no longer. "The other alternative, of course, is to stay right here."

"As I was about to mention," Lorene said.

Paul ignored the interruption. "Your child, Sarah, will be the first heir or heiress of that generation to Oakhurst Manor. If your baby should be a son, he'll stand first in line after Jeremy. I say he should be reared on the land that someday will be his. As for you, as of right now you'll enjoy all the prerogatives of being the wife of Jeremy Beaufort. As of this very moment, you'll become mistress of Oakhurst Manor, in fact as well as in name."

Sarah looked at each of them in turn. "First, I . . . I thank you for your love and support. There are parents who would have disowned me for what has happened. I'm not sure I deserve your loyalty, but I assure you I'll earn it. Papa, I appreciate the offer you and Lorene have made, but I can't accept it."

"Why not?" her father demanded.

"Because you and Lorene are beginning a new life of your own, together, and you'll be busier than ever moving your law practice to Charleston. It would be wrong for you to have the distraction of a daughter—and a grandchild—in the house."

Lorene went to her future husband and took his hand. "Sarah is right, Isaiah," she said. "She makes good sense, as she always does."

Sarah turned to Paul. "Papa Beaufort," she said, "I accept your offer, because I have no real choice. My child will come into this world with Beaufort blood in his veins. He must grow to manhood sharing your pride—and Jeremy's—in Oakhurst Manor. This will be his home, as it is Jeremy's—and now, as it has become mine."

Chapter 17

The friends and neighbors of the Beauforts, led by the entire Emerson clan, accepted without question the story that Sarah and Jeremy had been married in secret in Massachusetts. When Margot and Tom returned from their Savannah honeymoon, they showed no surprise, either; they, like everyone else, had been thinking of Sarah as Jeremy's wife.

There were subtle changes in Sarah's status. She sat at the dinner table in the place of the hostess, opposite Paul Beaufort. She assumed management of the household, buying new linens when necessary, ordering curtains, and assigning quarters to guests who visited Oakhurst Manor from time to time. Even the indomitable Cleo consulted her when planning menus, but didn't necessarily accept her suggestions.

There was a change in the attitude of friends and social acquaintances, too. The young women began to treat her with the respect due a matron, particularly when it became increasingly evident that she was pregnant. The young men of the area saw a distinct difference between a girl who was merely betrothed and one who was actually married. Perhaps their memory of Jeremy Beaufort's prowess with both sword and pistol was a deterring factor, but without exception they took care not to flirt with Sarah.

Members of the household staff were delighted. Cleo fussed incessantly over Sarah, supervised her diet, refused to allow her to exert herself, and even insisted on draping a shawl over her shoulders when she sat near an open window. Willie was equally elated and went to work at once, on what he called his masterpiece, a crib that could be disassembled and turned into a junior-sized bed when the baby grew old enough for it.

Mr. Higby became obsequious, sweeping off his hat and bowing low whenever he saw Sarah. His attitude set her mind in motion, and one morning at breakfast with Paul and Tom she decided to explore the matter.

"Why does Mr. Higby always carry that ugly whip? Jeremy always told me that the slaves at Oakhurst Manor are never beaten, and from what I've seen in the fields myself, that's true."

Paul shrugged. "It's always been the custom for an overseer to carry a whip. Call it his badge of office."

"It's more than that," Tom said. "Twice each year we buy a few new slaves in the Charleston market. They're husky brutes, field hands. Fresh off the slave ships from Africa, and only the touch of the whip has kept them in hand on the voyage. They're savages. The sight of Higby's whip reminds them to behave themselves."

"If they're savages," Sarah said, "the fear of the whip will keep them that way. Surely they would work harder and produce more if they lived happier personal lives and weren't in constant dread of being maimed."

Paul was faintly amused, but his interest had been aroused, too. "How would you achieve those ends?"

"Enlarge their houses as their families grow. Improve their diet by giving them more meat and fresh vegetables. Provide them with better clothing to wear on Sundays and holidays." Sarah warmed to her theme. "Above all, educate them."

Tom was startled, and stared at his sister-in-law. "How in tarnation would you do that?"

"Teach the newcomers from Africa to speak English. Teach reading and writing to those who have the ability to learn. Willie isn't unique, you know. If he were living in Boston, he'd be earning handsome wages, and for his sake and Amanda's, I hope they'll go north one of these days. My basic point is that many others can do what Willie has done. You can build a whole staff of proficient skilled workers who will improve the value of Oakhurst Manor in many ways and increase our income."

Tom shook his head. "In theory your idea may be sound, Sarah, but I'm none too certain it will work out in practice. For one thing, there's a feeling among plantation owners that it's bad to educate blacks. It makes them dissatisfied and causes problems."

She had no patience with such shortsighted views. "Rubbish! Ask Willie what he thinks, and you'll change your opinions!"

Paul was intrigued. "It may be just possible that you've latched onto something, Sarah, and I'm always interested in any innovation that will benefit Oakhurst Manor. How would you go about finding someone who would teach the Africans to speak English?"

"We already have someone right here. Amanda. We've had several talks, and she'd love to try. First thing each morning, she could give English lessons to the Africans for an hour or two, and later in the day she can teach the rudiments of reading and writing to those who are interested."

"You don't think field work will be disrupted?" Paul wanted to know.

"To an extent, perhaps, but not all that much."

"You're probably right," the plantation owner conceded. "One thing does worry me, though. The Africans can be wild, so what happens if they rise up in rebellion when no one is standing over them with a whip? Amanda could be murdered."

Sarah smiled. "Amanda isn't in the least frightened. She's sure they'll realize she's trying to help them, and there's no doubt in her mind that they'll be cooperative."

Paul made his decision. "It's a radical concept, but I'm willing to try it," he said, then grinned. "Higby will be mighty unhappy when he loses his whip. He's carried it so long, he thinks of it as a natural extension of his arm."

Sarah stiffened. "I'm not interested in Mr. Higby's views."

"Right," Tom said. "He does what he's told. I'll have a word with him as soon as I finish breakfast. We'll put up a new cabin today that Amanda can use as a schoolhouse, and she can start first thing tomorrow."

Sarah was delighted, and not the least of her pleasure was caused by her brother-in-law's attitude. Tom still went fishing and hunting when he should have been at work on the property, and she was growing accustomed to the worried expression in Margot's eyes on the all-too-frequent evenings when he drank to excess. But he was still a Beaufort: Oakhurst Manor came first, and he was willing to do anything that would improve the plantation.

One day soon he would settle down and become more like his father and brother. For the moment, however, as she had remarked to her sister only yesterday, he was still very young, so a measure of instability and a lack of responsibility could be excused. At least Margot was showing her mettle now that she was a married woman, her own conduct having become more sober, more considerate of others. So it was reasonable to hope that she would have a steadying influence on her husband.

After breakfast Paul retired to his library to go over his ledgers, and Sarah adjourned to her sitting room for her regular conference with Cleo. First, however, she had to tell Amanda the good news.

Meantime, Tom had a horse saddled and rode out into the fields to find the overseer. Ultimately he saw Mr. Higby at the western end of the property, where the rows of tobacco plants were growing higher under a benign early-summer sun.

They rode off a short distance together, out of hearing of the slaves who were weeding, and Tom explained what would be expected in the future.

The overseer shoved his broad-brimmed hat onto the back of his head and rubbed the stubble on his chin. "I don't rightly mind practical jokes," he said, "but not when I'm working."

"I'm dead serious," Tom told him. "My father has approved the whole plan, and a crew is already at work putting up the schoolhouse. You'll retire your whip."

Mr. Higby unleashed a stream of spittle at a tobacco leaf. "You and your brother were babies when I come to work here, and I'll be damned to hell if I'll go anywheres without my whip! Educate these slaves, and you'll have a revolution on your hands, but that's your lookout, not mine. All I know is that I got to protect myself if one of them attacks me."

Tom's face was set in hard lines. "If you should be attacked, you have recourse under the law. In the meantime, you've been given an order, Mr. Higby. A direct order."

The overseer shifted his weight in the saddle. "Who came up with this crazy scheme?"

"If you must know, the idea originated with my sister-in-law."

"Trust a goddamn woman to make a mess. What does any woman know about running a plantation? What does anyone from the North know about the handling of slaves?"

"Mistress Beaufort happens to be the wife of my brother, Jeremy. In his absence, she has a full voice in the management of Oakhurst Manor, Mr. Higby. As an employee, you're required to obey her direct instructions."

"Even at the risk of my own life?"

"It so happens these orders were issued by my father. If you choose to disregard them, that's strictly your own affair. But you've known my father a long time, and you know how he'll react. Regardless of what you yourself believe or want, either you'll do what you're told or you can leave us and find other employment."

The overseer's eyes narrowed. "Not many jobs are around in wartime. So I reckon I'll have to knuckle under. For now. But I won't forget what Mistress Sarah has done to me, and I'm not likely to forget your part in it either, Tom. One of these days you and me will have a personal score to settle."

"I'm available at any time," Tom replied curtly, and rode off in the direction of the manor house.

Lorene Small and Isaiah Benton were married in the presence of their families, and an intimate reception was held for them at Trelawney before they left for Boston. There Isaiah intended to close his law office and have his furniture and other household belongings shipped to Charleston, where he and his bride had just purchased a snug new home.

The reception was still in progress when the bride and groom departed, and Sarah spent a few moments alone with them.

"Papa," she said as she hugged Isaiah, "if I had selected a wife for you, it would have been Lorene. She makes me proud—as you do—to have been a Benton."

His daughter was so gallant, so generous, that tears came to his eyes, and he had to blink them away.

Sarah and Lorene embraced. "Thank you," the girl said, "mostly for giving Papa so much happiness. But for selfish reasons, too. You're the best friend I've ever had, and being related to you now makes me feel even closer to you."

It was a struggle for Lorene to keep her own emotions under control. "We're going to do our best to come back to South Carolina by the time you have your baby."

"Don't worry about me, Lorene. Cleo has already announced she's going to be in charge, and Dr. Pickens will consider himself fortunate if she allows him to come into the room."

The newlyweds departed before Tom Beaufort made a fool of himself. He drank more brandywine than was good for him, and in a reckless mood flirted with the always susceptible Alicia Emerson, who should have known better but was congenitally incapable of resisting the attentions of any man.

Had Paul Wellington Beaufort been aware of what was happening, he would have intervened, and so would Scott Emerson. As it happened, however, they and other members of the older generation were gathered in the parlor and were paying no attention to the young people, who were dancing on the side veranda of the manor house.

Sarah witnessed the incident, but lacked the physical strength to call a halt. Her baby, due in a month, was moving, and for Jeremy's sake as well as her infant's, she felt compelled to sit still in her comfortable veranda chair.

Margot's behavior was superb. Unwilling to separate her husband and Alicia, who were huddling in a dark corner of the veranda whispering to each other, she pretended to be unaware that anything was amiss. She danced with other men, she accepted a small cup of punch, and she chatted with various guests, never as much as allowing her glance to wander in Tom's direction. Above all, she conducted herself with dignity as well as aplomb.

When Paul Beaufort finally realized that Sarah was in distress, he insisted on taking her back to Oakhurst Manor without delay. She would have preferred to stay, hoping she could prevent the eruption of an ugly scene, but common sense prevailed, and she consented to be taken home.

Tom and Margot were among the last to leave the reception, and as he helped her onto the seat of their small carriage, which he would drive himself, she realized he was still under the influence of brandywine. So she curbed her anger, and seating herself as far from him as possible, rode home in silence.

Tom indulged in a steady prattle all the way home, apparently unaware of her anger. His continuing amiability gave way to stronger feelings after they reached Oakhurst Manor, and he tried to make love to his wife.

Only then did Margot actively resist, and Tom stormed alone into their bedchamber. She spent an uneasy night on the divan in their small sitting room.

The following morning, after bathing and changing into a daytime dress, Margot was still in the sitting room, sipping a huge mug of coffee, when a rumpled Tom appeared, clad in his dressing robe. His eyes were bloodshot, and he groaned, but she felt no sympathy for him.

"Coffee," he said, reaching for her mug. "Just what I need."

"Order your own," Margot said. "This is mine."

He blinked at her, then tugged at a bell rope to summon a servant who was already waiting in a pantry down the corridor to bring his breakfast.

Margot ostentatiously turned her back to her husband and tried to read a just-delivered Charleston newspaper, even though she was so upset that the words that danced on the page made no sense.

By now Tom realized trouble was brewing, but he remained silent until he had his own coffee and the servant withdrew. "All right," he said. "Tell me what I've done so I can apologize and we can forget the whole matter."

"I won't forget it," Margot said, "and I have no intention of allowing you to forget it, either."

"Was I that bad?" He grinned at her.

Her face remained masklike, and she flipped back a strand of red hair. "I married a man, not a boy," she said, "and I have a right to insist that you accept a man's marital responsibilities."

"If it comes to that," he replied, trying to place her on the defensive, "I seem to recall that you avoided me when we came home last night. A wife has responsibilities, too."

Until now she had been collected, but all at once her own temper began to rise. "Please understand, sir, that I shall have no more to do with you, ever, unless you mend your ways!"

He saw she was serious, and his broad smile faded. "It would be helpful if I knew the nature of the crime I committed."

"Someone who didn't know any of us," Margot said, "would have sworn you were courting Alicia Emerson. And succeeding."

"Oh, that." He tried to dismiss the matter with a wave. "Alicia and I have known each other all our lives."

"There's a difference between friendship and romance, even half-romance, and well you know it, Master Beaufort. I will not tolerate it when my husband flirts with another woman. Or slides an arm around her. Or whispers intimacies to her by the hour. All the while ignoring his wife, who must make the best of a most embarrassing situation."

Tom could think of no adequately convincing reply.

"If you wanted Alicia, you should have married her. Instead, you married me. If you've grown tired of me already, which is what I'm forced to assume, I'm prepared to leave Oakhurst Manor today. And if I go, I promise you, sir, I won't come back."

He realized she was in earnest, and was afraid he would provoke her still more if he asked where she would go if she left him. "Margot," he said, "I meant no harm and no disrespect to you, I swear it."

"The harm has been done," she said, "and I've been made to look ridiculous. By now half the state is gossiping about us, and I find that loathsome. Perhaps the name of Beaufort means nothing to you, but I've taken pride in it."

He straightened as though she had slapped him. "Surely you know I love you."

"I've thought so," Margot said, "but now I'm not so sure."

"You also know that Alicia Emerson means nothing to me."

She shrugged.

"If I paid too much attention to her, it was only because I was giddy."

"Then you should control your giddiness, which you can do best by drinking less."

"I'm sorry, truly I am." Tom paused, and his discomfort increased when his wife made no reply. "What must I do to make amends to you?"

Margot stood and faced him. "Grow up," she said. "Instead of finding excuses to drag Willie away from his shop to go off on hunting and fishing trips with you, spend all of your days at work. Learn your father's system of keeping books. Inspect our produce regularly. Make certain the workers are well treated and have no legitimate complaints. Visit the cotton and tobacco and sugar and rice markets in Charleston so you'll know what's being bought and what's being charged. Find ways to make this plantation more productive and efficient. You have a birthright, but you take it for granted, and it will dwindle and vanish unless you start earning your way."

Tom knew she was right, but still tried to defend himself. "I have many friends who work no harder than I do."

"They aren't Beauforts, and their families aren't owners of one of the greatest plantations in the South. If Jeremy were here, do you suppose he'd idle away his days going fishing? Do you for one moment think he'd spend his nights drinking and dishonoring Sarah by devoting his attentions to other women?"

"Ever since I was little, as far back as I can remember," Tom replied with heat, "everybody has asked me why I'm not more like Jeremy. Well, I'm not Jeremy. I'm myself. Tom Beaufort."

"Then Tom Beaufort will have to change and start living up to his potential. If he wants to keep me as his wife." Margot gathered up her skirts, and, not looking at him again, left the room. Her dignity had been restored, but she felt as though her heart was breaking.

Residents of Savannah claimed that the city soon would rival Charleston, Richmond, and New Orleans, and ultimately would become the leading metropolis of the South. Paul Wellington Beaufort doubted their assertion, and privately was pleased. Savannah had a charm that was distinctive, an air of its own. Industries were growing there, including iron foundries and cotton mills, but it was still primarily a clearing center for the agricultural produce of the Georgia hinterlands. And its seaport facilities gave it an international flavor.

Certainly it was a community that was pleasing to the eye. Its streets, even in the waterfront district, were laid out in neat, precise rectangles, and there were more parks than in any other American community. Office buildings were unobtrusive, and tree-shaded lawns shielded handsome private homes. In spite of its seeming gentleness, however, Savannah was tough. It had survived not only the years of British occupation that had started in 1778 and had lasted until almost the end of the War of Independence, but it had been rebuilt with remarkable speed and thoroughness after the terrible fire that had devastated it in 1796.

What Paul Wellington Beaufort liked best about Savannah was his ability to relax in surroundings he knew and enjoyed. He made two business visits to the city each year, conferring with exporters to whom he sold quantities of his cotton and tobacco. He always stayed at the same small inn, where his wants were known and where he was assured of comfortable quarters. A visit to Savannah was almost as pleasant as staying at home.

On this trip, however, Savannah failed to exert its customary magic. His suite at the James Oglethorpe Inn was large and handsomely furnished, the service was excellent and unobtrusive. He had no difficulty in disposing of his cotton and tobacco at fair prices that brought him a solid profit. And he enjoyed buying gifts for Sarah and Margot, as well as splurging on presents for his soon-to-be-born grandchild, including a set of two dozen silver mugs that would bear the Oakhurst Manor crest.

But something was missing, and he knew precisely what was wrong. He refused to dwell on his loss of Lorene Small to Isaiah Benton, and he was sincere in wishing them well, but those feelings didn't assuage his loneliness. Because he *was* lonely. Sarah was a great comfort to him, and he thoroughly relished Margot's lively company, but they were not substitutes for a woman of his own.

Returning to his suite from his last business meeting late one afternoon, he faced the issue squarely. He needed a woman who would help modify his loneliness, at least temporarily. He didn't want just sex, although that was important, but what he craved was sympathetic feminine companionship.

A pragmatist who never wasted his substance brooding when direct action could solve a problem, Paul settled his square-crowned hat on his head, picked up his gold-handled walking stick, and left the suite.

Visiting Northerners and seamen who came ashore from ships that had been sailing in cold waters found the summer heat of Savannah stifling. But the South Carolina plantation owner found the air balmy, the scent of jasmine and honeysuckle sweet. He walked at a leisurely pace, his mood already improving, and after strolling for three-quarters of a mile, he came to a large clapboard house, three stories high, that was protected by a stockade fence.

A pretty black serving maid took his hat and stick, then conducted him into a parlor, where the furniture was massive, the wallpaper boldly striped black and white. He seated himself in a leather armchair, but didn't have long to wait.

Three young women came into the room together, all of them attractive, although their evening gowns were a shade too revealing, their makeup too heavy. Each found an excuse to remain for a few moments. One lighted the candles in the wall candelabra, a second drew the draperies of stiff brocaded satin, and the third offered the guest a pinch of snuff from a porcelain box, which he declined.

A few moments later, a striking woman came into the room. Scores of Clara Hubbard's friends and acquaintances tried to guess her age, and most were mistaken. It was enough that there was only a sprinkle of gray in her dark brown hair, which she always wore in the same style, parted in the middle and gathered in a bun at the nape of her neck. Her brown eyes were clear, and there were remarkably few lines at the corners of her eyes or marring her smooth, high forehead. She was impeccably dressed in a full-skirted gown of peach-colored silk, and her only jewelry was a large cameo brooch that called attention to her full breasts. Her waist was still tiny, as a peach-colored sash attested, and she carried no extra weight on her tall, well-preserved frame. Only a faint wistfulness that appeared in her eyes at unguarded moments revealed to the sensitive that her life had been less serene than it appeared.

"Good evening, sir," she said as Paul stood. "Tell me which of my young ladies you like, and she'll serve you a drink."

She had failed to recognize him, and Paul concealed a smile. "I like all of them," he said, "but children don't appeal to me."

Clara Hubbard was surprised; most of her clients were middle-aged. "You prefer someone more mature, then," she temporized, wondering where she could locate an older girl on short notice.

"I prefer to chat with you, Clara," he said.

She was startled by his informality, studied him more closely, and gasped. "Paul Beaufort!"

He embraced her, and they kissed lightly. "You're as beautiful as ever, Clara."

"I refuse to entertain an old friend in public rooms."

247

She led him up a flight of carpeted stairs to a sitting room furnished in the old-fashioned colonial style, with pickled maple chairs, tables, and settees. "How long has it been since we last saw each other? At least ten years."

"Fifteen is more like it. My sons were climbing trees and learning to handle firearms when I last came here. Now both are married, and the elder has vanished. Probably impressed by the British Navy, although we aren't certain. His wife is going to make me a grandfather at any moment."

"You don't look like a grandfather, Paul!"

His smile was rueful. "Ah, but I do, and well you know it, so give me none of your soft talk, Clara."

"Very well, sir, you shall have a drink instead." She measured a small quantity of Madeira wine into a glass, then added water to it.

"What a remarkable memory for one's tastes you have. To your health, Clara!"

"And to yours, dear Paul." She toasted him, then continued to study him over the rim of her glass. "Oh, you've grown gray and a little portly, but you still cut a fine figure of a man. Have you remarried?"

"No, I had ideas along that line, but the lady preferred someone else."

"Then she was a bloody fool! Any woman in her right mind would be overjoyed to become the wife of Paul Beaufort."

He inclined his head in a gesture of thanks. "How goes it with you, Clara?"

"Life stays much the same. I've put aside enough—in gold napoleons and English sterling, mind you, not in our wildly fluctuating dollars—to retire. I talk about it often, but I'm not certain the bankers of Savannah, the Georgia planters, and the visiting sea captains could get along without the services my house offers them."

"Nonsense," Paul replied as he sipped his drink. "You're too good for them, Clara, and you always have been."

Clara Hubbard had spent a long career dissembling with others, but she refused to fool herself. "This is the only life I've ever known, dear Paul, and I'm fit for no other.

248

Would you marry me and take me back to Oakhurst Manor? Of course not! I've disqualified myself for marriage into the gentry, but I've been spoiled by my associations with gentlemen, and wouldn't marry an ordinary man. So there you have it. I stay in business from year to year, always putting off my retirement." She stood, excused herself, and went out into the corridor.

Paul heard her conversing at length with another woman.

Clara smiled when she returned to the room. "There, sir. I've ordered dinner for you, so you can't refuse my invitation to stay."

"You're kind. To tell you the truth, I have no intention of refusing. I was hoping you'd ask me to stay."

Again she studied him. "You're tired, Paul."

"A bit."

"Discouraged?"

"Worried over my elder son. His wife is a wonderful girl, bless her, and a great solace to me."

"You work and work and work. What else do you, dear Paul?"

"What else is there to do?" he countered.

Clara prepared another mild drink. "You need a wife."

"So you told me fifteen years ago," he said. "Just as I told you that you need a husband."

Clara's smile was weary. "What a great pity it is that we live in a world where people pin labels on everyone. Clara Hubbard, the mistress of so many men in her day and the owner of the fanciest bordello in Savannah, is so well-known and so notorious that she could never become the mistress of Oakhurst Manor. It's just as well, really. You and I can indulge in a little pretend romance, but we're no more suited to each other now than we were the first time you came here. More than twenty years ago, about a year after your wife died."

"How I hate narrow-minded people!"

"So do I, but there are so many of them in this world that we're forced to live with them, and that makes it impossible for you and me ever to live together."

They were interrupted by a serving maid, who announced that dinner was served.

Paul followed Clara into a small but elegantly furnished dining room, complete with mahogany furniture, highly polished, and copper candelabra that gleamed. The meals he had eaten here in the past had been memorable, and he had never forgotten any detail of the room.

He was astonished by the first course, fresh Savannah oysters wrapped in crisp bacon. "One of my favorites!" he exclaimed.

Clara merely smiled.

Other surprises followed. The soup was a gumbo, rich with chicken and okra. The fish was crabmeat, minced and mixed with a savory sauce before being baked in its shell. Then came beef, larded and smothered with wild mushrooms, and after it they were served pheasant, perfectly grilled, on beds of wild rice.

"Clara, you're astonishing," Paul declared. "For course after course you've remembered the dishes I like best."

Again she smiled.

"You didn't look up my preferences in notes. You simply remembered. How do you do it?"

"I refuse to give away my secrets." Clara was unexpectedly demure. "Let's just say it's no accident that I've become the best in my profession."

Paul didn't press her for a reply. It was enough that he was relishing every bite of his meal. They finished with a light fresh-fruit sherbet, then retired to the sitting room for coffee lightly laced with brandywine.

Gradually they filled each other in on the major events of their lives during the years they had been apart, and Paul unburdened himself. He told Clara about the disappearance of Jeremy, the solace Sarah had given him, and the high hopes he entertained for his grandchild. He spoke at length about his failed romance with Lorene Small, and most of all he talked about Oakhurst Manor, including his experiments that would provide greater crop yields and the splendid results that his humane treatment of his slaves was providing.

Suddenly he became aware of a clock chiming in another room, and he looked at his watch.

"It's midnight already! I'm so sorry, Clara. I didn't intend to overstay my welcome."

"That would be impossible, and I have no intention of allowing you to leave now."

She led him by the hand into a chamber dominated by a huge feather bed. Its furnishings were new, and Paul's only impression of the room was one of billowing, gauzelike curtains and frilly, flowered drapes.

"I've slept alone in this bed for longer than I care to recall," Clara said.

Then, deliberately and with tantalizing slowness, she began to undress before him, well remembering the delight he had taken, so long ago, in a ritual as old as man's desires.

There was no conversation now, and Paul's eyes gleamed.

When Clara was nude, she undressed him, and they moved together to the bed. The pace of their lovemaking was almost as deliberate as the scene that had preceded it, but as they became aroused, they responded to each other more quickly and with a depth of fervor.

They reached a climax together, just as they always had in bygone years.

At last Clara sighed. "I no longer envy the young," she murmured.

"Neither do I, dear Clara. They miss so much that only we who are older can appreciate."

They slept together all night, and Paul did not leave in the morning until he had eaten a hearty breakfast.

He walked quickly and with a light step to the shop of Savannah's leading jeweler, and there he ordered that a pair of gold earrings, set with sprays of small diamonds, be sent to Mistress Hubbard, embedded in a bouquet of gardenias and white roses.

He returned to his inn to pack his belongings, and not until he had taken his seat on the stage to Charleston did he realize the change that had taken place in him. His sense of loneliness was gone, his feeling of depression had lifted, and he felt better able to cope with the many problems that loomed ahead. His sons—and certainly his daughters-in-law—would disapprove of Clara Hubbard, but he knew her worth, and he would always cherish her special talent for renewing his spirit and making life worth living.

Cleo allowed no member of the household in the bed-chamber, forbidding even Margot to enter, while she herself carried in pail after pail of boiling water that members of the staff brought upstairs from the kitchen. Dr. Pickens thought he was in charge, but Cleo believed otherwise and gave him instructions. The only other person she allowed in the suite was Amanda, whose presence Sarah specifically requested. Cleo confined her duties to holding Sarah's hand and placing compresses on her forehead.

As the hours passed, the household became increasingly quiet, with servants walking on tiptoe. Tom was unable to tolerate the tensions, and rounding up Willie, went off for a day of fishing for eels in the swamps at the far end of the plantation, where two small streams converged and trickled toward the sea.

Julia Emerson had offered her services, but Cleo had rejected her help, so she and the other members of her family remained at Trelawney. Isaiah and Lorene Benton had not yet returned to South Carolina from Boston, and, as Margot observed, it was just as well. Her father's nervousness would have made the atmosphere even worse.

Her father-in-law was bad enough. Margot kept him company in the library, where she tried to distract him, but the task was impossible. Paul Beaufort refused to sit, and paced up and down ceaselessly, pausing only to refill his coffee mug. He could not forget the loss of his own wife in childbirth when Tom had come into the world, and that tragedy loomed large in his mind.

Margot tried to talk to him about the new strains of tobacco he had recently imported from the Ottoman Empire, but his mind was elsewhere. She launched a discussion of cattle breeding, a subject with which she was just beginning to familiarize herself, but he didn't hear a word. Even her attempts to drag him outside to inspect the new flowerbeds that had been planted under Sarah's supervision in the spring ended in total failure.

Trim in crinolines, her full skirt supported by petticoats and hoops, she was a model of composure as she sat near the open windows, even though she, too, was straining for sounds emanating from the suite directly above them.

"May I get you a little brandywine or rum, Papa Beaufort?" she asked.

Paul continued to roam. "I think not, thank you. The very notion of drinking liquor makes me ill."

"You've had more than enough coffee, and that will make you sick, too. Particularly when you've had no breakfast. Let me send for a dish of grits. Or some eggs. Or toast and honey."

He shook his head as he moved around the room like a caged animal. "Later, when we have good cause to celebrate, we'll have a banquet. For the present, I have no appetite."

Margot didn't know what else to say, and fell silent. She took a leather-bound book from the shelves, but could not concentrate on the adventures of Judge Fielding's *Tom Jones,* still as popular in America as it was in England.

Paul continued to pace.

Finally she could stand it no longer. "Papa Beaufort," she said, "I'm going to scream. At the top of my lungs. Until I'm too hoarse to scream anymore."

He halted at last, looking at her with concern. "Ah, you're as worried and upset as I am."

"I'm neither worried nor upset. I'm concerned, naturally, but I have no fears. Sarah is in the best of good health, Dr. Pickens is the most efficient physician in the state, and Cleo . . . well, Cleo simply wouldn't permit anything untoward to happen. The reason I'm going to scream is that you're driving me mad."

His smile was feeble.

Margot realized she was gaining the upper hand and pressed her advantage. "Be good enough to sit down, sir," she said sternly, and pointed to a leather armchair.

Paul was so startled that he obeyed.

Rising to her feet, she poured him a small glass of brandywine. "Now, drink this!"

Again he did as he was bidden.

She went to the door, summoned a servant, and ordered a dish of grits for her father-in-law, making certain it would be served as he liked it best, with butter, salt, and coarsely ground black pepper.

Soon the servant returned, and Margot handed Paul the dish, then stood over him.

"You're bullying me," he said.

She made no reply, but continued to loom above him, her hands on her hips and one slippered foot tapping on the parquet floor.

The master of Oakhurst Manor meekly ate the grits.

All at once the girl became guileless again. "There, sir! Isn't that better? Now you're fortified for the ordeal, and you'll be less likely to drive both of us insane."

He couldn't help laughing. "You're extraordinary, Margot. It never occurred to me, until now, but you're going to be a wonderful mother yourself."

A shadow crossed her face. "That will have to wait for a time."

He guessed what she meant, and refrained from questioning her. Her marriage was still stormy, her attempts to haul Tom into line and imbue him with a self-discipline, a sense of purpose, having shown no positive results. But he knew that if anyone could influence him and move him in the right direction, it would be this tiny spitfire who didn't know the meaning of fear.

"Tom is fortunate to have you as his wife," he said, "and I pray that one day he'll deserve you."

Before she could reply, they were electrified by the high-pitched wail of a newborn infant.

Paul leaped to his feet, and after they exchanged a startled glance, he started toward the door.

Margot caught hold of his arm. "Wait," she said. "We'll just be in the way upstairs for the moment. I'm sure someone will bring us word at any moment."

She was right. In a short time, a smiling Cleo stood on the threshold. "Missy have baby boy," she announced.

Margot hugged her, then hugged her father-in-law.

"How is Mistress Sarah?" Paul wanted to know.

Cleo regarded him with the contempt she reserved for the slow-witted. "Missy fine. Feel good. Very happy. But sad Jeremy not here. Soon you come up," she added, and climbed the stairs again.

An elated Paul Beaufort poured small quantities of brandywine into two glasses, handing one to his younger daughter-in-law. "Join me in a toast," he said, "to the future master of Oakhurst Manor."

They drank, and then Margot laughed. "How would you have felt if the baby had been a girl?"

"I never considered the possibility," he told her as they mounted the stairs together. "Sarah loves this place so much that I knew all along she'd have a son to carry on the line."

Dr. Pickens, who was rolling down his shirtsleeves, met them in the sitting room of the suite and admonished them not to linger inside for more than a few moments.

They went into the bedchamber.

A weak but clear-eyed Sarah was propped on pillows, her baby cradled in one arm, smiling at them.

Margot kissed her on the forehead, as did Paul.

Then they looked at the infant, who had a full head of dark brown hair. Jeremy's color.

"Jerry," Sarah said, "meet your grandfather and your aunt. They're Beauforts, too, and they'll help me to take care of you until your papa comes home to us."

Chapter 18

The seasons changed. The war dragged on, and Americans were heartened by the brilliant exploits of their nation's infant navy. The frigate *Constitution*, already known as "Old Ironsides" and commanded by Captain Isaac Hull, defeated the British ship *Guerriere* off the coast of Nova Scotia; some months later, under Captain William Bainbridge, she sank a British frigate, the *Java*, in Brazilian waters. Other Americans distinguished themselves at sea, too, and in September 1813 a small flotilla commanded by Captain Oliver Hazard Perry defeated and captured a fleet of six British warships. The country was thrilled by his victory message: "We have met the enemy, and they are ours."

Land forces fared less well. Victories were minor and defeats were partial. Both sides were handicapped by inadequate forces, and neither was strong enough to win decisively. The worst losses were yet to be sustained on both sides, but in January 1814 President James Madison accepted a proposal from London to engage in peace talks and dispatched a group of negotiators to Ghent, Belgium, where the conference would be held.

Oakhurst Manor continued to flourish, and enjoyed the greatest prosperity in its history. The humane treatment of the slaves instituted by Sarah Benton, universally known now as Sarah Beaufort, paid dividends that other, more benighted plantation owners regarded as remarkable. The cotton crop was increased by twenty percent, the tobacco crop by thirteen percent, and other produce, including cereal grains and table vegetables, also rose.

Little Jerry Beaufort grew rapidly. He was toddling now, speaking his first words, and his proud grandfather had already bought him a pony, which his mother refused to allow him to ride until his second birthday. She tried in vain to prevent the whole family from spoiling him, and continued to pray that Jeremy would return to her soon.

Some of the Beaufort friends and neighbors were beginning to think of her as a widow, and the attentions of men made her apprehensive. She clung to the conviction that Jeremy was alive and would come home, but it was becoming increasingly difficult to hold to that belief.

Worst of all, she had to fight her own inner nature. She was young, high-spirited, and desperately lonely, and it disturbed her when she enjoyed the attentions of various men and found herself attracted to them. But she continued to exercise strict self-discipline, and her principles remained intact.

The marriage of Margot and Tom was still rocky. She frequently forgave him for delinquencies that ran the gamut from overindulgence in alcohol to carelessness bordering on indifference concerning the assumption of his responsibilities. Each time, the pattern was the same. Tom was penitent, promising to improve and change, but the moment Margot relented, he reverted to his slipshod ways. Little Jerry was more responsive to correction than his uncle.

Tom meant no harm to anyone, to be sure. He was so amiable that his father and father-in-law, trying to deal with him as a man, found it difficult to chastise him. Sarah was troubled, but he played every day with her baby, enjoying himself thoroughly. The continuing absence of the child's own father caused her to recognize Jerry's need for a substitute, and she, too, was unable to bear a lasting grudge against Tom.

Only Mr. Higby was still on bad terms with the younger son of Paul Beaufort, and neither made any move to improve their relationship. Tom literally ignored the overseer when he rode out into the fields, pointedly giving direct orders to the slaves when cotton and tobacco were stored in warehouses or bundled for shipment. Higby, for his part, made it his business to communicate only with the master of Oakhurst Manor. He was withdrawn, his manner surly, but at no time did he shirk his duty or sidestep his responsibilities. As Sarah said at dinner one day, and her father-in-law agreed with her, as long as Mr. Higby did what was expected of him, they had no cause for complaint.

No one asked Willie's opinion, but the cabinetmaker expressed himself freely to Tom. "That Higby has blood in his eye when he looks at you or me," he said. "First chance he gets, when nobody knows about it, he's going to cause us trouble or do us in. He's white trash, and that kind never forgives an insult."

Tom merely laughed and shrugged. "Let him do his damnedest," he said. "The first time he crosses me—or you—I'll put a bullet through his forehead."

Spring came early in 1814, and birds that had spent the winter in the Caribbean, the Gulf of Mexico, and the Floridas began to move northward about a month sooner than was their custom. One Sunday morning, as the Beauforts were preparing to drive to church, flights of quail appeared overhead, and Tom abruptly changed his plans.

"We can go to church every Sunday of the year," he said, much to Margot's annoyance. "But quail are here for only a short time, and then they go again. Do my praying for me today. I'm finding Willie, and we're going off to the blind we've fixed up for ourselves in the swamps. Tonight there will be more quail on the table than we can eat!"

Amanda was less than pleased when Willie instantly agreed to go on the expedition. But she, like Margot, was helpless and was given no voice in the matter.

Tom and Willie changed into old clothes, then donned high, heavily oiled boots. They armed themselves with long frontier rifles, for almost forty years the most accurate weapon made and superior by far to the modern muskets being used by British and French infantry.

They rode off to the swamps at the southeastern end of Oakhurst Manor, and after tethering their horses, proceeded on foot. The ground became progressively softer and spongier as they walked, the reeds became higher, and the tangle of cypress and bushes was thicker. In places, the foliage was so dense that the sky overhead was hidden, and the odors of mud, stagnant water, and rotting vegetation that were peculiar to swamps were pungent.

The bird blind was located the better part of a half-mile from the spot where the two young men had entered the morass, and they waded toward it, their rifles carefully slung over their shoulders, their powder horns and ammunition bags suspended from their necks.

"In some places the rains have turned this creek into a real river," Willie said.

"I've never seen it this strong, and the mud is awful," Tom replied. "Some spots, we're sinking in it up to our knees."

"Good conditions for bagging quail," Willie said with a laugh.

"The best!"

As they drew nearer to the blind, they automatically fell silent and walked more slowly, taking special care not to splash or make other noises. They moved into single file, with Tom taking the lead, and every few minutes they looked up at the bright sky, searching for the quail they would bring home at the end of the day.

For at least ten minutes neither spoke.

Suddenly Tom gasped. "My foot is caught on a root," he said, his voice calm. "Both feet. My God! Stay where you are, Willie."

The cabinetmaker halted instantly.

"The flooring has shifted in some way," Tom said, "and I've walked into a patch of quicksand."

"I'll give you a hand." Willie extended the butt of his rifle, still grasping the barrel, and held on with both hands.

Tom took hold of the butt, and with Willie bracing himself and pulling steadily, tried to haul himself out. But the quicksand had already imprisoned him, and Willie could not gain a sufficiently firm footing in the mud to be of much help to him.

"I'll dig in as best I can," Willie said, "and when I'm set, you haul yourself hand over hand. It's the only way."

Tom was already sinking lower, but did not give in to panic. As soon as Willie nodded that he was ready, he exerted all of his considerable strength in an attempt to pull himself out of the treacherous mire.

But the very nature of quicksand doomed his efforts. The slightest movement of his feet and legs caused the flooring of the swamp to shift again, and he sank deeper.

They struggled against the terrible odds, and both were soaked to the skin.

By now Tom was waist-deep in the quicksand.

It was obvious to both of them that they needed reinforcements. Willie, in spite of his wiry strength, was slightly built and lacked the bulk to haul the other man out single-handed.

Both knew, however, that it was useless to shout for help. The slaves avoided the swamps, regarding them as haunted, and there were no poachers on the Beaufort property.

But reason no longer prevailed, and Willie shouted at the top of his voice. "Help! Quicksand!"

Tom tried to shout, too, but by now fear had overwhelmed him, and his voice emerged in a hoarse, inarticulate croak.

Again Willie shouted, then devoted what was left of his breath and his ebbing strength to the struggle against certain defeat.

He heard a sound behind him, paid no attention, then heard it again. Turning to glance over his shoulder, he saw Mr. Higby, a net and burlap bag in his hands. Obviously he had come to the swamp for eels.

The overseer halted, and instantly understood the situation. What to do about it was another matter. Here were his two enemies, each of whom had insulted and humiliated him. Unless he intervened, the white man would die in the quicksand. Then he could accuse the black man of murder, and no court in the state would believe Willie's story.

Tom saw Mr. Higby, but pride sealed his mouth. Under no circumstances would he beg for aid from someone he hated and who despised him. Surely he would suffocate in the quicksand, but he would die with his honor intact.

Willie was completely pragmatic. Paying no further heed to the overseer, he resumed his grim struggle against certain death.

Their contempt stung Mr. Higby to the quick, and his decision was made for him. Climbing onto hard ground, he took a knife from his belt and cut a long section of trailing vine from the undergrowth. Then, wading back into the swamp, he passed one end to Willie.

The cabinetmaker needed no instructions, and threw the vine to Tom. "Tie this under your arms," he said, "and be sure you make it fast. Quick, now!"

Tom needed no urging. He was chest-deep in the quicksand, and his hands trembled as he knotted the pliable vine.

Willie wrapped the line around his own body several times, and Higby did the same with the far end. Then they turned, with one accord, and straining with all their might, began to move away from the trapped Tom.

The line grew taut, but the victim of the quicksand did not budge.

Tom knew better than to struggle now, and relied on their efforts to rescue him.

The vine strained but did not break.

Willie and the overseer took tiny steps toward the hard ground that beckoned.

At last Tom felt himself being dragged a very short distance, perhaps a fraction of an inch. "It's working!" he shouted.

The encouraging word was all they needed, and they redoubled their efforts. The overseer grunted repeatedly, and Willie bent almost double as he strained and pulled.

Again Tom moved, and this time he was jerked a considerable distance.

The rest was almost anticlimactic. His left leg came free,

and he was able to help himself to a limited extent. A moment later he was staggering forward through the swamp.

His rescuers did not stop, however, until all three reached solid ground. Then they threw themselves onto the grass until they regained their breath and stopped shaking.

Willie reached into the knapsack on his back and drew out a flask of rum.

All three took long swallows.

Tom broke the silence. "Willie," he said, "you don't need me to tell you how I feel. Higby, I thank you from the bottom of my heart."

The overseer hauled himself to his feet. "I reckon you'd do the same for me," he said, and walked away.

Tom made no attempt to call him back.

There was no reconciliation in the real sense of the word. The overseer's participation in the rescue had constituted a pause in the feud, for humanity's sake, but neither side intended to forget or forgive. Someday, perhaps, when the odds were equal, there would be a final showdown.

Tom and Willie continued to rest, and although they emptied the flask, neither felt the effects of the rum.

A flight of quail passed overhead, and both looked up with indifference.

"I've lost my appetite for hunting today," Tom said.

"We had more than our share of quail last fall," Willie replied. "I reckon Amanda will be so glad to see me this early in the day that she'll fix breakfast for me right off, as soon as we get home."

Tom decided to make no mention of the incident to Margot or his father. They would be satisfied when they learned, gradually, that he was no longer hunting or fishing in the swamps.

Later in the year, a British force invaded the new American capital, Washington City, severely damaging the President's House and destroying the Treasury and War Department buildings before they withdrew. The heroine of the incident was Dolley Madison, the president's wife, who managed to take presidential portraits, silverware, and other valuables with her when she fled. It was said she escaped from the city to nearby Georgetown only minutes before the enemy arrived.

The humiliation had a beneficial effect. Recruiting had lagged, but now men by the thousands joined the colors, many flocking to the banner of General Andrew Jackson. Old Hickory publicly vowed to open the Mississippi River to American navigation, and the British were sending a force of seasoned veterans to meet him at or near New Orleans. These troops had just inflicted a severe defeat on Napoleon, sending him into exile, and many Americans were afraid their young armies would be crushed.

General Jackson did not share their fears. "We'll skin the redcoats the way we skin polecats in Tennessee," he told his troops. They believed in him and shared his confidence.

Meantime, according to reports published in the more responsible American newspapers, the peace negotiators meeting at Ghent were finally making substantial progress, and there was real hope they would reach an agreement in the near future. Neither President Madison nor Secretary of State James Monroe denied the accuracy of these stories.

The hopes of the family at Oakhurst Manor flared anew. Surely, if Jeremy was still alive, he would return home soon. If he was still alive. . . .

The better part of three years had passed since he had vanished, and Sarah's faith was beginning to falter. She had undergone previous periods of depression, but none had been so intense or so prolonged. Her son was more than two years old now, and might never know his father. She had to face the very real possibility that Jeremy might never return, that she would have to build a completely new life for herself.

In the meantime, she did not neglect her duties as the mistress of Oakhurst Manor. She was efficient, always controlled, and no detail of daily living escaped her attention. She rarely smiled, except when she played with little Jerry, and she performed her functions so meticulously that those nearest to her became concerned.

"She's become a robot," Isaiah Benton said as he and

Lorene sat in the manor parlor with Paul Beaufort, drinking after-dinner coffee.

"True," Paul replied. "It's as though she's been drained of all feeling."

"Small wonder," Lorene Benton said. "It would be better for her, after all this time, to receive definite proof that Jeremy is dead. At least she'd know. And in time, she'd recover her balance."

"I'll tell you what worries me most," Isaiah said. "Her self-control is so great that it isn't natural. She keeps her feelings bottled up inside her, and I'm afraid her mind will slip."

"She needs a distraction, even one that's temporary," Paul said.

Isaiah nodded. "I know. I've suggested she make a trip up to Richmond, even visit New York and Boston. But she simply won't travel. She won't leave Oakhurst Manor for as much as a single night, because she says Jeremy might come home while she's away. It's a slender reed on which to base her future."

Paul pondered for a time. "Peace is at hand, and everyone with whom I've spoken who has any knowledge of the situation seems certain the hostilities will end in the next few months. It would be premature to hold a peace party, but we need no excuse to give a ball."

"Splendid," Isaiah said. "Sarah will immerse herself in the details of preparing for the party, and if she's surrounded by enough young people, she might even break out of her straitjacket for one night."

Lorene failed to share their enthusiasm. "Give the ball if you wish," she said, "and I hope it will have the effect on Sarah that you seek. But she's burrowed so deeply into her shell that she may not respond at all. She's an exceptionally complicated person, and she's suffered far more than is good for her."

"I see nothing to be lost by trying," Isaiah said.

"Nor do I," Paul declared.

"I can only hope you're right," Lorene told them.

Preparations for the ball began the next day, and a special messenger was sent to North Carolina to engage the fiddlers. Work began in the kitchen, and Sarah herself wrote and addressed the invitations to two hundred guests.

From the outset, she decided that this party would be different. The menu would feature New England specialties instead of Southern fare. The outraged Cleo was temporarily ousted from her own kitchen, and Sarah, with the assistance of Amanda, herself prepared huge pots of chowder, rich in clams, onions and potatoes, as well as great vats of beans that were baked for hours and flavored with bits of pork. Meats included slabs of corned beef that were boiled, turkeys that were broiled and stuffed with sage dressing, and fish cooked over slow fires and basted with butter. Cleo was somewhat mollified when she was taught the recipe for brown bread, prepared with molasses and raisins, and when she learned the recipe for Indian pudding, she added her own touches, including a custard sauce flavored with Madeira.

The weather had turned cool, so the party would be centered in the ballroom on the top floor of the manor house, but Sarah decided that the garden should be decorated, and hundreds of colored lanterns were hung, each with a candle that would burn for many hours.

Margot, who was suffering from a series of headaches, took little part in the preparations. Her father and Paul privately told her the reason the ball was being given, and she approved. But she felt certain Tom would drink too much, and she had to steel herself for the coming ordeal.

On the night of the ball, Sarah suddenly lost her zest for the party. Empire dresses were no longer fashionable, now that Napoleon Bonaparte was living in exile on the island of Elba, but she still preferred them to more ornate gowns. Principally because Jeremy had admired her in them. So she had ordered a new cream-colored Empire gown, daring in its clinging simplicity. But as she sat in front of her dressing-table mirror, brushing her long blond hair and applying cosmetics, she no longer cared how she looked.

Amanda came into the chamber to see if she wanted assistance.

Sarah looked at her listlessly. "I feel like going straight to bed, stuffing my ears with cotton wool, and going to sleep," she said.

"You can't, Sarah!" Amanda was aghast. "People will never stop talking about you, and I shudder to think of the stories they'll tell."

"I just don't have the energy. Or the desire."

"Then find the energy! Look at yourself in the pier glass. You've never been prettier."

Sarah studied her reflection, reluctantly sliding large golden hoops into her earlobes. "If I must, I suppose I can do it with the help of a stimulant. Perhaps you'll be a dear and bring me a cup of that punch Tom has made."

Amanda looked dubious. "Willie says that's the strongest drink there is. It has brandywine, rum, and two kinds of wine in it."

"Just what I need. I can't feel any worse."

Amanda went off, returning with a cup.

The first swallow made Sarah shudder, but the taste improved, and by the time she was finishing making up, her spirits had risen. She went downstairs to be on hand when the guests arrived, and while she waited, she refilled her cup. By the time carriages pulled up in front of the portico, she was feeling giddy.

That was the beginning of the liveliest, most extraordinary evening she had ever known. When the younger people adjourned to the ballroom on the top floor, she took the lead in the festivities, dancing tirelessly with a score of partners and flirting recklessly with many of them. Those who had thought of her as a solemn, inward-looking person were astonished. Not even Margot, in the days before her marriage, had ever displayed such gaiety, such a sense of abandon.

"Thank the Lord," Paul Beaufort said when he came upstairs with some of the older people.

"At last she's relaxing," Isaiah Benton declared. "This party is just what she needs."

Lorene Benton kept silent. She had observed what neither of the men had noted, that Sarah's unusual high spirits were being induced by alcohol, not her own inner feelings. Whenever she began to grow quieter or to sag, she asked someone to bring her another cup of the potent punch. By now she was well under its influence, apparently without realizing it.

But there seemed to be no harm done, Lorene reflected. In the morning, Sarah well might be feeling less than chipper, and it was possible she would suffer remorse. But perhaps Isaiah and Paul were right, after all. She had bottled up her emotions for too long, and it did her good to stop grieving for one evening.

Margot, on the other hand, was behaving with modest circumspection. She circulated constantly, exchanging a few words with each of the many guests, but she refused invitations to join in the dancing, and her smiles were mechanical. It was not difficult to divine the reasons for her demeanor: Tom, as usual, was drinking heavily, and soon after midnight, Margot quietly slipped away to their suite, telling no one she was going to bed.

The supper was a huge success, the guests devouring the New England dishes. Sarah ate virtually nothing, however, and instead continued to drink cup after cup of the punch.

Isaiah and Lorene, who were staying at Oakhurst Manor for several days, retired as the guests began to depart. Paul bade farewell to the older guests, who were among the first to leave, but left Sarah and Tom to deal with the younger crowd. It was two A.M. when the last carriage rolled down the driveway and the lanterns in the garden were extinguished.

Sarah kicked off her high-heeled slippers, and staggering slightly, dropped onto the nearest divan in the parlor.

"Join me in a nightcap," a glassy-eyed Tom suggested as he came into the room.

"Why not?" she replied with a giggle, then couldn't stop laughing.

Instead of using punch cups, he filled two silver tumblers and handed one to his sister-in-law, then removed his swallow-tailed coat and over-the-ankle boots. "A great party," he said, and sat beside her on the divan.

"And a marvelous punch." Her judgment already warped, Sarah took a long swallow of the concoction.

"I was wrong about you," Tom said with a grin. "I've believed that both of the Benton sisters have cold water—very cold water—running through their veins instead of blood. But you, my angel Sarah, are a real woman!"

Again she laughed. "Don't tell anyone, but right now I

267

think I have brandywine punch flowing through my veins."
She raised her silver tumbler and took another long swallow.

Tom chuckled and stretched an arm across the back of the divan.

Sarah's head was spinning now, and his shoulder seemed the natural place to rest it.

All at once, without either of them realizing how it happened, they were locked in an embrace.

In Sarah's drunken confusion, as they kissed, she thought it was Jeremy who was holding her tight.

Their lips parted, their mutual desire mounted, and Tom, equally irresponsible, began to make love to her in earnest.

No man had touched Sarah in almost three years, and her ardor, inflamed by the punch, was explosive. She responded with vehemence, and soon they were stretched out together on the divan.

Jeremy was kissing and caressing her, fondling and stroking her.

But, all at once, before they commited sexual intercourse, she heard a door on the second floor slam shut, and the spell was broken. This man wasn't Jeremy.

It was her brother-in-law who was making love to her.

Shocked and horrified by her own conduct, Sarah struggled against him, managed to disengage herself, and pulled herself to her feet.

Tom protested feebly, then drifted off to sleep.

She paid no further attention to him, however, and suddenly she knew what had recalled her to her senses. Someone had started down the central staircase and had paused for a moment on the landing before retreating.

Instinct told her it could have been only one person: Margot.

Stunned into sobriety, Sarah climbed the stairs. Her fragile gown was torn, her hair was in disarray, but such things no longer mattered. It was imperative that she see her sister. Immediately.

She forced herself to organize her thoughts. The incident had stunned her into sobriety, at least for the moment, but the future of her family relationship was at stake, and she could afford to make no more mistakes.

Gathering her courage, Sarah tapped at the door of the suite. A lamp was burning inside, she could see under the door, so she felt certain her surmise had been right.

There was no reply.

Making a futile attempt to rearrange her neckline so the tear in her gown wouldn't be so obvious, Sarah took a deep breath and opened the door.

Margot stood at the windows, staring with unseeing eyes down at the garden. She was clad in a nightgown and robe, and did not turn when she heard the door open and shut.

Sarah continued to steel herself. "Margot . . ."

"Oh, it's you. I thought it was Tom." The younger sister still stood unmoving.

"An apology would be inadequate, and I won't insult you by offering one," Sarah said. "I just want you to know that I've humiliated myself, and I'll never recover from my mortification. This is no excuse, but I was drunk. So drunk that Tom looked even more like Jeremy than he does, and sounded more like Jeremy than he does."

"I understand." Margot's voice was still remote.

"Do you? I think not. No one can understand the torment I've been through for month after month after month. But I'm not asking for your pity, any more than I ask for your forgiveness. I just want you to know that I have no personal interest in your husband, I'm not attracted to him . . . and I thank God I came to my senses in time." Sarah began to weep. "It's enough that I'll have to live with this disgrace for the rest of my life."

Margot turned slowly and faced her. "Wait. Don't go yet."

"There's no more that I can say," Sarah whispered.

"Then listen to me for a moment." Margot's voice was firm. "I blame you for nothing that has happened tonight, and I swear I'll never blame you. Sarah, you've carried enough burdens, and you'll be wrong if you add a feeling of guilt to all the others. I'm surprised you didn't crack long ago, and you weren't at fault."

"You're generous." The tears streamed down Sarah's

face, adding to the ravages of her already smudged make-up.

"I assure you I'm not. For your sake, I'm relieved that you didn't actually . . . couple with Tom. That alone should make this sorry mess easier for you to put out of your mind. For all time." Margot reached out and touched her. "Go to bed, Sarah. Tomorrow will be a new day. I'll never mention this incident to you again, and I'll never think less of you than I always have."

Her composure was too great, her manner too controlled, and Sarah asked, "What about you . . . and Tom?"

"I don't know. As of now, I'm not sure what I'll do. I need time to think and plan. All I can say is that I've tolerated Tom's behavior long enough, and what he's done tonight is the last straw."

Chapter 19

Jeremy Beaufort's will to survive had prevailed, and he knew he was one of the luckiest men alive. The situation in which he found himself was far from ideal, but he was alive, his circumstances were comfortable, and he had been thrust into a position he was well qualified to handle. Certainly he could not quibble.

After he had been hauled from the sea, more dead than alive, he had discovered he was on board a triple-masted ship of unusual design, almost rectangular in shape, with a blunt prow and a square-cut stern. As he had recovered from the shock of the sinking of the bomb ketch, he had learned that the *County Mayo* was an oversized schooner built for a specific purpose. She was a blackbirder, the better part of her hold containing long benches used to transport slaves to the New World.

At this very moment she was sailing eastward across the Atlantic to Africa to pick up a cargo of slaves.

Not the least of the surprises that had awaited Jeremy had been the effusiveness of the welcome he had received from the ship's master, Sean Garrity. It hadn't taken long to find out the reasons for his warmth.

The man that Garrity had rescued from the Caribbean had been wearing the uniform of an officer in the Royal Navy. Garrity's first mate had just died at sea, and the young second mate, a Portuguese named Carvalho, lacked the experience to sail the ship.

It hadn't taken long to strike a bargain. Jeremy had accepted the post of first mate, and in return had been required to promise that he would not leave the *County Mayo* until she returned to the Caribbean and sold her shipload of slaves.

So here he sat, snug in his own cabin, which was twice the size of the quarters he had occupied on board the British bomb ketch. Even the clothes of the late first mate whom he had replaced fitted him well enough, and he could overlook the fact that the food was atrocious. As he kept telling himself, he was the most fortunate of men.

His return to the United States and his reunion with Sarah Benton were delayed by at least six months, but he couldn't really complain. Had he remained in the Royal Navy, he would have had to wait indefinitely.

The mission on which the *County Mayo* was engaged disgusted him. In his opinion, slavery was a necessary evil that supported the economy of Oakhurst Manor and all the other plantations of the South. But the men who actually engaged in the slave trade were loathsome, and now he was one of them.

Not that Garrity, a white-haired Irishman, was a bad fellow. To an extent, he was unscrupulous, willingly raising any flag, regardless of whether it was British or French, American or Dutch or Spanish, when he encountered a warship. It was true, too, that he had an unlimited capacity for the vile-smelling gin he kept in a locker in his cabin, but he drank only when off duty, and it wasn't a mate's place to criticize his captain's personal habits.

What bothered Jeremy was that Captain Garrity was an indifferent sailor. His seamanship was careless, his navigation was sloppy, and he was far too lenient in his treatment of his crew. There was the crux of the problem: the crew.

Ever since early boyhood in South Carolina, Jeremy had heard that only the scum of the earth signed on slave ships, and the stories had been right. There were forty-nine seamen on board the *County Mayo*, and all of them, from the boatswain to the newest recruit, were rogues and rascals, men without conscience who had been attracted by the high wages a blackbirder paid.

The majority were Portuguese who made such permanent homes as they knew in Portugal's African colonies. Some were Danes, others Dutch, and a handful were English and Irish. They were cutthroats and thieves, callous to the feelings of others. Captain Garrity kept his own cabin locked when he left it, and advised his new first mate to do the same.

Even the most vicious responded to sharp discipline, Jeremy believed after his experience in the Royal Navy, but Garrity was emotionally incapable of cracking down on his crew. The result was that trouble had been brewing for the past week, and Jeremy was convinced that sooner or later the master of the *County Mayo* would be required to take a firm stand.

At this very moment, as Jeremy donned boots and an oiled cape preparatory to relieving the captain and taking the next watch, he heard the sounds of an altercation on the quarterdeck. The argument grew louder, voices became uglier.

As a precaution, Jeremy took two pistols from the sea chest that had belonged to his predecessor, made certain they were loaded and primed, then jammed them into his belt, where they were concealed under his cape. Hanging from a bulkhead peg was a sword that had belonged to the late mate, too. It was a clumsy, old-fashioned blade, far too long and cumbersome to be practical, with too heavy a hilt. But it was a symbol of authority, so Jeremy buckled it on.

When he reached the quarterdeck, he saw that the situation was even worse than he had anticipated. A cowed master was being menaced by a dozen seamen who crowded around him, all of them armed with spars or clubs. One of Garrity's problems was that, in his sixties, he was too old for an active command at sea.

Jeremy crossed the quarterdeck in swift strides.

"Mate," one of the sailors called in broken English, "not your fight. You stay out."

Jeremy ignored the admonition. "What's happening here?"

Captain Garrity was badly frightened. "They object because I'm sailing to Luanda in Portuguese Angola instead of the Gold Coast, where they mistakenly think we'll make a better deal for a cargo of slaves, and they're threatening to take over the ship. They say the food is slop and they insist on an improvement, but they haven't told me where I'll find rations in mid-Atlantic."

"This is open mutiny," Jeremy said.

"Mate," a giant English sailor with a long, livid scar on his face said, "go about your own business, or you'll have a broken head."

Captain Garrity cringed.

The sailors inched closer, their spars and clubs raised.

An outraged Jeremy knew that the slightest spark would start a fight, and he realized he had to act quickly and decisively. Drawing his almost useless sword, he addressed the sailors in a clear, sharp voice. "Men," he said, "the captain determines where we sail. I'm as sorry as you are that the food is inadequate, but nothing can be done to improve your meals. So disperse. Now. And return to your duties."

The note of command in his voice caused some of the mutineers to hesitate, but the huge English seaman had a mind and will of his own. "I warned you, mate," he said, and stepped forward, ready to bring his spar down on Jeremy's head.

The clumsy sword had a practical value, after all. Reacting instinctively, Jeremy used the flat of the blade and knocked the spar to the deck.

The sailor had lost face in front of his peers and was livid. "Goddamn you, mate!" he roared. "I'll kill you for this!"

Jeremy realized he had no alternative, and before the man could leap, drew one of his pistols and fired. The shot entered the sailor's forehead, killing him instantly, and he crumpled to the deck.

There was no other way to deal with a mutiny, and Jeremy felt no remorse.

The other seamen backed away, their ardor for mutiny fast disappearing.

Jeremy drew his other pistol. "Wrap his body in a blanket and throw him overboard. Now. Then return to your duties. Step lively!"

Within moments the quarterdeck was clear.

A trembling Captain Garrity looked at Jeremy with deep gratitude. "Mr. Beaufort," he said, his brogue thicker than usual, "you've saved my life and my ship!"

Jeremy was embarrassed for him. "I'm relieving you, sir," he said.

Garrity nodded and slowly made his way to his own quarters.

"Two points south by southeast," Jeremy told the helmsman, and leaned on the quarterdeck rail.

The call had been close, and he needed the chance to relax. Never before had he killed a fellow human being in cold blood, but he had no regrets. The English sailor would have acted first and taken his life if he hadn't responded with vigor. Death was the price of mutiny, and every man who went to sea well knew it.

They were sailing in equatorial waters, the sun overhead was hot, and the sea was calm, so the sailing of the *County Mayo* required little of Jeremy's attention, and little by little he grew more tranquil.

Suddenly he realized that the sea around the schooner was seething. "All hands on deck!" he shouted.

The order was repeated, and soon pounding footsteps sounded everywhere.

"Man the nets!" Jeremy commanded. "We're sailing through a whole school of fish. Haul as many loads on board as you can gather!"

The men went to work with a will.

Perhaps the exercise was futile, Jeremy thought. It was possible that the small fish were *Italo bello*, pretty creatures but inedible. On the other hand, they might be *Italo blanco*, with fine-grained, firm flesh, delicious when grilled. There was nothing to lose, and a great deal to gain.

When three net loads had been hauled to the main deck,

Jeremy went down to investigate, and picking up a still-wriggling fish, he grinned. "Send the cook to me at once."

The cook, a Portuguese, soon appeared, but he spoke little English, so Jeremy gave his instructions to the Irish boatswain. "O'Hara, I want the portable stove brought up to the aft deck. Plant it in tubs of sand for safety's sake, and make certain you have buckets of water handy in case a fire breaks out."

"Aye, aye, sir." The boatswain, who had been on the verge of mutiny a scant two hours earlier, stood at respectful attention.

"Then put all idle hands to work scaling these fish and chopping off their heads and tails. That's all that needs to be done to them. The cook can put as many on the fire at a time as the grill will hold, after he dips them in oil. They're to be cooked until they're a deep brown."

"Very good, sir." O'Hara was puzzled. "Is this to be done at suppertime tonight, sir?"

"Right now," Jeremy replied as he started back to the quarterdeck. "We'll want to eat these *Italo blanco* while they're really fresh!"

Within minutes a fire was started, and a dozen sailors busied themselves cleaning the fish. Jeremy smiled to himself; the Royal Navy had the right idea. Keep a seaman active, and he wouldn't think in terms of mutiny.

Before long a grinning boatswain came to the quarterdeck and offered the first mate a heaping plate. "These are wonderful, sir."

Jeremy took a bite. "Indeed they are. Have a meal sent to the captain, with my compliments. And I'm sure that after I've finished this dish, I'll want another."

The members of the crew, he saw, were eating the fish as rapidly as the cook prepared them.

After a time the boatswain returned, and this time his face was solemn as he handed Jeremy a plate of fish. "Mr. Beaufort," he said, "there will be no more mutinies on this voyage. The men have taken a vote, and they'll follow you wherever you sail."

The *Italo blanco* had turned the tide, Jeremy thought, and was thankful for the miracle.

When his watch ended, he was relieved by Carvalho, the second mate, and started toward his own cabin.

But a shout from the master's quarters halted him. "Come in here, Mr. Beaufort! I want a word with you."

Jeremy saw that the captain had been consuming generous quantities of gin.

"Sit down, Mr. Beaufort, and join me in a drink."

Jeremy sat but refused a glass of gin.

"You may not know this, but I'm the owner as well as the master of the *County Mayo*," Garrity said in a thick voice. "It's been my plan to sell this ship after I make this last profit and retire to a house I've bought near Dublin. Meantime, I've racked my poor brains to think of some proper way to thank you for what you've done today—"

"I want no thanks, sir. I did my duty."

"Rubbish, boy! I've increased your first mate's share of the profits from ten percent to fifteen, and if I should die of my rheumatics or the bottle, which I pray the Lord I won't, I'm leaving the *County Mayo* to you. It's all here on this paper!"

Jeremy barely glanced at the drunken scrawl, politely expressed his thanks, and went off to his own cabin. The profits of a slave trader were of no interest to him. All he wanted was to return to Sarah and Oakhurst Manor at the first opportunity.

São Paulo de Luanda, capital of the colony of Angola, was said to be the most European city in Africa. Founded almost two and a half centuries earlier by the Portuguese, it lay south of the Congo River and north of the Kwanza River, so it was ideally situated for the purposes of slave traders who traveled inland on both of the great rivers when they made their raids on native villages.

The low-lying basin directly adjacent to the deep-water port was a native town, with primitive huts crowding each other, but behind this area stood the cooler, healthier hills, and there Portuguese merchants, government officials, and traders by the hundreds had built their homes, inns, and shops, most of them stucco buildings painted in pleasing muted pastel colors that blended with the gentle landscape.

Jeremy had not expected to find such a charming community, and was bemused by it as he rode in a creaking open carriage with Captain Garrity to the home of Pedro Fernandes Andeiro, a Portuguese slave trader. Andeiro, one of the most notorious men in Africa, was small and dark, with a face like a ferret, his hands in constant motion when he spoke, his gestures fluid and quick.

His house, solidly built and featuring jalousies in every window to admit breezes, resembled scores of other houses in Luanda from the outside. The interior was astonishing, however, because it contained only the most sparse necessities, all fashioned of bamboo. There were a few chairs and tables, and unadorned candles provided illumination at night; the floors were bare, and so were the walls.

Andeiro's indifference to his home did not extend to his person, however. He wore a suit of raw silk, his open-throated shirt was also fashioned of silk, and his boots were the most expensive Jeremy had ever seen. Rings blazing with rubies and sapphires flashed on the fingers of both hands, and like the buccaneers of the previous century in the West Indian islands, he wore a large diamond in one ear.

He offered his guests a mildly fermented root drink, which was served in chipped mugs by a slave woman. Jeremy didn't like the drink, telling himself the taste for it undoubtedly was acquired, but he was surprised by the appearance of the slave woman, whose ankle-length skirt was fastened around her middle and who was naked above the waist. Andeiro, Garrity, and the woman herself took her nudity for granted.

Andeiro wasted no time getting down to business. "So many ships have put into Luanda lately that I can only offer you an inferior lot of slaves right now, Garrity," he said. "But you may be in luck—although I don't see how I'll show a profit. Your friend Umbunga has been looking forward to your arrival, and I hear he's currently visiting one of his villages that's only a day's ride into the interior."

"King Umbunga," Captain Garrity explained to Jeremy, "is the principal chief of the Bantu, the most ferocious of the warrior nations in Africa. He's sold a number of slave loads to me. After he captures the prisoners in battle, he'd rather show a profit than follow the usual system."

"What's that?" Jeremy wanted to know.

Andeiro laughed at his ignorance. "Bantu prisoners are killed. Only a few of the women and girl children are spared."

The barbarity of Africa was appalling, Jeremy thought.

"The Bantu keep their plans to themselves," Andeiro said, "but there's a rumor that Umbunga intends to make war on the Watusi before long."

"Ah." Garrity rubbed his liver-spotted hands together and again turned to Jeremy. "The Watusi are a tall, sturdy people. They're strong, and many of them have been farmers. They're gentle, too, so they cause little trouble when they're transported to the New World."

Jeremy knew something about the Watusi, having accompanied his father to the slave market in Charleston on a number of occasions when Paul Beaufort had invested in members of the tribe.

"You may have a wait of several months, of course," Andeiro said, "because no Bantu campaign has started as yet."

"A shipload of Watusi is worth the wait," Garrity replied.

Jeremy had to swallow his indignation, and knew now how Sarah felt about the whole institution of slavery. These men were discussing human beings as though they were merchandise. Which they were.

"I'll make you a deal, Captain," Andeiro said. "Berth your ship at one of my wharves, and I'll provide you with guards guaranteed to admit no unauthorized persons on board. I'll also pay your men their regular wages while you wait for Umbunga to provide you with prisoners, and you'll have your full crew intact when you're ready to sail."

"How much?" Garrity demanded.

"Fourteen percent."

The Irishman became scornful. "I'll give you eight."

They bickered for a time, finally settling on a sum of eleven percent of the net profits, with a retainer fee of two thousand pounds in British silver to be paid immediately.

As soon as the deal was completed, all three rode without delay to the harbor. Jeremy elected to wait on shore while Andeiro and two of his men went on board to collect the retainer fee, which Garrity took from the safe in his quarters. Jeremy had seen the safe, but hadn't known there was a small fortune in cash in it.

Garrity came ashore again, announcing that he and Jeremy would start their journey to the Bantu village that same day.

Andeiro was agreeable, and promptly provided them with horses, supplies of dried meat and African beans, already cooked, that looked something like South Carolina chickpeas. He gave them weapons, too, Jeremy's consisting of a short sword that was more oramental than useful and a pair of silver-handled dueling pistols with hair triggers.

The pistols were gems, and Jeremy admired them.

"You may want to buy them from me after you return," Andeiro said with a bloodless smile. "Their former owner is deceased, and can no longer appreciate them."

Something in his manner told Jeremy that Andeiro had been responsible for the death of the previous owner of the pistols.

There was no chance to think further about the slave trader, however, Garrity being eager to ride inland without delay. Jeremy dismissed Andeiro from his mind; it was enough that the man was nasty and unfeeling.

Behind the hills of the Portuguese settlement stood a gently rising plateau, and Africa abruptly replaced the European community. Here was a vast meadowland, its grass knee-high, with not a tree to be seen anywhere. The soil looked black and rich to Jeremy's practiced eye, but he couldn't understand why there were no farms here.

"The Portuguese discourage native farming this close to São Paulo de Luanda," Garrity explained. "I suppose they're afraid they'll all be murdered in their beds during an uprising. Tomorrow morning we'll begin to see some villages, but the Africans hereabouts don't farm, not in our sense of the word. Game is so plentiful that they have ample meat when they hunt, and they gather all the wild fruits and vegetables they can eat. There's no need for them to cultivate the ground. On the Ivory Coast and

Gold Coast there's farming. And lots of it in the Watusi lands. But this is Bantu country, and they're strictly warriors. Too proud to be farmers."

About an hour or two after leaving the coast, they saw a half-dozen gazelles in the distance, remarkably graceful, agile creatures that leaped effortlessly through the high grass. Jeremy was even more fascinated, a short time later, when they passed a herd of zebra, horselike creatures with black and white stripes, grazing quietly near the banks of a small stream.

Late in the day, shortly before making camp for the night, they came across a large herd of the strangest animals Jeremy had ever seen. They stood four feet high, with manes like horses' and heads resembling those of oxen, with long, curved horns. They were incredibly swift, bounding and racing like antelope, and they showed no fear of the men on horseback, although they were careful to keep their distance.

Jeremy could not stop staring at them. "What are they?" he asked.

Garrity could understand his interest. "You'll see all kinds of animals here that you don't know in your world. Hippos, rhinos, elephants, not to mention lions and the like. These creatures are called gnus by the natives. The Afrikaners, descendants of the Dutch who live down at the southern end of the continent, have their own name and call them wildebeests. They can't be tamed, and they're not much good for food, so they roam where they please, and nobody molests them. They're too quick even for tigers, and I've been told the black panther is the only enemy fast enough to catch them."

They came to a broad river that meandered through the prairie, and when they stopped for the night, Captain Garrity insisted they use their swords to cut down the grass at their campsite. "You never know where there are snakes hereabouts," he said, "but they keep hidden in the grass, and this way we're safe. But we can't camp too close to the river, either. Sometimes alligators climb up the banks, and they've been known to chomp off an arm or a leg."

Soon after darkness fell, the night was filled with the sound of throbbing drums. Some were distant, others were closer, and they were beaten alternately, their rhythms constantly changing.

"That's how the natives talk," Garrity said. "You can bet they've already passed the word that you and I are traveling inland, and every village within a hundred miles knows where we are. The farther we go, the faster the word will be given. It's quite a system, and it sure beats our method of using couriers, I can tell you."

Unaccustomed to the sounds, to the proximity of wild animals, serpents, and alligators, Jeremy passed a restless night.

At sunrise, after a breakfast of smoked beef and African beans, they watered their horses at the river, fed them chopped grain from their saddlebags, and resumed their journey.

Stunted trees, many of them grotesquely shaped, began to appear here and there. Then they came to several miles of bushes, some of them bearing brilliantly colored flowers, and in midmorning they plunged into a forest. Trees towered high overhead, bamboo thickets and bushes were everywhere, and in places the foliage was so thick that the sun's rays could not penetrate the darkness. The smell of rotting vegetation reminded Jeremy of the Caribbean, but was even more pungent.

Occasionally they heard a rustling noise that told them an animal was prowling nearby, and at Garrity's suggestion they loaded and primed their pistols. "A lion will attack humans only when he's hungry, although a tiger may do it for sport. When they strike, you've got to be ready for them. Fire fast and with a true aim, because you won't get a second chance."

They followed a narrow path through the forest, which was fortunate, Jeremy thought, as he completely lost his sense of direction. Occasionally he had the strange sensation that they were being observed, and he mentioned the phenomenon to his companion.

"Oh, no question about it," Garrity said. "I'm sure the Bantu have been keeping watch on us ever since we left Luanda. One reason they're the leading tribe on the continent and win all their wars is that they never take chances with anybody."

Ultimately the sea captain halted, and standing in the path, directly ahead, Jeremy saw an African wearing an animal skin and two wide bracelets of beaten gold. Astonishingly, he carried an American long rifle, with a powder horn and bullet pouch slung around his neck. He was tall, about Jeremy's height, with a powerful torso, and muscles rippled in his bare arms and legs. His features were clean-cut, his hair was short, and he raised his arm in salute.

"Welcome to the land of the Bantu, gentlemen," he said, speaking in impeccable, London-accented English. "It is good to see you again, Captain Garrity. Mr. Beaufort, we hope you will enjoy your stay with us."

Jeremy gaped at him.

The Bantu laughed. "I am M'Bwana, in my own tongue, 'Water Buffalo Who Fights Forever.' The second son of King Umbunga. I was taught your language by missionaries, and spent two years at school in England."

The visitors dismounted, and when Jeremy shook the Bantu's hand, he liked M'Bwana's firm grip. There was something in his expression, too, that was heartening. Here was a forthright, honest man in his mid-twenties, obviously endowed with a quick intelligence.

They walked for a quarter of an hour, leading the horses, and M'Bwana brought the newcomers up to date. "Our plans for the campaign against the Watusi are completed," he said, "and my father will be ready to take to the trail in about a month. He hopes, Captain Garrity, that you have brought the arms and ammunition you promised us. Modern arms will make our task much easier and save many hundreds of lives on both sides."

Garrity grinned. "I'm ready to negotiate with King Umbunga," he said.

All at once Jeremy knew what was in the locked hold of the *County Mayo* that no one was permitted to enter. He had seen the key to the main lock on a chain around Garrity's neck, and he realized that the compartment undoubtedly contained large quantities of muskets or long rifles, gunpowder, and bullets. It was obvious the sea captain hoped to trade these munitions for a shipload of slaves he would transport to the new World.

They came to a bamboo fence more than eight feet

high, its main gate guarded by several spear-carrying warriors in loincloths, with streaks of white paint on their foreheads, cheekbones, and foreheads. They were tall, husky men, and it was apparent that the Bantu were formidable.

Inside the stockade was a sprawling community of huts with bamboo walls and thatched roofs, interspersed with communal cooking pits. Small naked children were at play, bare-breasted women in long skirts were weaving cloth on primitive but effective looms, or preparing food, and several groups of adolescent boys were practicing spear-throwing under the watchful eyes of massively built senior warriors.

Jeremy guessed that the village had a population of at least two thousand persons.

In the center of the community stood a hut much longer than the others, and there the white men were presented to King Umbunga, an older, more solidly built version of his son, who wore even larger golden cuffs and, over his shoulders, a cape of brilliant red feathers that appeared to be a badge of office.

Jeremy bowed to him, and the king rose from a tree-stump stool to clasp his shoulder and speak to him in Bantu.

"My father bids you welcome, Mr. Beaufort," M'Bwana said. "Every Bantu home is your home."

The hospitality of the monarch and his family was overwhelming. They ate in the open, outside the large hut, sitting in a circle, served by several women. Later Jeremy would learn that three of them were Umbunga's wives, while two others were slaves captured in past wars. All, it appeared, were on easy terms with each other and received the same treatment.

The main course, served in large gourds, was a piping-hot stew of water-buffalo meat that had simmered in a pot for many hours, and with it were cooked a number of root vegetables totally unfamiliar to the American, as well as many tiny, tender green leaves. With their meal they drank the mildly fermented brew made from another root.

Captain Garrity picked at his food, leaving most of it in

his gourd, but the ravenous Jeremy cleaned up every bite, then licked his fingers, and the delighted King Umbunga ordered him given a second serving.

After the meal the king and the sea captain began to bargain, and Garrity was determined to make the best possible deal for himself. In return for three hundred muskets, ammunition for them, and a single small six-pounder cannon, he demanded five hundred adult slaves, all but one hundred of them men.

It seemed impossible to Jeremy that as many as five hundred human beings could be crowded on board the *County Mayo*. It wouldn't be possible to observe even the rudiments of sanitation, and many of the captives would die on the voyage. The stories Jeremy had heard about the cruel, inhuman living conditions on board blackbirders were true, and he was disgusted.

The king and Garrity continued to dicker, with Umbunga's elder son and principal heir, M'Dolna, also taking part in the discussion. They continued until sundown, when the king adjourned the negotiations until a later time.

As they left the hut, Jeremy and M'Bwana happened to exchange glances, and it was apparent their thoughts were similar.

"It is wrong to treat slaves like cattle," M'Bwana said. "They must work for others because that is the law of the world, but they are not animals."

"Human greed is a curse," Jeremy said, and felt ashamed of Garrity.

That night the visitors were housed in a snug hut of their own, and they slept on pallets of a soft material that Jeremy found comfortable.

In the morning, after a breakfast of grilled river fish and an unleavened bread made from a root, the king announced that he was taking his guests on a lion hunt. He was following the strategy, it appeared, of postponing the prickly negotiations until another day.

The party consisted of the king and his two sons, the visitors, and about a dozen senior warriors. Each was given several handfuls of a ground cooked grain for his midday meal, and each was equipped with a bronze-tipped spear.

Jeremy had never before handled such a weapon, and after checking with M'Bwana to make certain it was appropriate to do so for purposes of self-protection, he slid his dueling pistols into his belt.

The warriors split into two groups, six acting as a vanguard and six bringing up the rear. They carried spears, too, but would not participate actively in the hunt unless it became necessary to dispatch a wounded lion that ran amok.

The elder of the king's sons proudly walked alone behind the screen of guards. His brother explained that M'Dolna was one of the greatest of lion hunters in Bantu history, and had already killed six, four of them males.

Then came Jeremy and M'Bwana, the American privately not caring whether they actually found a lion. He lacked Tom's penchant for hunting, and ever since childhood had been interested in the sport only for purposes of obtaining food.

They walked silently through a patch of deep forest, where the treetops were thick and long vines trailed down from the upper branches. Never had Jeremy felt so alien, so remote from Oakhurst Manor.

Suddenly a vine—or what appeared to be a vine—dropped swiftly from a tree. Captain Garrity screamed, and as a snake at least four inches in diameter sank its fangs into the back of his neck, he collapsed onto the ground.

The tragedy had occurred so quickly that Jeremy was stunned.

Then he saw another snake drop and start to wrap itself around King Umbunga. Its head reared back, and its fangs were plain to see.

Galvanized into action, Jeremy drew his pistols, took swift aim with one, and fired.

The snake's head disintegrated.

The serpent continued to writhe, however, so he fired again, and his aim was true. He destroyed a portion of the snake's body directly behind the head.

By this time the warriors had sprung into action, and

using short knives, they hacked away at the still-moving body of the snake.

Then, with one accord, they attacked the serpent that had bitten the Irish sea captain, and soon destroyed it.

Garrity was in agony, his whole body swelling and his face scarlet, but he managed to murmur a few words as Jeremy bent over him.

"The *County Mayo* belongs to you now, lad," he whispered. "May you prosper as you sail her through the seven seas." He tried to speak again, choked, and died.

Chapter 20

The lion hunt was canceled, and the entire group returned to the Bantu village. There the body of Captain Garrity was laid on a shield, and to the horror of Jeremy, was carried by an escort of warriors to a nearby open field. By morning, after the wild hyenas had finished feasting, only bones would remain.

"That is the Bantu way," M'Bwana explained. "Garrity died honorably, and the gods of the Bantu will guard his soul. If he had been a coward, we would have built a platform at the edge of the great woods and burned his body on it. Now he will be at peace."

Shortly before sundown, drums beat, and all the people of the Bantu town were summoned to the open space in front of the king's hut. Jeremy, still disturbed over the terrible death of the man who had befriended him, had no desire to attend, but was not given a choice. A delegation of senior warriors, their faces smeared with white paint, came to his hut, and their gestures with shields and spears were plain.

He accompanied them to the clearing, where the people of the community had already assembled. King Umbunga was seated on a throne decorated with a cured lion skin. His two sons stood on either side of him, as did several smaller children, obviously his offspring too, and his wives and slave women were clustered behind him.

As soon as Jeremy arrived, the king stood and began to speak, his deep voice sonorous.

M'Bwana translated. "Umbunga, Bantu king of kings, makes all of his people here gathered witness to his pledge. Beaufort-from-across-the-sea has saved the life of the king of kings. Umbunga can give his friend no gift great enough to repay him, but as tokens of his esteem he makes two gifts."

The king reached under his cloak, produced what appeared to be a necklace, and motioned Jeremy closer.

The American saw the pure, colorless gleam of gems, embedded in rougher stone, and realized he was being presented with a necklace of uncut diamonds. Over the years he had heard it rumored that such stones sometimes were found in southern Africa, and the stories were right. He was the recipient of an emperor's ransom.

Umbunga looped the necklace over his neck, then spoke again.

Again M'Bwana translated. "The king of kings has many sons. The first of these will rule the Bantu when Umbunga joins his ancestors. The second is M'Bwana. From this day forward, until he dies, M'Bwana will go where Beaufort goes and protect him from evil."

Jeremy was overwhelmed.

The young Bantu prince took a single step forward and extended his arms.

They embraced, and the drums beat a furious tattoo while the crowd roared in approval.

A feast followed the ceremony, including a roast wild boar, and the residents of the village sang and danced ceaselessly. But Jeremy was scarcely aware of what he ate or of the festivities. His mind raced.

The diamonds made him wealthy and would enable him to achieve the goal he had sought since being abducted. First, he would go back to Luanda and establish his ownership of the *County Mayo*. Certainly he had no interest in taking a load of slaves to the United States or the

Caribbean. Similarly, he had no desire to make an arms deal with the Bantu; instead, at the proper moment, he would present them with the guns and ammunition in the ship's hold.

The one thing he would do would be to sell a diamond or two in Luanda. The cash he received in return would enable him to hire a crew and sail back to the United States without delay. If all went well, he could rejoin Sarah in about six weeks and take her to Oakhurst Manor.

Knowing the Bantu would refuse gifts they regarded as payments for what the king had given him, he proceeded with caution. That very night he suggested to M'Bwana that they go to Luanda the following day, bring the arms to the Bantu Village, and then decide their worth. King Umbunga endorsed the plan, and the two young men departed the next morning, accompanied by forty bearers, all of them husky senior warriors.

Although they traveled on foot, they wasted no time and reached the city in three days. Going straight to the wharf where the *County Mayo* was tied, Jeremy made a search of the master's cabin and soon found the document he was seeking, the drunken scrawl Captain Garrity had written on the day of the mutiny.

He took the paper to the Portuguese authorities, and the colonial administrators made short work of the matter. M'Bwana testified that the former proprietor-master of the vessel had died of snakebite in the interior, and several of the older warriors corroborated the story. The Portuguese were at peace with the ferocious Bantu, and wanted nothing to disturb the state of amicable relations, so they hastened to take the word of King Umbunga's son.

In actuality, the transfer of property from one foreigner to another was of no consequence to them. Even if Jeremy had murdered Garrity, they wouldn't have cared, provided their own relations with the Bantu remained undisturbed. So they gave him a certificate citing him as the owner.

Armed with this document, he and M'Bwana returned to the *County Mayo* and descended into the hold. Many months had passed since slaves had been carried in these quarters, but the stench was still overpowering. By the light of flickering oil lamps they saw triple rows of plain wooden planking that served as sleeping quarters for slaves, and at six-foot intervals there were manacles chained to the bulkheads. Unfortunates who were incarcerated here were chained hand and foot throughout the entire voyage, except for the brief occasions when they were permited to go up on deck.

Jeremy was sickened by the spectacle, and M'Bwana was badly shaken, too. Hurrying though the slave pens, they unlocked the far hold. There, as Jeremy had anticipated, they saw stacks of muskets, bags of gunpowder, and bars of lead, complete with molds for making bullets. In a far corner, too, was a decrepit six-pounder cannon, which was more ornamental than useful.

The bearers were summoned, and soon the arms were being moved ashore.

When Jeremy and M'Bwana returned to the deck, they found Pedro Fernandes Andeiro awaiting them. The slave dealer was even more obsequious than usual.

"I felicitate you on your good fortune, Beaufort," he said. "I have heard you are now the owner and master of this fine ship."

"So it seems." It didn't take long for news to travel in Luanda, Jeremy thought sourly.

"I trust the arrangement I made with the late proprietor is still in effect."

"Of course. I intend to honor Garrity's commitments," Jeremy said.

Andeiro stared at the necklace of rough-cut diamonds the young American was wearing, but made no mention of them. "The Bantu are taking the arms you brought them, so I assume you've made a deal with them and soon will be returning with a load of slaves."

"We're still working out our agreement," Jeremy said, wanting to reveal as few of his plans as he could.

"I'll be waiting for word from you." The slave dealer couldn't resist reaching out and touching the necklace. "You've struck it rich, eh?"

"I haven't shown these stones to a jeweler, so I'm uncertain of their worth," Jeremy said. "I don't believe in getting a monetary estimate of a gift."

Andeiro realized he was being rebuffed, and soon withdrew.

His expression was so calculating that Jeremy promptly changed his own plans. Instead of staying in Luanda, selling one or more of the diamonds, and then offering cash to his crew, he would first return to the Bantu village. Otherwise Andeiro might claim he had been part-owner of the arms and try to charge an exorbitant sum. Even M'Bwana and his father, the most sophisticated of the Bantu, were relatively simple people, and it wouldn't be difficult for the slave trader to trick and cheat them. Jeremy's own departure would be delayed for no more than a week, and after the many delays and crushing disappointments he had suffered, he thought it only right that he wait a little longer so he could help the friends who were making it possible for him to return home.

The heavily laden bearers needed an extra twenty-four hours of travel time, so it was four days later before the party reached the Bantu village. There the arms were displayed, and Jeremy showed the king and his eldest son how to cut bullets, also explaining that gunpowder had to be kept dry.

He put on a shooting exhibition in the forest beyond the clearing for the benefit of the Bantu warriors. Then M'Bwana delivered a long, impassioned address on the subject of safety. Finally the arms and munitions were placed in a storage hut, under guard. The six-pounder cannon, which was so badly rusted it was inoperable, was placed outside the king's hut as a decoration.

That evening, only Umbunga, M'Bwana and M'Dolna sat down to dinner together.

"My father," M'Bwana said, "expresses his gratitude for showing your trust and bringing the weapons to him before you and he reached the sale terms. He wants to know how many slaves you want in return."

Jeremy took a deep breath. "None," he said.

All three of the Bantu stared at him in astonishment.

He explained that his one desire was to go to his own home and be reunited with the woman he loved. He had endured many hardships, but thanks to the necklace the king had given him, his most cherished dreams now would come true.

Umbunga nodded as his second son translated, and seemed satisfied. Then he made a few remarks, speaking slowly and with great dignity.

"The king of kings will grieve when you and I leave," M'Bwana said, "because he will lose two sons."

It was obvious that the Bantu prince would accompany him, and Jeremy didn't know what to say.

The king spoke again.

"Before we depart," M'Bwana translated with a smile, "the king wishes to give you one more gift, a pearl of great price."

"He has already given me the brotherhood of his son and these priceless stones. I can accept nothing more." Jeremy thought it wise to change the subject. "Tell him the warriors should practice with their muskets before they start their campaign against the Watusi. Delay for a month, two months, whatever may be necessary."

His comments were translated, and the meal came to an end.

It was night now, and Jeremy went off to his own hut, where several fat candles had already been lighted by someone who had used a coal from the cooking fire. There was nothing in the structure but his pallet and that which Garrity had occupied, but he liked the place. It was more homelike than anywhere he had been in his travels—except Lisa's bedchamber. And he couldn't allow himself to think about her, especially now, when he was about to begin his homeward journey.

It was enough, he thought, that he would miss the Bantu.

M'Bwana came into the hut, grinning broadly.

He was followed by a girl, and Jeremy could only stare at her.

She appeared to be about nineteen or twenty years old, and was ravishingly beautiful, with dark brown hair that fell in loose waves to her waist. She was of medium height, but perfectly proportioned, and like all women in the land of the Bantu, was naked above the waist.

Kohl encircled her eyes, making them appear enormous,

and her full mouth was a scarlet streak. She had daubed rouge of the same shade on her nipples, too, further emphasizing her large breasts. On her ankles and wrists she wore thin chains of fine gold.

As Jeremy gaped at her, it occurred to him that she was more white than black, and he guessed she might be a quadroon.

M'Bwana chuckled. "This is the pearl of great value my father promised you. She was a gift to him from the sultan of Algiers, and she grew to womanhood in his harem. No one knows who she was, or who her family may have been."

A feeling of panic swept over Jeremy. He couldn't imagine returning to Sarah Benton with this sultry, near-white slave girl in tow.

"Her name," M'Bwana said, "is Kai."

At the mention of her name, the girl prostrated herself on the ground at Jeremy's feet.

His embarrassment engulfed him. "Tell her to stand up, please."

M'Bwana laughed aloud. "She knows no English, and has learned only a little Bantu. Perhaps you will explore together to learn what tongue she speaks."

He tapped the girl on her bare back, and she rose, looking at Jeremy with liquid eyes.

His panic became ever greater.

M'Bwana moved behind her, and his smile faded. "She is truly a priceless pearl, my friend, and will give you much delight," he said, deep envy in his voice. Then he reached around the girl and fondled her breasts for a moment. "Observe. She has what the English call great passion."

Kai had made no move to get away from M'Bwana, and her nipples had hardened at his touch.

Jeremy swallowed hard. "I'll give her to you, my friend. Bring her along on our journey, if you wish, and when we reach Luanda, we'll buy her some European clothes so she isn't attacked by every man in the crew."

The Bantu prince had heard only a part of the remark. "My father would not forgive either you or me if you made me a gift of Kai and I accepted. Someday, perhaps, when you tire of her, you may wish to present her to me, and I will accept with great joy. Because no man has ever seen a woman more beautiful."

There was no denying her loveliness, which made the problem all the more difficult.

"I wish you a night of great pleasure," M'Bwana said, and left the hut.

Kai continued to stand motionless, her hands at her sides.

The night was cool, with a gentle breeze blowing through the hut, but Jeremy was sweating. He had known plantation owners who had bedded unwilling female slaves, but this situation was different. He simply couldn't have intercourse with this glorious creature, then take her off to America with him.

He pointed to the pallet at the far side of the hut, seeking some means of verbal communication with her. "Sit down over there," he said.

Kai continued to stand.

Jeremy lowered himself to his own pallet, then gestured toward the other.

Finally the girl understood, and reluctantly moved to the other pallet.

They were only a few feet apart, and her proximity overwhelmed him. "Well, Kai," he said, "this is a pretty kettle of fish, isn't it, now?"

Her provocative lips parted in an uncertain smile.

He was unsure how long he could keep his natural desires under control. It had been a long time since he and Lisa had slept together, and there was no denying this girl's sexual magnetism.

English was the only language Jeremy spoke well, but he had been tutored in French as a child, and dredged his mind, his desperation making him nimble. "Perhaps you speak this language," he said.

A beatific smile wreathed Kai's face, and she clapped her hands together in delight. "Ah, my new master speaks French!" she exclaimed. "May Allah be praised."

He had to speak slowly so he wouldn't miss any words. "In the first place, don't call me your master. My name is Jeremy Beaufort."

"A wonderful French name. I will like being your slave."

Jeremy couldn't keep her for any length of time, the thought of selling her was abhorrent to him, and he knew she would be helpless in the world if he simply set her free. "We must think together," he told her, "and decide what we're going to do with you."

"Kai will go everywhere with you," she said. "I will sleep with you when it pleases you, and I will attend you and wait upon you always."

He could imagine Sarah's expression if this luscious creature followed him into the drawing room of the Benton house in Boston, and inadvertently he groaned.

"Kai is ugly to you?" she asked. "Kai does not please her new master?"

To his horror, she drew a tiny knife from the top of her skirt, pointed it toward herself, and started to fall onto the blade.

In a swift motion Jeremy grasped her wrist, moving the knife out of harm's way.

As they grappled, Jeremy's free hand brushed across Kai's full breasts.

With a glad cry she threw her arms around his neck, her lips parting for his kiss.

Jeremy could resist her no longer, and in a moment they were stretched out together on the pallet.

In some inexplicable way, the girl wriggled out of her skirt and pressed her nude body close to Jeremy's.

He pulled off his own clothes, and only the immediate moment had meaning. He was thousands of miles from home, in an African hut far from any civilization he had ever known, but Kai spoke a universal feminine language, yielding to him, demanding that he ravish her.

Jeremy took her quickly, savagely, and was surprised by the intensity of his own ardor.

Kai's shining, liquid eyes looked up at him.

He made love to her again, deliberately taking his time, and she instantly suited her mood to his, teasing him and encouraging him to tease her. Their game seemed endless, but at last they became aroused, together, and the pace of their lovemaking quickened.

They exploded simultaneously, and then were exhausted.

"My new master likes Kai," the girl said at last, and it was a flat statement of fact, not a question.

"Too much," Jeremy replied, "which complicates the whole problem of how we're to deal with you."

Kai has no idea what he meant, but had her own way of treating a man who talked or thought too much at the wrong time, and her delicate hands became active.

Ultimately they achieved a third orgasm, and then drifted off to sleep. One of the candles was gutted, and the others burned lower, casting a feeble glow.

Neither heard Pedro Fernandes Andeiro creep into the hut. The Bantu system of sentry maintenance was primitive, and it had been a simple matter for him to sneak past the guards. Already familiar with the village, he had first located the large hut of the king, then looked into each of the dwellings near it, accurately guessing that the visitor would be housed nearby.

He crouched low over the sleeping couple, his eyes gleaming when he saw that Jeremy was still wearing the necklace of uncut diamonds. A swift slash of his long, curved knife cut the leather thong to which the stones were attached, and he stuffed the prize into his pocket, then sighed inaudibly.

All that remained now was to make certain that the American could not follow him to Luanda and start an action of some sort to reclaim the necklace.

Sucking in his breath, Andeiro took careful aim, and the knife swept downward.

At that instant Kai became aware of an alien presence in the hut, and, still half-asleep, moved one arm.

Her motion deflected the aim of the Portuguese slightly, but the long knife nevertheless plunged deep into the defenseless Jeremy's body.

The slave girl was wide-awake now, and emitted a high-pitched, piercing scream that shattered the quiet of the night.

Andeiro was unable to remove the knife from the body of his victim, and tried to silence her with his bare hands.

Suddenly a dark figure raced into the hut. M'Bwana

moved with the grace and speed of a panther, and taking in the situation at a glance, he leaped at the intruder, his powerful arms extended, his strong hands reaching.

Andeiro had no chance to resist, no opportunity to protect himself from the furious assault. M'Bwana landed on him, sending him crashing to the ground, and in a white heat of fury broke his neck. Andeiro died without making a sound.

Jeremy had no idea of anything that was happening. He lay unconscious, blood still pouring from his wound and soaking the pallet on which he and Kai had made love only a short time earlier.

Chapter 21

On January 8, 1815, General Andrew Jackson won the Battle of New Orleans, severely defeating the British conquerors of Napoleon and inflicting more than two thousand casualties on the redcoats. In an irony of history, an armistice had been signed at Ghent two weeks earlier by American and British negotiators, but the news did not reach the United States until February 11.

Critics of the American government claimed the battle had been fought in vain, but they were mistaken. Andrew Jackson, who overnight had become a national hero, had proved the worth of his nation's fighting men, and the whole country was thrilled by his victory. "Our nation has come of age," President Madison said. "Henceforth, Europe will tender us the respect that is our due."

Bonfires were lighted in hundreds of communities large and small, from the eastern seaboard to the Mississippi River, and entire towns joined in barbecues, fairs, and other festivities. But the celebrations at Oakhurst Manor were muted.

On February 4, a week before the news of peace was received, sickness struck the plantation and its neighbors.

The epidemic of Asiatic cholera that swept through Georgia and South Carolina was believed to have originated in Savannah, presumably introduced by a seaman from a foreign merchant ship, but no one could be certain. And no one really cared. All that mattered was that the disease, for which there was no known cure, inundated both South Carolina and Georgia, and some cities, Charleston among them, barred all outside visitors.

On a Tuesday morning, Scott and Julia Emerson were incapacitated by the sickness. By Wednesday they were spitting blood, and that night both died. Dr. Pickens had treated them with every remedy at his command, but none was effective.

The close friends of the Emersons at Oakhurst Manor grieved for them, but even before the funeral was held, they were overwhelmed by the same problem. In a single day, more than one hundred slaves were stricken, and a panicky Mr. Higby tied a bag of herbs around his neck and wore a cloth over his face when he rode out into the fields.

Then Paul Wellington Beaufort became ill, and a weary Dr. Pickens, who was working eighteen hours and more out of every twenty-four, diagnosed his ailment as cholera. "Give him apples to eat if he can hold them down," Dr. Pickens told Sarah. "For some reason we don't yet understand, they seem to have a beneficial effect when nothing else works."

Willie was dispatched into the countryside and returned with several large baskets of apples. Then he collapsed, too, and later that same day Amanda was also stricken.

Sarah and Margot worked tirelessly, tending their father-in-law, ministering to Willie and Amanda, and looking after the slaves. Sarah, with the help of Cleo, even more a tower of strength than she had ever been in the past, did her best to isolate little Jerry and keep him out of his grandfather's quarters and other sickrooms.

The sickness continued to spread, and at the end of the first week, only fifty of Oakhurst Manor's remaining four hundred slaves could be mustered for work in the fields. On two occasions Mr. Higby became hysterical, and Tom

Beaufort had to speak sharply to him in order to hold him in line.

Tom rallied to the crisis as he had never done in his life. He spent his days in the saddle, encouraging the slaves who were still well enough to function, and when necessary he pitched in with them, planting and weeding. After dark he spent hours looking after Willie and Amanda, and before each night ended he spent his fair share of time in his father's sickroom.

He became gaunt, but refused to quit, and it was obvious that he had given up liquor. Only his relations with his wife remained strained, and they spoke to each other when conversation could not be avoided, but were barely civil.

Then Margot contracted the sickness, too, and after Dr. Pickens confirmed that she had cholera, Tom broke down and wept. In her presence, however, he did his best to present a cheerful, optimistic facade.

Paul Beaufort had an enormous will to live, and for two weeks he struggled against the sickness, refusing to give in. He ate apples when even the sight of food made him feel worse, and his dogged determination was unflagging. After ten days, his high fever broke, he felt more comfortable, and it appeared as though he had weathered his crisis.

Sarah, her own nerves frazzled almost beyond endurance, was relieved beyond measure for his sake. At the same time, she was grateful that little Jerry had not succumbed to cholera. Most children in the neighborhood had proved vulnerable, and he was one of the few who were still untouched.

Amanda began to improve, and showing remarkable resilience, soon regained her feet. She refused to leave Willie's side, and spent all of her waking hours looking after him. Apparently encouraged by her example, he threw off the illness, too. Both were still so weak, however, that they could do nothing for the many others who suffered.

Sarah and Cleo held Oakhurst Manor together. Scrubbing and cleaning, tending the sick, and cooking, they labored without respite. In some miraculous way they had been spared, as had little Jerry, and they devoted all their energies, all their remaining strength to others.

Tom continued to work in the fields by day, then devoted his nights to his wife and his father. He aged by a decade, flecks of gray appeared at his temples, and his manner was somber. In the back of his mind he knew his youth had ended, that he had entered man's estate and had to live up to his full responsibilities.

His situation was driven home one cheerless morning when he left the mansion and went to the stables to saddle a horse, no servants any longer being available for such purposes.

He was surprised to see Mr. Higby standing near the stable doors, his usual bag of herbs hanging from his neck. He was wearing his best shirt, boots, and breeches, and as Tom approached, he forced himself to remove the cloth that covered his nose and mouth.

"This is the first of the month," he said.

"So it is." The calendar had lost its meaning.

"You pa still being abed, I've come to you for my pay. You owe me fifty dollars."

Tom was surprised by his abruptness, but wanted to keep talk with the man to a minimum, and reached into his purse. Ordinarily he carried several times that amount, but income these days was nonexistent, and after he paid the overseer, he discovered he had only ten dollars left. The sickness had eroded the prosperity of Oakhurst Manor.

"My belongings are packed," Mr. Higby said, "so I'll be on my way."

Tom was startled. "I beg your pardon?"

"I quit. I've been spared this damn plague, and I'm not going to hang around these parts until I come down with it. Anyway, you don't have enough healthy slaves in the fields these days to need an overseer. I'm heading up to North Carolina or Virginia as fast as I can get me there."

It was curious, Tom thought, that he felt no reaction of any kind. He had been acquainted all his life with this man he disliked so intensely, but at this moment he felt neither sorrow nor pleasure. His only thought was that, for the present, he would have to assume the duties of overseer himself. Well, he was ready, and at least he would save the sum of fifty dollars per month. Only a few weeks earlier he had squandered that much and more without thinking, but now he was grateful it wouldn't have to be spent.

"Good-bye, Higby," he said, and went into the barn to saddle his horse.

The overseer turned away silently, hurrying off to his own house to collect his belongings and leave. It did not occur to either to shake hands.

Late that evening, when Tom and a haggard, exhausted Sarah finally sat down to a supper of cold meats and tea that she had prepared, he told her of the incident.

"Higby is no loss," she said, choosing her words with care. "Provided you can fill in for him until we can hire somebody else."

"I'll manage," Tom said grimly, and paused. "Sarah, I haven't had the courage to apologize for the advances I made to you. A million years ago. My only excuse is that I was drunk—"

"So was I, and there's no need for apologies. The subject is closed." She was too tired to eat more than a few bites of her skimpy meal.

"Thanks, but it isn't closed. Not between Margot and me, anyway."

"What have you said to her?"

"Nothing. She . . . she discourages talk between us."

Sarah had seen so much suffering in recent weeks that she was able to speak calmly. "If she dies, you'll never forgive yourself for not making your peace with her. Go to her. Now."

Tom pushed away his plate and rose abruptly. "I reckon you're right," he said, and headed up the stairs.

Margot was propped on pillows, her expression listless, and she had lost so much weight that her face resembled that of a skeleton. Her husband had been coming to her regularly, but nothing of consequence had passed between them, and her eyes were dull as she looked up at him.

"I want to say something to you," Tom said, hooking his thumbs in his broad belt. "There's no need for you to answer, just hear me out."

Something unusual in his tone commanded the sick woman's attention, and she nodded.

"I've grown up since this disaster hit us," he said. "It's

about time, and well I know it. I'll never touch a drop of liquor again as long as I live, but that's the least of it. What matters most is that I've learned how much you mean to me. I pray day and night for your recovery, and if you get well and want to leave me, I won't be able to blame you. If you want no more to do with me, ever, I . . . I can accept that, even though I won't like it. Only one thing counts, that you get over this illness."

For the first time, a faint light appeared in her eyes.

"Margot," Tom said, "I don't deserve your love, but I do love you with all my heart and soul."

A painfully thin hand crept across the coverlet toward him.

He grasped it gently, and there was no need for either to speak.

As Dr. Pickens later said, Margot began to recover that very night.

Paul Beaufort's temperature remained normal, and he no longer displayed any of the symptoms of the sickness, but he was still so feeble he could not leave his bed. In spite of the coaxing of Sarah and Cleo, he had no appetite, either, and refused the meals they prepared for him.

After ravaging the countryside for a month and a half, the epidemic appeared to have run its course. No new cases were reported anywhere in South Carolina, and only in the back country of Georgia did the disease remain virulent.

The toll at Oakhurst Manor was devastating. Tom, who worked ceaselessly from dawn until late each evening, privately told Sarah and a convalescing Margot that more than two hundred and fifty of the plantation's slaves had died. Most of those who had survived were still too weak to work, and it would be another month or two before they could return to the fields.

"We can't tell this to Papa, of course," he said, "but we're in a perilous situation."

Sarah had been keeping the books since her father-in-law had fallen ill, and nodded. "We've had no income, and our outlay has been tremendous. We aren't bankrupt, since we own our land and buildings and livestock outright. But what worries me is that our means of raising cash are so limited."

Tom ran a sinewy hand through his hair. "To be blunt about it, we need new slaves to replace those we've lost, or we'll have no cotton and tobacco crop. This year, or next year, or as far ahead as we can see. But we just don't have the money to buy hundreds of slaves. Not at the current prices of a thousand to fifteen hundred dollars per field worker."

"Let's look on the bright side," Margot said. "At least we don't starve. There are enough of us here to plant vegetables and tend the livestock."

"We'll come damn close to starvation, I can tell you that," her grim husband replied. "I can see only one way out of this mess. We'll have to sell a good part of Oakhurst Manor."

"No!" Sarah sprang to her feet. "I won't permit you to sell even one acre. Oakhurst Manor is my husband's heritage, and it will pass intact to him. And to our son after him. If I've got to dig up the earth with my bare hands to plant cotton and tobacco." Her devotion was all-consuming.

That same day, Isaiah and Lorene Benton came to the plantation from Charleston, the state militia at last having lifted its travel ban. Sarah and Margot brought them up-to-date on all that had happened, sparing them none of the bad news.

"I can lend you five or ten thousand, if that will help," Isaiah said.

"And I have about seven thousand of my own," Lorene added. "You're welcome to it."

Sarah shook her head. "I don't mean to sound ungrateful, but we need so much more to get back on our feet. At least fifty thousand, perhaps twice that much. The figures make me dizzy. Besides, Lorene, maybe you can help young Scott. Tom has heard he may have to sell Trelawney."

"I'm afraid you're talking in terms of sums far larger than your father and I can possibly raise, my dear. It will break all our hearts if the Emersons lose Trelawney, but these are harsh times and we can't perform miracles. We thank God that so many of you have been spared."

"When can we go upstairs to see Paul?" Isaiah wanted to know.

"Not until tomorrow, if you don't mind," Sarah told them. "By the middle of the afternoon, Papa Beaufort becomes terriby tired and finds it difficult to tolerate visitors. He keeps dropping off to sleep."

"You told us in a letter that he had thrown off the cholera," Lorene said. "What seems to be ailing him now?"

"We aren't sure," Sarah replied with a sigh. "He was on the verge of death for many days, and only his great will to live helped him to survive. Dr. Pickens is afraid that some of his vital organs may have been damaged in the struggle, but we don't know as yet. We . . . we live with him . . . from day to day. And we keep hoping for signs that he'll recover."

Lorene sensed her attitude. "We won't press you, Sarah, but there's more to this than you're telling us."

"Yes, there is," she said. "Tom and Margot and I haven't even admitted this to each other aloud. But we're afraid Papa Beaufort is failing. Even if Jeremy were to appear out of the blue, I don't think it would save him. Dr. Pickens won't commit himself, naturally. You know how doctors refuse to be pinned down. But he's hinted that we should prepare ourselves for the worst."

They were glum, each of them withdrawn into private thoughts, until Lorene managed to rally their spirits.

The day of elaborate menus at Oakhurst Manor had come to an end. Sarah worked side by side with Cleo in the kitchen, as she did every evening, and together they produced a simple but substantial one-course supper of roast beef, vegetables, and baked sweet potatoes.

Tom came in from the fields while they were still eating, and by the time he had washed and changed his clothes, they were done. But they stayed at the table with him while he ate, and it was evident that Isaiah and Lorene approved of the changes in him. He drank only water and coffee, his speech was blunt and direct, and he rarely joked. Most significantly, he was obviously devoted

306

to Margot and was solicitous of her welfare. They had emerged from a fire together, and it had forged bonds far stronger than the fragile ties that previously had united them.

Isaiah and Lorene were doting grandparents, and Sarah allowed little Jerry to stay awake long past his regular bedtime. At last he tired of play, however, so she took him to his room, helped him undress, and tucked him into his bed. As she finished saying his prayers with him, a light tap sounded at the door.

Tom was waiting for her in the corridor. "Papa is awake," he said, "and has asked for you and me. No one else. He says he'll send for Margot shortly, and he wants a word with your father and Lorene, too. But first he insists on talking to us alone."

They exchanged glances, but neither spoke, and they hurried down the corridor to the master suite.

A wasted Paul Wellington Beaufort was propped up on the pillows that Cleo had just arranged behind him, and his smile of greeting was wan. "I don't have much strength, so I'll be brief. And I want no tears, either of you. Understand?"

They nodded and drew up chairs beside his four-poster bed.

"My time has come," he said. "An inner feeling I can't describe tells me the end is here, that I won't live through the night."

Sarah tried to protest.

"Quiet, daughter. There's too little breath left in me for arguments. Dear Sarah, you will never know what joy you've given me in the three years you've lived at Oakhurst Manor. Persevere in the belief that Jeremy will return to you someday. Now that the war has ended, that day should soon be at hand. But if he doesn't come back—and this is a possibility I've been forced to face—I've changed my will. In that event, his share of the plantation will go to your son, with you to act as his trustee and guardian, making all decisions for him until he reaches the age of twenty-one."

Sarah had promised she wouldn't weep, but she couldn't hold back the tears that came to her eyes.

"Tom," Paul said in a feeble voice.

His younger son leaned closer. "Yes, Papa?"

"I thank the Almighty you've become a man at last. Look after your wife and cherish her. Work hand in hand with Sarah to keep Oakhurst Manor prosperous."

"You have my sacred oath on it, Papa," Tom said.

Sarah thought her heart was breaking. Paul's condition was so perilous that they had not been able to tell him of the depths to which his beloved plantation had descended.

"May God bless both of you and watch over you," Paul said, "as I know He will. Send for Margot now. Isaiah and Lorene, too. I want to say good-bye to them. But not little Jerry. Let him remember me as I was, not as I am."

The tears streamed unheeded down Sarah's cheeks in scalding cascades.

"Don't cry, dear Sarah," Paul said. "My life has been rich and full, and I leave without regret. You have no idea how much I look forward to rejoining my own wife. I've thought of her constantly in the weeks I've been lying here."

Margot was summoned, as were Isaiah and Lorene. Paul bade farewell to each of them, then asked Sarah and Tom to take hold of his hands.

Soon he drifted off to sleep, a gentle smile on his face, and he did not awaken.

Two days later they buried him in a quiet plot behind a grove of willow trees on the plantation he had loved.

Sarah walked slowly through the house—her house—and the spiritual uplift it had always given her was gone. Oakhurst Manor no longer had a life of its own. It was sick, perhaps dying, and there seemed to be nothing she could do to save it. She emerged onto the portico, and for a moment she leaned against one of the sturdy Doric columns, but it failed to comfort her.

The plantation was being overwhelmed by its problems. The sickness had decimated the ranks of the field workers, and even though Tom was in the saddle from sunrise to sunset, he could not turn the tide. There simply weren't enough men and women available this spring to plant the crops on which the family's livelihood depended. She knew, too, that hope for the future was dim. They needed at least a third of a million dollars in cash to buy more slaves, but the strongboxes were almost empty.

Tom insisted they would have to sell at least a portion of the plantation, as young Scott and Alicia Emerson were being forced to do with all of Trelawney, but every fiber of Sarah's being cried out in protest. It would be sinful to part with as much as one acre.

I am a Beaufort, Sarah told herself fiercely, even though I don't have the name legally. My son is a Beaufort. For his sake and Jeremy's, I shall stand firm, no matter how great the odds against me. I shall not only survive, but I shall succeed. Somehow, even though I'm at my wit's end. Because I must. Because I have no viable alternative.

She had to depend on herself. And on the Almighty, who had shown her so few favors in recent months. No, that was wrong. Little Jerry had escaped the sickness, and she herself was in perfect health, too. Margot was recovering, little by little, and Tom had truly rallied in this time of need. She had ample cause to be grateful to God.

All at once she straightened and stood erect, her shoulders pulled back, her delicate but square-cut chin jutting forward. She had moped long enough, and the day would be hectically busy.

First she had to see what progress Amanda was making in the preparation of breakfast. Then she and Cleo would make their long, daily tour of the slave quarters to attend to the needs of those who were still ill. Then she would spend hours wrestling with the ledgers that haunted her. Finally, if she was lucky, she would snatch a few precious moments to play with her baby before taking her place at the head of the table when the family sat down to dinner. Sarah felt inundated by her cares and responsibilities, but she could not allow her steps to falter, not for a moment.

Chapter 22

Instinct told Jeremy he had been ill for a long time, but that he had turned the corner and was beginning to recover. He felt unaccountably weak, but his head was clear, and a sense of renewed energy flowed through him.

He opened his eyes and found Kai bending over him. All at once he remembered the attack of the Portuguese slave trader, and he looked up at her with concern. "Are you all right?" he asked her in French. "You have come to no harm, Kai?"

To his astonishment, she replied in English. "The gods have given you back your own mind. For many moons you have called me Sarah. Sometimes you also have called me Lisa."

Before he could reply, she raced out of the hut.

He could recall nothing of what she said, but thoughts of Sarah made him dizzy. And of Lisa.

M'Bwana came into the hut and smiled broadly as he helped Jeremy into a sitting position. "My friend, I knew you would be well again. Each day you have eaten the shredded bark of the *ginkano* tree, and now all will be well."

"How long have I been here?"

"For many months. Almost a full year."

Jeremy assimilated the news in astonished silence.

M'Bwana brought him up-to-date on all that had happened. The Portuguese was dead, and Jeremy had almost died.

The scar on the American's chest, long healed, told him how narrowly Andeiro's knife had come to his heart.

During all these months, the Bantu prince and Kai had looked after Jeremy, and M'Bwana had deemed it useful to teach her the rudiments of English.

His tone of voice when he mentioned her and the expression in his eyes revealed more than he intended. It was apparent that he had fallen in love with the Algerian girl.

There was much more to tell. The Bantu had won one of their greatest victories in their war with the Watusi, thanks to the weapons Jeremy had given them. In return, the Bantu were holding four hundred Watusi prisoners at one of their larger towns, a day's march from this village. These included the strongest of the men, the finest and healthiest of the women. They already belonged to Jeremy, and would be sent to Luanda when he was able to travel again and sailed for the New World.

Jeremy learned, too, that he had been eating regularly during the period his mind had wandered, so he was not as debilitated as he otherwise might have been. Now he had to concentrate on his complete recovery.

In the next few days, much occupied his mind. His necklace of rough-cut diamonds, each embedded in the rock from which it had been chipped, was intact. He knew he could sell one or two stones in Luanda and obtain all the money he needed to finance a voyage.

By now the crew of the *County Mayo* undoubtedly had been disbanded, so he would have to recruit others to take their place. M'Bwana confirmed that the seamen had been released to take other jobs, but felt certain there were many experienced sailors in the Portuguese colony who could replace them.

The four hundred Watusi slaves provided an additional windfall. After all that Jeremy had suffered, he was reluctant to take possession of them, but common sense told him it would be a far greater cruelty to refuse them. The Bantu had no use for their conquered foes, and rather than feed them, would put them to death.

In any event, the way would be clear at long last for Jeremy to return to the New World. His ship bore an English registry, so he was uncertain whether he would be required to sail to one of the British colonies in the West Indies or whether he could take the risk of trying to reach an American port. That was something he would have to discuss with the Portuguese authorities at the appropriate time.

What mattered most was that, in one way or another, he would make his way to the United States, join Sarah—provided she had waited for him—and take her to Oakhurst Manor.

His most immediate problem was Kai. Under no circumstances could he take an almost-white slave girl home with him. Certainly not one who was this beautiful.

Gradually, over a period of days, he thought he had found a solution. Kai was strangely silent and subdued when she brought him his meals. Only when M'Bwana also was present did she come alive, and then her violet eyes sparkled and her manner became animated. It dawned on Jeremy that she had fallen as deeply in love with M'Bwana as he had with her.

Perhaps, if Jeremy set her free, which she deserved, M'Bwana would elect to make her a member of his own household. The idea was worth exploration at the first opportunity.

Jeremy exercised in the hut for about a week, running in place and lifting heavier and heavier sections of log, which M'Bwana brought him. At last he was ready to venture out of doors, and not wanting anyone to assist him as he strolled around the Bantu village, he started out alone one morning shortly after breakfast.

In front of the hut adjacent to his he saw a sight that almost turned him to stone.

Kai was nursing an infant two or three months old, and did not see him. The naked baby, a boy, was pale-skinned.

He had Jeremy's hazel eyes, brown hair, and features. There could be no shred of doubt in Jeremy's mind that Kai had borne his son.

It was hot in the early-morning sun, but Jeremy broke into a cold sweat. Kai had not seen him, so he ducked back into his hut, his mind whirling.

Under no circumstances could he return to Sarah accompanied by a lovely slave-girl mistress and their child. Perhaps he could sell an additional diamond and give Kai the proceeds, which would be enough to keep her comfortably and take care of the child. But she was young, inexperienced, and so attractive she would be unable to take care of herself in a world dominated by strong men.

Jeremy was still pacing when M'Bwana arrived for his regular morning visit, and the Bantu saw at once that his friend was badly upset.

Jeremy gave him no chance to speak. "I wasn't told that Kai has had a baby. My son."

M'Bwana's expression became grave. "I waited because I was unsure whether you would be pleased or sad."

"I can't take her and the baby home with me!"

The Bantu shook his head knowingly. "In all lands it is the same. Women become jealous of other women. The Sarah woman you talked about so much would be angry. So would the Lisa woman."

Jeremy forced himself to stop pacing. "Before I learned about the baby, I had already decided to set Kai free. But she'd be helpless in this world, and I'm afraid to take the risk. Frankly, my friend, I'm so stunned I don't know what to do."

M'Bwana folded his arms across his chest, his wide bracelets of hammered gold gleaming in the sunlight that filtered in through the entrance to the hut. "If it is the wish of Jeremy to give Kai her freedom," he said, speaking slowly and with great dignity, "M'Bwana will make her his wife."

Jeremy could only stare at him. "Is that your wish?"

"It is." The Bantu spoke with finality.

"Is it also the wish of Kai?"

"More than all else in this world. I have assured her that if this can be arranged, I will take no other wife."

"I see." Only one stumbling block remained, but it loomed large. "What will become of her baby?"

M'Bwana became even more solemn. "The son of my friend," he said, "will become my son."

The matter was settled that same day. In the presence of three senior Bantu warriors, Jeremy formally announced that Kai was now free. She had prostrated herself at his feet, according to the ancient custom, and when he reached down to help her rise, he saw pleasure and gratitude beyond measure in her lovely eyes.

At sundown that same day, M'Bwana took the girl as his wife and formally made her baby his own. "His name," M'Bwana said, "will be Lance."

Jeremy absented himself from the wedding ceremony, the adoption of Lance by his new father, and the tribal feast that followed. He realized that both M'Bwana and Kai were disappointed, but he found it too difficult to explain to them that, according to the customs of his own world, it would be too embarrassing for him to be present.

Instead, he wandered out alone after dark in the direction of the stockade and listened to the Bantu drums sending their message deep into the jungles, where other towns and villages were being told that the second son of the Bantu monarch had taken a wife and had a son.

The night was clear, stars filled the sky, and never had Jeremy felt so alone. He rejoiced because Kai had found a mate worthy of her and because a secure future had been assured for the child he himself could not acknowledge as his.

But he was still isolated. He stood in the heart of Africa, thousand of miles from those whom he loved and who loved him. He had been absent from the United States for three long years, and he was afraid that by this time Sarah Benton had been forced to conclude that he was dead. He missed her desperately. He had to be truthful and admit he also missed Lisa, wherever she might have gone.

His days of waiting were coming to an end, however, and soon he would be able to start making concrete plans for the long voyage home.

Jeremy walked and fished, went on several hunting trips with the Bantu, and after weeks was restored to good health. Now he was ready to make his final plans. Accompanied by M'Bwana and an escort of warriors, he made the journey across the Angolan plains to Luanda.

There he found the *County Mayo* intact, still riding at anchor and under close guard. His next stop was the office of a merchant, where he sold one of his uncut diamonds for two thousand English pounds sterling, or more than twelve thousand dollars in United States currency. At last supplied with all the cash he needed, he paid a visit to the deputy governor of Angola, Don Henri de Savardes, whose comfortable, old-fashioned office faced the harbor.

"Your Excellency," he said after showing the ship's registry and his own proof of ownership, "I have a simple question. May I sail the *County Mayo* to the United States?"

The white-haired diplomat smiled. "Master Beaufort," he said in slightly accented English, "you place my government in a delicate position. The tax we impose on slave traders brings us large revenues, and ordinarily we don't concern ourselves with a ship's destination. But these are unusual times, and Great Britain is Portugal's oldest ally. You're required to give us a sworn statement and post a bond before you leave port, guaranteeing that you're sailing to a British port. If you refuse, and there is no way we can compel you to accept, we are obliged by treaty to notify the British Navy, which now bases a squadron here. You're certain to be intercepted at sea, and your ship will either be sent to the bottom or confiscated."

Jeremy was prepared for such conditions, and did not hesitate. "In that case, Your Excellency," he said, "I shall carry my cargo of slaves to the West Indian island of Jamaica."

After completing the formalities of clearing the port, Jeremy spent several hours shopping with M'Bwana, who insisted that he intended to make the voyage. Together they purchased clothing that would be suitable for the Bantu in the New World, and, equally important, bought a wardrobe for Kai, whose skimpy attire would create a scandal in the West Indies or the United States.

M'Bwana returned to the interior with his escorts. Jeremy took lodging at a local inn and began the process of putting together a new crew. From the outset, his luck was good, and the first to be hired was a mate, a Scot named MacDougall, whose papers were in order. Jeremy suspected that MacDougall well might be a renegade, but he knew, too, that the master of a slaver could not ask too many questions.

The sale of the diamond enabled the American to offer attractive wages and to reject any seamen whose attitude he did not like. In the next eight days, after interviewing scores of sailors, he was able to assemble a crew of Portuguese, Irish, Belgians, and Norwegians. He stressed to each man who signed on with him that the conditions normally observed on blackbirders would be suspended.

Slaves being transported in the hold would not be chained to their benches. None would be whipped, and, in fact, no member of the crew would be permitted to carry a whip. On most voyages, two out of every five slaves being transported died at sea, but Jeremy held the revolutionary theory that humane treatment would save lives.

He followed this same principle in his purchase of supplies. Instead of feeding slops to the slaves, he bought huge quantities of rice and millet, sweet potatoes, and the root of a wild jungle plant that, after being pounded into powder, made an acceptable bread. He also bought dried and pickled fish for the slaves, as well as the preserved meat of water buffalo, wild goat, and other animals whose flesh long had supplied the Watusi with their sustenance.

Members of his new crew worked day and night to prepare the *County Mayo* for her voyage, and Jeremy took the precaution of getting new sails, quantities of tar and a varied store of medicines. He spent the unheard-of sum of four thousand dollars and the merchants of Luanda began calling him the mad American.

On the ninth day, his crew began to repaint the *County Mayo*, and late the following afternoon the Watusi slaves arrived, convoyed by Bantu warriors. Leading the procession was M'Bwana, looking and feeling stiff in knee breeches, shirt, and swallow-tailed coat.

But Kai was ravishing in a gown of gray silk, complete

with multiple petticoats, and no one would have guessed that she had never before worn such attire. Jeremy marveled at the chameleonlike ability of women to adapt themselves to new circumstances.

Even Lance was dressed in the long gown that American and European babies wore, and nestled comfortably in his mother's arms as he was carried aboard the ship.

Jeremy ordered the frightened Watusi assembled on the main deck, and asked M'Bwana to act as his interpreter.

"Tell them," he said, "that no harm will come to them if they obey a few simple rules. They will be given three meals each day, and they will not be confined to the hold. When the weather permits, they will be allowed on deck for several hours each day in groups of fifty to one hundred. Every morning and every evening, the pharmacist's mate will pay a sick call to the hold, and anyone who is ill must report to him at once."

M'Bwana translated, and the panic of the slaves began to subside.

"Tell them," Jeremy continued, "that I will tolerate no violence. Any man who raises a hand against members of the crew or his brother Watusi will be confined in irons to a special part of the hold. He who kills will be killed. He who maims or injures will be maimed or injured."

Again the Bantu conveyed his message.

"The women will live apart from the men," Jeremy went on. "Now, I want ten of the women to stand forward. They will assist in the preparation of meals for all the rest."

Veteran members of the crew were astonished, and swore that never had slaves been allowed such freedom on board a blackbirder.

MacDougall, the mate, had already been told Captain Beaufort's plans, and was not surprised by them. What astonished him was that Kai, who looked white, would share a cabin with the husky M'Bwana, who wore a brace of pistols and carried a sword. The mate wanted to protest, but after looking at little Lance, he quickly changed his mind. MacDougall knew nothing about children, but even he could see that the baby strongly resembled Captain

Beaufort. It was wise, he decided, to keep his mouth shut and accept the unusual arrangement.

On the morning of the eleventh day, all was in readiness. The crew ate a hearty breakfast, as did the slaves, and Jeremy made a final inspection of the entire ship. M'Bwana accompanied him, and neither felt or showed fear when they descended into the hold.

Crew members were astonished when they emerged unscathed and smiling. Never before had the seamen known of a captain who dared to enter a hold occupied by slaves. But the master of this vessel obviously had a special way with the Watusi, who were peaceful and, so far, were causing no problems.

As the morning tide began to ebb, Jeremy made his way to the quarterdeck. M'Bwana still accompanied him, and did not even glance at the land of his birth, which he was leaving forever.

Crewmen waited at their sailing stations.

Jeremy was about to begin what he hoped would be his final adventure before he found some way to return to the United States. He stood on the quarterdeck, *his* quarterdeck, and it suddenly occurred to him that he had developed a love for the sea. Would he prefer such a life to the desk of a lawyer? He didn't know, and it troubled him that he was uncertain whether the existence of a planter would satisfy him, either. Those questions, however, belonged to the future. At this moment, his world was his alone.

"Mr. MacDougall," he said, "you may weigh anchor and haul in your lines."

"Aye, aye, sir!" The mate repeated the order, and the sailors sprang to life.

"You may raise your jib sheets, Mr. MacDougall."

"Aye, aye, sir."

Soon the *County Mayo* edged away from her dock and began to move out through the harbor to the open Atlantic. Only then did Jeremy ponder on the strange fate that had brought him wealth and made him the master of his own destiny.

Nature finally compensated Jeremy Beaufort for all that he had suffered. The seas were calm, the headwinds were gentle, and he encountered only two minor storms, which caused him no serious problems. The *County Mayo* plowed westward across the Atlantic without undue incident.

Twice Jeremy was challenged by Royal Navy warships. On both occasions he hoisted the Union Jack and was allowed to proceed.

The slaves remained docile and relatively contented. Two young males were confined to the brig after engaging in a brawl, and no other serious trouble broke out. No more than twenty were ill at any one time, except during the storms, and medication administered by the pharmacist's mate proved effective. Even the skeptical MacDougall was forced to admit that the master's unique methods prevented unnecessary deaths.

M'Bwana was eager to learn the principles and practice of seamanship and navigation. Jeremy was pleased to help him, and by the end of the third week of the voyage the Bantu was able to take command of the ship for brief periods, provided the master or mate remained nearby, ready to intervene if necessary.

Jeremy took double watches in order to keep himself occupied, and when not on duty spent most of his time alone. He saw little of Kai, who disliked the sun and remained indoors with her baby during daylight hours. Occasionally, however, he invited her and M'Bwana to dine with him.

On these occasions he found it odd that he didn't feel close to her in any way, even though they had been intimate and he had sired her child. She was M'Bwana's wife, her child had become M'Bwana's son, and Jeremy had become their joint friend and mentor, nothing more. He hadn't yet determined how they would fit into the scheme of life at Oakhurst Manor, but he refused to create a problem where none might exist. His experiences over the past three years had matured him so much that he realized troubles had a way of working themselves out.

Early in the fourth week of the voyage, the *County Mayo* entered the Caribbean Sea, and three and a half days later she stood off the familiar entrance to Kingston harbor, in Jamaica. Jeremy ordered sail reduced, and was surprised and puzzled by two strange phenomena. There were only two small Royal Navy warships at anchor in the outer reaches of the harbor, which he found extraordinary in time of war. And three merchant brigs flying the flag of the United States were tied to docks. He assumed they had been captured, but that didn't explain why their flags were still aloft.

As soon as the blackbirder was made fast to her berth, the harbormaster came aboard and accompanied Jeremy to the master's cabin, where he inspected the ship's papers.

"Surely these figures aren't accurate, Captain Beaufort," he said. "You and four hundred and nine slaves on board when you left Luanda, and you still carry the same number?"

"Indeed I do." Jeremy was proud of his achievement.

"May I ask why you've brought them to Kingston? Between you and me, Captain, you're a bloody fool. Buyers in the United States will pay at least double the prices you can get for them here."

Jeremy's smile was tight. "I prefer not to be intercepted and sunk by the Royal Navy between here and the United States, thank you."

The harbormaster stared at him. "Surely you're joking, sir. Surely you know the war ended eleven weeks ago!"

It was Jeremy's turn to stare.

"You're free to sail anywhere you please, sir!" the harbormaster said as he signed the landing permit.

The war was ended! Jeremy could think of nothing else. He was free to sail where he pleased, without fear that his ship would be intercepted or he himself returned to the Royal Navy for additional duty.

He immediately changed his plans. He would obtain fresh food, water, and other supplies and would sail on without delay to Charleston. There he would sell the cargo of slaves.

He granted twenty-four-hour shore leave to the better part of the crew, then went ashore himself to buy the provisions he needed. He still carried enough money to pay for what was necessary, but he wanted to take no chances, so he removed another of the rough-cut diamonds from his strongbox and took it to a trader on Duke Street.

To his delight, the man offered him fifteen thousand dollars in American currency for it, three thousand more than he had been paid in Luanda for a stone that had appeared to be about the same size.

Now Jeremy faced a dilemma. It was early afternoon, his business was done, and he had no need to return to his ship until the following morning. He fought hard against temptation, but lost the battle.

Hailing a carriage, he ordered the driver to take him to the Star Apple in the hills of Liguanea.

The ride seemed endless, but at last he arrived, and the place looked as he remembered it. A liveried servant admitted him to the ground-floor parlor.

Soon Mistress Ferguson entered, and looked hard at this stern-faced, full-bearded man with graying hair at his temples before she recognized him. The gold cockade of rank he wore in the bicorne confused her, too, but at last she placed him. "Captain Beaufort, I believe."

"The same, Mistress Ferguson." Jeremy wasted no words. "I've just put into port at Kingston Town today, and I've come up here in hopes of finding Lisa."

The woman shook her head. "She left soon after your last visit. A year and a half ago, or more. I have no idea where she may have gone."

Something in her expression indicated she was lying, but he had no way to compel her to tell him the truth.

"There are a number of attractive young ladies here," Mistress Ferguson said. "Perhaps you'd like to meet one of them."

"No, thank you," he replied. "There is only one Lisa."

Not until the carriage returned to Kingston and deposited Jeremy near the docks did he begin to recover from his disappointment. Perhaps it was for the best, as Lisa herself had told him so emphatically, that he didn't know what had become of her. His own future lay completely in another direction.

Chapter 23

Ladies infrequently visited the rough Charleston waterfront, particularly late in the day, when the harlots were busy soliciting business and the streets were filled with sailors on the prowl. But Lorene Benton feared no one, and was determined to buy the freshly caught crabs for which her husband had expressed a desire earlier in the afternoon. As any native South Carolinian knew, really fresh fish and seafood were available only in the waterfront area. Leaving her carriage and coachman nearby, Lorene walked the short distance to the shop.

She was glad she had come on the errand today. A huge blackbirder had just docked nearby, and she knew the adjacent slave market would be crowded the next morning. The whole area would be in chaos all day.

The fish shop was crowded, and the sun was beginning to set by the time Lorene emerged into the street.

Striding toward her were two men, and she glanced at them only because their appearance was unusual. One was white, dressed in the uniform of a merchant captain, and the other, who was black, was also handsomely attired.

They appeared to be equals, and both were tall, husky, and armed with pistols and swords.

Something about the white man, tanned and bearded, puzzled her. Perhaps it was his walk. Perhaps . . .

Suddenly she gasped, then caught her breath before she could speak to him. "Jeremy Beaufort!"

He gaped at her, startled for an instant, then swept her off her feet and enveloped her in a bear hug. "Lorene Small! What great luck! I've just come ashore, and you're the very first person I've encountered!"

"I'm Lorene Benton now," she said, "and we're related, in a manner of speaking. Is it possible that slave trader is yours?"

Jeremy was so excited that he could only nod. Then he recovered his manners and presented M'Bwana to her.

"I suggest," Lorene said, "that you come home with me for supper, and bring this . . . ah . . . gentleman."

There was so much to say, so much to ask, that Jeremy and Lorene babbled semicoherently on the drive to the yellow brick house. There Isaiah Benton had just arrived home from his law office.

He and Jeremy could only wring each other's hands in stunned silence.

Then, as they sat together over glasses of sack, Isaiah and Lorene brought Jeremy up-to-date.

Sarah was the mistress of Oakhurst Manor and had lived there for more than three years. She used the Beaufort name, and everyone assumed that she was Jeremy's wife. The deception had been made necessary because she had a son, now two and a half years old, who was the image of his father.

Jeremy winced slightly when they mentioned his son.

"Brace yourself," Lorene told him. "A terrible plague of cholera smothered us this past winter, and we . . . lost Paul."

Jeremy sucked in his breath. "My father . . . is . . . dead?"

They could only nod. Isaiah refilled his glass, and they gave him time to recover from the initial shock before they told him all of their other news.

Tom and Margot were married, Lorene said, and her

323

illness, combined with the troubles at Oakhurst Manor, had finally made a man of him.

"What troubles?" Jeremy asked.

They explained that the plantation, like so many others in the state, was suffering severe difficulties. Most of the slaves had died, and there was too little cash to buy new field workers. Sarah and Tom soon might be forced to sell at least a part of Oakhurst Manor, just as young Scott and Alicia Emerson had been compelled to put Trelawney on the market.

"I have other plans for Oakhurst Manor," Jeremy said with a tight smile.

Dinner grew cold as he told them of his own adventures, from which he omitted only the facts of his affair with Lisa, his affair with Kai, and the subsequent birth of her child. "The ship that rides at anchor yonder is mine," he concluded, "and so is her cargo of four hundred healthy Watusi. I have more than fifteen thousand dollars in cash, and my diamonds—thanks to M'Bwana here—are worth a fortune. A half-million dollars, maybe even more. So I can tell you this much—nobody is going to sell a single foot of Oakhurst Manor. That's Beaufort land."

Sarah had to admit, if only to herself, that she had reached the end of her rope. Wearily she pushed back her long blond hair, and sitting at the library desk that had been Paul Beaufort's, looked down at the ledgers. No matter how many times she added and subtracted the telltale columns of figures, the results were always the same. Oakhurst Manor was heading toward inevitable bankruptcy.

It was stupid to postpone the day of reckoning any longer, and she would have to sit down with Tom and reach a final decision. They could hold out a little longer, perhaps until summer, but the lack of manpower meant there would be no cotton, no tobacco to sell at the end of the growing season. No matter how much they hated the prospect, they would have to dispose of at least half of the property. There was no longer any other way.

The furious barking of King N'Gao interrupted Sarah's reverie. The dog seemed to be in a frenzy, which was unusual, so she went into the front hall to investigate. The animal was leaping at the front door in a futile attempt to batter it down.

She opened the door for him, and a gray streak shot off down the driveway.

At the far end, Sarah saw a strange procession, led by two men on horseback, one white and one black. Directly behind them was a carriage containing her father and Lorene, as well as a handsomely attired pretty girl holding a baby. Then came cart after cart filled with black men and women—twenty, thirty, more than she could count—stretching far out into the road beyond the driveway.

King N'Gao leaped at the bearded man, who halted the procession as he dismounted and greeted the dog.

At that instant Sarah recognized Jeremy, and a hand crept to her throat, her heart feeling as though it would burst through her rib cage.

He had filled out, he looked healthy and strong, and he was expensively dressed, so it was obvious that all was well with him.

Suddenly a thought struck her like a thunderbolt. Had he brought a wife and child home with him?

The black man who had been riding beside Jeremy helped the girl out of the carriage, taking the baby from her. Sarah could tell from the way he put a protective arm around her that she was his woman. The broad smiles of Isaiah and Lorene were reassuring, too, and Sarah began to breathe again.

Now her feet obeyed her will, and she walked alone onto the portico, halting when she reached the top of the steps.

She had no idea that Margot and Cleo had come behind her and stood in the entrance, the latter holding the hand of little Jerry.

King N'Gao became calmer, and Jeremy started to walk up the driveway toward the mansion, with the dog frolicking beside him. All at once he saw Sarah, halted for an instant, and then began to walk again.

It occurred to her that she hadn't washed her hair for several days, nor had she bothered with cosmetics that morning. And she was wearing an old dress, with an apron over it.

Then her eyes met Jeremy's, and nothing else mattered.

He slowed his pace as he advanced toward her, prolonging this moment. Their eyes held, and neither smiled, neither spoke.

Sarah stood motionless, her hands at her sides.

A boy and girl had been parted, a man and woman were being reunited.

All at once Jeremy bolted up the steps and crushed Sarah in a fervent embrace. Their kiss seemed endless.

Neither heard Margot happily weeping behind them, neither was aware of Cleo's sniffles.

Jerry broke loose, ran forward, and tugged at his mother's skirt. "Mama, Mama!" he cried, demanding his share of attention.

Sarah smiled and spoke for the first time. "Jerry," she said, "your Papa has come home to us."

Jeremy's laugh rolled across the lawn as he scooped up his son, embraced him, and looked hard at him. "Well, now, Master Beaufort," was all he managed to say.

It was Margot's turn to be hugged, then Cleo's, and suddenly everyone began talking at once.

Tom had seen the procession from a distance, and rode up to the mansion at a gallop, his boots dusty, his shirt sweat-stained.

As he leaped from the saddle, the brothers took each other's measure, and both were satisfied. Strong, hard hands were clasped, and that handshake reaffirmed Beaufort unity.

The next hour was chaotic. An ecstatic Willie and an equally delighted Amanda showed the Watusi to their quarters. A fire was lighted in the outdoor pit, and Cleo went to work with a vengeance, assisted by the surviving members of the household staff. Before long a side of beef was being prepared for barbecuing, and huge pots were put on separate fires to boil.

The library seemed the natural place for the family to congregate. Sarah and Jeremy sat side by side on the divan, never out of physical contact. They held hands, their shoulders touched.

Jerry gradually overcame his shyness and climbed onto his father's lap. King N'Gao continued to demand his fair share of attention, too, and had to be petted.

In spite of the many distractions, Jeremy again told his story, omitting only the mention of his sexual affairs. He was interrupted just once, when Willie came in to say that M'Bwana, Kai, and Lance were being comfortably ensconced in the house that had been Mr. Higby's.

Sarah was in a daze as she listened to Jeremy. The change in their fortunes was so startling that she could scarcely grasp the details. Thanks to the Bantu diamonds, they were wealthy beyond her wildest dreams. Thanks to the Watusi, the problem of obtaining new field hands was automatically solved.

Later she would appreciate the material miracle, the abrupt transformation of their situation. For the present, it was enough that Jeremy had been restored to her.

When he finished his tale, he surprised the family by rising abruptly to his feet. "If you'll excuse Sarah and me," he told them, "I have something to say to her in private."

She accompanied him out of the library, bewildered by the shift in his mood, and for the first time they were alone.

He led her to the seldom-used parlor, halted, and placed strong hands around her slender waist. "You and I need to go off on an errand," he said. "I'm sure there's plenty of time before dinner."

Sarah's bewilderment increased. "An errand?"

"Our wedding has been delayed long enough. Will you marry me, Mistress Beaufort? Immediately?"

She laughed through her unexpected tears. "I've been wondering when you intended to ask me, Master Beaufort. I do accept, sir, immediately, and with all my heart."

They were accompanied on the short drive to the church only by Isaiah and Lorene, explaining their mission to others merely by saying they wanted to offer prayers of thanks for Jeremy's safe return.

Sarah removed the ring she had been wearing for almost three years so Jeremy could place it on her finger. She was still so flustered that she barely remembered to take off her apron.

327

After the ceremony, Jeremy reached into a waistcoat pocket and presented her with the largest of the Bantu diamonds, which was dazzling, even in its rough-cut state and embedded in rock. "We'll have a jeweler in Charleston make this into a ring for you," he said.

The bride and groom kissed repeatedly on the return ride to Oakhurst Manor, much to the affectionate amusement of Isaiah and Lorene, but then became sedate.

At Jeremy's insistence, wholeheartedly supported by Sarah, M'Bwana and Kai were invited to dine with the family, as were Amanda and Willie. Cleo was asked, too, but indignantly refused, saying she knew her place and would keep it. Willie's presence at the table possibly marked the first time that a slave shared a formal dinner table with his master, but if the event was significant, none of the celebrators knew or cared.

Sarah surrendered her place at the head of the table to her husband, who assumed his position with a dignity and authority that had become natural to him. She sat at the opposite end of the long table, and could not stop smiling at him.

She was impressed by the incisive, masterful attitudes of M'Bwana, and could understand how he had become Jeremy's close friend. Kai was self-conscious and shy, but Sarah envied the girl's fresh, unspoiled beauty. It was strange to see a woman who was white—or almost white as Jeremy had explained to her—married to a black man, but their love for each other was obviously genuine, and M'Bwana was both protective and attentive.

After successive courses of fresh fruit, soup, fish, and the barbecued beef, Sarah called a temporary halt to the meal. No such banquet had been served at Oakhurst Manor for many months.

Jeremy took charge, telling the others some of this thoughts. "M'Bwana," he said, "is going to become our overseer. He not only shares my attitudes toward slaves, but he speaks Watusi, which is an enormous advantage."

Even the non-Southerners were startled. No plantation anywhere in the United States had ever utilized the services of a free black man as an overseer.

But Jeremy had grown indifferent to precedent. "There's

328

no one anywhere better able to handle the job," he said.
"Not only will the slaves be more productive, but they'll
be far happier in their personal lives. We'll build an addition to his house so he and his family will have more
space, and we'll assign them servants of their own. Tom,
I'll be grateful if you'll take M'Bwana out to the fields tomorrow morning, first thing, and start showing him what
needs to be done."

Tom agreed without reservation. Although he lacked his
brother's harrowing experiences, he, too, displayed a remarkably enlightened attitude toward slavery.

"Now we come to a major problem," Jeremy said. "Last
night, Lorene and Isaiah told me the younger generation
of Emersons have no wish to keep Trelawney, even if they
could."

"I'm afraid that's correct," Isaiah said. "The death of
their parents spoiled the plantation for them. Young Scott
has decided he wants to study law, so I'm giving him a
desk in my office. And Alicia is eager to move to New Orleans."

Jeremy nodded. "Before I explain what I have in mind,
let me tell you something of my own plans. I apologize in
advance to Sarah for not discussing them first with her.
But they've been in my mind for many months."

"Whatever you want is what I want for you," Sarah
said.

He looked at her, his expression so intimate that the
others glanced away.

"I've decided the law is not for me. I'm afraid that after
all the happenings of the past years, I'd have no patience
with a life of study, interspersed with court appearances.
Oakhurst Manor is in my blood, so I'll be a plantation
owner, first and foremost, for the rest of my days. But I've
also acquired a love of the sea, so I aim to sell the *County
Mayo*—for which I'm sure to get a very good price—and
use the proceeds to buy a merchantman. Perhaps two. Ultimately, I'd like to own a whole fleet. Now that we're assured of more or less permanent peace with Great Britain
and France, I'm sure our trade with the West Indian islands is going to increase a great deal, and I'd like to be in
a position to take financial advantage of that situation."

It was wonderful, Sarah thought, to see how much he had matured. She had said good-bye to a law student, and in his place she was married to a worldly man who had gained experience in many fields and, above all, who knew his own mind.

"Tom," Jeremy said, "you and Margot may want to talk about the idea I'm going to present to you. Naturally, if you want to stay on here, you're welcome to do so. Oakhurst Manor is as much your home as it is mine. But you might want to have a place of your own."

Margot and Tom exchanged a quick glance, and the younger brother smiled ruefully. "We've wanted our own plantation, but we can't afford even a down payment on a property. As you've discovered, we'd be in a pretty fix if you hadn't come home."

"I'm willing to buy your share of Oakhurst Manor for cash," Jeremy said. "What's more, I'll advance you whatever else you might need to buy Trelawney and restore it to an operating condition. We can have a chat with young Scott and Alicia in the next few days, and then work out our own details."

Tom sucked in his breath. "It sounds too good to be true, but how could I repay you, Jeremy?"

"That's easy enough. I'll take a small percentage of your profits—in the years you enjoy profits, that is—and I don't care how long it may take you to pay me back. Without interest. After all, I expect that both of us are going to be in these parts for the rest of our lives."

After the meal the ladies refrained from withdrawing while the men remained at the table for port and cigars. "I refuse to be separated from Jeremy for even a half-hour today," the radiant Sarah said, and that was that.

When the party came to an end, more than an hour of daylight remained, so Jeremy ordered horses saddled for Sarah and himself. He was pleased when he heard that Jerry had a pony of his own, so he insisted that the child accompany them.

Jerry rode between his parents, with his father holding the reins for him.

First they visited the slave quarters to make certain the Watusi were properly housed and that enough food had been provided for them. The new slaves, making themselves at home, were already familiar with Jeremy after the long voyage from Luanda, of course, and greeted him with smiles. It was obvious to them that Sarah was his woman, so their warmth extended to her.

Never before, Sarah thought, had new slaves settled into life on a plantation with less fear.

Leaving the slave quarters, Jeremy led his wife and son on an inspection of the entire property, and when Jerry grew tired, his father hoisted him onto his own saddle.

They halted a few minutes before sundown, and Jeremy dismounted, taking the little boy with him. Stooping, he picked up a handful of rich black earth. "See this, Jerry? Smell it!"

Jerry complied, pleased by what he regarded as a game.

"Do it again," Jeremy commanded. "Isn't that a wonderful smell, boy? This is the good earth of Oakhurst Manor, and no matter where you go or what you do in this world, you'll never forget that scent."

Father and son sniffed together, the child imitatively inhaling deeply.

Sarah turned away so they wouldn't see the tears that came to her eyes.

When they returned to the mansion, it was time for Jerry's supper. His parents sat with him while he ate, and accepted the scolding of Cleo, who rebuked them for delaying the child's meal.

Then they took Jerry to his room and put him to bed. They listened to his prayers, which included an automatic, "Please, God, bring Papa home."

Jeremy bent low over his son. "Papa is here, Jerry, and I'm going to stay here. I'll be here when you wake up tomorrow morning. And every morning. You and I are going to be making up for lost time, so we'll be doing all sorts of things together. Riding and planting and fishing. And someday I'll teach you how to sail a boat, too. A boat of your very own."

Sarah's happiness was complete.

When they returned to the ground floor, they discovered that other members of the family had discreetly retired to their own quarters.

"If you don't mind," Jeremy said as they headed toward the library, "I'd like to take a few minutes to look at the ledgers. I won't really study them tonight, of course, but I'll rest easier once I gain a general idea of the situation."

Sarah gave him the books that had been Paul's and that she had been keeping since his death.

Jeremy was soon immersed in them.

She left him there and went upstairs to the suite she had made her own. She changed into a silk nightgown and robe, and for the first time that day she used kohl on her eyelids, rouge on her lips and cheeks.

She was just finishing the arrangement of her hair when Jeremy entered.

"I almost knocked at the door first," he said with a grin, "but all of a sudden I realized that would be silly." He lowered himself into a chair, his mind still seething. "If you don't mind, Sarah," he said, "in the next few days, whenever it's convenient for you, I think we ought to move into the quarters that were Papa's—and my grandfather's before him. That's the master suite, and it's only right that we live there."

"I don't mind in the least," she said. "In fact, it's quite appropriate. It simply hadn't occurred to me."

"Splendid. Then we'll move Jerry in here. These rooms have traditionally belonged to the principal heir to Oakhurst Manor."

"Perfect," Sarah said, wondering when he would notice her. Just as this had been the most important day in her life, right now it was the most important night.

"I've had some other ideas, too," he said. "I want to experiment with some of the West Indian crops. I don't think their fruits will grow this far north, but their vegetables surely will. One type of sweet potato in particular is well suited to our climate and soil, I believe. It also occurs to me—"

"I wonder, Master Beaufort," she said, interrupting him in a sudden burst of annoyance, "if you might delay telling me these thoughts until later."

He was startled.

"Much later," she added pointedly.

Jeremy looked at her, looked again, and grinned. "Just

one more thought, Mistress Beaufort," he said. "You're not only more sensible by far than I am, but you're the loveliest woman on earth."

They embraced without embarrassment or hesitation, their long years of separation and all they had suffered suddenly evaporating.

With one accord they left the sitting room and went into the bedchamber, their arms around each other. They were husband and wife, and had been in all but legal name for so long that there were no barriers between them.

At first their lovemaking was gentle, almost serene, but gradually their long-suppressed mutual hunger overwhelmed them, and they wanted to devour each other. Their desire soared until it became almost unbearable.

The release was prolonged, an ecstasy greater than either had ever known. Now, at long last, they were truly united.

Jeremy's voice broke as he murmured, "Dear Sarah, you'll never know how much I missed you."

Tears of joy streamed down Sarah's face as they remained locked in an embrace, but she neither knew nor cared.

Chapter 24

There weren't enough hours in the day for all that had to be done as life at Oakhurst Manor was reorganized. Tom and M'Bwana spent their time together in the field, and soon the new slaves went to work. Sarah continued to keep the books but began to turn them over to Jeremy, who was everywhere. He took a hand in supervising the spring planting, he directed the workmen who were transforming the house of M'Bwana and Kai into a substantial dwelling. He directed the construction of a new stove for Cleo. He found time to play with his son, who was perched on his shoulder whenever he left the house. And every night he made love to his wife.

One evening after supper, as they sat together in the library going over the ledgers, Jeremy put them aside. "I think I should go to Charleston tomorrow morning," he said. "I want to dispose of the Bantu diamonds so I'll have the cash to buy Trelawney for Tom. And for all of the new projects you and I are starting here. We need all sorts of food supplies for the new field workers. I aim to sell the *County Mayo*, and I'll start looking at merchantmen tha might be up for sale, although I don't expect I'll find what I want right off."

"It sounds like a trip of about two days," Sarah said.

"No more than that. I also want to give your diamond to a jeweler so he can fashion your ring. Why don't you come with me? We'll stay with Lorene and your father, of course."

She considered for a moment, then shook her head. "There's so much to be done here that I don't think both of us should be gone at the same time. I'll wait until your next trip. Besides, you have so much to do in town that we'd be able to spend very little of our time together."

He looked, unexpectedly, like a small disappointed boy.

Sarah put a hand on his arm. "Dear Jeremy, after all we've been through, a separation of a single night will seem like nothing at all."

He was forced to agree with her, and the following day, after an early breakfast, he rode off on the two-hour journey to Charleston.

Sarah was on her own again, but what a difference her husband's return had made! She was lighthearted at breakfast, leaving the handling of the augmented kitchen staff to Amanda and supervision of the new household staff to Cleo. Later she would take part in the training of the new housemaids, butlers, and gardeners.

She made her regular daily tour of the slave quarters, and before dinner she played with Jerry, solemnly repeating Jeremy's pledge to return by the next evening.

After dinner she retired to the library to spend several hours at work on the miraculously improved ledgers. She was tired after her long, busy day, but one chore remained. Now that M'Bwana and Kai were settling into their house, it was incumbent upon her, as the mistress of Oakhurst Manor, to call on them and see if there was anything they wanted or needed.

Sarah walked the short distance, and was pleased to note that some of the old hands, experienced workers, had already erected the second floor of the dwelling. Masons, who had just stopped work for the day, were building a fireplace for the sitting room, and labor on a separate kitchen building was already completed. The home was unique, but so was the relationship that Jeremy and his Bantu friend enjoyed.

M'Bwana was still in the fields with Tom, but Kai was genuinely pleased to see Sarah, and they took chairs together in the sitting room, Kai having learned enough of American manners to offer the visitor a cup of tea.

The conversation was handicapped by the Algerian girl's limited knowledge of English. She responded eagerly to the suggestion that she join the English classes for the new slaves that Amanda was conducting.

When they ran out of small talk, Kai suggested that they tour the house, and as they rose, the fleeting thought passed through Sarah's mind that she envied the fresh, unspoiled beauty of this younger girl. She knew that she herself was still exceptionally attractive, but Kai still had an innocent, dewlike quality that could not be duplicated by someone who had suffered at length.

Lance was asleep in the new nursery crib that Willie had made for him.

As Sarah smiled down at the baby, the vague thought crossed her mind that the infant reminded her of Jerry at the same age. That was only natural; all small babies looked somewhat alike.

Then she looked again, and all at once she knew. Lance was Jeremy's son. The resemblance was so striking that there could be no doubt of it. Jerry had looked precisely the same way at that age.

Somehow the visit ended, and Sarah was in turmoil as she returned to the mansion. She couldn't imagine how M'Bwana could have married Kai and accepted Lance as his own son. But she knew so little of Africans, their customs, and thought processes.

She was unable to think clearly, but there was nothing else on her mind. Somehow she gave Jerry his evening meal and put him to bed. Somehow she joined Tom and Margot for supper.

It soon became impossible for her to keep quiet on the subject. "I visited Kai this afternoon," she told them. "Her baby is adorable."

"Indeed he is," Margot said, and seemed to be concentrating on her soup.

Tom nodded in agreement, but his gaze was elsewhere, too.

So, Sarah told herself, they knew, too. Which probably meant that Cleo and Amanda and Willie and everyone else at Oakhurst Manor also knew. She had been the last to find out. Because she had been so dazzled by her husband's return, she had seen and heard nothing but Jeremy, Jeremy, Jeremy.

Conversation became general, and supper passed without further incident.

Soon after the meal ended, Sarah excused herself and went straight to the master suite, into which she and Jeremy had just moved. There she calmed herself and made a supreme effort to analyze the situation.

She was jealous of Jeremy's affair with Kai; there was no question of that. The girl was so young, so pretty.

In her heart of hearts she could not blame Jeremy for having been attracted to Kai. After all, she herself had almost made a total wreck of her own life when she had slipped and had a near-affair with Tom.

Even more important, men were different. Their physical urges were stronger, more insistent than those of a woman who had taught herself—forced herself—to sublimate her urges. It was too much to expect that Jeremy had remained abstinent through the years.

Sarah had to be content with the knowledge that he had returned to her. That she was truly his wife now. That he gave genuine, sincere evidence of loving her as much as she loved him.

She could even understand his reluctance to tell her that he had sired Kai's son. It was too much to expect of any man after being reunited with the woman he loved for only a week.

What, then, should she do about it?

Absolutely nothing, Sarah told herself firmly. Someday, in his own way, Jeremy would come to her and tell her his story. Which she would accept. Completely. Without cavil. Without protest. Without as much as a look, a gesture, or a word of disapproval.

Until that time, she would never mention the subject, either to Jeremy or to anyone else.

It was enough that she and Jeremy had each other. That they had Jerry. That, in all probability, other children would follow.

Her great love enabled her to forgive Jeremy, even if she could not totally forget his transgression. Let those who had never sinned cast stones.

Weeks passed and became months. The spring planting at Oakhurst Manor was late, but not too late, and the cotton, tobacco, and vegetables grew under a benign summer sun. The autumn harvest was all that Jeremy and Sarah could have wished, and they were satisfied with a modest profit.

Trelawney was purchased, and in midsummer the younger Beauforts moved into their own home. Their marital misunderstandings seemed to be behind them, and in the autumn Margot told the family she was expecting a baby. Tom felt certain she would have a boy, and planned to name him after his father.

The choise of M'Bwana as overseer at Oakhurst Manor proved to be inspired. He worked as Mr. Higby had never done, but he was fair and compassionate in his treatment of the slaves. They, in turn, labored willingly and with zest. Neighboring plantation owners, who had raised their eyebrows when they had learned that a black man had become chief of the field staff at the Beaufort place, were willing to concede that the experiment, as they termed it, was a resounding success.

In the summer, Jeremy granted Willie his freedom, and the event was celebrated by Willie's formal marriage to Amanda. She still wanted them to move to Boston, but he hadn't yet made up his mind, and for the present they stayed on at Oakhurst Manor. Willie was being paid for his work now, and was making so much money that he was reluctant to leave.

Cleo was offered her freedom, too, but indignantly refused. She insisted that she had everything in life that she wanted, and she had no intention of making any changes.

Jeremy obtained a fair price for the *County Mayo*, but was finding it difficult to locate a merchant ship that met his demanding specifications. He began to think in terms of having a vessel built to order for him in Savannah, where the shipbuilding industry was booming.

Sarah knew he missed the sea and undoubtedly would go off on an occasional voyage once he became the owner of a new merchantman. But she could not deny him that pleasure. He had more than lived up to the promise of their youth, and was everything she could have wanted as a husband, family head, lover, and father.

It was true that he had not yet summoned the courage to tell her he had sired Kai's baby, even though Lance's resemblance to him and to Jerry was startling. But she was wise enough to show continuing patience, knowing that ultimately the day would come when he would make a full confession to her.

For the present, she was completely content. He was affectionate and considerate, always tender. He worked even harder than his father had done, and truly was the master of Oakhurst Manor. He and Jerry developed a close relationship, and for hours each day were inseparable.

Neighbors began coming to him for advice and help, too, and there was talk of organizing a movement to persuade him to run for a seat in the U.S. House of Representatives. But he showed no inclination to become active in politics, and did nothing to encourage those who wanted to send him to Washington.

It was summer before Sarah's diamond ring was ready, but it was worth the long wait. The gem was stunning, and visitors seeing the ring for the first time could not help staring at it.

Late in the autumn Sarah and Jeremy received a note from Lorene, inviting them to spend several days in Charleston, principally to attend a major dinner party that she and Isaiah were giving. Sarah had a new gown made for the occasion from a bolt of emerald-green velvet recently arrived from France. The dress had a deep, square-cut neckline and a tiny waist, with the full skirt falling in soft folds. When she tried it on for Jeremy, she looked so stunning in it that he persuaded her to wear it without the multiple petticoats that had become the rage throughout the South.

On the day before the party, they drove into the city,

using one of their smaller carriages, with Jeremy electing to handle the reins himself. The occasion marked the first holiday they had taken since his return more than a half-year earlier, and both were in high spirits. The day was cool, there were few other carriages or riders on the road, and they enjoyed themselves thoroughly.

Jeremy took the waterfront road to the Benton house, which was located in a neighborhood of aristocratic homes. The harbor was even more crowded than usual, but Sarah paid no attention to the ships, and was surprised when her husband slowed the horses to a sedate walk.

"Look yonder," he said. "There are the British warships that arrived a few days ago on the goodwill mission we heard about." He shaded his eyes as he strained to inspect the ships.

After his experiences in the Royal Navy, Sarah thought it odd that he should show any interest in a British fleet, but she kept her opinion to herself. "Whatever are you doing?"

Jeremy's laugh was a trifle sheepish. "I just wanted to see if I knew any of the ships. But I don't, not even the frigate that's flying an admiral's pennant."

They arrived at the Benton home in time for supper, and spent the evening exchanging family news. The following morning Sarah helped her stepmother prepare for the party. The guest list included members of the distinguished Pinckney and Marion families, as well as Congressman John C. Calhoun of Charleston, who would become Secretary of War under President James Monroe, and the rear admiral commanding the visiting British goodwill fleet.

Jeremy spent the morning visiting his father-in-law's law offices, and when they returned at noon, they found the house in a state of organized chaos. Lorene and Sarah had already vanished into their bedchambers to bathe and dress for the party. The long dining table was set, and three cooks were at work in the kitchen outbuilding. Thanks to the managerial talents of Lorene and Sarah, even the chamber in which women guests would primp before making their entrances was in readiness.

Isaiah and Jeremy checked the wines that would be

ished that no one else in the room was aware of it. Not Lord Saunders, not Lorene, not Isaiah.

Sarah's mind whirled as she sipped a cup of punch and tried to make small talk, her whole being feeling as though she had been hurled into space, where there were no supports beneath her feet, no columns on which she could lean.

She wanted to scream a warning to Lord Saunders, but couldn't disgrace herself.

She had been right to ignore Jeremy's inconsequential affair with Kai, even though Lance had been the result of their liaison.

But Lisa, Lady Saunders, represented a grave threat to her marriage, her happiness, her future. A threat to all she held dear.

The worst of it was her awareness that Jeremy and this lovely girl were in the grip of something beyond their own ability to control. The feeling was something that Sarah herself had never experienced, but watching these two as they struggled to keep their composure, she knew beyond all doubt that it existed.

A powerful chemistry was at work, no matter how many lives might be ruined.

Sarah realized she could not remain supine. She had to fight back. She had to use her own beauty, her wits, her lively imagination. She had to mobilize her femininity, her intellect, her cunning.

She faced the supreme test of her life, and she prayed she was equal to a task that, at this moment, seemed insurmountable. Yet she had to overcome all obstacles, she had to win. Love and life itself depended on the many talents she could muster.

More Big Bestsellers from SIGNET

☐ **THE FRENCH BRIDE** by Evelyn Anthony.
(#J7683—$1.95)

☐ **TELL ME EVERYTHING** by Marie Brenner.
(#J7685—$1.95)

☐ **ALYX** by Lolah Burford.   (#J7640—$1.95)

☐ **MACLYON** by Lolah Burford.   (#J7773—$1.95)

☐ **FIRST, YOU CRY** by Betty Rollin.   (#J7641—$1.95)

☐ **THE DEVIL IN CRYSTAL** by Erica Lindley.
(#E7643—$1.75)

☐ **THE BRACKENROYD INHERITANCE** by Erica Lindley.
(#W6795—$1.50)

☐ **LYNDON JOHNSON AND THE AMERICAN DREAM** by Doris Kearns.   (#E7609—$2.50)

☐ **THIS IS THE HOUSE** by Deborah Hill. (#J7610—$1.95)

☐ **THE DEMON** by Hubert Selby, Jr.   (#J7611—$1.95)

☐ **LORD RIVINGTON'S LADY** by Eileen Jackson.
(#W7612—$1.50)

☐ **ROGUE'S MISTRESS** by Constance Gluyas.
(#J7533—$1.95)

☐ **SAVAGE EDEN** by Constance Gluyas. (#J7681—$1.95)

☐ **LOVE SONG** by Adam Kennedy.   (#E7535—$1.75)

☐ **THE DREAM'S ON ME** by Dotson Rader.
(#E7536—$1.75)

THE NEW AMERICAN LIBRARY, INC.,
P.O. Box 999, Bergenfield, New Jersey 07621

Please send me the SIGNET BOOKS I have checked above. I am enclosing $_____(check or money order—no currency or C.O.D.'s). Please include the list price plus 35¢ a copy to cover handling and mailing costs. (Prices and numbers are subject to change without notice.)

Name_____

Address_____

City_____State_____Zip Code_____
Allow at least 4 weeks for delivery

Have You Read These Bestsellers from SIGNET?

- [ ] **SINATRA by Earl Wilson.** (#E7487—$2.25)
- [ ] **THE WATSONS by Jane Austen and John Coates.** (#J7522—$1.95)
- [ ] **SANDITON by Jane Austen and Another Lady.** (#J6945—$1.95)
- [ ] **THE FIRES OF GLENLOCHY by Constance Heaven.** (#E7452—$1.75)
- [ ] **A PLACE OF STONES by Constance Heaven.** (#W7046—$1.50)
- [ ] **THE ROCKEFELLERS by Peter Collier and David Horowitz.** (#E7451—$2.75)
- [ ] **COME LIVE MY LIFE by Robert H. Rimmer.** (#J7421—$1.95)
- [ ] **THE FRENCHMAN by Velda Johnston.** (#W7519—$1.50)
- [ ] **THE HOUSE ON THE LEFT BANK by Velda Johnston.** (#W7279—$1.50)
- [ ] **A ROOM WITH DARK MIRRORS by Velda Johnston.** (#W7143—$1.50)
- [ ] **KINFLICKS by Lisa Alther.** (#E7390—$2.25)
- [ ] **RIVER RISING by Jessica North.** (#J7533—$1.95)
- [ ] **THE HIGH VALLEY by Jessica North.** (#W5929—$1.50)
- [ ] **LOVER: CONFESSIONS OF A ONE NIGHT STAND by Lawrence Edwards.** (#J7392—$1.95)
- [ ] **THE SURVIVOR by James Herbert.** (#E7393—$1.75)

THE NEW AMERICAN LIBRARY, INC.,
P.O. Box 999, Bergenfield, New Jersey 07621

Please send me the SIGNET BOOKS I have checked above. I am enclosing $_____(check or money order—no currency or C.O.D.'s). Please include the list price plus 35¢ a copy to cover handling and mailing costs. (Prices and numbers are subject to change without notice.)

Name_____

Address_____

City_____State_____Zip Code_____

Allow at least 4 weeks for delivery

Other Big Bestsellers from SIGNET

SIGNET Bestsellers You'll Want to Read

☐ **'SALEM'S LOT by Stephen King.** (#E8000—$2.25)

☐ **CARRIE by Stephen King.** (#J7280—$1.95)

☐ **FATU-HIVA: Back to Nature by Thor Heyerdahl.**
  (#J7113—$1.95)

☐ **THE DOMINO PRINCIPLE by Adam Kennedy.**
  (#J7389—$1.95)

☐ **IF YOU COULD SEE WHAT I HEAR by Tom Sullivan and
  Derek Gill.** (#W7061—$1.50)

☐ **THE PRACTICE OF PLEASURE by Michael Harris.**
  (#E7059—$1.75)

☐ **ENGAGEMENT by Eloise Weld.** (#E7060—$1.75)

☐ **FOR THE DEFENSE by F. Lee Bailey.** (#J7022—$1.95)

☐ **PLAYING AROUND by Linda Wolfe.** (#J7024—$1.95)

☐ **THE SAMURAI by George Macbeth.** (#J7021—$1.95)

☐ **DRAGONS AT THE GATE by Robert Duncan.**
  (#J6984—$1.95)

☐ **TREMOR VIOLET by David Lippincott.**
  (#E6947—$1.75)

☐ **THE VOICE OF ARMAGEDDON by David Lippincott.**
  (#E6949—$1.75)

☐ **PHOENIX ISLAND by Charlotte Paul.** (#J6827—$1.95)

☐ **FEAR OF FLYING by Erica Jong.** (#J6139—$1.95)